THE BRIDE SERIES

THE BRIDE, THE WIFE, AND THE LOVER

S DOYLE

Copyright © 2017 by Stephanie Doyle

All rights reserved.

No part of this book may be reproduced in any form or by any electronic or mechanical means, including information storage and retrieval systems, without written permission from the author, except for the use of brief quotations in a book review.

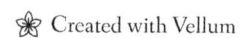

❦ Created with Vellum

To Molly and Simone... without you guys this wouldn't have been possible.

THE BRIDE PART 1

ONE

Ellie
January

MY DAD DIED. Wait. Wow. That was really intense. I should back up.

I'm Ellie Mason... and my dad was dead.

Here was the super bad part. My mom was dead, too. She'd died when I was nine of cervical cancer. She must have had a thought that she was going to die young, because she had planned ahead. She had worked for the National Park system in Montana for a bunch of years before meeting my dad. She'd had this life insurance policy that when she died my dad put in a trust for me for when I was twenty-one.

He'd said it was there to give me options. It wasn't like millions or anything, but enough to set me up with a place and a car if I didn't want to have to come back to the ranch after college.

Did I mention that my dad was a cattle rancher?

He was.

We were.

I was.

Over two thousand acres in western Montana. We ran about four to five hundred head a year. We had a barn, a chicken coop, some cattle-ready horses. A wide swath of grazing land and great irrigation. A full time employee plus my dad year round. For calving season and selling season we would bring in some extra hands: Javier and Gomez, two immigrant farm workers from south of the border.

They didn't say much because they didn't speak much English. But they worked eighteen-hour days. Never complained and took cash.

Our life was good. Sure, we were miles from everything. It took me over forty-five minutes to get to our nearest town to go to school every morning. Town was another three-hour drive from any city remotely resembling civilization. The nearest one being Missoula. Yep. To get to a Target was literally a four-hour drive there and back. I know because I did it once a month with my dad.

Except now my dad was dead.

Only that wasn't the worst part. The worst part was I was only sixteen years and eight months old. For those of you doing the math and need a calculator like me, that was one year and four months before I was considered a legal adult.

Which means I was an orphan. Like a for real orphan. I had this crazy urge to start asking for more and go looking for a dog named Sandy. It didn't seem like it could be a real thing in the twenty-first century. But it was. If your mom dies and your dad dies, then you are an orphan.

There had been no way to plan for this. My dad had died suddenly of a heart attack. Some artery that shut down. They called it the widow maker, only in this case it was an orphan maker.

He'd been a smoker, but quit years ago. I made him eat mostly healthy food, but he liked burgers and fries like everyone else. He drank some but not a ton, and he was only fifty-seven, which didn't even seem old anymore. Tom Cruise was in his fifties and he was still doing *Mission Impossible* movies.

My dad was not Tom Cruise.

My dad was not...

"Ellie."

I looked over my shoulder and saw Jake. His name was short for Jackson, which was a really cool name, but everyone who knew him since he was a kid always called him Jake.

He was my dad's foreman. The only full time employee who basically did everything my dad didn't do on the ranch. He was probably worried, too. About what was going to happen.

He nodded his chin and looked down at the rose in my hand. I was supposed to drop it on the coffin. That's what everybody was waiting for. Instead I was staring down at this hole in the ground, thinking...

That was it. I wasn't really thinking about anything. I wasn't crying, which was weird. All my friends from high school were. There were fifteen of them here, not because I was so popular, but because we had a really small class and most of us were pretty tight because we had all grown up together.

Although I guess most people liked me. All of my classmates had said or done something. A lot of *sorry* texts. Even from Riley, who was a grade ahead of me.

My friends were crying, my neighbors were crying. Jake wasn't crying, but he was a cowboy and cowboys didn't cry. Also he was probably really worried about what was going to happen to his job, and fear had a way of distracting you from your grief.

I suppose I was numb. With my mom I remember being so sad, but that was after months of her being really really sick. This was like someone turned off a switch on Sam Mason.

"We've got people coming back to the house," Jake said softly. "We'd best be getting back."

See, he even talked like a cowboy. Which was not how most guys in my class talked, but Jake wasn't like most guys. Not even when he'd been in high school. My dad used to say Jake had an old soul.

"Okay."

It was cold too. I was in a dress, my only nice one, and my legs were freaking blocks of ice because my nicest coat only barely covered my ass. Leggings versus Montana in January #leggingslose.

I held the rose out over the hole, careful to keep my feet on the green mat covering the ground, and opened my hand. The rose fell. I heard it hit the top of the coffin. I had this crazy idea that maybe I didn't do it right. Maybe I should jump in, get it, crawl out and do it over again.

But Jake put his arm around my shoulders and started moving me back to where the line of cars was waiting outside the cemetery. He'd driven me in his truck. We weren't fancy people who needed limousines to go to a burial.

Once I was inside, I buckled up and watched the line of people who were still dropping roses. There were a lot. That was good, I thought. It meant my dad was liked, and that was important.

Except I didn't know why exactly.

"Are there a lot of people coming back do you think?" I asked.

I looked over at Jake and he just raised his eyebrows.

"Yeah. I guess so," I answered myself. "We'll have lots of casserole and stuff. Mrs. Petty will bring her Bundt cake. You love that cake."

"Ellie..."

"I'm not crying. Why aren't I crying?"

"You're in shock still. It's natural."

"When are we going to talk about... you know. All of it."

"Not today. I told Howard today was for family and friends. About saying goodbye to a good man."

Howard was my dad's lawyer. A friend too, and basically the only lawyer in town. He'd be the one to figure out how all of this got sorted out. The ranch, me.

Because here was the really bad thing. Beyond being an orphan, beyond being underage, what Jake said about family wasn't really true. There wasn't a lot. There was my mom's crazy sister who lived in Florida, and I had only met her once at my mom's funeral.

She'd sobbed and cried, and then I think she'd tried to hit on my dad because he'd gotten really mad at her and told her to leave and never come back.

My dad wasn't Tom Cruise, but he had that kind of old-western cowboy look that I guess women were drawn to.

Since then, there had been nothing. Not a card, not a call. That was it. Both grandparents were deceased. My parents had met a little later in life. My mom was thirty-eight when she had me. My dad's mom was the only grandparent I could even remember, but she had passed away before my mom did.

A lot of death. Right? I'm too young for so many to have died.

What Jake said gave me a little bit of an out. I didn't have to be scared about what Howard was going to say today. I could worry about that tomorrow.

Ugh. Tomorrow. What a freaking orphan word.

No, I was going to try and smile, sadly of course, reassure everyone I was fine and eat some of Mrs. Petty's cake.

"You know I'm here, right Ellie? I'm not going anywhere."

Until someone said he had to go. Which would really suck for him. Jake had been part of this ranch for the last six years.

His dad and my dad had been friends growing up. Jake grew up on the property next to ours. The Talley River Ranch hadn't been as large as our operation, but it was a nice chunk of property on really quality grazing land. Only Jake's dad, Ernie, had been a drunk. A bad one. My dad had tried to support them both for as long as he could, but eventually the bank foreclosed.

After that, most folks said Ernest Talley drank himself to death.

My dad had given Jake a place to live and work. A chance to earn enough to someday buy back his family's land. Right now we were leasing the property to extend our grazing area. But really my dad had been holding on to it until Jake was ready to buy it back.

Yeah, Jake was shaking in his boots as much as I was

because we had both been reading up on things since Dad died three days ago.

Instead of answering his question, I nodded.

"Is Janet coming? I didn't see her at the cemetery."

"Yes. She was really sorry she couldn't be at the funeral, but she had to work. She got someone from Jefferson to come in and cover the afternoon shift so she could come out to the house."

Janet was Jake's girlfriend for the last two years, and a nurse at the urgent care clinic we had in town. The only place where someone could get immediate medical care until they could be shipped off to an actual hospital.

Riverbend had just about one of everything. Doctor, nurse, lawyer, judge, sheriff. We actually had two schools. K-7, then 8-12. It had been K-8 until the numbers shifted and there more young kids then teenagers. Nothing like watching a wide-eyed eighth grader see a senior in high school for the first time.

We were small. But we were tight. It made sense why Janet hadn't been there because getting people from towns nearby to provide coverage was never easy.

"Are you going to marry her?"

It was sort of none of my business, but I had been thinking about it lately. I knew they had been dating for a while, but I really didn't know how serious they were. I didn't know if my dad dying was going to mess up something else for him, too.

He shifted in his seat. One long movement of uncomfortable.

"I don't know. Maybe."

"She's nice."

"Do you like her?"

I made a face. He saw my face and winced. Which caused me to make another face. He saw that too.

"I don't *not* like her," I said quickly.

"You don't *not* like anyone."

It was true. When you live in a town of so few people, I found it a good strategy to like everyone. No enemies that way.

"She's just really intense sometimes. Like everything is always this big deal. She's the person who when you ask on a scale of one to ten, comes back and says a hundred. Or a million. Is that a nurse thing? I don't know. Maybe that's how she has to look at everything."

Jake smiled. "Intense is a good word for Janet."

He didn't seem to be mad that I was in some way calling out his girlfriend. Maybe this was good. Maybe now that it was only me, he would start treating me more like an adult instead of his kid sister. I took the opportunity to wow him with even more astute advice.

"And you are so not that guy. You see everything in perspective. I guess that's why sometimes when you two are together, I don't see it. But if you love her, you should marry her."

"A topic for another time. We're here. People have already arrived."

I could see it. The cars lined up in front of the house. The driveway was one big long U with house at the bottom in essentially what was the swell of the valley. The Long Valley Ranch brick archway announced the start of the property. Jake stopped the car before turning in.

"You ready for this?"

"No," I answered honestly. "Do we have to do this? Let's drive somewhere and let them eat each other's casseroles."

"But Mrs. Petty's Bundt cake. You wouldn't deny me that, would you?"

He was smiling. Sadly. I smiled back because I knew it would make him feel better.

"I mean it, Ellie. I promise you I'm not going anywhere."

Until he had to. I nodded and took a deep breath. "Let's do this."

TWO

Ellie

WHEN JAKE and I walked into the house, all conversation stopped. Everyone turned to me and I could see it, in each one of their faces... pity. No that wasn't fair. Sympathy. Which I interpreted as pity.

These were all the wives of the neighbors who hadn't driven out to the cemetery so they could set up the... what the hell was this, anyway? The after-funeral party? The Sad Reception? Whatever it was, it was weird.

I took off my coat, tried to rub some warmth into my legs, and walked into the living room where I imagined people would come and talk to me.

Or did I have to go and talk to them? Was this like a wedding where I was the bride and had to reach out to the guests? Or was this more like what I had to do at the church earlier, where I stood by my dead dad as everyone shook my hand and said *sorry for your loss?*

Some awkwardly hugged me, too. I mean people who would have never hugged me. Like my P.E. teacher, Mr. Kelly, was suddenly hugging me.

Now it seemed all these people would all do the same thing, except this time there would be the prize of food at the end.

Only no one who was already there came to see me. They were busy putting out dishes and plates and serving utensils. Jake seemed to be overseeing things, which was typical. Finally it was Mrs. Petty, of the famed Bundt cake, who found me first.

"How about I get you some hot tea?"

"Kay."

She smiled then. This really big smile, and I could tell it was because she was so happy that she could actually do something. TEA! Tea was going to make me feel better. Tea was going to warm me up. Tea was the thing that I needed and Mrs. Petty was going to make that happen.

She brought the tea with a softer smile, and I took a sip.

Tea did not make me feel better, but I didn't tell her that.

The doorbell started to ring, which was totally weird because I couldn't remember the last time I heard it. Most people who knew me or my dad knocked real hard and then opened it. It wasn't like the door was ever locked.

The Long Valley Ranch was in the middle of nowhere. We never expected people to come by and rob us.

Oh shit. I was going to have to live alone in the house. That was freaking scary. I guessed I would have to start locking doors. Keep Dad's shotgun next to the bed.

What if I had to shoot someone?

"Ellie?"

I looked up. It was Mrs. Nash.

"Hi, Mrs. Nash."

She opened her mouth and then shut it. I could see she'd been crying. This was super awkward too, because Mrs. Nash, who had been my freshman English teacher, had also been banging my dad.

"I don't know what to say," she finally managed.

"It's okay. You don't have to say anything."

"I'm so..."

"Sorry. Yep. I guess... Well, you know. I'm sorry too. For you."

She looked at me and I could see she realized that I knew about her and my dad. For a moment she looked alarmed. Like I would start telling everyone my dad had been banging a married woman.

"It's okay," I told her.

"Did your father..."

"No. He never said anything. It was an accident that I knew. I wouldn't tell anyone."

My dad had this hunting cabin on the property. A one-room cabin with limited amenities. I can't even remember what had caused me to head out there. I'd been riding Petunia—yes, my horse's name was Petunia—and I'd figured I would check to make sure the cabin was stocked in case Dad wanted to go hunting as the season was coming up. I saw his truck parked out front and then I watched as Mrs. Nash drove up and got out of her car.

The reason she was called Mrs. Nash was because of Mr. Nash.

Mr. Nash ran the grocery store in town that everyone was always complaining about because he only ever had two of any one brand. If you didn't plan your food shopping around restock day, then forget getting your hands on Kraft

Mac N Cheese. You got the generic brand instead, which tasted like shit.

Shit. My dad didn't like it when I cursed.

Anyway I'd sat on Petunia from about fifty feet away on an overhang and had watched the whole thing go down.

Oh no, gross. Not the WHOLE thing!

I meant I saw my dad open the cabin door and let Mrs. Nash inside. He patted her on the ass—I could tell she'd liked that—and then he'd closed the door.

Luckily, I was a sophomore when this happened so I didn't have to worry about my grades being corrupted by how good or bad my dad was in bed.

Everybody seemed to know Mrs. and Mr. Nash were not a happy couple. But they had two kids, so I guess they wanted to stick it out for them. Neither Mr. Nash nor the kids were here today.

Today was for her.

She patted my shoulder and then she walked away. I could hear her hiccup a sob into her handkerchief.

See she was crying. I should be crying.

There were more comers. More *I'm sorrys*. My friends stayed on the other side of the room, all huddled together. Talking and whispering. Sometimes daring to look over at me. I felt like I had this contagious parent dying disease they were all afraid of catching. I wasn't mad. I figured I would feel the same way if one of them had recently been made an orphan.

Ugh. That word. *The sun'll come out...*

"Ellie! There you are. Oh my god, I'm so sorry. What can Jake and I do? We have to do something!"

It was Janet. She was loud and she was making me stand up to hug her. Then she was bawling and I was patting her on the back to make her feel better. Totally intense Janet.

"I mean what's going to happen to you?" she cried.

That was actually pretty funny, because she was loud enough that almost the whole house heard her. All these people who were all thinking the same thing but no one would actually say it. Hell, I was thinking it but wouldn't even come close to letting myself say it out loud.

Not Janet. She just let it rip. The one-million-dollar question. What was going to happen to Orphan Ellie Mason?

"Janet, I didn't know you were here," Jake said, coming up behind her.

Seeing them next to each other, I kind of saw what he saw in her. Objectively, Jake was hot. Tall, built in the way a man gets from working a ranch. Short dark brown hair, hazel eyes. Square jaw. It wasn't something I thought about much because he was... well, Jake. However, there was no getting around the fact he was pretty much the biggest catch in Riverbend.

He and Janet made sense. She was pretty with long blond hair, a nice round body without being chunky. Sweet and nice. I shouldn't have been so hard on her. Only now she was sobbing hard and it was not a good look for her. I could actually see little bubbles of snot in her nose.

She turned to him and hugged him. He patted her on the back too, and I think I saw her rub her nose on his dress shirt.

Gross.

"Why don't you go help in the kitchen," he told her when she came up for air.

"Okay. I can go help with dishes and stuff," she said.

"That's a good idea."

And so totally sexist. His girlfriend was freaking out and his answer was to send her to the kitchen? Normally I would have taken the opportunity to point this out to him. I feel like as a new generation of women, it's our duty to educate men every chance we get, but because I wanted her to go away I kept my mouth shut.

Sorry Gloria Steinem, I'll get him next time.

She left and everyone got back to the business of eating beef stroganoff and three layer bean dip and not saying the thing they were all thinking.

WHAT THE HELL WAS GOING TO HAPPEN TO ME?

"I don't want to wait," I told Jake as soon as it was the two of us.

"What do you mean?"

"I want to talk to Howard. Tonight. I don't want to wait."

"Ellie..."

"No. I know you're going to say I need more time. But the thing that's going to happen me after all of this, *time* isn't going to change that. I need to know now. The sooner I know my options, the better."

I looked at him then. I needed him to see I was serious. As I said before, I'm a pretty nice person who gets along with everyone. Very easygoing about most things. Until I wanted something hard. When something really counted and I really wanted it, I got stubborn.

My dad had said this was a good thing. He'd said I had grit, and for a person to get what they wanted out of life they needed grit.

I'd told him he watched too many John Wayne movies.

All I knew was in that moment I wanted to know what

was going to happen to me. Only Howard had those answers.

"I'll go find him," I told Jake. "But we should probably both talk to him together."

Because it wasn't just my life. It was Jake's too.

Our life.

"He's in the dining room with Mrs. Nash. I think we should wait until everyone leaves first, but I'll ask him if he can stay after."

I nodded. "Thank you."

Jake stared at me hard but I couldn't tell what he was thinking. Maybe trying to see if I was strong enough to handle whatever Howard said. I had no clue. How do you know if you can handle anything until you have to... handle it?

IT WAS three more agonizing hours of tears, whispers, *sorrys* and hugs. I was like a hugging machine. Which is weird for me, because outside of animals I'm not really a touchy feely kind of girl. I found this out when I was going steady with Mick last year, because he always wanted to hold hands.

He had this thing where he would show up at my class as the period let out and walk me to my next one, which was sweet but he had to hold my hand the whole time. This meant I had my backpack on my right shoulder and my books in my right arm so my left hand was free for holding. Mick was a right-hand hand holder. Anyway I always felt overloaded on my right side.

Mick and I didn't last very long.

When the last guest left, it was me, Jake, and Howard. I

called him Howard like I used to call Jake's dad Ernie. Because they were part of the family. Like Ernie, Howard had grown up with my dad. They had been a posse for a long time. Howard had tried to save Ernie too, only he stopped trying long before my father gave up.

I don't know if Jake resented him for that or not.

We made our way to my dad's study. It was a typical man cave, with a lot of brown leather and a big old cherry wood desk. There was a bar in the corner and Howard helped himself.

"Make mine a double," I said, and Howard turned to glare at me disapprovingly. "What? I'm kidding."

I sat on the couch and Jake sat next to me. Not close, but close enough I knew he was ready to act in case of emergency. If he needed to hold me or catch me if I fainted.

Not that I had ever fainted in my life, but who knew what was coming next. I guess I felt slightly lightheaded.

Although thinking about it, that was actually kind of sexist of me. I mean, his whole life was possibly about to be upturned too. What if Jake fainted?

"I just want you to know, I'll catch if you faint," I told him.

"Ellie, this is serious," he replied as if I had been making a joke.

Right. He was probably too heavy for me to catch.

"Okay," Howard started. "Let's cover the basics. Obviously the ranch and all its property goes to you, Ellie. The will is very straightforward. There is a provision to continue leasing the Talley property until such time that Jake can afford to buy it back. To that end, Sam bequeathed you twenty thousand dollars, Jake."

Jake let out a whoosh of breath.

"Is that good?"

I mean, I knew what the ranch was worth generally. Which was weird. We weren't rich people. We certainly didn't live like it. However, the ranch itself if we were going to sell it would be listed for about two million dollars. That was the thing about ranches though. You only got that money if you sold it. No one I knew would ever choose to give up land for money.

Jake was nodding. "It's a lot. Especially in cash. Your dad knows... knew... how much I had saved already. That plus the twenty thousand and I can put a down payment on my land."

Then why did he sound so weird? Tight or angry. It was hard to tell. I only knew that the muscle in his cheek was twitching and his hands were locked together.

"Now we need to talk about what happens with you, Ellie," Howard said.

Yep. The part about me. That's what I wanted to hear. Not that I wasn't happy for Jake. Being able to get his land back was huge. But you know...

WHAT WAS GOING TO HAPPEN TO ME?

"There is your aunt in Florida..."

"Not going to happen," I said quickly.

"Ellie," Jake said softly, "let Howard finish."

"Okay. He can finish but I'm not going to Florida."

Howard sighed. "I don't think it's an option anyway. I've been working on this problem since your father passed. After your mother passed away he made Ernie your legal guardian, but he never updated the will after Ernie died. I blame myself for not pressing him to fix that... but that's spilt milk. Anyway I managed to track your aunt down, but she's currently in a rehab facility. She also has a criminal record for possession of drugs."

Right. Not going to the druggie. "That means I can stay here?"

Sure it might be scary and yes I would have to lock the doors. But as long as Jake stayed nearby in the bunk house then I would be fine.

Except Howard was shaking his head. "You can't. You're a minor and legally you have to have guardianship. In the absence of any family there is a foster family in Paradise..."

"Paradise!" Yep, still not letting Howard finish. "Foster family! No way. Paradise is like a three-hour drive. How would I get to school and back? And I would have to stay with some strange family? Definitely not happening."

"I know this frightening for you, Ellie," Howard said calmly.

"Why can't Sheriff Barling... you know, forget about me? I mean, we're talking about a year and a few months. What is the freaking big deal?"

"It's the law. He can't ignore it. Everyone in town knows your situation."

"Then fine. I'll stay with my friends. I'll bounce around between them until they get sick of me."

Again with the head shake. "That's not sustainable. Not for over a year. Also those families would have to be cleared by the State Child Protective Agency as foster parents."

"Couldn't Jake do that?"

"Jake is not eligible. As a single man, he would not be qualified to be your guardian."

This time Jake had his hand on my knee to steady me. Except I had already crossed my arms over my chest and shut up. I started running through the scenarios as fast as I could. I needed to run away. I needed to take all the cash we had in the bank and run away for a year and four months.

Jake could run the ranch while I was gone and then once I was eighteen I could come back and take over.

"The foster family really is the best option, and as you said it's only a year and a few months."

I shook my head. Remember that stubborn part about me? When something counted. "I'm not going to Paradise."

"Ellie..." Jake started.

"I'm not. I'll leave Riverbend. Everyone can think what they want, but I'm not living with some strange family. I need to know how much cash my father has."

"Ellie, you're not running away." See, that's how close Jake and I were. He totally got where I was going with that. Except it wasn't his call.

"Jake, no offense, but you have no say in this. You got your out. You've got your money, you can buy your land. You're cool. But this is my life and I'm telling you I'm not going to live with some strange family."

"There is another option..." Howard started, then stopped.

I wanted to hit Howard in that moment. All this time there was another option and he was only now getting to it? What kind of monster... and why was he looking at Jake like that?

"You've been researching this too, haven't you?" Howard asked him.

Jake nodded. "As soon as you told me there was no legal guardian in the will."

"Okay. Time out. Holy shit, what is happening right now?" I was screeching. I knew I was screeching and it did not sound good. But this was my fucking life!

Howard leaned forward in his chair. "There is a provision in the Montana State Constitution that says with parental approval a sixteen-year old-can apply for a marriage certificate."

My first thought was *eww*. I don't know why, but my mind immediately went to one of those religious communes where the creepy old guys have all these young child brides.

"Now, you obviously don't have parental approval, but I think I can petition the judge to waive that in this case."

"What? Wait. You're going to marry me?"

Super gross. Howard was the same age as my father and plus there was his wife. Mirry would not be happy.

"No," Jake said. "I would."

Okay less gross, but still weird. "No way."

"In name only," Jake said. "Obviously. We get married. You get to stay here. When you turn eighteen we get divorced."

"Let me get this straight," I said, turning back to Howard. "The state won't approve him as my guardian, but it's okay if he's my husband?"

"Legally, yes."

"That's jacked up."

Howard huffed out a laugh. "I agree. But it is the law. What do you think, Jake?"

"I think there isn't a thing in this world I wouldn't do for Sam Mason and Ellie too for that matter."

I leaned back against the couch. Only this time more in shock. "You would do that?"

"I would."

"What about Janet?"

"I would explain the situation. We're only talking a year and four months."

Married. To Jake. Only not really *married* married. Basically it accomplished what I wanted. I got to stay in my house, stay in my school. There would be some legal document that said we were married, which would make it all okay. And he was right, it was just a year and four months. If he wanted to propose to Janet tomorrow, they would probably be engaged for at least a year anyway.

"What about your land though? You wouldn't be able to work both this ranch and your own."

"That can wait too. The leasing rights mean no one else can swoop in and buy it out from under me. Another year of saving at my current salary and I'll have more to work with to get it going again. I've been patient this long. I can wait another year."

"And four months."

He smiled at me. "And four months."

There was only one thing left to do.

"Jake Talley, will you marry me?"

Because it was the twenty-first century and a girl could ask the guy if she wanted to.

THREE

Jake

THIS WASN'T GOING to be fun. I knew it going in, but as soon as I opened the door to the diner I felt dread settle in my stomach. Janet and I had lunch here every Sunday. It was our standing "date."

Not that it was much of a date, but the diner was the only place in town to get food unless you counted the hot dogs at the gas station.

She never complained, though.

Sometimes I would think about taking Janet somewhere nice. A place with cloth napkins and candles, but between her schedule and mine there never seemed to be the time.

She hinted at getting away and taking a real vacation, but that would cut into my savings, and my savings was everything. Except when I said the word *savings* she would get this shy smile and I could guess what she was thinking. That part of what I was saving for was a ring.

I had thought about it. Taking a chunk of money and buying a nice diamond ring. But every time I did the math in my head, a ring cost me at least a year in getting my land back.

That was unacceptable.

My land was everything, and now because of Sam Mason I was closer than ever.

Which meant no matter how bad this was going to suck with Janet, I wasn't not going to do it.

Janet was already in our booth. Third one on the right. She heard the bell ring overhead when I opened the door and lifted her head in anticipation. She smiled like she always did when she saw me.

She had a menu in front of her, but I never understood the point. It wasn't as if we both didn't know every item on the menu and everything Frank would make for us that wasn't.

Still, every time she needed to see the menu, and she would change her mind at least three times before Kathy came over to take our order.

I took off my coat, hung it on the hook on the side of the booth, and sat down across from her.

"What?" she asked me straight out.

This was why I was not a very good poker player. I was going to start with some small talk and work my way up to the news, but she saw it on my face.

"We need to talk about something."

"I can see that."

"You know about Ellie's situation..."

"How is she?"

She was strong. More settled now that she knew her future. But it still hadn't hit her. The reality of what had happened. That her dad was gone. Forever. She was still in that numb period where your brain understands what has happened but the rest of you still wasn't buying.

I knew because it was how I felt when Ernie had died.

"She's okay."

"What's going to happen to her? You told me her father hadn't updated the guardianship from Ernie. That's really irresponsible of him. Especially as a single parent."

I didn't have anything to say in Sam's defense other than taking the time to update your will when you're dealing with your friend's death, helping his son, raising your daughter, and running a ranch... stuff like that falls through the cracks. Besides, no one thinks they are going to die.

"That's what we need to talk about. In Montana a sixteen-year-old can actually apply for a marriage certificate. With parental approval, but Howard thinks he can get that waived."

"A marriage certificate? What does that get her?"

I gave her a moment to figure it out. Easier than having to say I was going to marry Ellie Mason.

Her mouth opened as it dawned her. "You. You're going to marry Ellie so she can stay on the ranch."

"It's either that or a foster family in Paradise." Which in my mind had never been an option. I agreed with Ellie. She was my family. My only family now, and I wasn't about to send her away. The fact that I had to make it legal through marriage was semantics. Still, it helped to point out how extreme the other option would have been for Ellie.

Janet sat back in the booth. "I'm not sure what I'm supposed to say."

"There is nothing to say. Nothing is going to change between us. This is a legal situation to protect Ellie. Nothing more."

"It's marriage, Jake. Marriage. Which means if you're married to her, you can't be married to... anyone else."

"Sixteen months. That's it. Sixteen months and she'll be legal and we can get a divorce."

"I'm supposed to wait? Put my life on hold while you do this? I thought we were working toward something, Jake."

"We are," I admitted. I wasn't ready to say I wanted to marry her now. I wasn't there yet. I wanted my land back first. I wanted to have a better sense of the future before I made that commitment. "But I have to do this. There is no choice. Sam saved me. Hell, he left me enough money to buy my land. I'm not going to abandon his daughter to some foster family in Paradise."

"Have you considered the idea that we could get married, apply to be foster parents, and then we could be her guardians together?"

I had. I had thought about it. But being married to Ellie was a sixteen-month commitment. Being married to Janet was for life.

I didn't say that.

"I don't know how long that would take. Or if it would be a guarantee. I can't take that risk. Not with Ellie."

"So Ellie is more important than me."

I sighed. It was typical Janet to take it to that level. Black or white. Her or Ellie. "Yes. Ellie needs me more right now than you do. You have to see that."

"No," she snapped. "Don't make me the bad guy here. We've been dating for two years. I've been patiently waiting for you to save up for the land and get everything you wanted in place. I know you, Jake. You're a planner. But I thought we were close, and now you're telling me I have to sit back and wait sixteen months. I'm twenty-seven now."

It was a thing with her, being a year older than me. I got

it. Most of her friends were either engaged or married and already had babies. She felt like she was late to the race.

Maybe I wasn't being fair to her. I liked Janet. I really liked Janet. I thought about marrying her all the time in a logistical manner. I just never had the definitive moment when I thought *yes, she's the one I want to be with forever*.

The truth was, I liked our lunch dates and I liked the regular sex. When we didn't have the extra staff for calving and sell off, the bunk house was mine. For most of the year we had all the privacy we wanted, which was key since Janet still lived with her parents.

I wouldn't let her stay over though. I thought it was disrespectful to Sam. He had a young impressionable daughter in the house, after all. Not that Ellie didn't get what it meant when Janet came to the bunk house on her nights off. She wasn't stupid. Still, it was the principle of it.

She was right. It wasn't fair to make her wait so I could get off when I wanted to.

"Janet, I understand if you need to move on…"

She slammed her hands on the table. I could feel the other folks around us turn and look.

I lowered my voice. "What? I'm trying to do the right thing by you. If you don't want to wait, I get it. But this is happening. Ellie is my family. The only family I have left, and I'm not sending her to strangers. That is never going to happen, so you need to decide now what works for you."

She was nodding, but I could see her lips were quivering. She took a few shallow breaths and reined it in.

"Are you going to live with her? In the house?"

It wasn't a question I was expecting, so I answered without thinking. "I guess so. She might not like being alone in the house. And she should probably have some supervision. She's only sixteen."

"Almost seventeen."

"Yeah. So what."

"Has it occurred to you what it's going to look like? You're twenty-six, Jake, not seventy."

"I'm not following."

"You've known Ellie since she was born, but have you looked at her lately?"

"Of course I've looked at her."

"No, have you *looked* at her. She's growing up, Jake. She's not an adult, but she's not a girl either. Tall, thin, long brown hair, perky little breasts."

I saw red. "Tell me you're not suggesting that I would take advantage of an underage girl. Of Ellie."

I could see her back up, but it was too late.

"You think that of me?" I asked her. "You think that's who I am? Then what the fuck have you been doing with me for two years?"

She reached across the table to grab my hands, but I pulled them back out of her reach.

"Of course I know you're not that guy. But think of the visual, Jake. You're a strong attractive man, she's growing into a beautiful young woman. You'll be married, living together."

"She's like my fucking sister," I snapped.

"But she's not," Janet said, gathering her purse. "People will talk."

"I don't give a shit what they say. You'll know the truth. That's all the matters."

"I need to think about this," she said, scooting out of the booth. "I love you, Jake. I thought I was going to spend the rest of my life with you, so I'm not ready to give up on us, but I need time to process this."

I nodded. "That's fair." I needed time too. Time to think about what it meant that Janet was actually jealous of Ellie.

It was absurd and ridiculous. And wrong.

I WALKED into the house and made my way back toward the kitchen. Ellie was sitting on a stool at the center island, working on her laptop.

"Homework?" I asked. Because even after everything she'd been through, life still went on. She'd already missed a week of school and I knew her teachers had sent her some work to help her try and keep up.

She lifted her head and I tried to *look* at her. Janet was right. I hadn't really thought about Ellie in any particular way other than as Ellie. This girl who was in my life, who was part of my family.

She had grown up. And she was very pretty. Long honey-brown hair. She had her dad's eyes. Dark blue. Her mom's chin, a little pointy. She was taller than most girls in her class, which I knew she hated, because it also meant she was taller than a lot of the guys. She'd once informed me, as if it were a biological fact, that guys did NOT date girls taller than them.

Would people talk? I didn't think so. Too many people knew our story. My dad dying, then her mom, now her dad. People would talk more if I let anything happen to her.

No, it didn't matter that she'd turned into this young beautiful woman while I wasn't looking. I knew me. I knew Ellie. I knew what we were to each other. Janet's jealousy was unfounded.

Only now I had to worry about the guys who would eventually come sniffing around her.

"How did she take it?" she said, not answering my question.

"Not great."

"Figured."

I walked to the fridge and took out a beer that had been left over from the wake.

"Why did you figure?"

"Jake, she's twenty-seven. Around here that's almost ancient to be married. She's waiting for you because you're the best. Only now you told her she has wait *another* year. You had to assume she was going to be upset. You shouldn't be mad at her."

"Why would I be mad at her?" I was.

"Because you think she should understand. You know, because I'm an... ugh... orphan. Except you made a choice to put me above her. That was going to hurt no matter what."

When the hell had Ellie become so damn smart?

"For sixteen months," I reminded her. "You over her for sixteen months."

"Doesn't matter. Which means you don't get to be mad at her."

I let it drop. "Hey, have you thought about what we should do after the wedding? In terms of me living here."

I had been sleeping on the couch in the study since Sam died. It seemed presumptuous to take the guest room. But the couch was lumpy as hell and wasn't sustainable.

"I have, actually. I know you're going to balk, but I think you should take Dad's room instead of the guest room."

"Not happening."

"Hear me out. It's got a private bathroom, so we wouldn't have to share. A TV. You could have your own space that's separate from me. It makes sense, Jake. I can't take it. It would be too weird and I don't want to move all my stuff anyway. I like my room."

I hated it when she made sense. "Okay."

"I'll start going through his stuff tomorrow."

"School," I instinctively said. It was Monday.

"One more day. I have what I need to catch up," she said, pointing at the laptop. "I think... I need one more day. Then I can do it."

"Okay. One more day."

I took my beer and was about to leave her to her homework when I thought about what Janet said. What people might think about us living together.

I wanted to ask her if she had concerns, but I didn't want to invite the ugliness of it inside. Of course it wouldn't have occurred to her that people might talk. She was growing up, but she was still innocent. I wasn't going to change that.

"Dinner in few hours?"

"Yep," she said. "Lots of casseroles. We have casseroles for life or something."

I laughed and thought it was the first time. The first time since Sam died. Ellie could always do that.

Yeah, I was doing the right thing.

FOUR

Ellie

I LOOKED at myself in the mirror. I didn't think I looked like a creepy teenage bride and I knew I wasn't a creepy teenage bride, but still...

I didn't look like me.

It was the same dress I wore to my dad's funeral—weird, I know—because it was still my nicest dress. Blue velvet, capped sleeves, with a belted waist. I wore my hair up because I thought it made me look older.

You know, because I was getting married today.

MARRIED.

I should at least look like I knew what I was doing.

I kept going back to my mantra. *It's no big deal. It's no big deal. It's no big deal.*

Who was I kidding? It was a big freaking deal. On a scale of one to ten, this was a full-on ten.

I was getting MARRIED.

I guess I always thought I would someday. Fall in love. Find my guy. Have kids. It was all out there as the *most likely future.*

Sure, sometimes I thought about leaving Montana and heading to New York and becoming some major advertising executive. I would work in this high rise building in a corner office. I would have people fetch me coffee and handle my dry cleaning. I would wear five-hundred-dollar shoes and thousand-dollar pant suits. And I would have someone blow out my hair every day because it always looked nice when Bella at the Hair Stop in town blew it out.

Only I knew that was never going to be my reality. My reality was cattle, horses, hay, chicken shit (literally chicken shit), and Montana.

So here I was, standing in front of a mirror in my blue velvet dress, leggings (because still January) and my hair up because I thought it made me look older.

Shoe choice was a no-brainer. Flats. Because guys did NOT date girls who were taller than them even if it was only because of shoes. It was a biological imperative.

Jake was pretty tall. I guess could have worn heels, but I didn't have any.

I didn't want to buy anything new for the wedding either, because then it might make it seem more than it was.

It was no big deal.

There was a soft knock on the door. "Ellie, you ready?"

It was Howard.

"Another minute?"

"Sure."

Howard had been great. He'd written up the pre-nup. What was mine was mine, what was Jake's was Jakes. It would make the divorce a lot cleaner. He'd gotten Judge Michaels to waive the parental consent on the marriage certificate. Howard and his secretary were going to be witnesses.

I wanted to keep it professional. No friends or anything. Besides, then I would have to chose between Karen or Chrissy, who were my two best friends. Either one would have been mad if I picked one over the other. If I had them both come, then it would have been a thing and Lisa might have felt left out.

No, it was best to make it business.

Janet definitely wasn't coming.

Jake said she was cool with the situation now. That she understood he was doing what he had to do and was willing to wait for him.

What he had to do.

That's what he'd said. *What he had to do.*

I didn't like it. When he said that, it made me feel like this charity case. Like that football player from the movie with Sandra Bullock. You know the one where she won the Oscar and was all like *I love my husband Jesse so much* only to find out practically the next day he was banging a porn star behind her back.

I felt like the football player. I needed to be saved.

Only what if he didn't need to be saved? What if I didn't?

He was a big freaking dude. What if he found a way to get into football without the rich blond?

I wasn't homeless. I wasn't poor. I was sitting on land worth two million freaking dollars. What if I could have made it on my own for sixteen months?

I had it so much easier than that football guy did. Yet, still I needed to be saved.

Jake was going to do what he *had* to do.

Another gentle knock. "Ellie? We're running a little

late now."

Right. Because we had one court, one judge, and he had way more important stuff to do.

Like traffic tickets and parking violations.

There was no point in putting it off, though. This was what *I* had to do.

I walked over to the door and opened it. Howard gave me a weak smile. No compliments, no anything. He started walking and I followed him through the hall into the open courtroom. There were a few people in the benches, waiting for their turn at whatever.

Jake was standing in front of the judge's desk.

Judge Michaels, who had made this all possible, was wearing jeans and a chambray shirt. He didn't do the whole robe thing, which was a little anticlimactic. A looming judge in a black robe might have been more ominous.

Because that's what this felt like. More like a sentencing than a wedding.

I ran through my options again.

Foster home.

Running away.

Or Jake.

Jake gave me a chin nod and I guessed that meant he was okay with everything. He was clearly my best option. If only we didn't have to be married.

Finally I shuffled toward him and stood next him. He was actually way taller than I was. My head only came up to his shoulder. I guess I hadn't realized that. Jake was the type of a guy a woman could wear high heels with if she had them. Which I didn't.

"You okay?" he asked me.

I nodded, but the truth was I felt nauseous. That would

make for some interesting wedding photos. Me puking on Jake's cowboy boots.

He was wearing his suit that he'd worn to Dad's funeral. Same suit he'd worn to his own father's funeral. His only suit. What if he wore it to his next wedding? That would be too awful. I would have to tell him that. *Do not marry Janet in the same suit you married me in.* I knew instinctively Janet would not like that.

"Is everyone ready?" the judge asked us.

I nodded. I could see Jake nod out of my peripheral vision because I didn't want to look at him directly. I didn't want to watch him as he made this sacrifice and essentially gave away a year and four months of his life.

For me.

"You don't have to do this," I blurted out. I turned to him but kept my head down. "I'll go to the foster home. It's only a year and..."

His hand was under my chin, lifting my face, forcing me to look at him. Until I reached his eyes. Those eyes, which I had known for as long as I could remember, told me everything.

"We got this," he said.

"You're sure?"

"Yep."

"I'm going to be your wife." I know I made a face at the word *wife*.

"You're going to be my family. Legally. That means I can protect you. Legally. That's all we're doing today."

"Right." *It was no big deal.*

"We're ready, Judge," Jake said. Then he took my hand.

"Hookay," I breathed out. "Let's get hitched."

It was short and simple.

Do you?

Yes.

Do you?

Yep.

By the powers invested in the judge by the state of Montana, we were legally a family.

But then the judge said it. The *kiss the bride* part. Probably out of habit. It wasn't like he was trying to be lurid or anything. Jake turned and kissed my forehead right in the center.

My dad used to do that. Whenever I was the most upset. Screaming or carrying on about anything. Crying. It didn't matter. He would hold me by the shoulders until I calmed down, and then kiss my forehead.

He was never going to do that again. He wasn't just gone. He was dead.

He was dead and he wasn't coming back ever. I was never going to talk to him or hug him again. I was never going to hear his voice when he called my name. He wasn't going to be at my real wedding. I wasn't going to dance with him. He wasn't going to know my kids.

I could feel this horrible ugly thing rolling around inside me. Like all the air and blood and guts had suddenly been sucked out of me. I was breathing and my lip was wobbling and I couldn't think hard enough to stop any of it.

"Ellie..."

I was holding on to Jake's forearms. Squeezing them as hard as I could to stay standing.

"My dad is dead," I sputtered out even as I felt the tears start pouring out of me. Except I didn't want to do this here. Not in front of Howard and his secretary, Sue Anne.

Not in front of Jake, because he might think I was weak and he wouldn't want to be married to a weak person. But I couldn't stop it. "He's....really dead..."

Except when I looked down at her, I realized I did feel different. More connected to her. More bonded to her than ever before. She was officially my responsibility.

Our marriage would only ever be a piece of paper.

But the immediate future was about us being a team. Me helping her through her grief. Getting her up to speed on what it meant to run a ranch. Her helping me figure out all the things Sam did that I probably didn't know.

Team JakeandEllie.

It was crazy, but I really liked the sound of that.

"I got snot all over your suit," she said when I got to the truck.

"If I put you down to open the door, are you going to be able to stand?" I could feel her nod against my neck.

I set her down and had her lean against the truck. I opened the passenger side door and then lifted her in. She felt like a limp doll.

I rounded the truck and got behind the wheel. She'd managed to get her seat belt on.

I took a deep breath. "I know this sucks to hear right now, but I swear you will get through this."

She didn't say anything. Just leaned her head back against the seat.

We had planned to have dinner in town. With Howard, as a thank you for arranging everything, rather than any kind of celebration. I was pretty sure he would understand if that didn't happen.

"Can we go home?" she asked.

Home. To our bizarre new world.

"Yep. Let's go home."

FIVE

Ellie

"I CAN'T BELIEVE you're married to Jake Talley," my friend Chrissy said.

It was Saturday and she'd come over to the house to work on a science project together. We were supposed to be creating water or something from ingredients, but I was pretty sure we were going to blow something up.

Science was not my strongest subject. Right behind math. I kept my average up with English, History and Spanish. Spanish I rocked because Javier and Gomez, who came to work during calving and sell-off season, helped me to be almost fluent.

"Get over it," I said back.

I pretty much had. It had been a week since the wedding. I was back in school. Jake was living in my dad's room. For the most part, things were settling back into normal. Weird normal, sad normal, but normal.

I was still crying myself to sleep every night, but I did it into a pillow so Jake wouldn't have to hear.

"Are you, like, allowed to drink now?"

Not according to Jake. Which I thought was lame.

"Uh, no. I'm married, I didn't suddenly turn twenty-one."

"Oh. Are you going to have to take him to the prom?"

I looked up at her. "Are you for real?"

"No, I mean seriously. He's your husband. And he's like super hot. You should totally take him to the prom."

"I'm not taking Jake to my prom."

Chrissy seemed to mull that over. "Do you think Riley will still ask you now that you're married?"

Ugh. That word. I was officially putting *married* in the same category as *orphan*.

"Who's Riley?" Great. Figured Jake would take that minute to enter the kitchen.

"Uh, I hate to break it to you, Jake, but your wife has a crush on him."

I slapped Chrissy's arm. "I do not."

"Who's Riley?" Jake asked again. Only this time he was asking me.

"He's a senior. He's nice. We talk every once and a while between classes. It's no big deal."

"If he's taking you to the prom, I want to meet him."

I had no idea why, but this rush of anger rolled over me. "Fuck that."

"Watch your mouth," Jake said, completely startled.

"You're not my dad, Jake. Please do no start acting like one."

"Uh... I'm going to head out now," Chrissy announced. "Sounds like you guys are about to have your first married fight."

Now my anger turned toward her. "Chrissy, we're not done yet with the experiment."

"Dude, it's okay. We have study period before class. We'll figure it out then."

Before I could say another word she'd gathered up her stuff and left. Which had me focusing my anger once again on the person responsible.

"That was so not cool."

He opened the door of the refrigerator and pulled out an apple.

"You're right. You weren't being cool at all. But you're still grieving, so these little outbursts and temper tantrums will continue to happen."

I hated when he did that. When he tried to explain everything I was feeling. "You can't do that. You can't make everything about me being sad. My point is if I want to go out with a guy, I do not need your approval."

"Like hell you don't. I am your family. I watch out for you. You want to go out with some guy, fine. But I get to meet him."

"That's so unfair. You get to have rules but I don't."

"I have rules because I'm the adult here."

"Yeah well, the law says I'm an adult now too because we're married. And marriage is supposed to be a fifty-fifty thing, not a dictatorship."

He seemed to consider that. "Okay. Fine. You can have rules. What do you want?"

Of course I drew a complete blank. Then I thought of something. I don't know why I said it, but it just came out.

"I don't want Janet sleeping in Dad's room. I get that you have sex and stuff. I just don't want to walk out of my room in the morning and bump into her. It would be super weird."

She hadn't stayed over since the wedding. Not before it either. They were still doing their Sunday lunches, and I knew he had plans to go out with her tonight. Maybe that's why I thought about it. This would be their first real date since the funeral. Their first opportunity to do it.

Then I thought about them doing *it* in my dad's room and got freaked out by it. I wasn't planning on saying anything. I figured it was something I would have to live with. He and Janet were a couple. They would have sex. My dad's room was where Jake lived now.

Of course he'd want his girlfriend to stay over.

Although now that I thought about it, she'd never stayed over all night when he was living in the bunk house.

That house was a two-level structure about a hundred yards out behind the barn. The first level was where my dad used to keep tractors and other equipment he didn't want in the barn. The second floor was a bunch of rooms with one bathroom and a kitchen.

It's where Jake had lived for the last six years, and for two of those years he'd been dating Janet. I got up sick early to be able to get my chores done and still get to school on time, and I never once saw her car parked in front of the bunk house when I knew she'd come over the night before.

I was about to let him off the hook. It was kind of stupid. I was probably being immature, which I hated. It was so stereotypical teenager... immaturity. I needed to get beyond it. Because in sixteen months, when Jake and I did get divorced, it was going to be all on me to run this place and make a life for myself.

"Forget it," I said. "It was stupid."

"No. It's not. And it's a rule. Your rule. I won't let Janet stay over. I never have out of respect to your dad. Now it's a matter of respecting you. This is your home, Ellie."

"It's yours too. I don't want you to feel like it's not. I guess... I mean it's not like you would let me have sex with my boyfriend and he could stay the night."

He didn't like that. I could tell, because that muscle in the back of his jaw started working hard. I got it. Older brother complex and all that.

"Right. Sorry. I have to remain a virgin until death, but you get to have all the sex you want. No double standard there."

"Ellie..." He clearly wanted to say something, but stopped.

"What?"

"I can't have this conversation with you right now." Then he did the immature thing and left.

That's right. I scared Jake Talley out of the room with sex talk.

I smiled what I hoped was one of those little evil smiles, because seriously that was fun. Then I got back to work on my project, because Chrissy and I always used that study period before Science to gossip.

Jake

"THAT WAS FUN!" Janet had her hand on my leg, on my thigh. Pretty high up on my thigh actually.

We were driving on the highway after dinner and some country line dancing. This being our first date since the wedding, I wanted to step my game up. Jefferson had this new country western bar for people who liked to drink hard and dance hard.

Tonight Janet was one of those people. She'd decided

for our first real date since Sam had died that tequila was a good idea. I had fun watching her dance moves slowly digress until she found herself stepping right when everyone else was sliding left.

It was just after eleven, but it had definitely been time to call it a night. Right now she was fun drunk Janet. I knew from experience that one more shot and she would transition to difficult drunk Janet.

However, this is where the situation got tricky. If I took her back to the bunk house for some drunk sex—and drunk sex with Janet was fun because she tended to loosen up a little more in bed—there was no way she was going to be able to drive home.

The new rule was she wasn't allowed to stay over in the house.

I understood. Ellie knew Janet, but to have her in the house in the morning when Ellie was doing her morning thing would be weird.

But if I took Janet home back to her parents' place, then no drunk sex.

"I want you so bad, Jake Talley," she said, leaning over the truck's console. She actually bit my ear.

Yep. Fun drunk Janet and sex.

Decision made, I took the exit for Long Valley. The problem was as soon as I pulled up to the house and was about to explain that we needed to use the bunk house, Janet was already out of the truck and heading up the front porch. She opened the front door, which wasn't locked, and walked right in.

A few things went through my mind.

One, Ellie needed to lock the door when she was home at night. Yes, Long Valley Ranch was in many ways quite literally in the middle of nowhere. But the guys from her school presumably knew where she lived. Guys who knew she no longer had a father to protect her.

What would they think of me? Sure I was the husband, but I had spent Saturday night out with my girlfriend.

They would know that too. They would all know I was still with Janet, which meant Ellie was out here by herself. Unprotected.

I didn't like that. Hell, I didn't like this guy Riley and I hadn't even met him.

I didn't look too closely at it. Ellie was basically a little sister. What older brother wouldn't be protective? It's because I knew what guys, especially seventeen-year-old guys, thought about.

We wanted pussy. All we wanted was pussy. And we wanted to tell as many guys as we could when we got pussy, that we'd had pussy.

I never told any of the guys when Dinah and I finally did it my junior year. My father had drummed that much manhood into me.

But I'd wanted to. Which was so stupid in hindsight.

So I knew Riley wanted Ellie and I knew Ellie was vulnerable right now. Not a good combination. I was going to have to change that. Make sure she was more protected.

Because she was mine now.

My second thought was how Janet could be in the living room right now with Ellie, who was probably in her tank top and pajama bottoms watching television.

Fun drunk Janet walked into Ellie's house thinking she could, because she was my girlfriend. I needed to hustle her out of there fast. Especially since I knew Ellie wasn't exactly her biggest fan.

I jogged up the steps of the front porch and followed

Janet inside. She was in the living room, sprawled out on the couch. Her cowboy boots on the arm rest.

Thankfully, Ellie was not there to see her. Hopefully she was sound asleep in her room. Oblivious to any noise.

"Janet, this is not cool," I said as I picked up her ankles and turned them so her boots were on the rug and not on the furniture. "This is not your house."

"No, but it's yours now isn't it?" She was twirling a finger in her hair, trying to look seductive. It was working. Then again, anything would. It had been a few weeks of stress and sadness and I wanted to get laid.

I could feel my dick getting hard and thought I had maybe two or three rounds in me before I had to drive her home. Because while letting her stay over in the bunk house wasn't technically breaking the rule... I still didn't like the visual.

Because Ellie was right. It wasn't fair. I got to have sex. She didn't because I said so. The last thing I needed to do was rub it in her face.

"Come on. Let's get out of here. We'll head over to the bunk house."

Janet sat up. "Why? You have a room here. In fact it looks like we're all alone now. You know that thing that I never do that I know you really like..."

She was leaning forward and reaching for my belt. That thing she hardly ever did but I really liked was a blow job.

Fun drunk Janet was undoing my belt and running her tongue around her lips as if she was about to give me a blow job in the living room.

Now I was rock hard, but I had to stop this.

"Janet stop," I said, trying to push her hands away from undoing the buttons on my jeans.

"Why? You know you want it. I can see your hard peen."

Janet called my dick a peen, her nickname for penis. It was one of the more annoying things about her when it came to sex.

Call the damn thing what it was. A cock, a dick, an erection, a penis.

Peen was not sexy.

Since she was not getting the picture, I finally had to grab her hands and take a solid step back. "Not here," I snapped.

"What?" she screeched. "We're alone."

"She's freaking upstairs. What if she comes downstairs for some damn water?"

Her face got hard then. "Oh sorry. Wouldn't want to upset your *wife*."

And there it was. Fun drunk Janet was gone. Apparently that last shot had finally kicked in. I, however, still wanted to salvage the night.

Translated, I wanted to fuck someone. And my girlfriend was Janet.

"Look, let's just go to the bunk house. We'll have all the privacy we want."

"The bunk house? We can't even have sex in the house where you now live because you're afraid of what...? Ellie is going to find out that you have sex?"

"She knows I have sex," I muttered. Not really even comfortable with that.

"I got it. Sam was old fashioned, so you wouldn't let me spend the night. But get real, Jake. Ellie is a big girl who I'm sure can handle me being here."

"Actually she asked that I not let you stay overnight in the house."

That was probably the wrong thing to say. I literally watched my chance to get laid evaporate in front of me.

Janet's arms were crossed over her chest, her face was hard. Not the image of a woman who still wanted to give me head.

"Are you fucking kidding me?"

"Look, it's her house. She knows we date, yes. But it's not like she knows you that well. How would you feel if you woke up and some stranger was making coffee in your kitchen?"

"I'm not some fucking stranger, Jake. I'm your girlfriend of two fucking years. And I'm not going to hide out in the bunk house like I'm... I'm... your fucking mistress!"

I really hated it when she cursed. She didn't do it often. But when she started, she couldn't stop herself.

I lowered my voice in an attempt to get her to do the same. I did this so I wouldn't have to tell her to be quiet, which whenever I did that with difficult drunk Janet, she invariably got louder.

"I don't get what the big deal is. You've always been fine with the bunk house. It's nice in there with the fireplace going."

She stood, wobbled on her feet a little, but steadied herself.

"Take me home."

"Janet..." I sighed. I really wanted to get laid.

"Now."

"Yeah. Okay." The night was over. I could see it in her face.

I drove her home without a word between us. There was no point. She was too drunk to really listen or understand anything I might have said. I thought about the hand job I would give myself when I got home as a way to distract myself.

The reality was that by the time I took her back to her place, then drove all the way back to Long Valley, I was too tired to do anything but crash. A rancher worked seven days a week, three hundred and sixty-five days a year, and I needed to be up at dawn.

I made a mental note to talk to Ellie about always locking the door before I fell asleep.

SIX

Ellie
February

"THIS IS WEIRD. Do you think everyone will be staring at us?" I asked Jake as I sat in the passenger seat of his truck while I looked across the parking lot of Nash's Grocery Store.

"Why would people be staring at us?"

"Uh, it's our first official appearance as a married couple in town."

Jake huffed as he popped open his door. "We're at the grocery store, Ellie. It's not like we're going to walk in as they announce us Mr. and Mrs."

Fine, he didn't have to be freaked out, but I was. We were three weeks into our fake marriage, with only fifteen months and one week to go.

Javier and Gomez were back. It took a little bit of explaining in my best Spanish that my dad was dead and I was married to Jake. They didn't blink. Like it made sense that we would marry and carry on with the ranch.

They called me boss lady. They called him boss man. They did the work as always, with little conversation and no complaints.

But as soon as the calves started to drop the work increased by threefold. Protecting the newborns, watching for predators who had a penchant for calf afterbirth, constantly monitoring the weather for sudden drops in temperature. During calving season a rancher had to be super hyper-focused on all of it.

It was a big deal to take time out from that, but today we decided we would go grocery shopping together. This way I could get a handle on what he liked and him the same with me.

Which meant that one us (which would be either of us at times, because the idea that only women grocery shopped was sexist) could do grocery shopping in the future and we would be confident we knew what the other person liked.

As it was restock day at Nash's, I was feeling pretty confident they would have at least one of everything I typically bought.

We grabbed a cart and started with fruit.

"I like apples," Jake said. "Any kind."

"That's fine, but a few bananas too. Also I'm allergic to anything berry."

"No berries, got it."

We moved on to produce.

"Vegetables suck," Jake said. I had to cut him a little slack because he was a cattle rancher and meat was his passion. "I know vegetarians exist, but don't try to actually convince me this shit is good."

"It's good for you," I said. "That's the point. You shove

enough broccoli and asparagus down and you don't feel guilty about french fries."

Jake looked super serious when he said, "I never feel guilty about french fries. I can handle lettuce, spinach, and broccoli. Bring home Brussels sprouts and you're on your own."

So noted. We didn't have to worry about the meat aisle, because we obviously butchered and ate our own. However, I did point out the need for chicken. Because I was a girl and couldn't live on red meat, and because chicken parmesan was delicious.

"Why? We can just kill one of the chickens no longer laying eggs."

"No," I said. "I like the chickens."

Then I got the rancher frown. My dad had mastered this look by the time I was three.

Ellie, you don't get attached to the product. Cows are meat, chickens lay eggs until they become meat, and the horses are your employees. You want a pet, we'll get a dog.

"I know, I know. I'm saying every once in a while packaged chicken instead of having to slaughter the dinner I fed that day is easier, okay?"

"Fine."

That's when things got a little dicey. We cleared shampoo and conditioner no problem. I liked Fruictise Rainforest, and yes I needed both shampoo and conditioner. He liked Dove shampoo because it was the cheapest.

I needed body wash, any brand would do.

He needed Irish Spring soap.

He showed me the razors he liked. I showed him the deodorant I had to have. Fresh Scent.

Then we got to feminine products.

"Awkwaaaard," I sang.

"Get a grip. You're married now."

I laughed. I think that was actually a joke. Jake didn't really do jokes very often.

"Always pads, Tampax tampons." I showed him the right color bag and box.

"Yep."

We walked past the condom section. Did not say a word. Just kept walking right past it.

Joey at the register bagged us up and we made it back to the truck without anyone stopping us or staring at us or in general being weirded out by us.

On a scale of one to ten, I called the shopping trip a resounding nine.

Jake thought my whole scale stuff was stupid.

Jake
March

"TELL me what I'm watching again?"

It had become a thing, I realized. Ellie and I would either cook or clean up. We went back and forth based on whoever felt like doing what. Sometimes that came down to a coin flip, then we changed into our comfort clothes (she called them jammies—I refused to reference any article of clothing I had as jammies) and watched TV.

I was a rancher, I was up at dawn so I was in bed by nine at the latest, but sometimes it helped to drift off to something mindless.

She had her phone in her hand and was feverishly texting someone. "*Scandal*," she said without look up.

"Catch me up. What's the plot?"

She lifted her head and gasped. Actually gasped. "I can't catch you up on *Scandal*. Do you know how many things have happened? It would take months, it would take essays."

Essays? On a TV show?

"I can't get a general grasp?"

She sighed and set her phone aside. "Well, okay, that's Olivia Pope and she has this badass law firm, sort of? Anyway she was in love with the President, and they had an affair, but he of course was married and then she fell in love with Jake, I think. Or she's still been in love with the President the whole time, it's hard to know. But Jake is a serious badass and no one is sure if he really loves her or if he is just loyal to her father."

"Who is her father?"

She looked at me like I had two heads. "Hello, he's the bad guy. There, that guy. He runs like this super spy agency, which does really bad things. Oh, and he killed the President's son."

I tried to think about what that meant. "So Olivia was having an affair with the President, but then her father killed his son."

"Yes. But I think at the end of the show she's ultimately going to end up with the President and not Jake. You know. True love."

Her phone started buzzing again and she went back to texting.

I didn't know much about true love. My mother left my father when I was five. Still, if my true love's father killed my son, I'm pretty sure I would have a problem with it.

"Who are you texting? Chrissy?" I wasn't sure why I asked. I guess because it wasn't like her to be so distracted. She wasn't one of those girls pinned to her phone all the time. She had too much work to do around the farm for that kind of stuff.

I wasn't certain if she was even on Facebook. I sure as hell wasn't.

"Riley."

The boy. Now it made sense. "I want to meet him at some point."

"Yes, Jake," she answered, but I could tell she was humoring me.

Still, I figured I would leave her to her... conversation. All that typing. I don't get why he didn't man up and call her.

"I think I'll go up and watch ESPN."

She smiled at me. "Okay."

I got up and started to head out of the living room when she said, "Jake?"

"Yep?"

"*Game of Thrones* is coming back soon. You like that show, right?"

"My favorite."

"Okay, so we can watch that together."

She was lonely, I thought. The texting Riley aside, this was different. Being in the house with someone. Sam had been more than her father, he'd been her whole world. Except for me.

"Yeah," I told her. "We can watch that together."

Ellie
April

"NOT BAD," Jake said as I showed him the numbers. We

were at the kitchen table. It was Sunday night, which meant we were working financials of the ranch.

Expenses, our calf yield, the current market rates for beef, and what we needed to sell to hit our goals.

It was strange because I wasn't the best at math in school, but for this stuff you could use a calculator and I seemed to have a head for it.

Like now I was showing Jake how we were overpaying for hay. My dad had always stuck with Mr. Johnson, but they were charging almost ten dollars more for a large bale than the McCurdys.

I had no intention of being disloyal to Mr. Johnson, but I told him if he didn't come down on the price I was walking.

He crumpled like a tin can under extreme water pressure.

Jake could care less about that kind of stuff. Until he saw the result.

"You really called Mr. Johnson up and started haggling for hay cost," he said smiling as I showed him what it meant in savings per year.

"Girl's got to do what a girl's got to do.'"

He looked at me then and I could see he was thinking something serious.

"You're really getting into this. I wasn't completely sure if you would or not."

"Uh, hello? Like I sort of have no choice. Future here."

He nodded. "I guess it never it occurred to me if this was the future you wanted?"

"Of course it is."

Right? I mean I always knew ranching was my future. I suppose I wanted it. Or maybe I hadn't really thought it out because I was supposed to be way older before I started having to do any of this stuff.

And it was a lot of stuff.

So I thought about it. Really thought about it and answered him again. "I'm a Mason. Long Valley is Mason land and has been for five generations. It's mine to have and work for future Masons. I don't know if it's about wanting it so much as knowing this is my destiny. It all came way faster than I was expecting. But it doesn't mean I can be any less responsible about it. Does that sound corny?"

He smiled, then reached over and ruffled my hair, which I hated.

"Stop!" I smacked at his hands.

He laughed and seemed to come to some conclusion about something.

"When school's out I'll start taking you around more. Showing you every aspect about the ranch. I want you to be as prepared as you can be."

Yep. That's what I needed to be. As prepared as I could be because we were counting down time now. Only twelve months and two weeks left.

SEVEN

Ellie
April 22

IT WAS OFFICIAL. Today was going to be the best day of my life. On a scale of one to ten, a total ten.

First, it was my birthday. Jake promised to make me my favorite for breakfast. Eggs and ridiculously burnt bacon. Normally we fended for ourselves in the morning. He was always up before me anyway.

Especially during calving season, because those little suckers were always popping out.

He could be up around the clock some days. But calving season was always exciting because it meant securing the future. Which was good news, something we needed around Long Valley because we hadn't had it in a while.

Either of us.

Janet had broken up with Jake a couple of months ago.

Then she asked him to get back together. Then she broke up with him again.

It was all very intense.

As of today I think they were officially on again, but one thing was quite certain.

She hated me.

Like next-level hated me. My first official enemy in Riverbend. She would call the house line because cell service was spotty out on the ranch, and I could hear it in her voice.

Hi Ellie! How are yooooo?

So chipper. So peppy.

Translated.

I hate you, Ellie... please divorce my boyfriend soon.

One more year to go. Anyway, back to my birthday. I was seventeen. Jake was taking time to make me breakfast this morning. I wasn't expecting a gift, but you never knew with him. Some times Jake did (remember my horse Petunia—that was a Jake gift) and sometimes he didn't. Just a simple 'happy birthday kiddo' instead.

Point of fact, I hated it when called me kiddo.

I made sure he had a gift on his birthday every year he lived with us, because he was... Well, he wasn't an orphan. We all figured his mom was alive somewhere in the world, but no one knew that for certain. What was certain was that she would never step foot inside the state of Montana again. She had hated living here. A transplant Ernie had picked up from Seattle and brought home.

Not a good fit.

Since he was basically as good as an orphan, I would make my dad give me money so Jake had a present on his birthday and for Christmas.

Today, first time as my husband, who knew what to

expect. But it didn't matter. Because no gift was going to be as big as tonight.

Tonight was prom night. We didn't do proms by grades. Just one big dance where everybody could go. In the gym, which was a little old-school cheesy, but the only place in Riverbend that would fit us all for an event.

Riley had in fact asked me to go with him. We weren't dating, but we were officially hanging out. With some kissing. Hanging out and kissing. Tonight was going to be our first real date.

I had a dress. I had an appointment with Bella to get my hair blown out. But the best thing was... I was going to lose it tonight. The V card. I was going to tell Riley I wanted to have sex. Actual sex. Full on penetration. His dick, my vagina. We were going to do it.

Chrissy had done it. Lisa had done it. Karen hadn't done it yet, but she'd given her boyfriend a blow job.

I had done nothing! Nothing except the kissing and I was ready for more.

I had condoms. I would be safe. I figured it wasn't going to be as good as Bella and Edward's first time, but Riley was hot and I was really motivated.

Jake had met Riley and had instantly shut him down with a man glare. Of course. Worse, I could tell it had made Riley uncomfortable. When I'd called Jake out about it, he'd said a man shouldn't be intimidated by a look. I would have reminded him that Riley was only eighteen, but it didn't matter. Jake was not going to like any boyfriend I brought home. It was how he was built.

And truth was, he didn't get to have a say in this part of my life.

We had been clear from the get go. Our sex lives were separate. Sure, he didn't think I had one, and if he knew what I was planning tonight would probably do something to make that not happen. I figured what he didn't know wouldn't hurt him.

I knew entirely far too much about his. Thanks to a pretty loud Janet several months ago I knew his girlfriend called his dick a peen and that Jake liked blow jobs.

Things I figured out pretty quickly about myself: I would never call a guy's dick anything other than what it was. A dick, a cock, a penis, whatever. Janet had sounded like an idiot.

Also I took it for granted that most guys liked blow jobs. I thought I wanted to start with some straight-up sex first, but I was of the opinion I should be open minded in all things related to sex.

How could you know what you liked or what you didn't if you didn't try it all?

I had even tried doing it to myself, but I was not having a whole lot of success pulling off the orgasm thing. I could finger myself and play with my nipples, and that felt good, but it never went anywhere, which I knew it should. Which meant I probably wasn't doing it right, but it's not like I was going to ask my girlfriends how to jack off and it certainly wasn't a conversation I could have with Jake.

In some ways I was hoping he would be cool with me about guys and sex. He wasn't that much older than I was. It's not like he didn't remember high school at all. I thought I could talk to him as one soon-to-be non-virginal adult to another.

It took that one hard macho staredown when I introduced him to Riley to seal the deal.

He couldn't *not* be that guy. The overprotective, wrap me up in bubble wrap and let's pretend that I wasn't going to be on my own in a year running this ranch, guy.

I bounced out of bed washed my face and brushed my teeth and headed down for breakfast. I could already smell the bacon cooking. I would eat first, then chores, then get ready for school.

"I smell bacon," I sang.

"Burning as we speak," he said over a popping and sizzling frying pan.

I sat on the stool at the island and waited patiently. "Eggs, eggs, eggs," I said, pounding the counter with my fists. Okay, maybe not so patient.

Finally he put a plate in front of me with eggs over easy, burnt bacon, and toast that was more butter than bread. My total favorite!

I dug in and after a few bites looked up at him and smiled.

"Birthday breakfast rocks," I said.

"Happy Birthday, kiddo."

Okay, that meant no gift. And let's face it, I was seventeen. Not really a big deal year. Last year had been Petunia. Still, a part of me was a teensy bit disappointed. I was the guy's wife after all. And since my dad wasn't here, that meant no one was going to give me a present.

Well, I suppose Riley was. The gift of sex. I tried to hide my smile.

"One more year to go," I said, shrugging off the no-gift thing. "We should find a place in the house and make those lines like they do in prison movies, counting off the days. Three hundred and sixty-five left."

"Absolutely. Because living here with you is almost as bad as prison."

Jake left the kitchen then, and came back with a wrapped package in his hands.

I clapped and squealed, because really it was my birthday and who didn't want a gift on your birthday?

I took it. It was square and fairly heavy. When I opened it, it was a framed picture of my mom and dad that I had never seen before. It looked like Christmas, because there were lights up on the porch. My dad was standing behind my mom with his hands over her stomach, her hands on top of his.

They were both beaming into the camera. Oh my God I missed them.

"Turn it over."

I did and I could see the frame in the back was clear. So I could read my dad's handwriting scrawled on the back of the photo.

We're pregnant!

I put the picture down on the counter and walked over to Jake. He had his arms open and I stood in them for five solid minutes crying on his chest. Finally the crying turned to sniffles.

"Where did you find it?"

"It was stuck in the back of the top dresser drawer. It was pretty creased, but I found a good frame person who made it look nice again. I thought you would like it."

"I love it."

He stroked my hair and rocked me in his arms because I wasn't ready to let go yet. I guess we didn't hear the front door open, but Janet walked into the kitchen and made this little gasping sound.

I'll never know why I did it. I mean it wasn't like Jake and I were doing anything wrong. He gave me this awesome and kind of sad picture of my mom and dad, and was comforting me through that sadness.

Totally legit.

Still, as soon as I heard that gasping sound, I pushed him away. So hard he stumbled back a step. We stood next to each other looking at Janet and it was officially weird.

"Hey Janet," he said.

"Hey."

"Janet, look at this awesome picture Jake gave me for my birthday." See the reason why I was hugging him. Why he was holding me. I picked it up and showed it to her. She was looking at it, making this humming sound in the back of her throat.

"I brought cupcakes," she said. "For your birthday."

That was super nice. I wondered if there was arsenic in them.

"I'm making eggs," Jake said. "Want some?"

"Sure."

Jake went back to the stove. Janet sat next to me. I tried to eat my eggs, bacon and toast as fast as I possibly could, but I wasn't leaving a crumb behind, because it was my birthday breakfast. Eight minutes later I was done.

"Okay, I'm out. You remember it's prom tonight, right?"

The deal was Chrissy, Karen, and Lisa were coming over and we were all going to get ready here. Then we were going to take Chrissy's Jeep, because she had the coolest car, into town and meet the guys at the dance. Then Riley was going to drive me home, by way of my dad's hunting cabin where I was going to have sex for the first time.

The cabin was prepared with five stolen beers, to get in the mood. Sorry, Javier and Gomez. A strip of five condoms —thank you, Karen's boyfriend—and a really soft blanket. And a bag of Combos in case we got hungry after.

"Yes," he said as if I hadn't been reminding him all week, which I had. "Midnight, Cinderella. Not a minute later or I come looking for you with my shotgun."

The plan was to leave the dance at ten. By the time we got back to the cabin, that left a solid hour and fifteen minutes for sex.

"Yep. It's a deal."

I grabbed my picture and hugged it to my chest as I scrambled out of the kitchen.

Totally the best night ever.

Jake

GUILT. I was feeling guilt. I was looking at the eggs frying in the grease, trying to understand this emotion, and finally I had to call it what it was.

Guilt.

There was absolutely nothing to be guilty about. I gave Ellie the picture, I knew she would love it, but I knew it would hurt in a weird way, too. She cried, I consoled her. That was it.

"I think the eggs are burning," Janet said from her seat at the kitchen island.

I was on top of them and I didn't see it. The edges were burning. I slipped them onto a plate. Added less burnt bacon and turned around to serve her. Slowly I set the plate in front of her.

Like she was this unpredictable animal and I didn't know what was going to happen next.

She said nothing. Just took the fork I offered and started eating.

"That was nice. The cupcakes and all," I said.

"Hmm," she nodded.

"Ellie was shook up about the picture but I think she really liked it."

"Yeah."

I didn't do this. I didn't play games. I was a man who on any given day had about a hundred tasks that needed to be completed. Otherwise animal lives could be lost, human lives could be lost, money could be lost. Which meant I always had to cut to the chase to get the work done.

"Why don't you say what you're upset about and have at it," I snapped. "Yes, I was holding Ellie, who was crying because of a picture I gave her of her dead parents."

Janet put the fork down on the plate as if it was sterling silver. "You know what, Jake? I think you're mad because I told you this might happen. I think you thought it couldn't happen to you. No, not the honorable Jackson Talley. Never him. You were so above it."

"What in the hell are you talking about, Janet?"

You know how you do that thing. When you ask someone a question like they are crazy, but really you know exactly what they are talking about. Yes, I knew exactly what she meant, but she was wrong.

Me holding Ellie meant nothing. I didn't feel anything other than deep affection for the person who I counted as family.

It was guilt that made this awkward.

"I don't know, you two looked awfully guilty when I walked in. Hell, she nearly toppled you over. And you, you can't even look at me."

She was right. I had evaded all eye contact.

"You're falling for her."

I shook my head. "You are so ridiculous right now, I can't have this conversation."

Because the conversation wasn't going to end well and I

had too much shit to do today. This wasn't about me falling for Ellie. The truth, the real truth was I liked her more than Janet. That was where the guilt came from.

There. It was out. At least in my mind.

At some point in these last few months of our on-again, off-again relationship, I had stopped liking Janet. If there was someone I wanted to spend time with, it was Ellie.

Only I couldn't have sex with Ellie, so I needed Janet. Which was wrong on so many levels.

And wait, did I just think about sex and Ellie in the same thought in my head?

Oh shit, I wasn't...

No. Ellie was Ellie. This wasn't about her. This was about Janet. I felt guilty that Janet caught me liking someone way more than her.

Janet opened the bakery box she had brought and took out a cupcake. She peeled the paper away from the cake and bit into it.

"Chocolate with vanilla frosting. I knew that was her favorite because you told me."

"Janet, for real, I have to get to work. We can talk about this later."

"No, I think we're done talking." She threw the cupcake at me and it hit me squarely in the face. "You fucking wasted two years of my fucking life."

Fuck the drama.

I was wiping icing out of my eyes as she breezed by me. I was pissed enough and small enough to shout at her as she left.

"FYI, you suck at sucking dick."

The front door slammed and the house rattled. I was toweling the frosting off my face when Ellie reappeared, dressed in clothes to feed the chickens.

"Don't say a damn word," I snapped.

"Okay. But I super hope you're okay being broken up for good with her, because trust me when I tell you no girl is getting over that."

I didn't care. Because I was super over her.

IT WAS eleven thirty that night when the front door was slammed shut hard for the second time that day.

I looked up, surprised to see Ellie. I checked my watch to be sure but yes, it was a full thirty minutes prior to midnight. I didn't think she would be home a minute sooner. It had been tough to watch her leave tonight.

In some ways she looked all grown up in her pretty blue long dress with the thin sleeves. Her hair all blown out and hanging down her back. In other ways she looked like a girl trying to be a woman. Except she wasn't a woman. Not yet.

That's what seventeen was all about.

Seeing her as dressed up and as sexy as she could make herself put the whole morning into perspective. I didn't have to worry about myself or my feelings for her. Not when she was still a girl.

I was about to comment on the thirty minutes when I looked at her face. It was red and blotched. Her lipstick was smeared around her mouth and her mascara, which she'd applied too much of, was smudged around her eyes.

She looked pissed and I thought someone was going to die that night.

That someone being Riley.

I stood up slowly, and calmly, again because I was dealing with an unpredictable animal. A teenage girl/woman.

"Ellie," I said as I moved toward her.

"I don't want to talk about it!" she screeched and bolted up the stairs before I could catch her. But this was something she didn't get to *not* talk about. Not when she'd been on a date with an eighteen-year-old guy and came home looking like that.

She'd shut the bedroom door, but hadn't bothered to lock it. Maybe because she didn't think I would ever dare to come in. I had lived in this house for four months and I had not once seen the inside of this room.

For that matter, it had probably been four months since she'd stepped in what had been her father's room.

She was lying facedown on the bed. When I came closer, she turned her head so she wasn't looking at me.

"Ellie, talk to me. What happened tonight?"

My gut clenched. What the hell was I going to do if that prick actually hurt her?

"I mean it, Ellie. You don't start talking, I'm going to find that boy and make him tell me."

"Nothing," she said and scrambled up until she was sitting on her knees. Yep, she was all sorts of pissed off. "Okay. Are you happy? Nothing happened."

"Was something supposed to happen?"

She put her face in her hands. "Yes, I was supposed to have sex. There, I said it. I didn't want to be a virgin anymore and I really liked Riley. So I told him we should go to the hunting cabin, and I had beer and condoms, and we could do it. And he said no. He said I was married and that it would be adultery and it was against his fucking religion! He said he liked me but he could never do that with me ever while I was still married. Which is so ridiculous. He can kiss me and make out with me even though I'm married, but not have sex with me?"

I didn't catch much beyond beer and condoms. And it was so horribly sexist. I had sex when I was seventeen with Dinah. There had been beer and condoms. But the thought of Ellie in the hunting cabin...

I took a breath. Raised my eyes to heaven, asking Sam for inspiration, and then sat on the bed next to her and tried to get a grip on my feelings.

"Okay, let's break down what you said. You didn't want to be a virgin anymore. Why?"

"Because everyone has done it except me."

"And that's the reason to have sex with someone?"

"Oh please, don't give me the *if everyone jumps off a bridge am I going to jump off a bridge* speech. Yes, everyone is having this huge life experience and I wanted to try it too. I mean, it's supposed to feel good and be fun. As long as it's safe and no one gets hurt or pregnant, what's the big deal?"

"Wow. You are a virgin."

"Uh, hello. What I'm telling you."

"Ellie, yes sex can be fun and feel good, but man, it's way more than that. Especially the first time. That first time there has to be huge amounts of trust. Have you ever gotten naked with a guy?"

"No."

"It's scary. The first time. For the guy and the girl both, it's like oh shit... we're both naked and you can see and touch everything."

That made her huff out a laugh.

"And the other part. When a woman lets a guy inside her body for the first time, obviously I'm not a woman and I can't imagine how that feels, but for me it's like this huge gift from the woman. Like she opened herself up completely to me and my body. Every time it happens I think wow, she is the bravest person for letting me do this.

For trusting me with this. Then all that goes out the window because it does feel pretty good."

She leaned against me as if all the adrenaline had left her. Which let's face it, the adrenaline must have been pumping through her all day if she thought this was how the night was going to end. Because no one went into that first time without a lot of nerves.

Dinah and I had both been trembling. Before, during and after.

"I thought it was going to be the best night ever."

"I can't say I'm sorry it didn't go as planned. But trust me, Ellie, it's the person who you're with that will tell you when it's the right time to have sex. Not a day on a calendar, but a man who you can trust implicitly with something so important."

She lifted her head off my shoulder and looked at me. "You were surprisingly good at that. That was a legit sex talk."

I was. Because I cared about her and I was honest.

"Go wash your face before you fall asleep. You've got gunk everywhere."

I got off the bed and made my way to the door.

"Thanks again for the birthday gift, Jake. And thanks for being cool about tonight."

"No problem."

I shut the door behind me and thought that went about as well as it could have, and then I didn't think of it again. Because Ellie having sex in the hunting cabin... holy shit.

Right now it was my job to protect her. For better or worse, richer for poorer, for the next three hundred and sixty five days.

That was it.

EIGHT

Ellie

IT WAS the next Tuesday after the prom. I was no longer hanging out with Riley. Obviously. In a lot of ways Jake was right. I wanted to have sex. Riley was the guy I was hanging out with, but I didn't know how much I wanted to have sex with Riley. I liked him. I liked kissing him. But all that stuff Jake said about Riley penetrating my body and was I cool with that?

Truthfully, I think I probably would have freaked out.

Fine. I didn't yet know which guy was the one. I would wait. It wasn't like sex was going anywhere. There would be all kinds of chances in the next forty or fifty years. I wasn't sure at what age people stopped having sex. My dad was still going strong at fifty-seven, so that had to mean something.

I sat down at our normal lunch table in the high school cafeteria. Karen, Lisa, and Chrissy where there. They all knew what didn't happen. They all knew about how cool Jake had been about the whole thing. They were all supportive.

They were my friends.

Now it was behind me. We had all vowed to never speak of what became known as the Great Prom Debacle again.

Except in that moment Bobby MacPherson showed up at our table. Sitting down next to me on the bench, facing away from the table.

"So Mason, hear you are looking for some action?"

My face flushed as I realized what he meant. Seriously, that's how you know you're a virgin, because it takes you that long to realize what he's asking you.

Bobby MacPherson was the best athlete in the school, which really didn't mean much as team sports weren't that big of a thing in Riverbend. Mostly because we were too far away from other schools to have regular weekly games, but also because non-traditional sports like rodeo were bigger in Montana.

Still, we had a football team that mostly scrimmaged amongst themselves and played the team from Jefferson twice a season. Bobby was QB One and like some bad cliché in a high school TV drama, QB One thought his shit didn't stink. He made everyone in class call him Mac, which was stupid because his name was Bobby. So I called him Bobby.

"Screw you, Bobby."

And screw Riley for blabbing. I mean really? He rejects me then has to tell everyone about it. What kind of douchebag move is that?

"No, screw you. That's what I'm offering," he snickered at Chrissy's horrified gasp.

As I previously mentioned, I was mostly liked by people but let's face it, it was high school and the weird kid was always separated from the herd. Weird enough I had no mom going in to high school. Now no father. Weirder still I had a husband and everyone knew it. I suppose they had been giving me an obligatory amount grieving time before dismissing any considerations for my feelings. Now the gloves were off and I, the weird married high school student, was fair game.

"Although I don't get it, is Jake not doing a good job of plowing you every night? Or is that even legal? I mean you're his wife, but you're also still jail bait. What's a guy to do?"

"You're disgusting. And you're not worth my time."

I turned back to my lunch and ignored him. Or at least pretended to.

"Every guy in school knows you're fair game now, Mason. That you're hot for it."

He'd said it quietly in my ear. Like it was some kind of threat. Yeah, most people liked me because I got along with most people.

Not with Bobby. Because he knew I didn't buy his bullshit and because I called him by his fucking name.

"You're a dick, Bobby. Go be it somewhere else. You're ruining my appetite."

After that I continued to ignore him until he left.

"Are you okay?" Chrissy asked.

"He's such an asshole," Karen added in support of me.

Lisa didn't say much, because I knew Lisa secretly still liked Bobby. That's who she had given it up to for her first time. He'd taken her virginity and then dumped her a week later.

Asshole.

"I'm fine. Empty threats, but wow what a jerk Riley turned out to be."

"They're guys. They can't not talk about this shit," Karen said wisely.

"Whatever." I said it like it didn't matter.

Except it did. It seemed like every single guy who passed me in the hall or sat in class with me was smirking at me. Like by admitting that I wanted to have sex, I was already tagged as easy. Fair game when I wouldn't even remotely consider doing anything with any of them.

My inner feminist wanted to tell them all that I would not be slut shamed. That as a woman I had just as much right to be interested in and want sex as boys did. But the truth was I felt a little sick at the way everyone was treating me.

Shamed.

That Scarlet Letter thing was no joke.

That afternoon, I didn't linger at school like I normally would, shooting the shit with my girls. They understood. Instead I went home to Jake. I pulled up to the house and figured I would have to wait until tonight to talk to him—there was no way to know where he would be on the property.

I changed into my work clothes and went out back to the barn, figuring I would give Petunia a good brush. Brushing a horse was the closest thing to therapy a person could have in Riverbend.

I was about fifteen minutes into rubbing her down, after feeding her an apple which she loved, when I heard the barn door open and Jake was leading his horse Wyatt inside.

"Hey," I said and suddenly everything made sense. The barn smelled like hay and horse with a hint of shit. Jake mucked every morning, but there was never getting around the essence of it.

And Jake.

This ranch, this barn was all him too. And he was here to have my back no matter what.

"You home early?" he asked.

I took off the hand brush I was wearing and put it back on the shelf.

"A little."

He must have seen it on my face, because as soon as he had Wyatt secured in his stall he came to stand in front of me.

"What?"

I huffed. "I hate that... I hate that I'm upset by this."

"Spill it."

"Right? That's exactly what Riley did. Why do boys do that?"

His jaw got tight and that muscle in the back of his cheek started going.

"Riley told everyone in class that I wanted to have sex, and then Bobby MacPherson was all like *You're a total slut looking for action*. Slut shaming is out, Jake. Everybody should know it, but just the way he said I was fair game creeped me out. Seriously? Because I'm seventeen and wanted to have sex, now I'm a target for rape? How completely unfair is that?"

Jake pulled me against his chest and I thought about how good it felt. To be held in his arms. It wasn't like it was with Dad. It was different, but the space felt the same.

Warm. Safe. Protected.

"You're my husband, so I think you should beat Bobby up," I muttered against his shirt.

"I'm going to have a conversation. That's for certain," he

said over my head.

Which immediately had me pulling away. "Oh no. I was totally kidding. You can't say anything to him. It will only egg him on and make it worse."

Jake's face was no joke. Super scary.

"Bobby was only... being mean. I should have been prepared for it. It was a bad day. I mean it, Jake. You can't fight my battles."

"Why not?"

"Because. Uh hello, parenting 101, I have to fight my own battles so I learn from them. In three hundred and sixty days, I'm on my own. If I can't figure out how to stand up to the creeps like the Bobby MacPhersons of the world, I'm never going to able to handle running this place."

He opened his mouth as if to say something but stopped.

"I got this. I was...sounding off. You know."

"Yeah, I know."

I let out a breath. "Okay. I'll go get dinner started. Pasta and meatballs tonight. I already made the meatballs."

"Sounds good."

I left the barn feeling lighter than I had when I first stepped inside. It was a strange thing with Jake. He was family, but not my parent. He was a friend, but not a girl. He was without a doubt the first person I wanted to tell about my crappy day.

And I had to admit it, if I truly did need someone to put Bobby MacPherson in line, Jake would absolutely be my first choice.

The thought of him wailing on Bobby's smug face kept a smile on my face all through dinner.

Jake

I KNEW THE MACPHERSON KID. His father had at one time worked for mine. Now he was working one of the corporate cattle ranch operations outside of Jefferson. Which meant he was away for the week and only home on weekends. The money was probably pretty good, but that meant the kid had free rein in the house. I hadn't met Mrs. MacPherson. Didn't know if she was the type to keep a handle on a seventeen-year-old.

I knew Bobby and his boys liked to hang out near an open lot by the gas station. I saw them there frequently when I was in town. My guess was they tried to get people who were over twenty-one to buy them beer. I didn't know how successful they were, but I knew other than that there was no reason to hang out at the gas station.

I parked my truck across the street and thought about what I was doing. Ellie was going to be pissed. That much was obvious. Except I wasn't doing this as some knee-jerk macho thing to say stay away from her.

Ellie was my wife. She wasn't my girl. But she had to know there was legitimate risk out there for her.

Did I think Bobby MacPherson was going to try something? Yeah. Seventeen-year-old guys weren't mean to girls. Seventeen-year-old guys wanted to get in their pants. It was how they went about accomplishing it that said something about their character.

I'd thought Bobby had a thing for her for a while. It was the way his name kept coming up through the years. Always pestering Ellie, always in her business. Except she never gave him the time of day.

Did I think Ellie could handle herself? Yes. At least that was what I told myself. She was a strong girl, tall for her age.

Worked beside me and her dad long enough to know she wasn't weak. She wasn't someone who was going to be bullied into sex either. That much was obvious with her behavior with Riley. She wanted to experiment, she set the scene, and she went for it.

She'd been in control. Which meant if she was in a situation where she didn't want sex, she'd be in control of that too.

All of that sounded rational and reasonable in my head.

So why was I parked across the open lot next to the gas station, watching MacPherson and his friends shoot the shit?

Because it needed to be said. It needed to be understood that Ellie was not without protection in this world. It needed to known far and wide that she was the opposite of fair game.

If I did this, it would get back to her. If I did this, I would feel the brunt of her anger. If I did this, she was probably right. They would probably give her more grief for it.

But if I did this, despite whatever they might say, they would think twice before acting. That's what counted.

I got out of my truck and walked across the street. Never much traffic in Riverbend. I watched as Bobby hit his friend's hands hard, sending a hot dog flying in the air. I could hear the friend bitching, but not much.

I stopped at the edge of the lot and waited for them to notice me.

"Hey, isn't that Jake Talley?" one of them said.

"Oh shit, Mac. He's coming for you."

"Dude doesn't scare me."

I could scare him. I could scare the shit out of him. But that's not what this was about.

"Bobby," I called out to him. "A word."

He sauntered, because seriously it was the only word for it, over to me. I wanted to tell him men in Montana did not saunter, but I was certain the nuance would've been lost on him. I got it. He was saving face in front of his friends. I was going to handle this totally cool.

"Jake," he said once he was standing a few feet away.

"You know why I'm here?"

"Yeah, did the little woman send you?" He started laughing at his own joke, which wasn't actually funny.

"Look, I'm going to keep it simple. She's had a rough time these last couple of months. Maybe you could lay off her."

"I'm sorry did you say lay her?" He laughed again, and I didn't want to hit him. He wasn't man enough to hit. I wanted to slap him in the face like the bitch he was. "Isn't that your job, dude? Tell us, what's it like banging jail bait? Is she nice and fresh?"

I clenched my jaw and counted ten before I said anything. I was not going to rise to a kid's taunt.

"Don't talk to her. Don't look at her. I hear anything else, we'll have more than words, and I have a feeling your father would back me up on that."

"Yeah, good luck finding my dad. If he's not working he's fucking some trash from Jefferson every weekend."

That was a shame. For Mrs. MacPherson, and Bobby who was obviously impacted by it. It was not, however, my problem.

"Stay away from Ellie. Or I'll know about it."

I turned and started to walk away. I waited for whatever shot he was going to fire. I knew his type. Bobby MacPherson was the kind of kid who waited until your back was turned to feel brave.

"You know what, screw you. I wouldn't touch her with a

ten-foot pole. No one around here wants used goods. Jake Talley's sloppy seconds."

I kept walking. There was no point in responding. No point in telling him I would no sooner touch or look at Ellie like that ever. It's what he thought.

Think of the visual, Jake. You're a strong attractive man, she's growing into a beautiful young woman. You'll be married, living together.

Janet had said it, but I hadn't wanted to believe it at the time. I didn't really believe people would think that about me. I wasn't even entirely certain Bobby believed what he was saying.

Words were weapons. I got that. Insinuations could be as ugly as they wanted to be, but they weren't based in fact.

I almost did it. I almost turned around and asked an obnoxious seventeen-year-old with a bad attitude if he really thought I would do something so... dishonorable. I didn't, because then it would give him even more power. Knowing how much what he said hurt. I didn't, because what if he did believe that of me?

What if I married Ellie thinking I could save her, but instead ruined her life because people thought she was the type of girl who could be seduced?

Riverbend was small. Ridiculously small. The options for both the men and women in this town were limited. Hell, it was probably why I had dated Janet as long as I did.

Ellie would have all the limitations I had, only she would have something else.

An ex-husband and possibly a reputation.

In all of things I had considered when making the decision to marry her, I never thought of that.

I should have thought of that.

NINE

Ellie
June

SCHOOL ENDED with pretty much a whimper. None of the guys hassled me anymore, which was cool. But they also didn't talk to me either. Even the guys I was friendly with. I think I had officially gone from the girl most people liked, who most guys thought was pretty cool, to Weird Married Ellie.

The truth was, I probably got away with being Weird Married Ellie longer than most girls would have. This was because most people liked me and most guys thought I was cool. Had I been bitchy or nerdy, that transition no doubt would have happened much sooner.

Only three hundred and twenty-two days left of my marriage. Counting the days instead of the months made it seem like a much smaller frame of time.

Jake didn't get it. He said the time would come when it

came, and there was no use rushing it to get here. Which was such a cowboy thing to say.

Anyway, it was summer and that meant I needed to start learning about ranching full time. This morning after breakfast Jake was going to introduce me to semen.

Don't be gross. Not that kind of semen. Bull semen.

I was following Jake to the pen, wearing my cowboy boots, jeans, and a T-shirt. I followed his tradition of using a baseball cap to keep the hair out of my eyes and the sun off my face.

I realized how much I liked this. I liked working outside. I liked that we had this thing we needed to do every day. Of course I had grown up with chores. Feeding chickens, gathering their eggs, mucking the stable, taking care of Petunia. I knew what ranch life was. But I didn't know what being a rancher meant.

Maybe because I hadn't ever thought of myself as a rancher. That was my dad. What I told Jake was true. I had come to grips with understanding that this was my destiny. My responsibility.

What I didn't know was if I was going to enjoy that destiny. It was a little scary to think... what if I hated it? What if this was my life, and I was totally not good at it. Or freaked out by it.

We were talking about bull semen here. I was going to have to handle bull semen.

I wrinkled my nose and tried to be cool about it. We got to the pen and I followed Jake up the wood slats so that I was above the fray of cows. Currently we had a little more than four hundred cows, which translated to sixteen herd bulls. Jake explained everything I needed to know about cow fucking.

"See that one there, that's Guss, he's your most fertile,"

he said, pointing to one of the large bulls, who was currently doing the nasty on the back of a cow.

"Tell me how you can tell again?"

"He's the strongest, and tracking the DNA through the calves each year he's inseminating over thirty cows per cycle. That's a lot. But Hank over there, he's getting on in years. He's probably going to have to be replaced next year."

"And I want a four-year-old?" Jake had been through this, but the more I went over it the more it helped to stick.

"Four is okay, you have to be careful he's not getting in the way of Guss. Sometimes the younger ones will get a little ornery. If they're doing all the breeding and you're not getting calves from it, that's a problem. And remember you have to check the..."

"Penis. Yes, I know."

That's right. Some bulls overworked their dick, and it broke their penis. Seriously, this was information I had in my head now.

We watched for a while as the bulls kept banging it out. You could tell by the cows' tails, which were up and crooked, which ones had already been tapped. The best part about using herd bulls was that you didn't have to worry about knowing when the cows were in heat. Evolution and biology took care of all that, and the bulls just knew when the time was ripe.

All this sex, even if it was cow sex, made me squirm a little. I looked over at Jake, who I knew was taking all this banging very seriously. This was work, after all. Our livelihood, when you thought about it. We needed baby cows to grow up and become sellable meat. That's how we lived.

Still.

"Does it get to you at all?" I asked him.
"What?"

"You know... all this sex. I mean it's this constant stream of... well, sex. Does it make you think about it? After all you and Janet have been broken up for months now..."

I stopped talking. He was giving me that *I'm disappointed in you, Ellie* look. Not one of my favs.

"This is serious business, Ellie."

"I know. I'm taking it seriously. I'm only asking, is it hard for you? Literally?"

He huffed. "I'm not having this conversation with you."

"Fine. I'm saying it's a little hard for me and I don't even know what sex is like. You must be on edge."

"I'm fine." He said it, but it was this clipped hard *I'm fine*. Like he wasn't really fine.

"Maybe you should do something about it."

He gave me a hard look. His jaw tight. This was territory we didn't typically encroach on, but I thought it was important to... give my permission, so to speak.

"Dude, I get it. You're a guy. You don't have a girlfriend and your job for the foreseeable future is to monitor animal breeding. If you need to find a little relief... well, you should feel comfortable doing that with someone. We're married, but we're not *married*."

He didn't say anything and I didn't press it.

"It's time to show you artificial insemination," he said after a few moments of quiet.

Remember the bull semen? This was something Jake wanted to try. The semen was from a particular bull that had been bred to produce a leaner, lower-cholesterol-generating beef. More like buffalo. We were going to inseminate a select group of cows and monitor the result.

This was going to happen. I was going to shoot spunk into cow junk.

I was so badass.

THE INSEMINATION WORKED. Nine of the ten cows we picked got pregnant. And two weeks later Jake took three days off to go to Missoula. I was completely cool with it. No problem at all.

AT ALL.

He didn't look at me the entire day after he came back, but the day after that we were fine.

Only three hundred and four days to go.

Jake
August

"JAKE! Jaaaaaake. I know you can hear me!"

"Is she fucking serious?"

I asked the question of no one in particular, as I was currently alone. Ellie was in the kitchen, studying up on some breeding research I had given her. At first I thought it was some background noise on the television.

"Jake Talley, you bastard! Come out here and face me like a man!"

Janet. Janet was outside the house, screaming. Resigned, I got up and walked over to the front door. Ellie was coming out of the kitchen with an expression on her face that basically alluded to how completely awkward I felt in that moment.

"Maybe she found out about your trip," Ellie offered.

What the fuck? Why would she even suggest that? Technically, Ellie didn't even know about what happened on that trip. That trip was not to be discussed. It happened. It was over.

"Did you tell people..."

She was shaking her head. "Nope. Not a soul. Not even Chrissy, who is probably my biggest vault, and when I say vault I mean she tells all my secrets to anyone who wants to know them."

"Why are we talking about my trip?"

This didn't make sense. It was like Ellie was bothered by it, which would have been a complete contradiction since she was the one who encouraged it.

She shrugged. "I don't know. Why is Janet out front calling you a bastard?"

Because she was Janet. The past few weeks I had been getting texts, which I suspected were written under the influence of alcohol. Apparently this was going to be the culmination of those texts.

I opened the front door. And she was in her car, not cool, sitting on the driver seat door, shouting at me over the roof of her car.

"Janet, what the hell are you doing here?"

"I wanted to tell you in person you ruined my fucking life. You ruined my life, Jake!"

That's when I saw the bottle in her hand. If I had to guess, this was a result of tequila. On the plus side, there weren't a lot of cars on the road at night in Riverbend where she could have hurt someone. On the downside, driving into a ditch and getting stuck, she could go days without being found.

Not cool.

"I'm going to get my shoes and drive you home."

"Fuck you!" she screamed back.

I stepped back inside the house and made my way upstairs. Ellie followed without saying anything, but when I came back down the stairs she also had a pair of cowboy boots on over the leggings she was wearing.

"I'll follow in the truck so she has her car."

"It would serve her right to leave it out there. She'll sober up and realize what an ass she made of herself."

Then Ellie laid her hand on my arm. "Don't be too harsh, okay? You guys were together for two years and if it wasn't for me..."

"Ellie, this isn't about you." The truth was I had been procrastinating the whole time with Janet for this reason. I never saw her as *the one*. I wasn't so romantic that I thought magic was waiting out there somewhere for me, so yes, I had considered marrying her and building a life regardless. Except I never pulled the trigger, which I always suspected was my gut telling me to walk away.

"It is," she insisted. "You don't know what might have happened if I had gone to the foster home. You wouldn't have had all this pressure on the relationship. It could have been different. Which is why I'm saying give her a break. She loved you."

Did she? Did Janet love me? Or did she love the idea of being married to me?

We came out to the front porch and I shut the door behind me. Ellie would be following, so no point in locking up.

Except when Janet saw Ellie it only egged her on.

"Oh goodie! The wife. Hi Ellie! What's it feel like knowing you stole my future? My life. My children's lives!"

The closer I got to her I realized what rough shape she was in. Her face was blotched, her eyes swollen. Worse was costs going into the next season, I had a pretty tight cash margin to live on for the next year.

It made me understand my dad better. In so many ways Sam Mason was one of the coolest, most easygoing guys around. Living with him, obviously I knew there were layers under all that. I saw the stress in his eyes each year before he went to market.

I understood it now, the pressure he was under year in and year out. I knew what it meant to budget. To want things and know what I could and could not afford.

I remember asking my dad when I was fifteen if I could have a new car when I turned sixteen, because I knew my destiny was not my mom's ancient Subaru.

He laughed in my face. Now I got how ridiculous I was.

It was fine. I wasn't really into clothes and stuff. Jake and I replenished what we needed. Which was mostly jeans and work shirts. Except today was Jake's birthday, which meant we could splurge on dinner out.

The diner was a big deal for us, because Jake hadn't been back since his standing dates with Janet ended. Janet, who by the way, had officially left Riverbend. Word had it she'd gone to work at a hospital in Missoula. I did really wish her the best. Maybe I never thought she was the one for Jake, but it didn't mean I didn't want her to find happiness with someone.

When Jake pulled up the truck to park at an angle in front of Frank's, it seemed weird to me.

Every summer except this past one I would have spent most of my time in town. Hanging with Chrissy, Karen, and Lisa. Sitting in the diner for hours, gossiping and eating cheese fries. Frank made cheese fries with real American cheese. Delicious.

This summer I had barely made it in to town. And only

then because Jake had insisted I get away from the ranch. Chrissy, Karen, Lisa, and I had gone to see a bad movie.

It had been fun. But in some ways it had been sad. Because everything they had talked about seemed like a million miles removed from my life.

Boys and clothes and hair and who did we think was going to hook up this year. What was senior week going to be like? What was going to be the theme of the homecoming dance?

Meanwhile I was worried about beef prices, ranch expenses, being on my own once I turned eighteen... and well, just about everything they weren't concerned about. It was sobering.

"You okay?" Jake asked me.

"Yeah. It's been a while since I've been to Frank's. I hadn't realized."

"I know. I'm craving some chili."

He got out of the truck and I followed. When we walked into the diner, heads turned. Jake got a bunch of chin nods and hat tips.

Me... I could feel it. The Weird Married Ellie vibe. Jake and I had been living together out on the ranch now for nine months. Something that had become totally normal for us. Except when I saw it through the lens that folks in town saw us through, we were weird again.

I wasn't going to let it ruin dinner though. We picked a booth on the left and got in on either side. Just then Bobby MacPherson, who was dating Susan (having dumped Lisa again) passed us to pay for their dinner at the counter. Jake's gaze on him the whole time was ominous. Dare I say deadly.

"Will you stop," I whispered. "You're going to make a scene."

"I'm reminding him, it might be a new school year but the rules are the same."

Right. I was officially not open for business. Which should have been super upsetting, but again it really wasn't. Right now boys did not compare to the importance of cows in my life. How sad was that?

"Yep. Got it. I'm going to be a perma-virg," I muttered as I opened the menu.

"Ellie, I'm not having—"

"This conversation with me, I know. I think I want pasta."

"Hey Jake. Hey Ellie. Long time no see." Kathy came to our table. She wore jeans and a nice T-shirt. Frank didn't bother with waitress uniforms.

"Hey Kathy," we said at the same time.

"I don't think I've seen either of you two in here all summer. You two keeping busy at the ranch?"

It was such an innocent question, but as soon as the words left her mouth I could see her face turn red as she realized what a double entendre that was. It wasn't intentional. She wasn't trying to be salacious, but if you took it the wrong way, keeping busy had a whole new meaning and Kathy knew it.

Jake, however, was impervious.

"Yep. Big ranch, a lot to do."

Kathy quickly recovered. "Oh, that's good. Glad it hear it. Coke for you, Jake and diet for you, Ellie."

We both nodded and she left.

I looked at him then and wondered. Did he really not see it? Did he really think people weren't a little suspicious of us?

Or maybe it was me, and I was the one overthinking it.

"Going to head out to the property this weekend. I want to check on the house."

The property was code for Jake's land, only he didn't want to call it his land because technically it wasn't his yet. It was like he was trying not to jinx himself.

"How was it last time?"

He grimaced. "Standing, but that's about it. I only need four walls and roof, and it will do until I can get up on my feet. I'm worried about the condition of the barn, though."

I had no doubt he would see to Wyatt's comfort before his own. That's the kind of cowboy Jake was.

"You should have taken the raise I offered. You could start fixing things up sooner."

"There will be plenty of time come May."

I nodded. May. When this whole thing would be over and we would move on with our lives.

It was good that he was so focused on that. On the future. On his dream.

Really really good.

I had spaghetti and meatballs and he had the chili. When we got back to the house I gave him his birthday present. Fur-lined work gloves for winter. He loved them.

And red velvet cake with cream cheese icing.

It was his favorite.

Ellie
October

SO LIFE WAS ROLLING ALONG. School continued to be school, boys continued to ignore me, and I tried to focus on my grades, mostly because Jake insisted, but really what was the point?

I was going to be rancher. Did I really have to know geometry?

It was so crazy to think about the things that used to upset me BDD (Before Dad Dying) and now.

BDD: When was I going to finally lose my virginity?

Now: Did I know enough to handle running a fairly large cattle ranch? Was I making a mistake even trying to do this?

BDD: Were Chrissy and Karen hanging out without me? More importantly, were they talking about me?

Now: I hoped Chrissy and Karen got to hang, because I had no time to see them. I hoped they wouldn't forget me completely. Maybe talk about me once and a while.

BDD: Was Jake going to marry Janet?

Now: Who was Jake sleeping with?

Yeah, I'm not going to lie. Those thoughts started to creep in. I guess it happened after the trip to Missoula, because I knew why he'd gone. I knew he'd had sex with someone else. Heck, I was the one who encouraged him to do it.

I hadn't accounted for how it was going to make me feel. I tried not to think about it.

I tried really hard.

Then, what I came to forever refer to as #penisgate, happened.

"HEY," I called out when I heard the back door open.

"Damn it Ellie! The shoes." Shoot, I had made a mental note to get them before Jake got home. Jake always griped when I left my shoes by the door because he inevitably tripped over them and Jake didn't like tripping.

"Sorry! My mental note got lost."

"Whatever," Jake returned.

"How cold is it outside?"

Weather was a new thing in my life.

Again, BDD I didn't think much of it. Certainly I knew I had to respect it. Dad had taught me that much. Winters were no joke—snowstorms could be deadly to people as well as cattle, and as a ranching family our livelihood depended on having the cattle survive each season.

So yeah, weather was something I understood. Now it was something I obsessed about. How cold could it get? What could cattle survive in and what couldn't they? How many calves could we store in the barn, how many head could survive in the pen? When did we hook up the running line from the house to the barn and the barn to the pen? Before it started snowing, or could I wait to see how bad it got?

All of these things were new to me. Things I had always trusted my dad to take care of for me.

"Colder than a witch's tit," he said as he came into kitchen.

"I don't even get that. You're saying what? That witches have cold skin in general or is it just their tits?"

He thought about it. "Yeah, I don't know either. It's October. It's cold, kiddo. What do you want me to tell you?"

I glared at him. "You know I hate *kiddo*. You know I hate it. Every time you say it I tell you I hate it, and you still say it."

He smiled fiendishly. "Chill out, kiddo. It's a term of affection."

"It's a term that identifies me as a child, which I'm not. One hundred and eighty-nine days, Jake."

"Yeah, yeah. What's for dinner?"

It was my night to cook so I was standing at the kitchen island, mincing garlic. That's right. This girl could mince garlic with the finest chefs in the land. Inseminate cows, heard cattle, mince garlic.

It was an all-around education I was getting.

"Steak and mashed potatoes."

"Awesome. I'm going to go up and take my shower. I'll be down in ten."

"You have to use my shower."

"Why?"

"I'm cleaning yours with special stuff that gets mold off the tile. You should have told me how gross it was getting in there."

"What were you even doing in my room?"

I looked at him then. It wasn't an accusation. Like, *how dare you, what the fuck were you doing in my room*, but I could hear the surprise in Jake's voice.

We'd lived in the same house together since last January, and I had never been in his room. Because I wanted him to know he had his privacy. Because I was afraid if I walked in there it would no longer smell like my dad, and that would make me sad.

It didn't smell like my dad. It smelled like Jake. It was a little sad.

"You said you wanted me to pick up cotton swabs. I shopped today and went to put them in your vanity. Then I saw how dark the corners of your shower were. I have this stuff that will take it off, but you have to give it twenty-four hours to sit."

"Okay. You have extra towels in your bathroom?"

"Yes, I put one up there for you. The green one. Do not use my blue one or I will kill you."

"That seems a little extreme over a towel."

"I'm very particular about my towels, and I don't want your man parts touching the blue one."

He shook his head, but didn't argue and left. A couple minutes later I heard the water turn on overhead and went back to chopping garlic. I was running the knife over what I had already cut to make it even finer, and I slipped and caught my thumb with the knife.

Instantly the blood started to gush, and I quickly set it under water before it ruined the work I had already done. Only the damn thing kept bleeding. I wrapped a towel around it and that helped, but if I was going to finish cooking I needed a band aid. I listened for it and I could hear the water was off upstairs. Jake was finished with his shower. Hopefully back in his room already.

I jogged up the stairs and froze.

I froze because as I was rounding the steps Jake was leaving my bathroom with a towel around his waist, and as he took a step the towel came loose and I saw it.

His penis.

I saw his naked penis.

"Ellie, what the hell?" he said as he gathered the towel around him.

"I'm cut. I need a band aid."

I could see it then. The indecision of wanting to see how bad the cut was, but not wanting to get any closer. Because he was naked except for a towel. More naked than anyone I had ever seen.

Chest, legs, and penis. Only the penis was now covered.

I hoped to hell he couldn't see me blushing as I headed

toward the bathroom. "I'm fine. I needed a band aid and I thought you were done."

I closed the door and gave him the opportunity to return to his room without worrying about another towel-slipping incident. The mirrors were fogged up, which was good because I didn't want to see my face.

I didn't want to see how red and blotchy it was because I saw my first human male penis.

And it was Jake's.

It was no big deal. I shook my head and decided I was being stupid. We lived together. It had been bound to happen at some point. We were family. Family sometimes had to see shit. That's the way it was.

I grabbed the band aid and worked it over the cut until it was secure, and then I went downstairs to finish the meal.

Ten minutes later I had steak cooking in the skillet and Jake came in dressed in jeans and a flannel shirt. The universal uniform of cattle ranchers everywhere.

"Should be ready in another few minutes," I said as casually as possible over my shoulder. As casually as possible for someone who had just seen her first penis, that is.

"Ellie," he said quietly. "Do we need to talk about that?"

"Nooo," I said quickly. "It was no big deal. I'll have the gunk off your shower tomorrow and you're back to having your privacy. Let's not make something out of nothing."

He waited a bit, then sighed. "Okay."

Which is when I started to have all these thoughts in my head. Like I shouldn't have said it was nothing. No man wants his penis referred to as *nothing* and *no big deal*. The truth was, it had actually been pretty big...

No, no, no, no. I wasn't thinking about his dick. I wasn't going to think about the size or the shape or the dark hair around it. He was a man. He had a penis. I knew what it looked like. Story over.

I served him his steak and mashed potatoes, like he liked them with extra butter and garlic.

I ate my own steak but didn't really taste much of it. When I was done I let him clean up and I headed to my room. Normally I would change into my flannel PJ bottoms and my tank top.

Never once had I thought about it. The tank top had a bra shelf, so it wasn't like my boobs were flopping in the wind. Still, I was a respectable C-cup. It never occurred to me that it bothered Jake. That I sat every night with him watching TV, not wearing a bra.

If it had bothered him he would have said something, right? Or he wouldn't have said anything, because that would be calling attention to something neither one of us wanted to call attention to.

He wasn't a man. I wasn't a woman. We were Jake and Ellie.

We didn't think about each other's parts. That's not what we were.

Except I had seen his penis and his hairy chest and his hairy legs, and something inside me shifted.

Like I wasn't looking at Jake. Like instead I was looking at a naked hot guy. My very own personal porn.

And I wanted to touch...

No, no, no, no. I had to lock down any and all thoughts about that. I would not go there. I could not go there.

Jake was my older brother. Jake was my way older brother. Jake was MY BROTHER.

I pounded the thought into my head so that it was louder than all the other ones. I couldn't go downstairs and hang with him, naturally. I knew enough about myself to know I needed distance. But he would think it weird if I bailed this early for bed.

So I did what smart girls everywhere did when they wanted to get out of an awkward situation. I lied.

I walked out of my room and called down to Jake from the top of the stairs.

"Hey, no TV for me tonight. I've got a book I'm behind on for English."

There was a beat. A moment when he said nothing and I cringed.

"Okay," he finally called up to me.

But that's when I knew something had changed. I had seen him not as Jake but as a man, and now he knew I was freaked out by it, enough that I needed some distance.

On a scale of one to ten, this event was definitely a solid eight.

ELEVEN

Ellie
November

WOW. Whoa. Holy freak. Eww, gross. Was that even humanly possible?

You probably want to know what I was doing. Frankly, I was watching porn. That's right, porn.

I was a healthy teenager, not having sex, but I had... curiosity. Given that every guy in school had completely frozen me out, thanks to Jake. Because even though he said he didn't say anything to anyone, I know he must have said something to someone because this was not just retaliation to Bobby being an asshole.

This was something else.

Whatever. It didn't matter. I had already reconciled that cows were my future, but now that I had seen my first penis I was simply curious how it stacked up.

Hello internet. Google search porn and penises and... Voila.

All the dick a girl could ever want to see. And no lie, there was some dick I hoped I never saw again.

I was so focused on what I was seeing that I didn't hear Jake calling to me as he came through the back door.

"Ellie didn't you hear me?"

"Eeek!"

Obviously I didn't hear him or I would have shut off my laptop well in advance of him coming into the kitchen. Instead I made that horribly girly noise and slammed down the lid of the laptop as fast as I could, which immediately made me look suspicious.

Also my blazing red cheeks.

Girly noise.

Slamming laptop lid.

Red cheeks.

It all spelled porn surfing.

However, I was a girl. Which meant I might get away with it if Jake didn't suspect I would ever be doing such a thing.

"What were you doing?" Nice leading opening salvo by him.

I looked at him—well, at his left ear. I shrugged. "Nothing."

"Ellie."

"Jake."

"Do I want to see what you have up on your laptop?"

"I'm going to go with a solid no on that."

He sighed. It was his dad sigh. Something I'm sure his future children would learn to hate.

For me it ranked with being called *kiddo* and him ruffling my hair.

"Ellie, do I need to worry about you getting into some online trouble? You know the internet is dangerous. You have to be careful."

Was he kidding me? Did he tell me I had to be careful on the internet?

It made me angry. Angry enough that I wanted to hurt him.

"Fine, you want to know what I was doing? I was checking out porn."

"Ellie..." I could see him closing his eyes.

"What? I'm curious. I saw your dick and I thought I would compare it..."

Then his eyes blasted open. "Compare! Compare? Ellie, for fuck's sake don't ever say that to a guy. You never ever say the word *compare*!"

Hookay. That was a life lesson. I had never seen him get so freaked out. Now he was pacing back and forth in front of the island, hands on his hips.

"Geezus. Compare? With porn stars. Those men are professionals, Ellie. What the hell."

I'd started out being angry with him for treating me like a child, but this was freaking hysterical.

He must have seen me trying desperately to hold back my laughter.

"This is serious. This is not a joke. You don't... say things like that."

"I'm sorry. I didn't know you would freak out like this."

"Any guy would freak out." He ran his hand through his hair. "Any guy."

"Got it."

"And... porn is for guys. There, I said it. Call me a sexist, call me whatever. But it's meant for and geared to guys."

"You mean guys also like to look at other men's penises?"

He winced. "Some guys. I don't know, it doesn't matter. Just... cool it. And stay away from that crap. It's not real."

I rolled my eyes. "You're such a prude, Jake."

"I'm not a prude," he mumbled. "I asked you if we had to talk about what happened and you said no."

"Because we didn't. Why can't you get it through your head that I'm interested in sex? It's a highly normal, healthy thing. Stop making me out to be a perv."

"I'm not making you out to be a perv. I just don't—"

"Want me to have sexual thoughts. I got it. You know why? Because you want to think I'll be ten forever. Well, I'm not." I held up my hand. "Five months, Jake. Five months and I'm an adult and this is all mine. When that happens, and I'm no longer under your *protection,* I hope to hell there's a line of guys waiting out that door for me because I plan to bang every one of them."

His jaw got tight and hard and I knew what was coming next, so I beat him to the punch line.

"You know what?" I said, grabbing my laptop. "I can't have this conversation with you right now. You're on your own for dinner."

I left and felt particularly justified in my fury.

Then once I was in my room, I suddenly felt like shit. I didn't want to bang every guy in town. I didn't want to be some slutty girl. I wanted to...

Be normal.

But I wasn't. I was Weird Married Ellie.

Some days it sucked.

Jake
A few days before Thanksgiving

"HEY, we have to decide what we're going to do for Thanksgiving," Ellie told me.

She was sitting across the kitchen table, cutting her steak, and I thought—I hoped—that things were starting to get back to normal between us. It had been a few chilly days after the whole porn incident.

"What are our options?" I asked.

"The Pettys invited us over."

"Perfect. Mrs. Petty means good food."

I looked up. She was pushing peas around on her plate, biting her lower lip.

"You don't want to go to Mrs. Petty?"

"Well, Chrissy also sort of asked if... *I* wanted to go to her place. You know, hang out and stuff."

It was odd, but something sank in my gut. "You don't want to spend Thanksgiving together," I realized.

It was our first major holiday. Or family holiday. The first real holiday where she would be missing Sam hard. We'd had great Thanksgiving open houses here at Long Valley for years. There was no way this day wasn't going to back up on her. I needed to be there for her.

Unless she didn't want me. Unless she wanted Chrissy.

"No. I mean... I do. Want to. It's ... I didn't know if you thought that was important or not. Like maybe you wanted to do something else. With someone else."

"Who the hell else would I want to spend Thanksgiving with?"

I hated this. She had an agenda. I knew she did, but instead of coming right out and saying it she had to girl that shit up.

That's right. I said it. Girl that shit up. If that made me a sexist I had to own it.

"I don't know. A girlfriend I don't know about. Maybe that girl you met in Missoula."

We were still talking about Missoula. This was a problem. A potentially big one, but I wasn't going to let it get that far. Simple and basic. That's how I liked pretty much everything. Including my Thanksgiving.

"I don't have a girlfriend. I want to spend Thanksgiving with you because you're my family. I want to go to the Pettys because neither of us can put together a decent Thanksgiving meal and we both know it."

She beamed at me and I knew I had said the thing she wanted to hear, but I wasn't sure which part.

"Okay. I'll let Mrs. Petty know we're coming."

LATER THAT NIGHT, in my bed, I stared up at the ceiling. Sleep eluded me completely.

Ellie was checking out porn. Ellie was hedging around to find out if I had a girlfriend.

This was not good. We were not that. We were something else entirely and she had to know that.

I closed my eyes and thought, *I really hope Ellie isn't thinking about having sex... with me.*

Ellie
That same night

SO I WAS THINKING about having sex with Jake.

In my defense, there were a number of valid reasons.

He was hot.

He was my best friend.

He was the one person I trusted most in this world.

He had a nice penis. I know because I did compare (sorry Jake) and thought his was way better than anyone else's.

I liked him.

I also loved him.

I was married to him, so I was pretty sure it was legal even though technically I was still under eighteen.

It was a bad idea. I knew that. I knew *how* I was supposed to think about him. I knew how he thought of me.

It was probably a phase. Or a crush or something totally teenager.

I'm sure I would get over it.

Soon, I hoped. You know, before he divorced me.

TWELVE

Jake
Christmas Eve

ONE HUNDRED AND eighteen days left.

It was Christmas Eve and we were at Howard and his wife's open house party. Ellie had said I should buy a bottle of nice wine, so I did. We walked up the steps together and I rang the doorbell and Mirry, Howard's wife, opened the door with a big smile.

A lot of the neighbors were there. Their heads turned toward us. Ellie got the sad smiles. I got the I-did-the-right-thing smiles. These weren't the people who thought the salacious things about us, because these were the people who had known us our whole lives.

Howard came up and clapped me on the back.

"How's the ranch?"

"Fine, sir."

"Good to hear. And Ellie? She keeping her grades up along with all the extra ranch work she's doing?"

"Three point six. I won't let her get below it."

"You won't *let* me," she said as she joined us after taking off her coat and leaving it on the coat rack near the door. I had braved the cold for the twenty-foot walk to the door. I hated taking my jacket with me where I went, because anytime I did I invariably forgot it and had to go back.

"Try again. I earned my GPA because I work hard at it. A decision *I* make."

Yeah, but I made sure she had time to study every night. And I made sure she at least thought about college, even though it probably wasn't an option for her. I couldn't see her trusting the ranch to anyone she hired after I left, enough to actually move away to college.

In a few years, after she got some of her mom's life insurance money and was comfortable with whoever they hired, maybe.

The point was, I wasn't really thinking about any of this. Not Christmas, not whether she would like what I got her as a present—I knew she wouldn't. I had done it intentionally too. I wanted to get her something practical rather than something sentimental that would make her cry. The day was going to be hard enough for her.

Thanksgiving hadn't been easy. Christmas would be just as bad.

I went with a pair of smaller wire cutters I thought she might be able to use to work the fence. I had no doubt she was going to bitch about them all morning because she hated working the fence. Mostly because she didn't have the hand strength to do it.

The wire cutters might help.

Except I wasn't thinking about any of that. Instead all I could think about was that my life with her was going to be over basically in another four months.

Four months, which meant we needed to bring someone on soon. We had decided in addition to Javier and Gomez, we would add that potential full time person for calving season. This way we could see how he handled himself over the next few months before making a decision to pull the trigger.

It was complicated. I wanted someone older and more seasoned. Someone who could be a mentor to Ellie. Someone like her father.

The problem was, a man like that might be unwilling to live in the bunk house. Especially he might be unwilling to share space with Javier and Gomez, even if it was on a part time basis.

Maybe a divorced rancher? Although I had to say there weren't many people that fit the bill around these parts. We were going to have to make our search country wide. Thankfully with the internet, that wasn't as much of a problem as it might have been in the past.

Then there was the Ellie factor. I didn't often let myself think it, but there were times I couldn't avoid it. She was beautiful. Not just pretty. Not just cute. She was beautiful and growing more so each day as she matured.

She was going to be eighteen. The sole owner of a multi-million-dollar cattle ranch, and stupid hot.

The man we found who was going to work for her, respect her, keep his hands off her... Well, I wasn't sure who that was other than me. Which is why I was going for age. The older the better.

For her.

"Drink?" she asked me. I gave her a chin nod and she was off. She knew what I liked. A while later she came back with a Corona and lime for me, lime already pressed inside, and a cup of what appeared to be punch.

"Is that spiked?"

She smiled a did this jiggle thing with her eyebrows. "You bet your ass it is. And not a word from you. It was spiked last year too, and Dad didn't have any problem with letting me have a cup or two."

She was only going to be eighteen in the next few months, not twenty-one, but still I didn't really have a problem with it. I had started drinking when I was eighteen and no one thought anything of it.

In fact, unless you were being unusually stupid the twenty-one age limit was for the most part ignored in these parts.

Pete's was the only bar in town, and on Friday nights it was filled with as many under-twenty-ones as over. If you got stupid and got kicked out, your fake ID was confiscated. Otherwise, Pete looked the other way.

It occurred to me I might actually run into Ellie at Pete's once we were divorced. I had only been a few times in the past year, but it was a place I liked to go on occasion. I hadn't let her, but once she graduated that's where her friends would most likely hang out on the weekends.

She would want to hang out there too.

That would be cool. Sharing a beer with her out in town. And strange, because she would also be my ex-wife.

Because it was one of those things I thought about all the time when she counted down the days.

I thought about getting my hands on twenty thousand dollars. I thought about the feeling I was going to have when the land was mine again. I thought about how the hell was I going to fix the house, because it was a mess, find enough cash to start buying up cattle, and have a place to actually move into. I thought about a lot of things. Exciting things. Things that drove me forward to making my own dream come true.

And then I thought about how I would miss Ellie. Miss her. It wasn't wrong of me to think it. We lived together. She was my roommate. We ate together, worked together, watched TV together. Of course I would miss having her in my life.

Had things been weird since the towel incident? A little.

I struggled for a while to figure out what it was. I knew she was a virgin, so yeah my dick was the first one she probably saw. Maybe that had freaked her out. Or the weirdness of seeing me basically naked. We'd always been close but never intimate.

Since then I could tell she was more cautious around me. She had this sweatshirt thing I'd never seen before that she started wearing at night, complaining the house was too cold. When the temperature had never bothered her before.

When I said something she decided was sexist—I did it a lot mostly to egg her on—she used to rub my arm and tell me what caveman I was and how sorry she was for my next wife.

Not one touch since the towel incident. And I had said a lot of sexist things.

I hated the shift.

In our not-normal world, we had found a way to be normal.

Janet accused me once of falling for Ellie, and I was so damn proud to say that I hadn't. That she'd been wrong. That all men weren't assholes with dicks and no brains.

That it didn't matter that Ellie was beautiful because she was still freaking seventeen. And that when she turned eighteen that wasn't going to magically change anything either.

I wasn't a man waiting for a number.

Not going to lie, when I went to Missoula for those few days this past summer I had felt a little... guilty wasn't right. Awkward, maybe? Not because I picked up some girl in a bar and basically had nonstop sex with her for three days. That I had no guilt over.

I had needed that, and it felt good. It was just that coming home to Ellie reminded me that I wasn't so noble I couldn't abstain for sixteen months while we got through this thing.

So I was a man, and I did have a dick. But I wasn't some damn animal who couldn't restrain myself with my brain when I needed to.

Yay me. The problem was, since the towel thing, despite her caution, Ellie had been giving me these looks.

Sometimes I would actually catch her staring at me, like she didn't even know she was doing it, and I wanted to know what the hell was going through her head.

Only I didn't want to know. I didn't want to know for a second that she had thoughts like that. Which if I verbally communicated to her she would say was sexist.

She was going to be eighteen. She was allowed to have sexual thoughts. I was a man who was very much in her world. I wasn't an asshole, but I knew I was attractive to most women.

I had had zero problem picking up... what the heck was her name? Sherry? Shari? Something like that.

It was not unheard of that she'd seen me and realized I wasn't some eunuch she was living with. I wasn't her father.

And though we'd basically been raised together I wasn't her brother.

Which sucked if that turned into some kind of crush. Imagine having a crush on your husband, only to have him turn around and divorce you in a couple of months.

Because that had to happen. I could not stay in that house one day past her eighteenth birthday or everyone would think something was going on. That something had been going on.

No, I was leaving on April twenty-third, and I really hoped when I did, I didn't hurt her.

"I'm going to go mingle," she told me.

"I'm going to stand in this corner and drink my beer."

Her head tilted in that way it did when she was disappointed in me. "You're so predictable. Do you realize that about yourself?"

"I do."

"It's a party."

"And I'm here. Don't overdo it on the punch."

She sighed. "Kay."

I did as I said I would. Nursed my beer because I was driving and checked out the room of people. The same room of people who were here last year, all in different sweaters.

"Hi Jake."

"Mrs. Nash," I said as she walked over to me. "No Mr. Nash?" There was never Mr. Nash when there was Mrs. Nash, but still I had to ask because it was polite.

"At home with the kids. I'm coming here for a while, then he's going to another party later and I'll take the kids."

Right. Because Riverbend didn't have about twenty age-appropriate babysitters.

"How is Ellie doing?"

It was a common enough question. No one ever asked her directly. So much easier to do it with me. It pissed her off actually and I could see why. I wasn't the boss of Ellie. I wasn't the caretaker of Ellie.

I was only her partner. For this part of our lives.

Still, I had to be polite so I gave the standard answer. "She's doing great. Grades are good and she's learning a lot about ranching."

Mrs. Nash smiled. "No, I meant *how is she doing*?"

Right. Because not eleven months ago Ellie had lost her dad. Sometimes as strong as she was, even I forgot that.

"She's okay. She's strong. She's determined. She's more of a rancher than I would have thought. Takes to all of it, even the ugly stuff. She hates to go in my room for any reason, I think because it makes her sad. If our laundry gets mixed up she leaves my stuff folded outside my door. She cries at the weirdest things on TV and I know it's because something reminded her of Sam. If I ask her if she wants to talk about it, she lifts her chin three feet up in the air and says she's fine. Like her dad. She's grown up a lot. And in a way that's good, because come April this all falls to her, but in a way I'm sorry she didn't get to experience her senior year. I doubt she'll go to the prom. She didn't bother with the homecoming dance. She's focused. Which is important. Mature for someone so young, which is also important. But she's not as goofy as she used to be. She doesn't laugh as much. It bothers me sometimes."

Mrs. Nash made a sound in the back of her throat and I looked at her.

"Jake Talley, I've known you your whole life and those are more words in total than you have ever said to me."

I wasn't sure I understood why that was important.

She put her hand on my shoulder. "She's lucky to have had you through this."

Yeah. She was. I didn't say it because I thought it would make me sound like a jerk, but regardless of what weirdness was happening now between us, Ellie and I were solid.

We were family.

For another one hundred and eighteen days at least.

"CAN I ASK YOU A QUESTION?"

It was late. We were driving home from the party. I could tell she was drunk on punch and eggnog. It was ruthless of me really, but I thought it might be the best way to get to the truth with her defenses a little down.

"Go for it," she said. She was twisted a little in her seat, on her side and looking at me, smiling.

"Did you have fun tonight?"

"I did."

She said it like it was a surprise.

"Is that because you're hopped up on punch?"

"Yes," she laughed. "No. It was nice to be around... people who know us. Who get us. Who don't think we're weird."

"Ellie," I had to tell her. "We're weird."

"I know. Even the way we showed up at the party. Me with a bottle of wine. You driving and being all manly. Like we were some normal married couple celebrating Christmas with the neighbors."

"Do you think of us that way?" I asked it gently because I knew this was poking into a sensitive area.

"No," she answered quickly. "I know we're not. We are so *not* a couple."

"You've been acting a little different with me lately, and I wanted to make sure..."

Now she was tilting away from me. "Make sure what?"

"Ellie, are you really ready for April? For the divorce. Because it's going to happen. I can't see any way around that."

She nodded. "I know. I'm ready for it. I want you to have your chance. You've worked so hard this year to make my place a success and to teach me everything you know, you deserve to be able to put all that work into something of your own. I know you have to go and do that."

"I'm not dying, you know. I'm going ten miles south, remember?"

Again a nod, only she was looking out the window, not at me.

Maybe that's what it was. Maybe this had nothing to do with a crush or seeing my dick or any of it. Maybe she was pulling away because she was scared about being on her own.

"Talk to me, Ellie. What are you thinking?"

She leaned her head back. "Sometimes it just hits me. I'm really all alone."

That made me immediately angry. "You're not. You're always going to have me."

She looked at me then, her smile gone, and I could see it in her eyes. All the sorrow and weight of her grief had changed her. Made her older, made her wiser. I missed goofy Ellie, but serious Ellie was a woman to be reckoned with.

"I'm not, Jake. I'm not always going to have you. And you, you are not always going to have me. I think we need to realize that. We think April twenty-second isn't going to change anything, but it is. We should start preparing for that now."

I didn't say anything. How could I when I was essentially trying to get to the same point. Of course I had been worried about potentially hurting Ellie.

I really hadn't considered how I was going to feel.

I thought I was going to feel like shit.

THIRTEEN

Ellie
March

ON A SCALE of one to ten, it was a full-on ten. Possibly maybe ten and a half.

Except I never do this. I never break the scale because I think it makes the scale invalid. Then any number is acceptable and representative of being bad or good.

What's the difference between eleven and a thousand, really?

But for the first time, this seemed to warrant it.

Remember my obsession with the weather? I had started to ease up once we rolled into March. The worst cold should have been behind us.

They called this an anomaly. A major Arctic air mass that moved down over the Rockies with virtually no warning.

Right now the temperature was twenty below freezing,

and it was snowing hard. The wind gusts were brutal. I couldn't feel my hands despite being covered with heavy work gloves. I couldn't see the house from the barn. I couldn't see the pen from the barn, where Jake was working to save the calves.

All I knew was that this was bad. Because according to every prediction we'd gotten before the satellite kicked out, it was supposed to get worse.

Which made this storm on a scale of one to ten a full-on ten. And maybe a half.

I tried to focus on my work. I needed to put blankets on Petunia and Wyatt, make sure they had plenty of food. I had to thaw the trough water with boiling water I had hauled from the house to break up the ice so they could drink it. This would have to be done throughout the day and night as the water started to freeze almost immediately.

Of course, not realizing what was coming, Javier and Gomez had left before the storm. While their help would have been huge, we also didn't have to worry about the generator powering the house and the bunk house.

All we had to do was make sure we could keep the calves as warm as possible. Which meant moving them from the pen to the barn. As many as we could fit. Jake knew from past storms the barn could hold about thirty.

We had nearly ninety calves born so far. Eighty-nine, to be exact.

One by one Jake was hauling them across his shoulders from the pen to the barn. He'd made it through seven. And those seven had taken him almost three hours.

The barn door opened and the blast of cold and fury hit me in the face, but I pushed through it to get to Jake. He was hooked to the line that ran between the pen and the barn. I unhooked the karabiner and he lifted the calf off his shoulders and pushed it deeper inside the barn.

He was bent over and breathing hard through the mask he wore over his face. He also had ski goggles over that to keep the snow out of his eyes.

I handed him the thermos of hot coffee I had brought with the boiling water. Then I said it. The thing I had to say. "You have to stop."

He lifted the goggles over his eyes, looked at me, and shook his head.

"It's getting dark and the temperature is dropping. The wind gusts have to be at least a hundred miles per hour. You can't keep doing this."

He stood and rolled his shoulders. Each calf, especially the older ones, had to weigh at least sixty pounds. Jake was strong, but no man was that strong.

"It's too cold," he said. "And projected to stay that way for too long. We have to save as many as we can."

"Then let me help."

"You can't lift a calf, Ellie." He barked it. Like he was angry at me for being so weak.

"What about the rope? I can tie it around the neck and lead it."

He'd shot it down before. The calf would be too skittish. It wouldn't be easily led. Especially with these gusts, but I didn't see any other way. "I have to try. You're not going to be able to do this yourself." Then I said the thing we were both thinking. "They are my calves, Jake. This happens next year, I would be doing this anyway. Alone."

He looked at me, and no lie it was so creepy with that mask hat on. Like he wasn't Jake underneath it but some kind of mean bank robber. A mean bank robber who knew I was right.

"Hook up."

I pulled my own hat down over my face, found an extra set of goggles and grabbed the rope. Then we opened the barn door together. The cold was so intense. More powerful than anything I could remember. Then again, any time these storms flared up in the past I had been safely inside, while Dad and Jake had done all the work.

Those days were gone. My land. My cattle. My work. I had about a foot of belt around my waist that was hooked to the karabiner. I clipped the hook to the line that ran from the barn to the pen.

Jake shook it a few times to make sure it was secure, then hooked his own line and did the same.

I didn't have to be told the importance of staying connected to the line. This would prevent a gust from taking me off my feet. It would make sure I got to the place I was going, which I couldn't see, and most importantly it was how I was going to get back.

Jake moved out first. He knew I would be slower and probably thought he could do multiple trips there and back to my one. Still my one, was one more run he didn't have to do.

It literally felt like I was pushing up against a wall of wind that barely moved. Step by step I plowed through the fury of it. Finally when I was as close as a foot to it, I saw the fence lines of the pen. The rope line allowed us to climb over it, and into the mix of animals. The line also ran from one end to other so I could move my way into the center in search of the freezing calves. I found one, hooked the rope around his neck in a loose noose, and started to pull.

The calf was strong but I was stronger. I made it to the end of the pen and Jake was waiting. He knew he was going to have to lift the calf up and over. He did, then I was over, and me and the calf were moving again.

I had almost made it to the barn when Jake came up behind me. He had to unhook his karabiner to get around me, then quickly rehook. He made his way to the barn, dropped the calf, and started out again. I made it to the barn, took the noose off, and started out again after him.

We had done this two more times. He had brought back three calves to my two but that was because he had to wait for me at the pen, to help get my calf over the fence. I was on my way back to the barn with another one, only this one was being even more stubborn. I was fighting the wind and fighting the damn animal.

"Move it, asshole!"

Like that might work. All it did was cost me precious hot air. Then the damn rope slipped from my hands. My fingers were getting so numb I had no strength left, so I had wrapped the rope around my hand. But it unraveled and the calf took a step away.

I reached for it, but the foot of line at my belt kept the rope just out of reach. I needed to grab it now before the calf moved again, otherwise I would lose sight of it. I unhooked myself and grabbed at the rope.

The calf took another step back, then another. I followed and lunged for the rope. This time I secured the end of it, wrapping it several times around my hand. Only a gust of wind hit me in the face and I could feel myself moving. Although I wasn't sure in what direction.

I reached for the line all around me and felt nothing. I tried to move forward and reached again, but nothing. I looked in front of me, behind me, but I saw nothing.

Don't panic, don't panic.

I shouldn't have unhooked myself. Okay. But I needed

to think. The pen was directly east of the barn, which means I had been heading west. I knew the winds were coming out of the north, which means the gust most likely took me south. If I continued to head in a northwest direction I would eventually hit the barn.

Visibility was zero, but I wasn't talking miles. The barn literally had to be a hundred feet in front of me.

But each step got scarier. The calf was no longer fighting me, but that might have been because she was getting weaker in the cold. I was moving in a total whiteout, and every time I reached my hand out to feel for the line, there was nothing.

Snow started to seep through my winter gear. I could feel it in the back of my neck and down my back. I stopped for a moment and once again tried to get my bearings. What if I was going in the wrong direction? What if I had gotten turned around?

Why didn't I bing a compass? What if I let calf go? Would I have a better chance of making it on my own?

This was bad. This was serious.

"Jake! Jake!"

I was screaming. As loud as I knew how to scream, but there was no way he could hear me. Not over the wind and bleating cows.

"Jake! Jake!"

Another gust of wind pushed at me, so hard it knocked me off my feet. I could feel the snow at my back even as it covered my face. In another five minutes I might be fully covered by it.

I thought about my dad. I thought about how hard this all was. But then I thought about Jake and what it would do to him if he lost me this way. I was the only thing Jake had left.

I pushed myself up and I moved forward, dragging the calf behind me. I had no idea if forward was right or not, but it was the only direction I could think to go.

Jake

I GOT BACK to the barn and hefted the calf over my neck, my shoulders screaming with pain. I set it down and swatted it on the ass. I fell to my knees and dropped to my elbows and took a few breaths.

I didn't want to think about it. I certainly didn't want to say it, but I was pretty sure I was done. Mentally, I counted what Ellie and I had carried in my head. We weren't close to filling the barn. Maybe only half capacity.

But it was getting too dangerous out there. Hypothermia was legit and could happen so damn fast. And Ellie was at least a hundred pounds lighter than me...

Ellie. I didn't unhook around her. I came straight from the pen to the barn and I didn't pass her. That wasn't possible. Unless she was in the barn already.

I hopped up on my feet. "Ellie!"

Nothing but crying calves and horses. I took the goggles off my head and searched again. "Ellie!"

Think. Would she have gone back to the house? Without telling me?

It was so damn cold, maybe on her last trip she'd called it quits.

Ellie wouldn't quit.

Right? I knew that much about her. When it was important, when it mattered, Ellie dug in. Hard.

Last I left her, I had taken a calf over the pen fence. She

had the rope and was moving back. I got another calf and started back after her. Which meant if she had gone back to the house I might follow the line close enough to get a visual. I put my goggles back on, hooked myself to the line heading to the house, and started out knowing, full on knowing in my gut, this wasn't right.

She would have waited for me at the barn.

Which meant somehow, at some point, she had unhooked herself from the line that led from the barn to the pen.

The damn calf got away. The calf got away and she unhooked herself and went after it.

That's what she would have done. I made my way back to the barn, unhooked my line, and rehooked myself to the pen line. As fast as I could I moved against the wind and the snow.

"Ellie! Ellie! ELLLLLLIE!"

I waited and listened. There was nothing. Nothing but wind and...

There it was. A crying calf. Off to my right. I unhooked the karabiner and moved toward that sound. "Ellie! Ellie"

She was exactly ten feet away. I know because I counted.

She was facedown in the snow, the damn rope still wrapped around her hand. I lifted her up to sitting.

"Ellie! Ellie!"

I saw her body startle, my voice finally penetrating the cold. I hauled her up to standing and then dropped her over my right shoulder.

"Calf," she moaned. "Calf."

"Fuck this." I took the rope and pulled the calf behind us. I made it back to the line, ten feet from where I left it. I hated wasting the time it took to get to the barn first, but I couldn't be certain if I tried to head directly for the house I would make it.

I dropped the calf off, shut the barn door, hooked myself to the house line, and moved as fast as I could. I could feel her like dead weight on my screaming shoulder. I saw the house and almost cried out.

I got us both inside and shut the door. The warmth was almost too much. Not stopping, I moved us through the back of the house to the stairs. I took them two at a time and made my way to my shower. It was bigger.

I turned the hot water on and sat Ellie on the toilet seat. She didn't fall, but she was out of it. I slapped her face a few times.

"Ellie, I need you to wake up for me. Listen to me. I have to get you in the shower."

Her eyes drifted closed. "Jake. So cold."

I started removing her clothes. All of it. Her mask, her coat. I got her on her feet to remove her snow gear, then sat her down to get her out of the boots. As damp as everything was, it was only helping to keep the cold locked inside.

Then her shirt, her sweatpants. Finally her bra and panties. I shoved her into the shower and she slid against the wall until her ass hit the tub. I undressed and followed her. Then I moved her so her back was to my front and the hot water was hitting her directly.

It felt like a hundred little pin pricks all over my body. I knew it was the same for her because she started writhing in my arms and crying out.

"Hurts," she cried.

"I know, baby. I know. But we have to get your temperature up."

It was like holding a block of ice in my arms.

Finally, eventually the hot water did its thing. I could

see her skin turning pink and her breathing was sound and even. Her head was on my shoulder and I knew I wasn't going to lose her when she started crying. Soft cries that shook her whole body.

"You're okay," I crooned.

"I'm naked," she sobbed.

Yeah, like that was important, but it was to her so I lifted her out of the shower and wrapped a towel around her and sat her back down on the toilet seat. I hadn't taken off my boxer briefs to spare her that, but truly as soaked as they were I wasn't hiding much.

I grabbed a thermometer from my vanity, rinsed it off, and stuck it in her mouth. It was an electronic one and after a few seconds it beeped.

95.7. Not great but probably better than she had been.

"We need to get some hot liquid into you. Can you stand?"

She looked at me and shook her head. "I'm sorry."

I left the bathroom, took off my wet briefs, found sweatpants, a sweatshirt and some socks. I got dressed and made my way downstairs. I needed sugar and heat. Hot cocoa. Instant. I threw the powder and water into a mug and put it in the microwave.

Our power was gone, but the generator was working. Normally I wouldn't have wasted energy on the damn microwave but I needed fast. After a minute and a half it dinged. I took a sip, burned my tongue and figured that was a good thing.

As fast as I could without spilling it, I took it upstairs. She was still sitting on the toilet, only now she'd started to shiver.

Which was actually a good sign. It meant she'd gone from frozen to cold.

I got on my knees in front of her and slowly fed her sips. She was through about half the mug when the shivering stopped. Another few sips and she could hold the mug on her own.

I pulled her wet hair off her back and took the mug out of her hands when it was empty.

"You unhook yourself from the line?" I asked her.

"It got away from me. It was so close," she said quietly. "A couple of feet."

"You unhook yourself from the line?" I asked again.

She nodded.

A rage, unlike any I had ever felt, swept over me. Any lingering cold I had in my body was gone in that moment. She had unhooked herself. She had lost sight of the line. She had kept moving with the damn calf tied to her arm.

I pulled her off the toilet seat until she was also on her knees. My hands were tight around her arms and I wanted to shake her. I wanted to shake her so hard so she would never ever do anything as stupid as that again.

"I could have lost you," I shouted at her. "Do you understand that? You could have DIED!"

Her lip was quivering, but I didn't care. I had so much feeling inside of me, so much of everything all at once.

And then it happened. I couldn't shake her. I couldn't beat her. So I bent my head and I kissed her.

I took her lips and her tongue. All of it. I took every ounce of my anger and fury and I growled it into her mouth.

I was kissing her. I was kissing her and this was Ellie.

Fuck!

I don't know if I pushed her away or she pushed against me, but suddenly we were apart. Each of us breathing hard, looking at each other, neither one of us knowing what to say.

"Jake..."

I stood up. I took the mug.

"Get dressed. Something warm. You're going to be tired, lethargic, but you can't go to bed. I need you to get to ninety-eight degrees before you can sleep."

Then I walked out of the bathroom, walked downstairs, and threw the mug against the fireplace as hard as I could.

Watching it shatter felt good.

Cleaning it up sucked.

FOURTEEN

Ellie
March

SO THAT HAPPENED.

Jake and I didn't speak the rest of the night. I didn't have the energy for it, and he was still really mad at me. The snow let up eventually, but the cold lasted another brutal three days, getting as low as forty below freezing.

Jake went out the next day to try and save more calves. He told me not to bother to ask to come with him, but the truth was I didn't have it in me.

He came back three hours later with a grim expression.

We still didn't talk.

It was now four days PK (post kiss). Jake was still sullen, only I'm not sure who he was more mad at, me or himself.

Today we were going to assess the damage.

He was standing in the kitchen, waiting for the coffee to

brew, when I came downstairs. He stared at me for a few minutes before asking, "Can you do this?"

I shrugged. "I have no idea. I've never had to do anything like this."

Death on a large scale. Animal carcasses filling the pen. We were going to count up what was left, and then Jake said he would have to hire equipment and a large truck to get the dead cows out of the pen. Then another machine to dig a mass gave.

Filled with coffee and dread, we made our way outside.

I'm not going to lie, as we crunched our way through the snow I felt the anxiety of that day rushing up at me. I didn't want to be anywhere near snow. I didn't want to come close to feeling that cold ever again.

Fear of the cold for a rancher in Montana was not a good thing.

When I shared this with Jake I got a very sympathetic... "You'll get over it."

I know, I know. You don't want to hear about all the gruesome shit. The dead calves, the dead cows, the brutal work of clearing it all out.

You want to know about the kiss.

We couldn't talk about it. I think we were both too raw from the experience in general. Jake had not been wrong. I could have easily died. There was emotional fallout from that.

I tried to tell myself the kiss wasn't really anything.

Like on a scale of one to ten, maybe like a five. Sure, it happened. It was weird for us. But it had more to do with me almost dying than any feelings Jake had for me. Or I had for him.

Still, it was a pretty hot kiss. My hottest kiss ever. Sure, I had kissed guys. Four of them, if you want a running total, but nothing in my life had prepared me for that. That was... that was...

Intense.

Okay, so maybe it was more like a six on the scale. It was an event. It happened. It was powerful but it didn't have to change anything.

Unless it changed everything.

We were at thirty-eight days. Thirty-eight days until my eighteenth birthday. Until I was legally an adult.

Thirty-eight days until Jake left.

"Stop," I called out to him.

He turned around. "We have to do this, Ellie."

"I know, but we have to do the other thing too and I want to do it first."

He put his hands on his hips, then he turned around and started walking toward me. The crazy thing was, every time he did that now, any time he started moving toward me, I couldn't help but wonder if he was going to kiss me again.

Fine. On a scale of ten our kiss was probably more like a seven in terms of overall life impact.

Instead of kissing me (which I knew he wasn't going to do) he grabbed my hand and pulled me back toward the house. "If we're going to do this, we might as well be warm."

THIS. Suddenly that word had colossal meaning in my brain.

This could mean hashing it out, which is what I intended.

This could mean more kissing.

This could mean sex.

Because kissing led to sex. Because I wanted sex. Because secretly in that place I don't like to think about too hard, I wanted sex with Jake.

There, I thought it. I don't know how it happened. It wasn't seeing him naked. It wasn't any one thing. It was that day in and day out, he'd become the one person who understood me. The one person I wanted to see in the morning, the one person I wanted say goodnight to at night. When we watched TV on the couch, I wanted to cuddle. When we drove into town, I fantasized about holding hands.

When we went to Howard's Christmas party, I'd pretended we were a real couple. Only in my head.

Because I knew he didn't feel the same way. Worse, not only did he not feel the same way, he knew how I was feeling. So embarrassing. I guess men have a sense of things when they know a woman wants them.

He'd been walking on eggshells around me for months, while I desperately tried to tell myself I didn't care that he didn't want me. I didn't care that we were going to get a divorce. I didn't care that I was going to have to do this all by myself.

We still had no foreman, because Jake had dismissed all of the candidates as either too inexperienced (young) or too creepy (which who knew what that meant) or too set in his ways (he didn't do things like Jake wanted him to do them).

Javier and Gomez agreed to come back in May to help me out, but they were always going to be temporary, as neither one was willing to commit to full time. Probably because full time meant legal papers neither one of them had.

So all of this had been building up and building up. Then the storm happened and Jake kissed me and now we needed to talk about it. Because it was day thirty-eight and this was more important than a lot of dead animals.

This was good. I was angry. I was pretty sure this whole

conversation would be better with pissed me than pathetic me.

We were inside the back room, going through the routine of taking off our coats.

"I need a drink," he said.

"It's eight in the morning."

He hit me then with his expression. "Are we going to have the conversation I think we're going to have?"

"Yes," I snapped, my arms crossing over my chest.

"Then I need a fucking drink."

The only place we kept real alcohol was my father's study. A room we never went to because I think it hurt us both too much to be in there without him. Any bookwork we did was always at the kitchen table.

Across from the living room Jake opened the door to the study and made his way toward the bar in the corner. The same one Howard had gone to the night of Dad's funeral.

"Make mine a double."

Jake glared at me.

"Oh you get to drink, but I don't?"

He said nothing and poured me a splash of something brown.

He handed me the glass even as he took a healthy gulp of his own.

I smelled fire and fumes. Then I tasted fire and fumes. I coughed and set the glass aside.

"Okay, Ellie. We're here. You want to talk, talk."

"Don't make this about me being dramatic about something. You kissed me, Jake. Not the other way around."

His jaw clenched. "I was so... so fucking mad at you."

"Then that's it. That's all it was. Because we're getting divorced in thirty-eight days. Do you get that? That means you move out. Completely. You go to your ranch, I stay on mine and we see each other... whenever. Which with all the work you have and all the work I have means hardly ever. We will hardly ever see each other. Is that what you want?"

He started laughing at that. A harsh and ugly sound. I never wanted to hear it again. He sat on the couch like his legs couldn't hold him and looked up at me. "Are you that fucking naïve?"

That hurt. Like he'd slapped me.

"Not cool, Jake," I said stiffly.

He sighed then and stood up. He walked over to me and took my hands. I was tempted to snap them back but I thought it would make me look immature, and after having just been called naïve, I was trying to avoid that.

"I'm sorry. I'm... I don't know what I am. But I've been taking it out on you and I know that. It's fair for you to be pissed off."

"I didn't do anything wrong."

He glared at me. "You fucking took yourself off the line, Ellie."

"To save a calf, Jake. I'm a rancher. That's what we do. That's what you would have done."

"I'm a hell of a lot stronger than you."

This time I did pull my hands back. I didn't want him touching me.

"I can't control that! You know that. You know I can't cut fence, even with those stupid wire cutters you got me for Christmas. You know I can birth a calf, but I can't lift one clear off the ground. You know all of this. So why don't you just say it? I can't do this. You're mad at me, really mad at me, because you know I can't do this by myself and you feel guilty for leaving. Admit it."

"Ellie... I drove out to my old home yesterday."

He'd left. I knew that. I presumed it was to do a check

in with some of the neighbors. But that made sense. The wind had been brutal. It didn't look like we had sustained any damage to the house or barn, but where his house was located it was a little higher up on a ridge. More exposed. Of course he needed to check on it.

Still, I didn't understand what that had to do with anything. "Okay."

"It's gone."

"What's gone?"

"The house. The roof is gone or collapsed. The north facing side is also collapsed. It was in bad shape when I left it six years ago. I've only been barely doing what I could to keep it livable for when... it doesn't matter. Now it's gone."

"But you can rebuild it?"

"In time."

That muscle in his jaw was still ticking and I knew it. I knew he was seeing a completed puzzle while I was still looking at individual pieces. That was Jake. Always the man with perspective on everything.

I was sick of it.

"Fine, I'm stupid. I'm naïve. Whatever. What aren't you telling me?"

He lowered his eyes. "I didn't take a hard count, but it was easy enough to see... we lost about half the herd. Saved only those calves we managed to pull out that first day."

This time I sat down. I tried to wrap my head around the numbers. I knew what we'd made last year with double that. I knew what losing so many calves would do to us next year.

I knew that in thirty-eight days I had pay Jake twenty thousand dollars he was owed so that he could buy his land.

Land that no longer had a place for him to live. Because his house was gone.

Which seemed fitting, since I knew I no longer had twenty thousand dollars to give him anyway.

Then he said the thing he'd already figured out. The conclusion I was struggling to get to.

"I'm not going anywhere in thirty-eight days, Ellie."

I can't explain how it hurt. It was really sharp and piercing. Like being back in the hot water when I had been so cold.

He sat down next to me and I shifted away from him. Suddenly it all made sense.

He knew what damage the storm had done. He knew he had nowhere to go and there would be no money to pay him off anyway.

Which meant there was no point in getting divorced. Which meant everyone would think...

The worst of him. That he'd been screwing me all along.

"We can still get divorced..." I said, and stopped when he put his hand on my knee.

"I'm not sure what's worse. I stay here and we're not married. I stay here and we are. But what I do know is I can't leave you. Not now. You're right, you can't do this on your own, and now there is no money to bring someone on to help. Storms like this are once every twenty, thirty years. They happen, and ranching operations survive, but it's going to take years, Ellie."

I nodded. "You're trapped. Wow. It's like a fucking prison sentence. Sure, Jake. Marry me. Sixteen months. What's the big deal..."

He squeezed my knee to stop me from speaking, but I couldn't hold the words inside.

"You'll hate me. When all this is done, you'll resent and hate me."

"I will not. Not ever."

But he would. How could he not? I could feel tears happening and I swallowed a bunch of times to try to force them down. "The whole time I thought you were mad at me because... but really you're mad that you're stuck here."

"I'm not mad about that, Ellie. I promise you. You are my family. You need help right now and so I'm not going anywhere. Hell, not that I have anywhere to go to. With what your father was going to give me I barely had enough money to put down on the land. I can't buy the land, buy cattle, and build a house from scratch all at the same time."

He was trying to make me feel better, but it wasn't working. I felt like shit. Then I said the scary thing. The thing I had to consider.

"I can sell it. The operation, the land."

Jake closed his eyes. As if what I had said was blasphemous. Worse than any curse I had ever shouted. Masons had been on this land for five generations.

Until it got to me.

"Ellie..."

"No, Jake. Don't you see? It's the only way. I can sell it and give you the money and then you don't have to worry about me anymore. I won't have to lift a calf, or cut fence line or any of it... You would be free."

He looked at me then and I could see I had shocked him.

"You would do that? You would give up all of this, your legacy, your future... you would do that for me?"

I nodded. It was only fair.

He reached up with his finger and brushed my cheek. Like I was some odd fairy he discovered in the forest. But then he was shaking his head. "Ellie, you and I both know you come into some money when you're twenty-one. That money is there for you so you can have choices. If all we have to do is wait another three years..."

"Three years! Jake, that is three more years of your life. You'll be thirty!"

He smiled then and I wanted to hit his arm.

Instead he bumped his shoulder against mine. "Yes, I'll be thirty, but I won't be dead. You do this drastic thing now, you can never undo it. We wait three years and then you'll have the money I need..."

"It's not enough. If you're going to give up another three years of your life, then you deserve more. You have to give that to me. You have to make this so it's not all about me taking, but giving back to you too."

"Okay. We'll talk to Howard. We'll work something out. Something that's fair for both of us."

We sat there then quietly as reality started to close in around me. I had started crushing on Jake hard, pretending I wasn't because I knew he was going to be leaving soon. Jake knew I was crushing on him and was being gentle with me because he didn't feel the same but didn't want to hurt my feelings when he left.

Through it all we seemed to have had this light at the end of the tunnel. April twenty-second and it would be behind us.

Instead, it was three more years ahead of us.

"What are you mad about, then?" I asked him.

He turned his head to me. "What?"

"You said you weren't mad about being stuck here, but you're obviously upset about something."

He nodded. "Yeah, I guess we have to talk about that too. I am angry with myself that I kissed you."

"But you said it was just a reaction to the situation."

"It was."

"Then you don't have to worry about it."

"Ellie, I'm angry at myself that I kissed you. But I am fucking furious with myself... because I want to do it again."

My head shot up but he didn't wait to give me chance to say anything. He left and slammed the door of the study behind him.

"Oh no," I whispered to an empty room. "That's a problem."

THE WIFE PART 2

ONE

Ellie
Two weeks after the storm (aka the day Jake kissed me)

SO THAT HAPPENED.

Oh. Wait. I should probably catch you up with everything. Well, you remember my dad died, I was underage, so Jake stepped up and married me. We agreed to the arrangement until my eighteenth birthday.

Except a month before my eighteenth birthday, a major Arctic blast took out half my herd and two thirds of my calves. Oh, and Jake's old house on the property he was going to buy back—as soon as we got divorced and I gave him the money my dad left him in the will.

No house.

No money to buy the land.

Massively in trouble cattle ranch.

What did all of that equal?

No divorce.

Which meant Jake and I were going to stay married. And you might think what was the problem with that? After all, we did it for sixteen months, no problem.

Okay, one problem. About a year in I started to have... feelings. Yeah. *Those* feelings. I fought it. He mostly ignored it, but I could tell he was a little upset about it. He liked me. He didn't want to hurt my feelings when he... you know... divorced my ass.

So we pretended I didn't feel anything, which was fine because the divorce was only a couple of months away. Then he would leave, I would get down to the business of running my ranch, and all those...feelings would fade away.

Except now we weren't getting divorced.

Enter problem number two.

Jake had kissed me. I had unhooked my karabiner from the safe line and lost my way in the storm. Thankfully, Jake had found me. But he'd been pissed.

Super pissed.

Angrier than I had ever seen him. And he'd kissed me. It was hot. It was—well, this is probably going to sound super profound... but the kiss was about life. Two people who had survived, and while the whole feeling thing was weird between us, there was no question we loved each other.

We were Ellie and Jake. Jake and Ellie.

Now there was this elephant in the room. Because while the kiss had happened under extreme circumstances which we might have been able to write off, him telling me he wanted to do it again...

Leading to problem number three.

We're married. Jake didn't want folks to think he would ever take advantage of an underage girl, because he wouldn't. Except now I was very close to not being underage, and we had kissed.

You're thinking sex was the natural conclusion to that day?

You would be wrong. Instead we'd rented equipment and pulled dead cows out of a pen all day, then buried them in a mass grave. Totally not sexy times. We'd fallen asleep after being dead on our feet and we didn't talk about the kiss, his stunning confession, and his very real anger at himself for feeling that way.

Anger that kind of, sort of, leaked out towards me.

It was not fun times.

Which gets us to now.

Two weeks later.

"I don't think I understand what that means," I told Mr. Connelly.

Mr. Connelly was the Vice President at Heartland Bank. Heartland Bank held the note on Long Valley. I had done some research and had come up with a plan to free Jake. Jake didn't think the plan would work. Still, he'd come with me to the bank.

"You're asking for a loan? Correct?"

That's what it means when you go to the bank and ask them for money. We were going to have to do this anyway. We had to buy more cows if we were going to restore the operation within the next few years. Since I was taking a major hit on what I was going to be able to sell at the end of summer, I was going to have to borrow the money anyway. Not a big deal. We had the land as collateral, and that was worth a lot.

"Yes," I said, like he was a little thick.

"And you and Jake and have worked it out and decided to stay married? Correct?"

I hated the way he said *correct* after every question. But I was digressing. This was part of the plan. I was just going to borrow more money than I needed. Jake and I worked out the numbers. The least amount we needed to borrow to buy the cows to replenish the herd. Then I added twenty thousand to that number.

I would pay him his money and we could get divorced.

Because FYI, being married to someone who didn't want to be married to you... also not fun.

Which meant we fought about it constantly, because I apparently was the only one looking for a way out.

I'd told him he had a hero complex and that he should divorce me.

He'd told me to shut up.

I'd told him I was going to divorce him and he had no say in the matter.

He'd told me to shut up.

I'd told him about my bank plan, and he'd said it wouldn't work. And now it seemed it wasn't working.

"Uh, does that matter?"

Mr. Connelly laced his fingers together and gave me what would be my first, but not my last, what I would come to know as the banker smile.

"Ellie, I knew your dad... well, just about my whole life. He was a good man and he ran a solid cattle ranch operation."

"Thank you."

Jake had warned me to be polite to Mr. Connelly. I hated that it felt like Jake already knew the outcome when I hadn't even asked the question yet.

"So you'll forgive my... hesitancy in allowing you, a new rancher, to take on a loan of such size without knowing that you'll have Jake's experience working beside you."

Jake's experience? Horseshit. Jake was only ten years

older than I was. Then I realized Jake had something I didn't have.

A penis.

I know. Because I saw it. Naked and everything.

Not going to lie. I spent a lot of time thinking about Jake's naked penis.

"This is because I'm a woman," I said.

"Oh, here we go," Jake muttered.

"Ellie, no, absolutely not. We would never make any kind of decision based on the sex, race, or sexual orientation of a person applying for a loan."

That didn't sound practiced at all.

Mr. Connelly continued. "You have to understand we're a small bank, and that storm was hard for a lot of folks around here. We have to make good decisions. Giving an eighteen-year-old *person* a significant amount of money on the hope that you can return the ranch to good standing on your own—well, that's a risk we can't take. If we knew two experienced *persons* were working toward that effort, we would be willing to consider a loan given the value you have in the land."

I leaned forward to make my point. "I don't think you get it. He doesn't want to be married to me."

"Ellie, shut up," Jake interjected. "We're fine, Mr. Connelly. We're going to stay married for the time being. Until we can get Long Valley back to what it was. What happens now?"

The banker smile was back. Now all of Mr. Connelly's attention was focused on Jake. Even though it was my ranch and my loan.

Mr. Connelly walked us through everything that would be required while I sat and basically seethed. Because little did Mr. Connelly know, I ran the money in our house. I anymore. I'm going to be eighteen next week. You have needs. I get that. What about me? I have needs too, Jake!"

It was very unfortunate timing on my part, as Kathy chose just that moment to come by to take our orders. Her expression was as awkward as I felt.

"Like right now I *need* a tuna open-melt sandwich with American." I smiled at Kathy.

"Got it. Open T with Am. You, Jake?"

"I'll do the same."

"Yep. Be back in a few. Minutes. It should only take a few minutes," Kathy said, basically letting us know her schedule so we could plan our sex conversation accordingly.

Jake just gave me the look.

"Okay," I said. "Awkward. Fine. But that doesn't change anything. We've mutually agreed we're not going to satisfy those needs for each other, so I want to know how we're going to do this. For three fucking years."

"You shouldn't swear."

"Fuck you."

That made him smile. "Okay. You're saying we need new rules. But do we have to do this now and here? At Frank's?"

"No," I allowed. "I only wanted to put it out there that we can't run away from the conversation. And the kid card no longer applies. Next week I'm an adult and I want to be treated that way."

"Fine."

"Fine," I returned. "Speaking of, what are you getting me for my birthday? We don't have any money left, so you're going to have to be creative. Like baking a cake would totally count this year."

"I'm not baking you a cake."

"I love cake."

"I'm not baking you a cake," he repeated.

"Because *men* don't bake? Some of the world's most famous pastry chefs are men."

"I don't bake because I burn stuff."

"Well, you have to get me something. I am your *wife*."

Weird. I used to throw that line around all the time as a joke. Now it didn't feel anywhere as funny.

"I have an idea, but it's a surprise."

I clapped. I loved surprises. I especially loved guessing what the surprise was going to be.

"Just so long as it's not practical," I reminded him. Wire cutters for Christmas. What had he been thinking?

"Yep."

Kathy came back with our tuna melts, and luckily we were back on to the basics of the ranch and the myriad of things that still needed to be done to clean up from the storm. There we sat. The two of us at Frank's, where it was now officially concluded we would remain married for the next three years.

Yep. Me and my husband (not really), Jake. In our booth at Frank's.

All of it was gut-wrenching. It sucked because I couldn't control it.

Nope. Once the switch was on, it stayed on. There was no going back.

That kiss had changed things. That day had changed things, too.

Now I was stuck in this marriage, platonic of my own choosing, lusting after my wife, who was dancing with other guys.

I should ask Ellie where she would put that on the scale of one to ten of suckiness, because I was going with a solid nine.

The last dance ended and the girls peeled away from the crowd. Ellie searched the bar for me, and it felt good when her eyes landed on me. Like it was important to her to know I had her back.

She bounced over, tipped her cowgirl hat back on her head, and tried again.

"Come dance with me."

"I don't dance," I replied. Just like I had every other time she asked.

"I'll show you the moves. It's so easy, and you're in a line of people so it's not like you stand out or anything."

I turned to her friend. "Chrissy, what one particular thing do you know about me?"

"You don't dance," she said, then giggled. It was a funny giggle. Like a drunk giggle, even though she was wearing the pink wrist band which announced her age.

"I don't dance," I told Ellie, and then I watched as Chrissy swayed a bit on her feet.

That wasn't dance swaying. That was drunk swaying.

"Shit."

"What?" Ellie asked.

"Chrissy, what are you drinking?"

"Diet Coke?" she said, holding up her red solo cup.

"Chrissy, another thing you should know about me. I'm not an idiot. What are you drinking?"

Ellie turned to her friend. "You're drinking without me? That's so not fair. It's my birthday."

Chrissy winced. Apparently she saw the selfishness of her actions. "Okay, so maybe this guy bought a shot of rum for me and put it in my drink. Okay... maybe there were like four shots."

"Not cool." I looked at my watch. "It's after eleven. I don't want to ruin your birthday or anything…"

"No. It's fine. I'm getting kind of tired and my feet hurt in these boots."

"Noooo," Chrissy protested. "I think I'm in love."

"Point him out, then go wait for me by the door."

Ellie narrowed her eyes at me. "Jake, let it go. Chrissy was just being Chrissy. She probably asked for them."

"A shot I let go. Maybe two. Not four, and knowing Chrissy, it was more like five. Which means some asshole is trying to get her drunk so he can take advantage of her. What do I always tell you?"

"Trust no one. Great motto by the way."

"Trust no one. Never a guy and not with your drinks. It sucks that there are creeps out there in the world, but they exist and you have to watch for them. Now, hold on to her while I go deal. Chrissy, which one?"

Chrissy lifted her hand in the guy's general direction. I saw who it was instantly, as he was staring at Chrissy. Not a good kind of stare either. He was waiting for the booze to do the trick.

It wasn't until I was almost on him that he straightened up. When I got up close and could see the face under the cowboy hat, the motherfucker was easily over thirty.

"You like to feed underage girls drinks," I said to him. It wasn't a question.

The guy got his back up. "She asked for a drink, so I bought her one. Big deal."

"Even though her wrist band clearly showed she was under legal age."

"Whatever. Dude, I'll move on if you're upset."

"What I am, is sickened by the thought a man almost, what... double her age... tried to get her drunk so he could do... What was the plan, anyway?"

"Dude, go fuck yourself. I was trying to have a little fun."

I nodded like I was in agreement. "Yeah, I get it. No confidence. Or self-esteem. Or whatever it is you're missing that makes you think a girl will only like you if she's drunk. You're a pathetic piece of shit and I'm sorry people refer to you as a man."

"Fuck you, I can get any piece I want."

I turned to the bartender. "I'll take..." I turned and eyed up the guy. "Seven shots of Fireball."

The bartender lined them up quickly in front of me and just poured through the glasses.

"You want to show me what a man you are? You fed the girl who is half your age and half your size four shots. Let's see how you do after seven?"

The man grimaced. As if seeing the numbers made him realize exactly what he'd done. Or at least I hoped I made my point.

Then the man sneered. "Fuck you."

"Dude, trust me. The only thing you're going to be fucking tonight is your right hand. Have a solid jerk off, douchebag. Try not to think of me when you do." I took one of shots and fired it down. "Yeah," I drawled, "little pussy like you ... you probably don't want to drink those. Bartender, you want to pass those out to those pretty ladies in the corner and tell them I said to stay away from this guy?"

"Sure thing, bro."

I made my way to the girls, where Ellie was talking to the bouncer and pointing back at the asshole.

He nodded. "Yeah, I know the guy. Comes here all the time on Under Twenty-One night. He's an asshat. I'll take care of it, honey."

"Thanks, Bob."

"Have a nice rest of your birthday."

She beamed at the guy. "It was the best birthday ever!"

That made me happy. That I had given her a fun night.

I followed the girls to my truck as Chrissy bobbed and weaved from side to side.

"I'm still so pissed at you for not sharing," Ellie was hissing at her.

"You know I can hear you, right?"

She turned and gave me her what-I'm-so-innocent smile.

And I wanted her.

Nope. Not a switch you can turn off.

WE DROPPED drunk Chrissy off at home. It wasn't pretty. After who knows how many shots, she was wasted. The good news was her parents were in bed, so it went down with little drama.

Ellie and I poured her through the front door, and she was on her own. Make it to her bedroom or bust.

Then we drove back to Ellie's...*her place...our place...my place?*

I called it *the house*. Long Valley was the ranch. The house was the house. It wasn't hers or ours. It was just the house. Not a home either. Which in some ways made me sad, but I was a guy and we typically don't get sad. For myself I simply try to force it away.

Forcing away sadness was a lot like trying to force away desire. It wasn't always easy. I had set the wrapped gift up on the kitchen island before we left for the bar. I wanted it to be the first thing she saw when we got home.

Ellie always poured herself a glass of water right before bed, so as soon as we got inside she made her way to the kitchen.

I heard the gasp and smiled.

I liked that I'd made her gasp.

I followed her into the kitchen and she was holding the box to her chest. Like it didn't matter at all what was inside it. Hell, I probably could have wrapped an empty box and she would have been happy with that.

I liked that she was that kind of girl. The kind of girl who understood that it was truly the thought that counted.

"What is it?"

"Open it and find out."

She started to tear through my very bad wrapping job. "Did you get me what I asked for?"

"You asked for a vibrator. No, I did not get you what you asked for."

"The gift of pleasure, Jake. You shouldn't mock it."

She opened the lid on the box and slid out the Styrofoam. Then when she opened that, she gasped again.

Nestled inside was a beautiful silver scale. Two disks balanced on either side, and two containers with five silver disks in each. She set it up on the able and opened the silver disks. Holding one in her fingers.

"You're always going on about your scale of one to ten..." I felt a little awkward. Because she wasn't saying anything. Just looking at it thoughtfully, as if it were a puzzle to be solved instead of scale. "Figured now you had the actual physical representation of it."

"I love it," she said quietly. Then she turned to me. "You always give the best gifts."

I nodded and waited for it. My hug. Every year I gave her a gift and every year she hugged me for it.

Not this year, apparently. Because instead of hugging me she was playing with the disks and putting them on the scale.

All ten on one side.

"Today," she said.

That had to be enough, because it was all I was going to get.

"Good night, Jake."

"Good night, Ellie. Happy Birthday."

She got her water and went upstairs and I stood there like a statue for what was definitely too long, fighting off the disappointment that I didn't get my hug.

Because it was all I would let myself have...I wanted it really badly.

THREE

Ellie
June – Graduation day

I WAS NOT GOING to be disappointed. He told me he would do absolutely everything he could do to be here today, but he couldn't control when the foal was going to come. That's right, I forgot to say—we were having a baby.

Well, not us. We weren't having a baby because we weren't having sex. No sex at all for us. No sirree Bob. I went to school and we worked really hard and we never ever considered having sex.

Jake didn't, anyway. Me, not so much. I thought about it. A LOT!

A LOT!

Are you feeling me?

Anyway, Jake put Wyatt to stud on Isabella, who he'd bought just for that purpose, and now Isabella was due any moment. Javier and Gomez were back and living in the bunk house, but I knew Jake wanted to be there for the birth.

After all, this was his precious Wyatt who was about to become a father. Let's face it. Jake was most definitely hoping for a boy that would one day fill Wyatt's shoes when he was too old to carry Jake.

So I understood completely if he couldn't make it to my graduation. It was a stupid thing anyway. Caps and gowns, long boring speeches, and then everyone having their name called out.

If he could make it, he was going to take me to dinner afterwards to celebrate and then we were going to go to Pete's for drinks.

That's right. I said we were going to Pete's for drinks. It seemed as a high school graduate I was now mature enough to have a few beers.

If he couldn't make it though, then plan B was to go out with Chrissy and her parents for dinner and then go with Chrissy to Pete's.

Either way, Pete's was happening. It was a Riverbend tradition that Pete officially started not caring about fake IDs once he knew you were no longer in high school. A bunch of kids from my class would be there tonight.

Then, if he could, Jake would meet me at Pete's later.

Which was pretty much what it looked like was going to happen, because as I sat on the stage behind the principal and looked out over the crowd I didn't see him anywhere. It wasn't a large group. We were only a class of eighty-six, and since we all knew each other's families it wasn't hard to see who was here and who was not.

I noticed Bobby MacPherson's dad was not. Just his mom. It almost—almost—made me feel for bad for him. I knew there was trouble there, and I knew Bobby had spent the last year basically being angry at the world.

He'd left me alone, so I shouldn't have cared at all. I guess I knew what it was like not to have a parent in your life. His dad wasn't dead, but sometimes it was harder if they chose to leave you.

For my dad there had been no choice. He'd be here now if he could be. I knew that. Or not. Because if he'd had a mare about to drop a foal, he probably would have told me the same thing as Jake.

I smiled and lifted my head to the ceiling of the auditorium and smiled at him and hoped somewhere in the universe he saw it.

Then, as we all stood for the Pledge of Allegiance, I saw him. He was jogging down the row of chairs, holding his tie against his chest. Still in his neatly pressed jeans, but he'd gone so far as to wear a tie and jacket.

He found an empty seat along the aisle and stood in front of it.

He looked up at the stage to find me, and when his eyes hit on me I waved.

He raised his chin and smiled.

He made it. To my graduation. Which meant we were going to get to have dinner and then he was going to take me to Pete's.

I thought about my scale that I kept in full display on the kitchen counter, and mentally moved all my disks to the right side. (The right side was for good stuff. The left for bad.)

Then it occurred to me that Jake, just by being Jake, gave me a lot of ten days.

I WAS in my best dress. Blue with small white flowers all over it, a deep V in the front, and a wrap-around tie at my waist. I paired it with white wedges and I hoped, I thought, I looked anywhere as close to as nice as Jake did in his jacket and tie.

I mean, this wasn't a Frank's dinner. This was a real restaurant with cloth napkins and really nice silver and everything.

The Chop House was a legit steakhouse. It had taken us over an hour to drive here, but it was so worth it. I felt like... I mean, the whole thing had the feel of... a date.

Not that it was a date. It was my graduation dinner. Logically I knew that, but still I was going with it.

"You're not eating," Jake pointed out.

"I'm excited to see the baby."

Jake smiled and it almost took my breath away. "Amazes me every time it happens. One minute I'm sliding this big ball of goo out, and the next it's up on these little spindly legs, looking at them like *what the heck am I supposed to do with these things?*"

"I'm glad it worked out."

"Me too. I would have been heartbroken thinking I missed your graduation."

Heartbroken. Hmm. That was an odd word choice.

I cut into my steak and took another bite and closed my eyes it was so good. I must have made a noise too, because when I opened my eyes Jake was looking at me funny.

"It's a steak, Ellie."

"It's a good steak, Jake."

He smiled again, but a little tighter this time.

"And we still get to go to Pete's after this."

"Yes, I will happily buy you your first beer. Or wine. Or cooler. Whatever it is you drink."

I shrugged. I didn't know what I "drank". Other than spiked punch and eggnog at Christmas, the only time I'd had a real drink was the day after the kiss... I meant the storm. The storm was the bigger event that day.

It burned my throat the whole way down.

The drink. Not the kiss.

"What if I like wine?"

"What of it?"

"You're a beer guy."

"So?"

Right. That was stupid. Just because he was a beer guy didn't mean I needed to be a beer girl. It's just that I always figured Jake would be the kind of guy to like hanging out with a girl who could sit back and drink beer with him.

Where a girl who drank wine he might consider snobby.

"What did Janet drink when you guys used to go out?"

He looked up at me like I was crazy. "Why are you asking about Janet?"

I shrugged. "I'm curious. When you guys went out, what did she drink?"

"She liked beer. Shots every once and a while, tequila. But mostly beer."

See. Jake had previously been with a beer girl. I was drinking beer tonight no matter what.

He had a small smile around his mouth.

"What?" I asked.

"I think I always knew it," he muttered.

"What?" I demanded.

"I think you're a wine girl. I can feel it."

"I'm not!" I insisted. Ridiculously. This was the stupidest conversation ever. And *I* was not the type of girl who drank something or ate something because the guy I was with liked the same thing.

It was horseshit. You were who you were, you liked what you liked.

"Okay, so maybe I am. I don't know. We'll have to wait and see tonight when I try both."

"That's fine. We'll see. But I'm still going with wine."

I had the urge to stick my tongue out at him, but we were in a really fancy place and I was an adult now so I resisted.

BEER WAS GROSS. Cold white wine was delicious. I hated that Jake was right, but as I said I wasn't going to change what I liked to match what he liked. After all Jake loved blondes, and at best my hair could be called honey brown. It's not like I was going to dye it.

Wait, should I dye it?

Ugh. Boys. They messed with my thinking. Or at least Jake did.

We were at Pete's and I have to say it was a little strange. When we walked in a lot of my friends from high school were there, but I sort of stuck by Jake's side. I didn't want to leave him to hang by himself and, well... I didn't want to leave him. We were having a really nice night hanging out together.

So when he asked me if I wanted to sit at the table with Chrissy and some of the other girls from school, I shook my head and we went to the bar instead.

I'd had my first beer, hated it. Now my first glass of wine, loving it and Jake was sipping on his beer.

"This is fun," I said.

"Yeah. I knew hanging with you at Pete's would be a trip."

"You want to play pool?"

Jake's eyes shot up. "You can play pool?"

No. But how hard could it be? You poked at the balls with a stick. I was fairly certain I could do that. "Sure."

"Okay. What are we betting?"

"Wait, there are stakes in this?" I asked. This could be interesting.

"It's the only way to make it fun."

I ran through several scenarios in my head.

If I won, Jake had to have sex with me.

If I lost, I would have to have sex with Jake.

I was fairly certain he wouldn't go for it.

I shook my head. "You decide."

"Loser has to grocery shop for a month."

Typical Jake. There was no sex in any of that. I huffed. "Fine. But if I lose, I'm buying everything you hate. Vegetables. Lots and lots of vegetables."

"I don't care. I still won't be doing the shopping. Let's go."

He led me to the back of the bar where the pool table was. He put a dollar of quarters on the table and after the last group finished we were up. He allowed me to break, which I did and actually got one ball in. It was solid, so he was stripes. My second attempt was not so great, and then Jake took over and cleared the entire table.

Snickering... because there was no other word for it... the entire time.

Apparently Jake was good at pool. Sometimes it freaking seemed like Jake was good at everything.

And he was my husband. Mine.

"Best two out of three?" he offered.

"No thanks. You'll have me doing the shopping, cooking, cleaning, and laundry. Not a chance."

He laughed. "You want another glass of wine?"

"I can have one?"

"Yes, you can have one."

"Then yes, my dear husband, I would love another glass of wine."

"You're a goof," he said as he brushed by me, but I knew it was a compliment.

I was distracted by rolling the ball along the felt when I could feel someone approaching. I looked up to see Bobby MacPherson standing in front of me, and it probably showed on my face that I wasn't thrilled to run into him because he started by raising his two hands in the air as a surrender.

"Hey Ellie, just hear me out."

"Okay."

"Look... I know was kind of an ass to you last year..."

"Kind of?"

"Okay, I was a major ass. I'm not making any excuses or anything but I was going through a lot of shit with my dad... and I was angry. A lot. I don't know why I took that out on you. But I wanted to say... sorry."

Wow. Bobby MacPherson was apologizing. That was something I never thought would happen. Which meant I had to be classy.

"Apology accepted."

"We're cool?"

"We're cool."

He smiled and nodded his head. "Then maybe I can buy you a beer?"

"She prefers wine," Jake said, coming up behind him. He moved around Bobby and put the glass in my hand. Then he stood next to me and basically glared at Bobby until Bobby got the message.

The message I read was *back the hell off*. Bobby must have gotten the same message because he eventually did.

"Right. See you, Jake. Ellie."

"See you, Bobby."

Jake waited until he'd left to growl in my ear.

"What the hell did he want?"

"He actually came to apologize," I told him. "You know, all that stuff happened a year ago. He could have grown up."

"Maybe, but I'm not buying it. Watch yourself with him. He's got a thing for you."

"A thing for me? Hardly."

Jake looked at me then with a hard expression. "Ellie, why wouldn't he have a thing for you? You're beautiful, smart, funny... and he looks at you... Well, let's just say I know the look. He's got a thing for you."

OH. MY. GOD.

Jake thought I was beautiful and funny and smart. But beautiful came first on the list. Which as a feminist I should be affronted by, but as a woman I knew how important that was to guys.

It made me think maybe I had this all wrong. For the last few months, since the storm... the kiss, I thought he wanted to go back to the way things were before. Because of that I had been trying really hard to not make any moves.

Seriously, just because I *thought* about sex with him all the time, didn't mean I wanted him to know I thought about sex with him all the time. If he did want things to go back to the way they were, then it would make him uncomfortable to know I was super attracted to him.

Mostly I pretended that I was cool with our situation. But what if that was the wrong approach? What if he was waiting for me to let him know what I wanted? That I was okay changing our relationship?

Today felt special. For the first time, we were acting like a legitimate couple. Doing things like a couple. We had the nice romantic dinner, now we were hanging at Pete's.

He made Bobby go away in a quick second, and now he seemed...

Jealous?

"I still think you're crazy," I told Jake. "But since I don't want to talk about Bobby anymore I'll let it go."

"Good idea," he grumbled.

I sipped my wine and decided then and there that tonight was it.

Tonight I was going to make a play for my husband.

I was probably going to need another glass of wine.

FOUR

Ellie

I PRACTICALLY SKIPPED into the kitchen. I had taken my wedges off in Jake's truck because they were hurting my feet and dropped them by the front door as soon I got into the house.

"Damn it, Ellie, how many times do I have to tell you not to leave your shoes by the door? I'm constantly tripping over them."

This was true. My preferred state of being was barefoot, so any time I came into the house my first order of business was to remove my shoes. My last order of business was to take them upstairs to my room.

Thus, a tripping Jake.

Which was not good because I was gearing up here to make my big move, and it wasn't the best idea to start such a romantic gesture with him cursing at me.

I walked over to my scale—my most favorite gift, outside

of the picture of my parents and my horse Petunia, all given to me by Jake—and moved all ten disks to the right side.

Jake huffed out a laugh behind me. "Good day, then."

"One of the best," I said although it came out more like *bessts* because I was a little tipsy.

Liquid courage was no joke. I felt like I could conquer the world right now.

This whole time, I had been so afraid I wasn't looking at what was right in front of me.

Jake knew me. Better than anyone else alive. He liked me. I knew that because as long as I wasn't watching what he referred to as girly shows, he hung out with me every night.

Beyond that, Jake cared about me. No one who didn't could be so completely thoughtful.

Most importantly Jake, I knew for a fact because he said so, liked kissing me enough that he wanted to kiss me again.

We were freaking married! The way I saw it there was nothing wrong with us changing our relationship.

I was leaning against the kitchen island while I watched him pour himself a glass of water.

"Want some?" he said, holding up the Brita container.

"Sure. Except... could you put that down for a second? I... I wanted to talk to you about something."

He did as I asked and turned to me. There he was. Jake Talley. The hottest guy in Riverbend. Maybe the hottest guy in the county. Maybe all of Montana.

My scale present guy.

My guy.

I walked up to him, put my hands on his waist.

"Ellie what are you..."

Then I did it. I kissed him. It was weird too because it was my first time initiating the kiss. All throughout high she was hurting enough from my words that it wouldn't have registered with her that I did kiss her back.

Don't think about it. Don't think about it.

If she stopped looking at me like *that*, then maybe I would stop wanting to pound the ever loving crap out of her.

What a fucking asshole I was.

I made my way to the living room, sat in my chair, and drank my beer. It did absolutely nothing to make me feel better. Knowing nothing would, I got up and went to bed.

I heard her, of course. Through the door. Even though she was trying to muffle it. Crying because of me.

I remembered when she'd cried for days after Sam died. Always under the covers or into a pillow. I never really understood back then why she had tried to hide it from me. Her father was dead, it was only natural she would cry.

Had she thought I would think less of her? I hoped that wasn't the reason.

Now, I knew she didn't want me to hear her because it was a matter of pride.

Yeah, I told myself, this was good. Exactly what I needed to happen. She'd be angry and pissed. A little heartbroken. Then eventually she would get over it.

As long as she didn't come to hate me. As long as that didn't happen, we would be okay.

Ellie

THERE WAS something to be said for physical labor. I was in the barn, hacking away at a bale of hay, thinking what it would be like if I took said pitchfork to Jake's head.

Okay, maybe that was a little over the top, but I was still super pissed at him. He was pretending to ignore it and mostly we were civil to each other, but after three days I was still not over what had happened.

At this point I was done crying over him. At least I hoped so. But it wasn't just about the pain of rejection. Sure, my feelings were hurt. Sure, I was sad that what I thought had been changing between us was only changing for me. Those were things I could rationally deal with if I had a semblance of the maturity I claimed to have at my age.

What lingered was the anger.

Because I think, for the first time in my life, Jake lied to me.

"Ellie, I need you," Jake called from outside the barn.

That would have been nice to hear the other night.

I set the pitchfork aside and made my way out of the barn to where Jake was standing behind Wyatt, facing away from him with Wyatt's left hind hoof in between Jake's hands.

"He's got a rock stuck in his hoof. I have to get it out but he keeps shifting on me, I need you to settle him."

I walked over to Wyatt, took his reins in my hands, and gently started to stroke his nose. That always calmed him.

"There, there, Wyatt, be a good boy for daddy. You know how upset he gets if he thinks you're in pain."

"Don't talk to my horse like that. You'll soften him."

"Whatever," I muttered under my breath.

Wyatt remained still and a minute later, Jake informed me that he got it out. I dropped the reins and started back for the barn. The less time spent around Jake at this point the better.

"Ellie?"

I stopped but I didn't turn around.

"What?"

"It's been a few days. I know you're upset, but you need to get over it. You'll see. We're going to be fine."

Get. Over. It.

Furious, I turned to him then and I could see it. There in his eyes. This look of pity mixed with his Ellie-doesn't-know-any-better expression. I wanted to hit him. I wanted to slap him upside his fucking smug face.

I walked toward him with purpose and I could see him get his back up. Ready for whatever attack I might lodge at him.

Only I didn't have to hit him. I didn't have to leave a single mark on him. Because I knew the freaking truth. I invaded his space. I wanted him to feel uncomfortable.

"You're full of shit, Jake Talley," I said even as I pushed my finger into his chest.

"Ellie..."

"Don't! Don't you dare say anything to me right now. I'm talking. First, you were mean to me the other night. Flat out mean and cruel. To me. Your best friend. You could have handled that so differently, but you didn't. You know why? You were turned on. You think I couldn't tell? I have a bruise on my freaking ass cheek. So you can tell yourself how I made up *this* in my head, and how much you don't want me, but don't think you can lie to me."

He said nothing and I didn't wait. I went back to the barn to finish my chores and let him stew on that.

Jake

CRUEL AND MEAN. To my best friend. She was right. I

had no comeback, because she was so damn right. She was my best friend and I'd hurt her. Intentionally.

Apparently I had also hurt her physically, but the last thing I wanted to think about was her ass. Still, I couldn't leave it like this, and it was wrong to think she would simply get over what I did.

She was right. I had lied. It was time to man up.

I followed her into the barn. She didn't look up from what she was doing.

"Ellie, I'm sorry."

"Save it," she snapped.

"Put the fork down and please come talk to me." I sat on one of the long benches and patted the spot next to me.

She stopped driving the fork into the hay and glared at me. "Aren't you afraid I might try to ravish you? I hear barn sex is supposed to be smoking hot. All raw and earthy."

I closed my eyes and struggled for patience. "Please."

Finally, she relented. She sat, nearly a foot away, crossed her arms over her chest and didn't look at me.

"Look, I'm sorry about what I said that night. I shouldn't have yelled at you. And I shouldn't have been..."

"Mean," she reminded me.

"Mean. I was taken aback. It took me a few minutes to wrap my head around what you were trying to do, which is something I've been trying *not* to do for months."

I could see the flare of victory in her eyes when she faced me. "You're admitting it then. Physically, you are attracted to me."

I nodded.

"Then what the hell, Jake?" She sounded so exasperated I nearly smiled. If this wasn't so damn serious I might have.

"Ellie, just because I am doesn't mean I want to be."

Victory turned to confusion.

"I don't understand. We live together. We hang out together. We feel like a real couple. Didn't you have fun on graduation night?"

"I did. I had fun."

It was the truth. Being around Ellie was as much fun as I had ever had being with anyone else. Partly because I knew her so well. Because she knew me so well. We had all this shorthand for speaking that it made being around her so easy.

"Then I don't get it. We like each other. We have fun together. We're attracted to each other, but I'm not supposed to want anything else or think about anything else?"

"Look, I know all of this is super confusing. Because everything you said is true. But you have to believe me when I tell you if we add sex to that mix, it's going to be even harder. Because this has to end, Ellie. You and me."

Her face fell a little at that. "Oh."

"Yeah. Oh. We went into this as an arrangement. A temporary one. We didn't *really* get married. Can you say now you want to spend the rest of your life with me? Only me and that's it, even though you've never had sex with another guy, never seriously dated anyone else?"

She was thoughtful for a moment and I thought that was a good sign. She was actually listening to me.

"You didn't want to marry me," she said. "You didn't plan to spend your life with me either."

"No," I said quietly. Truthfully. "I didn't. I wanted to help you. I succeeded. *We* succeeded. Circumstances changed, and I'm trying my best to continue on. But if I take your virginity, if we start sleeping together... then it's like we'll have this weird marriage in which neither one of us had a choice. Then if one or the other wants to walk away..."

"Ugh! Why do you have to make sex seem so complicated? You banged some chick in Missoula and it wasn't a big deal."

Shari? Sherry? Something like that.

"I don't even remember her name. Yes, sex can be simple and uncomplicated. It wouldn't be that way between us, because we care about each other. I think you know that. The other night was... intense."

Her eyes narrowed.

"You think I'm being really immature about this."

"I hate to remind you, but you are in fact a virgin. I'm not saying you're a kid, but your sexual experience is nonexistent. You have to take my word about this."

"And you're really okay with me losing my virginity to someone else?"

No. No, I wasn't. "I'm a guy, Ellie. Cut me some slack with that question."

"Fine."

"We good?"

"We're... okay."

"I'll take that." I stood up, then chucked her a little on the shoulder. See, I thought, a couple of buddies. "It's just a few more years. We've got this."

I left the barn and made my way back to Wyatt and tried not to think about how long three years actually was.

"I've got this," I told myself.

Too bad I didn't believe me even a little bit.

FIVE

Ellie
July

I WAS ROLLING my cart down the supermarket aisle when Bobby MacPherson turned the corner coming toward me. Normally I would have kept moving forward, head straight, not saying a word, but I figured we were cool now so I had to at least be friendly.

"Hey Bobby."

He smiled and came over to me, a small cart hanging from his arm. "Hey Ellie, what's up?"

"Nothing much."

Nothing at all really. Since graduation it had been all work and no fun. Jake and I were managing, but it was there. Between us now. This weird thing. A mutual attraction we were not going to act on for good reasons.

We were both trying to pretend it wasn't there. That wasn't working either.

"What about you?" I asked him.

"Helping my mom out. I don't know if you heard. They are officially getting divorced."

"Oh. I'm sorry. That sucks."

"For her it does. That's why I'm trying to help out. Make things easier for her." He lifted the basket of food.

"That's nice of you." Bobby MacPherson and nice. Two words I would not normally put together. "Are you still heading to school next month?"

I knew Bobby was planning to go to University of Montana. It was where most of the kids in my class who were going to college were going.

For the first time, I found myself a little jealous. The idea of getting away from home. Being some place new and different. Right now it was very appealing.

"I'm not sure. Might have to put things off a semester. We'll see."

"Oh, that sucks." I wasn't sure what else to say. "Well, good luck. With everything."

He gave a chin nod and I started to roll forward.

"Hey can I ask you something?"

I stopped. "Sure."

"What is the deal with you and Jake?"

It was weird, but I got this horrible feeling in my stomach even thinking about what we were. "No deal. Same as always. We couldn't get divorced because of the storm..."

"No, sure. It's a money thing. But at Pete's on graduation night... I don't know, I thought maybe things were different between you two."

They were. They were totally different. Not in a good way either.

"Nope. Nothing different." Then I said it. The dreaded line everybody who has ever been in this situation fucking simple but sexy dress. All her hair falling down around her back.

Helpless to stop myself, I wrapped my hand around my now-hard cock. Stroking myself hard while I thought about her.

I told myself I could replace with her with some actress. Scarlett Johansson. Charlize Theron. Blondes. I liked blondes and Ellie had honey brown hair.

Ellie's hair. All down her back, her ass in my hand, her tongue in my mouth. It had been so fucking hot. Just a kiss, too.

I pumped myself faster. I needed this done. I need to come so I could stop thinking about her. Stop thinking about her like this. My balls got tight and I started snapping my hips as if I was actually fucking her. Then the punch came, the one that felt like it started in my lower back and ran down through my balls as my come shot out of me. So damn good.

This time I put both hands on the tile and rested my head again while I caught my breath. While I let myself feel my body. How good and sated it was. The guilt would come eventually. That I had done that, thinking about her. Wondering how it would feel if it was her hand.

Her mouth.

Her pussy.

Oh God.

I turned off the water, dried myself off, got dressed, and made my way downstairs where *my wife* was making us dinner. Some taco pie casserole recipe she found on Facebook she knew I would like.

Because she always knew what I liked. It was that simple with her.

"Hey," I said.

She turned away from the pan she had on the stove and smiled.

"Hey, this is going to be so freaking good. You are going to cry."

I thought about her smile. It was pretty. It would always be pretty. But it wasn't the same. Not since I shut her down. Not since I drew a line between us and told her to stay on her side.

"Smells good," I told her.

Then I let myself think it. Just for a second I let myself think, what if this really could be our life? What if we stayed married? What if we made it real? I could buy my land and we could add it to Long Valley Ranch.

Have kids, raise them together. Two best friends. Two lovers.

I waited for how it felt in my chest. I expected I would have a sense of claustrophobia. That I was putting myself in a situation I would never be able to get out of. That even if at some point I realized I was never going to love her like a husband should, I would never let myself leave because of how guilty I would feel doing that.

Hurting Ellie hurt me. I'd felt like crap after the kiss, because I knew even though she had eventually understood why I'd shut her down, I'd still hurt her. If we became lovers, if we tried to turn this into something real and it didn't work, I would go to my grave never letting her know how I felt.

That wasn't even considering her feelings. I showed up on a damn white horse and saved her from a foster home. Was it all those feelings of gratitude that had morphed into her thinking she wanted me like that? Hell, was it plain teenage horniness? She was a young woman. Living with me. Was it circumstances that made her believe she wanted me?

If I crossed the line, if I took her to bed, would she ever really know the difference between loving me or forever being grateful to me?

I didn't consider myself much of a romantic, but I had to think it would suck if I knew deep in my gut that Ellie never truly loved me. That she couldn't know if she loved me because she never had a chance to see what anything else was like.

I could see it there. Right in the middle of the damn kitchen floor. The line I had drawn between us. I could step over it, turn off the gas, take her hand and lead her upstairs. To my room. To my bed.

She wouldn't say no. In fact she'd be happy. Excited.

I could do that and potentially trap each of us into something that was no less than a life sentence.

"I need to head out to the barn for a second. Is that okay?"

"Sure. This thing needs to bake for another fifteen minutes. You've got time. Jake, everything okay? You've got an odd look on your face."

I looked at her. I thought of how hard I'd come just thinking about kissing her.

I thought the line was so damn thin.

"Fine. I just need to leave."

It probably sounded stupid and made no sense to her, but I knew if I didn't walk out the back door....

If I didn't head to the barn and take a few seconds to get myself under control...

I might cave.

I couldn't do it. I had to be strong enough for both us. I walked outside, made my way to the barn, got to the center of it and I sunk down on my haunches. I counted it out. From a hundred down to one.

That's how I would get through this, I realized. This wasn't about me and what might happen to me if I crossed the line. This was about her. I had to protect Ellie. From myself. From herself. I had to be strong enough for her.

That, I thought I could do. That, I knew I could do.

SIX

Ellie
September (Or as I came to know it... The month Carol came to town and ruined everything.)

YOU KNOW how stuff can just happen to you one day? You're going along with your life, and everything is fine if not great, but you're still moving. One foot in front of the other.

My scales were constantly set to five and five. Nothing was either good or bad, they just were.

Jake and I were mostly doing okay. There was tension yes, but there wasn't anger. At least not on my part. I don't think on his part either.

Then one day I was pulling the truck into the portico next to the house and I noticed a strange car in the driveway. I made my way into the house, but it was empty. Out to the barn, but it too was empty. That was strange. Not that it was empty. Jake could be off anywhere doing anything, but if someone had come for a visit where would they go?

I wandered out from the barn down to the pen, and that's when I saw them. Jake and a woman were standing on the fence, and Jake was pointing out various different calves.

She was young, thin, and blonde. Super blonde. His preferred type. And she appeared to be laughing at everything Jake said.

Jake was not that funny.

I put away the feeling in my chest and did the grown-up thing. I headed out to meet them. When they saw me they both hopped down off the fence. She was wearing dark skintight jeans that wouldn't last a day working a ranch, these adorable cowboy boots, and some cool light coat I would have no idea where to even think about buying.

I hated her immediately.

"Hey, Ellie, we were just talking about you."

Were they?

"Ellie, this is Carol. She's a travel vet staying with her family in town for a while. Carol, this is Ellie."

"His wife." Okay. I know I said that too loudly. Then I tried to cover it up with a stupid joke. "Yep, the old ball and chain."

"Hi Ellie." Carol stretched out her hand, and so I had to take it. Shake it. Let it go. "I didn't think you guys were *really* married."

"We're not," I said quickly. Too quickly. "That's just my little joke."

"Yeah, it's hysterical," Jake said.

"I heard..." Carol said, "that Jake married you after your dad died to save you from having to go to a foster home."

Yep. That was the story. Good old Jake.

"Which is very cool you would do that," she told Jake. A soft smile playing around her lips.

Wow. This was happening. Actual flirting was happening in front of me.

"So what brings you out to Long Valley?" I asked.

Did you hear in town there was a married but not really married hot guy out here and decide to give it a shot?

I, of course, did not ask her that question.

"Oh, I was at the Simmons ranch down in Colorado and heard about what Jake was doing with his different breeding techniques. I knew I was going to be in town and I couldn't help myself. I'm sort of a geek about that kind of stuff."

I nodded. Don Simmons was rancher in Colorado that Jake emailed frequently as the two men were both enthusiasts when it came to cow breeding.

"Don gave me his information and I emailed Jake to see if it was okay that I stop by to check out his operation."

"I told you about this," Jake said to me.

He told me about this? He told me Carol, the hot vet, was coming to the ranch to flirt with my husband?

I tried to think back. Then I remembered. A vet from Colorado was coming. He would have known she was a woman. He couldn't have known how pretty she was.

"Well, what do you think?" I asked her.

"It's really amazing. Especially knowing what you guys suffered last spring."

"Yep, Jake has a really high birth rate on his insemination program. He knows how to work the ladies, if you know what I mean."

Wow, another really bad joke.

"Well," Carol coughed. "I don't want to take up any more of your day. Thanks for letting me come check it out, Jake."

"You said you wanted to ride out and see the property," Jake reminded her.

She tilted her head and smiled at him. "Another time?"

"Sure."

I wanted to vomit.

"Really nice meeting you, Ellie."

I hope you fall into a ditch on your way home and die, bitch.

I, of course, did not say that. That was awful of me really. I wasn't that person.

"You too, Carol. Definitely come back and Jake can show you the land and the full operation."

"Great. See you both around."

She left, her butt swinging from left to right as she did. I didn't have it in me to look to see if Jake was watching her go. Instead I said, "I've got a bunch of supplies in the truck I'm going to need help with."

"Yep."

We took care of emptying the truck and went about the rest of our day.

LATER THAT NIGHT I was sitting on the couch thinking about what I wanted to watch for TV when Jake came in and sat in the chair closer to the TV. It had been his turn to clean up from dinner.

"What are we watching?"

"There's this new show on Netflix that's supposed to be awesome."

He nodded his chin as if that was fine by him. I started the show, and as the opening credits came on I couldn't not say what I had been choking down my throat all afternoon.

"So Carol seemed nice."

"Hmm."

See, that was how it started. A hum. A small sound that acknowledged what I said was true without actually agreeing with me.

"Pretty, too. Definitely your type."

"I don't have a type," he grumbled.

"You so have a type, Jake."

"Whatever."

"I'm just saying it's okay to admit you thought she was attractive."

"Ellie, what's this about?"

Right. Another excellent strategy. Make this about me. I'm thick. I'm stupid. I didn't see what I clearly saw.

I stood then and faced him. "Can we not do that thing?"

He sighed. "What thing?"

"The thing where we lie to each other."

"I'm not..." He stopped himself. "She was cute."

Cute. The word felt like this little pinprick. It hurt, but it wasn't so bad.

What I didn't know was that pinprick was going to turn into a gutting. But that would come later.

The key to this moment was understanding guy speak.

If he'd said she was hot, well, hot meant a girl was hot, but you didn't particularly think you had a shot with her. There weren't many girls Jake didn't have a shot with, but still.

Hot could also mean she was blatantly sexual. Sometimes with blatant sexuality, men liked to look at it but it didn't necessarily mean they wanted to hit that. For some the blatant sexuality was actually a turnoff to guys who preferred their women a little more demure.

Jake didn't say Carol was hot.

If Jake had said she was attractive…he would have never said that. *Attractive* was too clinical of a word for him. And *beautiful* was too over the top.

(See, this is me not remembering the time he once casually referred to me as beautiful.)

No, Jake said Carol was cute.

Cute to Jake meant he thought she was hot and that he had a shot. That she wasn't just some sex object, but rather someone worth getting to know. To see if his attraction for her was something he wanted to pursue.

Carol *was* cute.

At least he hadn't lied to me.

"I totally agree."

"Can we stop talking about this?"

"You bet." I walked back to the couch and grabbed the remote. I tossed it to him and smiled when it landed on his lap hard when he wasn't expecting it. "I changed my mind. I think I'm going to head up early. I'm really tired."

"I thought you wanted to watch this show on Netflix."

"You go ahead, I'll catch up. Night Jake."

"Night Ellie."

I WAS RUBBING down Petunia in the barn when I heard them. Sure enough, two days later Carol had made good on her promise to return, and Jake offered to take her out for a ride around the property.

They both, of course, asked me to come.

Because I was the cool marriage of convenience wife, I said no.

I had to, right? I had to let him have this. He'd said we couldn't be a thing. He'd said it would hurt too much later when it all ended. Which meant I was free to pursue other relationships, so he was too.

I was doing the upright thing. I was doing the fair thing.

I hated every minute of it. I was jealous as shit and mad at him for making me feel this way. But I couldn't deny him this opportunity.

They were coming back down around the pen, laughing about something. I cut Petunia's grooming short and walked her back to her stall with a silent promise to make up for my halfhearted attempt later this week.

I didn't want to have to deal with them. I didn't want to see the mutual attraction thing going on. I didn't want to hear anything that would be really awful.

As I made my way out of the barn I could see them dismounting. Jake was helping her off Isabella, but it was clear to see Carol knew what she was doing on a horse. No jerking, no sudden movements.

Then I looked at Jake and what I saw there nearly ended me. He was smiling. Really smiling for the first time in... I couldn't remember when. He looked so free and easy, it was only then I saw how much the tension between the two of us impacted him. Like around me he was constantly holding in his breath and sucking in his gut and now, with Carol, he was finally able to breathe.

I had done that to him. I had made him tight and cautious because I had done this stupid thing and kissed him.

I looked away. It hurt too much. I made my way inside and I didn't look back at them again.

WE WERE EATING dinner and it was awful. I had been

sullen and bitchy all night and he wasn't calling me out for it at all. He was simply dealing with my mood like it didn't bother him. Quietly eating the food I made for him without comment.

"So are you going to ask her out? Or should I say have you asked her out already?"

I heard his fork clank against his plate. With a little more force than if he'd placed it down.

I had to know. I couldn't stand around waiting to see something or hear something or suddenly have him announce her to me as his girlfriend. This wasn't like Janet. Janet was a known commodity. They had been dating before our marriage. Before we were anything.

Carol was new. A brand new person he met, who he thought was cute, who he spent two days hanging out with on my ranch.

"Ellie..."

"I want to know. I'm not saying you shouldn't. I'm not saying anything. Although it seems to me she was awfully sure that our marriage wasn't a real one when she came out to the ranch to meet you. It's one thing to hear a rumor in town and just take it for granted that you know the situation on the ground."

"Ellie..."

"Just tell me. Have you asked her out yet?"

"I haven't."

I nodded.

Then it came. The knife slash right up the middle.

"Yet."

"Hookay."

Slowly I got up and took my plate to the sink. Gingerly, as if I really had been cut with a sharp knife. Fuck this hurt. I had never experienced anything quite like it. Then suddenly I was numb and I wasn't feeling anything at all.

I rinsed my plate off but I knew I had to get out of there. Knew I couldn't look at him again. Except it was my turn to do the dishes. Fuck the dishes.

"I'll clean up later. I'm going to go take a shower."

"Ellie..." He was up and out of his chair. I could hear the scrape of it as he bounced up and reached out to grab my arm. "Listen to me."

I tried to pull my arm back. I didn't want him to touch me, but he wouldn't let go. It's like he wasn't done with whatever awful thing he wanted to say to me.

"I heard what you said. We don't have to talk about this. You're free to date whoever you want. I am too, for that matter."

"Just... I know this is weird. I know things haven't been... easy... between us. But I'm thinking this might actually help. If we stay in this kind of rut, then it's only going to get harder... you know what I'm saying? But if we snap this... thing... and I take Carol out, it could be better. It could normalize things. Like how we used to be."

He was rambling, and I didn't get much, but what I did get was that he thought taking Carol out was not only a great idea for him. But for me too. That I should fully support him because it was going to make things easier between us.

That's how he was justifying this.

He used the word *snap*. It was a good word. To snap something was to break something. That was exactly how I felt.

Broken.

In a way it was like when he'd rejected me. That had hurt too, but this went deeper. This wasn't him rejecting me to spare me what he thought would be pain later on down the road. This was him moving on from me. Moving on from us.

No, that wasn't fair either. There had never really been an us. There had just been a me wanting him and him not wanting to want me back.

Now he wanted Carol instead. Somebody should have explained to me how much this could hurt.

I nodded. "Good point. You're right. This probably a really good idea. For us."

His expression was nearly desperate.

"You see that, don't you?"

"Sure, Jake. I'm good. You can let go."

He dropped his hand as if he hadn't realized he had it wrapped around my arm the whole time.

"I'm still going to go take a shower. Long day today. Leave everything by the sink and I'll do the dishes later."

"I can do the dishes..."

"No," I snapped. Because that was him feeling guilty and I wouldn't have it. I wouldn't have his guilt or his pity. "It's my turn to do the dishes and I'll do them. I just want a damn shower first. Is that too much to ask?"

"No," he said.

"Fine. Good." I started to leave the kitchen, but I stopped myself as something occurred to me. "The rules are the same, Jake."

"What do you—"

"The rules," I said. "She doesn't get to stay the night in this house. I don't want to... wake up in the morning and run into her."

His expression tightened. "Jesus, Ellie, as if I would..."

"Just promise me."

The muscle in his jaw flexed. "I promise."

SEVEN

Jake
October

IT WAS FREEING. Being with Carol was like being released from a cage I hadn't known I had locked myself into. This was what it was like to have simple feelings. This was what it was like to act on them.

It had been so damn long I had forgotten.

She had come out to the farm again for another ride. I asked her if she wanted to get lunch in town. She said yes. So easy. Like riding a bike.

We were having lunch at Frank's, not in the booth where I usually sat with Ellie, but another one along a different wall. Kathy may or may not have given me an odd look when she turned the corner and realized I wasn't here with Ellie.

Another positive thing about Carol. She was the statement Ellie had wanted to make to everyone. She was the signal that said to all the citizens of Riverbend that our marriage was still platonic and in name only.

That I had never taken advantage of Ellie and that I still wasn't.

Carol was two years older than me, a professional working vet, and exactly the type of woman I had always imagined I would be with.

Okay, so maybe I did have a type.

Anyway, we fit better than Ellie and I did in many different ways, and it was easy for anyone looking at us to see that.

This way all the gossip about me and Ellie could be shut down once and for all. Yep. This was a win-win for everyone all the way around.

"Uh hello, Jake?"

I focused my attention on Carol. "I'm sorry, I drifted there. What did you ask?"

"How long have you been doing the insemination program?"

"The last four years. I had to convince Sam first. Ellie's father. He was pretty old school about things. Thought that cows bred from insemination couldn't possibly taste as good as cows that came from Mother Nature."

She laughed, maybe a little too much, and put her hand on mine. "That is so funny."

Was it? It didn't matter. She could touch me all she wanted. No harm, no foul. No guilt.

No. Fucking. Guilt.

It was heavenly.

"Anyway, we've been expanding the program each year. This year in particular because we took such a loss with the storm, wanted to get the most bang for the buck in bull sperm."

"How bad was it? The storm?"

I had a flash of stumbling upon Ellie in the snow. Not awake. Nearly frozen to death. I forced it out of my head.

"Bad. It was bad."

She made a noise that I guess was supposed to be sympathy. Like she understood when she couldn't possibly. But it wasn't like I was going to touch on my relationship with Ellie with the woman I was currently on a date with.

"What about you? How long are you in town for?"

She shrugged. "I'm helping my aunt out for a while. But probably not too long. Eventually I have get back to work."

"Where do you call home?"

She smiled and did her head tilt thing. I knew she traveled with her job a lot. She was essentially a contracted vet who could work anywhere in the country. Small rural communities mostly, where large animal vets were needed desperately.

"I have an apartment in Denver, but I'm rarely there. I should give it up, while I'm with this job, but it's the thought of moving everything into storage until I finally settle on a place that bothers me. I like my stuff. Even though I only get to see it occasionally, I like knowing it's there."

"I hear you."

Carol talking about her stuff made me think of the scales. The scales I had given Ellie for her birthday that had sat on the kitchen counter ever since. Five and five. For months now.

After I had given them to her, when she'd recorded her first ten day, she used to change them every day.

Right was the good side, she'd explained. Left was the bad side.

She had nines and eights. She had twos and threes. She

once told me day one of her period was a guaranteed four and the day could only get worse from there.

Information I hadn't wanted at the time, but I made a mental note when the right side was below five to be a little more sympathetic.

Then after the kiss, it stopped. Five. Always five.

"This is fun, being out with you," Carol said with a shy smile.

She had no idea. This was sheer and utter bliss. I wasn't thinking about anything beyond her pretty hair, her pretty face, her pretty lips.

"Soooo... can I ask about your marriage?"

I tightened a little bit. "What do you want to know?"

"You're really married, but not *married*?"

"Platonic. Platonic I think is the word you're looking for. And yes. Ellie and I are... friends."

I paused. Why did I pause?

"That's got to be tough. For you I mean. For her too, when you think about it. And it's really okay that we're out like this? I don't want to cause any kind of trouble for you."

"No trouble at all."

She smiled then. "Okay. Then this is the part where I say I like you, Jake Talley. You intrigue me."

"Can I take you out for dinner then?"

Her smile flashed even brighter. "That would be a definite yes. I have to confess it's been a really long time since I've done anything like this. I broke up with my boyfriend over a year ago. Let's just say that trying to meet new people when I'm only in a place for a few weeks at a time is a... challenge. You know what I mean?"

It took me a second to process what she said. She broke up with her boyfriend a year ago. She hadn't been on a date since.

Which probably meant she was as hard up as I was.

"I'm sorry," she chuckled and then reached for my hand again. I liked that she kept touching me. "Oh my gosh, did that seem forward of me? I didn't mean to be so...blunt."

"No, that's fine. I get where you're going."

See? This was even better. Carol was NOT a virgin. She was like an anti-virgin. A sexy mature woman who I think was telling me I could tap that if I wanted to.

A man, who had been trapped like I had been in the stickiest situation imaginable for months, couldn't have dreamed a better solution to the problem than Carol.

"You're honest," I said. "I like that. I'm looking forward to getting to know you. Taking our time."

I turned my hand and our fingers linked together. I didn't think about how odd it looked. I was making sure I was on full charm.

She smiled. "Time, huh? Let me guess, you're a guy who wants to be wooed."

I smiled at the word. "I do like to be wooed. Possibly even seduced."

"Seduced? Oh, now I get it. You don't put out for just anyone."

"Only when I like someone."

It was the truth. Carol wasn't going stay in town permanently, but she was going to be here for a while. So this wasn't like my one-and-done weekend to Missoula. This could be a nice little affair for a couple of weeks. If that was going to be the case, we didn't have to rush anything.

"Okay. Fair enough. I like that you want to take things slow. It's very old fashioned of you."

"Not too slow," I said. "I don't want you to think I'm a tease."

"Thank God!"

We finished our lunch and I gave her a small peck on the cheek. Again, no need to rush anything. I told her I would need to check and see what the best night was for dinner. She was heading back to her aunt's. It occurred to me I hadn't thought to ask who that was. A town this small and I probably knew the woman.

I needed to head over to the post office before heading back to the ranch, so I left the truck at Frank's and walked on foot.

I opened the door and grimaced when I saw Bobby. I wasn't even really sure why. He'd done the solid thing and had apologized to Ellie. I even knew about the issues with his parents. Still, it had been the language he'd used when I had talked to him last year. The way Bobby had talked about me screwing Ellie.

I felt it. In my bones. That's who Bobby was. The civil Bobby, the one who apologized and offered to buy beers—that Bobby had an agenda.

"Bobby," I said nodding.

"Jake."

That was it. It was clear Bobby was putting something together to be shipped. He was taping up a box pretty soundly. Maybe sending some of his dad's things to Jefferson. Rumor was Mrs. MacPherson wouldn't let Mr. MacPherson back in the house.

I moved around him to the counter. It was a small post office, like anything else in Riverbend, and only had what a person needed.

"Hank," I said. "There should be a package for me."

I had ordered a new type of insemination device. Basically I had been using what amounted to a turkey baster, but this new thing was something Don had recommended that I wanted to try. Anything remotely exotic when it came to ranch equipment had to be ordered online. It had been a few days and I had to think it would be here by now.

Sure enough, Hank was walking back with a box that looked to be the right size. I didn't even think about it. I took the box and assumed it was what I had ordered. There was a pair of scissors on the table where Bobby was finishing up. I took them and cut the tape and split the box down the middle. I was anxious to see what it looked like.

I opened the flaps of the box and maybe the pink should have given something away. Something that would have made me stop.

But I was so certain of what it should have been that when I pulled the pink box out of the larger box, I froze.

I heard Bobby snorting, then full-on laughing.

I shoved back what had clearly been a female sexual device, and covered it with the packing paper.

"Guess that's proof enough you're not fucking her."

My face was without doubt as red as it had ever been, but as I looked over at Bobby, who was still snickering, suddenly the embarrassment was gone, replaced by anger.

"Shut your fucking mouth."

"Poor Ellie is so desperate she needs toys now. Why don't you just put her out of her misery? Oh wait. I forgot. Didn't I just see you out on a date with someone else?"

I moved toward him and he had the good sense to take a step back. "I was right," I said. "All that shit about growing up was a cover for what you really want and can't have. Someday you will figure it out, Bobby. You are nowhere near good enough for Ellie. Deal with it."

I took the box and shoved it under my arm. I stormed to my truck and tossed the box onto the other seat, realizing the whole time I was going to have to go home and tell Ellie I opened her freaking dildo in front of Bobby MacPherson.

I had a suspicion that was not going to go well.

Ellie

"YOU WHAT!" I screamed at him even as I took the box he was holding out.

"It was an accident. I didn't intend to... I thought it was this new inseminator I ordered."

I looked down at the open box. "It has my name right there. RIGHT THERE!"

At least he had the decency to look ashamed.

"I'm sorry. I didn't even think to look. And there is something else..."

I closed my eyes. "Oh god, tell me you weren't with Carol."

"I wasn't with Carol. I picked it up after our lunch."

I glared at him. The way he said it so casually.

Our lunch.

Their date. Like those words weren't soul destroying. Except of course he didn't really know what they were doing to me, because I was putting on a brave face. That was me. Ellie the Brave. All crying was saved for late at night under the covers and in the shower.

At this point I didn't even care what he said. He was officially dating Carol, and nothing really mattered. I didn't even want the damn toy anymore. It's not like I could imagine kissing Jake to work up any arousal. Not when I knew he was kissing someone else.

Had he kissed her? Like he'd kissed me. Had it felt the same way? Was it always like that for him? He said it had been intense between us. Was it intense with Carol?

Oh god, I couldn't stand this feeling. I had to find some way to stop thinking about him.

"What?" I asked snapping at him. "What is worse than you opening my dildo in public?"

He couldn't even look at me when he said it. "Bobby MacPherson was there."

"Shoot me now."

"Look. It's embarrassing. It was embarrassing for me too. But he said some shit... I'm telling you, I'm right about this guy. I want you to be careful around him."

"Because he has a thing for me."

"Yes."

"So stay away from the guy who actually wants to hook up with me. That's not the greatest strategy in the world for losing my virginity."

He winced, and that felt good. Hurting him a little felt really good. Which was awful I knew, but he had no idea what he was doing to me.

"Don't get squeamish, Jake. That is my end game. It's why I bought the damn thing in the first place. I'm having a hard time with... well... it doesn't matter. I'm saying a girl should practice when she's getting ready for the main event."

His head snapped up. "Are you dating someone?"

"Why would you care?"

"Ellie, if you're dating someone... if you're thinking of having sex with someone..."

"Condoms. I know."

He winced again.

"I meant to say that if you're seeing someone, I should know who he is."

"Oh right." I laughed, but it sounded harsh. "So you can give him the classic Jake stare-down. Like you did with

Riley last year. Like you did with Bobby on graduation night. Trust me when I tell you, you will never know the name of the first guy I fuck. I've learned my lesson."

That was a direct missile to his gut. I actually saw it land. This time he didn't wince. It was like his whole body shuttered.

"I thought we were friends," he said, as if he was asking himself and not me.

I swallowed. We were friends. But I was in too much pain because of him, and it was really hard to be in pain and not want to inflict some back. Two people inflicting pain on each other could not be friends.

"I get it, Jake. You want to be with Carol and you want me to be with some guy, who you approve of course, so that we can go back to the way things are. That is a fantasy *you* have. It's not reality. We can never go back. Only forward. Whatever we're going to be, we're only going to know what that is going forward."

He closed his eyes. "I'm trying so hard to do the right thing."

I walked by him and patted him on the shoulder. "I know you are. I know. You're a good guy, Jake. Don't think I've forgotten that."

I left him and took my sex toy upstairs, shoving it under the bed, so I wouldn't have to think about it.

Forward. That's what I had told him. I couldn't see what that looked like, but I didn't think if we kept doing this to each other, hurting each other, that it would be very friendly at all.

EIGHT

Jake
October

I WAS HURTING ELLIE. That wasn't supposed to happen. Me seeing Carol was supposed to help things. But it wasn't until after the package fight I realized it. She was angry and she wanted to hurt me. The only reason Ellie would do that is if I was hurting her.

She didn't like me seeing Carol. Hell, I hadn't even done anything with Carol yet. I wasn't lying when I told Carol I wanted to go slow. We'd had lunch. That was it. I was taking her out to dinner tonight. Nothing else.

But in the two weeks since that fight over the dildo, things had changed. It had been subtle at first. Ellie stopped watching TV with me at night. Said TV was a waste of time and she wanted to spend more time reading. Which was horseshit, because Ellie loved TV. Except now she didn't.

And because the TV distracted her, she did her reading in her room.

I didn't think too much about it at first. In fact it was probably a good thing we didn't hang out as much as we used to.

Then she stopped eating with me. Breakfast and lunch we were on our own. However, we always ate dinner together. Then she started finding excuses to cook in the middle of the day, leaving a plate for me in the fridge with a note.

Or if I was cooking, she usually picked those nights to head into town to see her friends.

Except I had no idea who she was seeing because Karen, Chrissy and Lisa, who I knew were her best friends, were all at different colleges around the state. Which led me back to this guy she might or might not be dating who she was planning to fuck (her words.) Not that I could ask about that.

Still, I made sure to cook for both of us and leave her a plate. Sure enough the next morning she would have eaten it, cleaned the plate and put it away.

During the day, forget about it. All her tasks were getting done but I never saw her. If I was moving cattle she was back at the house. If she was moving cattle I was fixing fence line.

I could have forced the issue. I could have said we needed two people to push the cows to different grazing areas.

I didn't because it was obvious she didn't want to see me.

That had to change. I was doing this thing with Carol to help us, not to hurt her. And I had absolutely no plans on getting the silent treatment from her for the next three years.

Which was why I was waiting in the kitchen this morning for her to come down. I had shit I needed to do, but I was done playing this game.

I was on my second cup of coffee when I heard her coming downstairs. When she came into the kitchen and saw me, I knew she was startled.

"You're usually gone by now."

Yep. No *good morning Jake*. No smile. God how long had it been since I had seen her smile?

"I wanted to talk."

"About what?"

"I'm not going to be home for dinner tonight. I'm taking Carol out."

I watched her face, but it was carefully blank. Too blank. She was hiding something.

"You waited around the house to tell me you had a date with your girlfriend? Seriously?"

I balked at the word. "She's hardly my girlfriend. We've hung out a few times and had lunch."

"I don't need a recap."

"Look, this thing with Carol... this is not going anywhere. She's only in town for a couple of weeks at best."

"So?"

"Well, if you're worried that this is going to turn into something, that we will be back in the same position we were with Janet, I want to make it clear that's not the case. You're pissed at me. You've made yourself as loud and clear as possible by being absolutely silent. What I'm trying to find out is why?"

"First, you don't know where this is going with Carol. People start dating and plans can change."

"Trust me. I know what she does for her job. She's not settling down anytime soon. This is just…"

"Sex?"

"I don't want to go there. I'm only saying if you're worried about things changing around here because of her, you don't have to be."

"Got it. Are we done now?"

This wasn't working. "Can't you talk to me about this?"

She sighed then, and it sounded sad and it broke my heart. Then she shook her head. She had her hair pulled back in a ponytail, like she usually did when she worked outside, and I could hear it swish against the coat she was wearing.

"Trust me, Jake. There is nothing to talk about. There is nothing that will fix this. It is what it is. I'm dealing the best way I can. What more do you want from me?"

That was when it hit me.

I wanted my Ellie back. I wanted my friend back. I wanted my partner on the ranch. My buddy who I watched TV with, my family who I ate dinner with. I wanted the girl who smiled so wide it made you feel good when you saw it.

I wanted the scales to change.

"I miss you," I said.

It was honest. It was how I felt. That was supposed to be a good thing. I was a man. Men didn't normally share their feelings so openly like that. I figured by putting myself out there, by showing her how important our relationship was to me, she might understand.

The look of horror on her face suggested something else.

"Fuck. You. Have on fun on your date with Carol tonight. Asshole."

She turned and headed out the back door before I could get another word out.

That hadn't gone like I hoped.

"DO YOU LIKE MY DRESS? I wore it especially for you."

I looked at Carol's dress. It was a nice dress. Black and sexy.

"Very nice," I said with a smile. At least I think I was smiling. I know what I wasn't doing. I wasn't focusing on Carol very much, and that wasn't fair. I was still reeling from the full-blown loathing I had gotten from Ellie that morning and trying to understand it.

Sure, I *understood* it. I wasn't stupid. She thought... she had feelings for me. Feelings that I shot down. FOR HER OWN DAMN GOOD. Now I was trying to show her we both had to move on if we were going to get back to any kind of equilibrium, and it was hurting her.

Okay. It sucked. I remember being a sophomore in high school and crushing hard on Alice Samberg. I had done everything I could to show her I liked her and then I'd found out she had started dating Joey Eastman, who was a junior. It had totally blown.

I was not oblivious to the feeling of rejection. But Ellie had to understand something too. She hadn't been rejected. I did care for her. I did want her. I simply could not have her. To protect her. To protect her future. My future, too.

She needed to get over this Carol... "Bullshit."

"I'm sorry?" Carol asked.

"Huh?"

"You said bullshit. Are you saying you don't like my dress?" Carol was smiling as if she knew that couldn't possibly be true. What man wouldn't be into a woman looking she did in that dress?

So different from what Ellie had worn when we'd been here back in June. (That's right. I took Carol to the same restaurant I took Ellie. It's fucking Montana. My choices are limited. Get over it.)

"Of course not," I said. "You look amazing."

"I hope I'm the reason you don't seem to have an appetite tonight."

I looked down at my steak. Barely half-eaten. It was something to do, so I picked up my knife and fork and cut into it.

"Tell me more about your life, Jake. I know everything there is to know about your approach to cow insemination, but I'm assuming there has to be more to you than that."

"I hope so," I laughed.

"Well?"

"Well, what do you want to know?"

I shifted slightly in my chair. I didn't want to talk about Ellie with Carol, and really Ellie and the ranch had been my life for the past year and a half.

"Have you ever been serious with someone?"

"Sure. I had a girlfriend, but we ended it."

"Before you were married?"

"No. While I was married. Remember, it's only an arrangement."

Carol reached for her wine. She preferred red. She could order a glass here because she was obviously over twenty-one. Where Ellie could only drink at Pete's.

I wondered if that's where she went when she left at night. I should remind her about drinking and driving again. Really reinforce how important that was. Although Ellie wasn't an idiot. She had to be more responsible than any girl her age for a lot of things.

"How did your girlfriend feel about you getting married to someone else while you were with her?"

I looked up at Carol instead of down at my plate. "She wasn't crazy about it. But that's because she was hoping we would get engaged. She understood eventually. I did what I had to do."

"But it didn't work out in the end."

"No."

You're falling for her.

The accusation was pretty loud in my head, but I dismissed it. Carol had no right to any of that.

"What about you?" I asked in return. "What happened with your boyfriend?" *Please tell me anything so I didn't have to talk about myself.*

"We wanted different things. He wanted to settle down and start making babies, and while I want that some day, I wasn't ready at the time. He said he didn't want to wait and I can't really blame him."

"I'm sorry."

"Thanks. I was sad. For a long time. Now I'm... ready to move on. You know?"

Yeah I knew. I could fuck her. If I wanted to, I could take her back to... well, I didn't know where she was staying, as I picked her up in town because she had to do something at the bank before we could leave.

But I was pretty sure I could take her back to her place and do that.

"Do you want dessert?" I asked instead.

She smiled. "Oh yes, Jake. I definitely want dessert."

I PULLED my car over to the side of the street. The town was dark, empty. The only place that would still be open would be Pete's, and even that shut down at midnight during the middle of the week.

Since Carol had her car, I took her back to the bank where she had left it in parking lot.

"This was fun, Jake," she said.

"I'm glad."

"Do I get a kiss goodnight?" she asked, leaning towards me with a quiet sexy whisper.

"Absolutely," I said, turning my head to her. I tried to get into it. She was hot, she was pressed up against me in this sexy-as-hell dress, her tongue was in my mouth and I was stroking it with mine, and it was fine. Then I pulled back and she pulled away too.

"You make me a little crazy, Jake. Which is actually kind of hot."

"I like that we're building to something here." I had no idea what that meant, but it was something to say.

"When can I see you again?"

"When do you want to?"

"I would love another ride on Isabella..."

"Come out to the ranch tomorrow early. I'm talking sunrise early, and I'll make time for another ride."

"Perfect. Night, Jake."

"Goodnight, Carol."

She got out of the truck and I made sure she made it to her car safely. That it successfully started and I watched as she drove away. There were no thoughts in my head. I knew because I was making sure not to think about anything but the road in front of me.

I made it back to Long Valley and pulled up in front of the house. I was pleased to see Ellie's car already under the portico. I got to the front door and pulled my keys out only to find the door wasn't locked.

Damn it! How many times did I have to tell her she needed lock the door when she was home alone? I let myself inside and glanced at the clock. It was not yet midnight and I had absolutely no problem waking her up to have this fight.

This wasn't like her annoying habit of leaving her shoes and boots by the door, this was dangerous and I wasn't having it.

I took the steps two at a time and got to her door. I stopped when I heard a sound on the other side.

A whimper. Then a gasp.

Holy shit. They were sex sounds. It was happening. She was having sex with someone else right now while I was standing outside her door. I reached for the door handle with this instinct I had to stop it. I had to protect her. Except I could see the door was slightly ajar.

Sometimes her door didn't close right unless she locked it.

I was helpless against it. I had to know. I looked in (it was not peeking). Just looked through the fissure and I could see her on the bed.

She was alone.

Thank God! The relief was so stunning I almost fell to my knees. I was literally breathing hard and it was because I had been holding my breath. Alone. Not with another guy. She was having a dream or something?

I took another look.

No. She was awake. Her back was arched, her head angled back. She had her hands between her legs and she was...

Oh shit.

I immediately backed away from the door. Good bet I was a sick fuck for looking in the first place, but I wasn't going to compound my mistake. I stood there against the wall and I heard her groan.

Only it wasn't a satisfied sound. More like she was annoyed about something. I heard this loud thump as if she'd thrown something across the room. Then the house was silent.

As quietly as I could, I made my way down the hall and back to my room.

I got undressed, brushed my teeth, and got into bed. I took a couple of tissues with me.

When I wrapped my hand around my hard dick, I told myself the whole time I was thinking about Carol in her sexy black dress. About what I was going to do to her the next time I saw her.

Yeah, when I spit on my hand, then worked the head of my cock hard, it was all about Carol.

Not Ellie. Not that picture of her hands between her legs. Not those noises she made.

Not that fucking gasp.

"Oh fuck," I moaned as I shot my load. I cleaned myself up, turned over in bed, and did not let myself feel a damn thing.

NINE

Jake

IT MIGHT HAVE BEEN because of last night. Because of what I saw, because of what I did. I only knew when I woke up I was pissed. At everyone. Myself, Ellie, even Carol even though she had done nothing to deserve it.

Then I smelled it. Bacon. I turned to my clock and saw that it was early. A few minutes after six a.m. Ellie was never up this early. But she'd gotten up and decided to make bacon?

Last thing she said to me to was *fuck you, asshole.*

Now she was downstairs making bacon.

I took this as a good sign. I hopped out of bed and pulled on a pair of jeans and a t-shirt. I barely brushed my teeth because I wanted to know what this was about. Was this an apology for cursing at me? Was this some grand gesture to ask for my forgiveness for yelling at me so rudely?

Because I didn't deserve it. The cursing. She didn't

understand the sacrifices I was making for her. She didn't know what this was costing me. I got that, but it still didn't give her the right to be a bitch to me.

I skipped down the stairs with a sense of anticipation and when I turned the corner I came up short.

"Hey. Morning," Carol said with a smile. "You said come early for my ride, so I thought I would surprise you with breakfast. The door was unlocked, so I took that as a sign. Hope you like bacon and eggs."

Because I had forgotten to lock it last night. Because I had been so angry with Ellie. Then I saw Ellie...

Carol looked adorable. Leggings with a long shirt draped over it, her hair down loose around her shoulders. She wasn't wearing her riding boots. Probably left them by the door.

Shit. I had completely forgotten about our date.

I stood there like an idiot watching her flip the eggs, put them on a plate and add the bacon to it.

She set the plates down and turned to me. Her head tilted as if she was trying to understand my expression.

"I think you need something a little stronger to wake you up," she said, coming towards me.

I didn't move and then she leaned in and kissed me. I was standing there in the kitchen with the smell of bacon and her perfume and suddenly I was furious. Furious that she thought it was okay to kiss me. Furious that I was kissing her back because it felt good. Because I couldn't have Ellie but I could have Carol.

Because Ellie thought I was an asshole.

I wasn't an asshole.

She peeled away from me and lifted my t-shirt over my head. I held my arms up and let her. Then I wrapped my arms around her waist. I hauled her up against me, turned her and sat her on the counter, pressing between her legs.

Her hand must have come down to balance herself, and she knocked off the scales, sending them and the disks crashing to the floor.

It was the sound of the disks crashing that broke me out of whatever the hell I was doing.

I pulled away from her and thought about the sound the damn scales had made and looked to the kitchen doorway.

It was too late. Ellie was standing there in the doorway, wearing her kitten pajama bottoms and tank top and a stunned expression on her face.

"I smelled bacon," she whispered.

I looked around to see what she saw. The two plates on the island. Breakfast. Me, in a pair of jeans only. Carol on the kitchen counter with a swollen mouth.

"Ellie..." I began.

But it was too late.

Her eyes welled up and I watched as the tears just came rolling down her cheeks even as she scrunched up her face in what could be called nothing less than fury.

"You promised!"

"Ellie..."

"You FUCKING PROMISED!"

"I... this isn't..."

She ran out of the room and I was about to follow her when I realized I still had to deal with Carol. I ran my hand through my hair and looked back at Carol, not really sure what to say.

She was slowly getting off the counter, about to the reach for the scales she'd knocked off.

"No, don't touch those. I'll get them."

"I'm sorry," she said. "I thought...you said it was okay that we were doing this."

"It is. It is okay. We had this rule and she thinks... it doesn't matter."

"I think I better go," she said.

"Yeah, that would be for the best."

I watched her grab her bag and head out. Heard her stop for her boots and then heard the door close behind her. Once she left I turned and made my way up the stairs.

I knocked on Ellie's door. "Can I come in and explain?"

"Go away."

"It wasn't what it looked like. She came over early for a ride and decided to surprise me with breakfast."

"Go the fuck away."

"She didn't stay the night. I didn't break any promise. It was just a kiss."

Which might have gotten out of control. If Carol hadn't knocked over the scales. If the sound of them crashing hadn't gotten through to me. Would Ellie have come downstairs to see me screwing Carol on the kitchen counter?

I grabbed my head with both hands and again the fury raged through me. This was not my fault. I was not this guy.

And then it came out. All my anger and rage. All of it spewing up and out. I banged on the door hard.

"You know what Ellie, FUCK YOU! I did this thing FOR YOU! I married you! I kept you out of the foster system. *I* did that! I kept your ranch running. I kept your legacy alive for you. I put my life on hold FOR YOU! And now I'm trapped in this fucking *marriage* that I can't get out of. I can't touch you. I can't fuck anyone else. And I'm the bad guy. Always guilty. Always doing something wrong no matter what I do. No matter why I'm doing it. And I fucking hate you for that! Can you hear me behind your locked door, Ellie? I hate you for that!"

Ellie

"AND I FUCKING hate you for that! Can you hear me behind your locked door, Ellie? I hate you for that!"

I couldn't even cry. The breaths were coming so fast.

Jake hated me. Jake hated me. Jake hated me.

Then I couldn't breathe at all. It was like the day of our wedding. I couldn't handle what I was feeling inside. I knew it. I was going to faint.

What if I died? What if I died because I couldn't breathe anymore?

I heard him stomp off. A few seconds later I heard a door slam. He was out of the house. It helped. It helped when he wasn't shouting at me any anymore. I started to sob, these horrible gut-wrenching deep sobs. A sound I had never heard myself make before.

Eventually I fell back down on to my bed. Eventually I cried myself out. Eventually I fell asleep.

When I woke up my throat was raw, my mouth was dry, and my eyes were nearly swollen shut.

But I knew what I had to do.

The first thing was pack.

Jake

I WAITED until as late as I could before going back to the house. I walked up the stairs of the porch and inside. It was quiet. Dark. I made my way to the kitchen. The scales were still on the floor, the disks scattered about.

I picked them up, glad to see the scales weren't broken. I very decidedly put ten of the disks on the left scale.

Because on a scale of one to ten regarding how shitty of a day this was, it was definitely a ten.

I didn't know what I was going to say to her. How to begin to apologize. For all of it. What I did, what I said.

But I was a man. At least I hoped so. Although I couldn't imagine Sam or Ernie being too proud of me in this moment. Men owned up to their shit. With a sick feeling in my gut, I made my way upstairs. It was late. She was probably in bed. It occurred to me that the front door wasn't locked again, but I was not going to bring that up.

"Ellie," I said as I knocked on her door. "I know it's late, but we have to talk."

Nothing.

I knocked louder. "Okay, how about you need to let me grovel at your feet. I'm sorry. So damn sorry."

Still nothing. I reached for the handle, expecting it to be locked, but it wasn't, although this time the door was closed. I opened it expecting to see her sleeping, except she wasn't there at all. It hadn't even occurred to me when I pulled up that her car wasn't under the portico. I was too focused on finding the words I was going to say.

I could see her alarm clock from here.

It was after ten.

She could have gone out. She would have been upset. She probably would have wanted to talk to someone. Tell them what an asshole I was.

This time she would be right.

Except usually she was home by ten. My day started at six, but hers didn't start much later than that.

By ten thirty I was getting nervous.

By eleven I was done waiting. I sat on the couch in the living room, the TV on in the background, and grabbed my phone. Thinking she might not want to talk to me I tried texting.

Hey where are u?

Nothing.

Look, I know u r mad, but it's late and I'm worried.

I waited for the three dots and clenched my jaw when nothing showed.

I called. It rang five times and then her voice mail clicked in.

Hi this is Ellie. Three reasons I might not be answering, I'm not near my phone, the reception where I am is garbage, or I just don't want to talk to you right now. Leave a message.

"Ellie, no joke. It's eleven. I don't know where you are. Call or text if you don't want to talk to me. But I need to know you're safe."

I waited until eleven thirty before I called again.

Five calls. At least twenty texts.

By midnight I was coming out of my skin. Where would she be? I called Pete's. He was just closing up, but no he hadn't seen her there tonight. Where the hell else would she go?

Her friends were still at college. Would she have done that? Left completely?

The nameless boyfriend? Some guy, who I had never met, who was with her and now wasn't letting her answer her phone? Why wasn't he letting her answer her phone?

I needed to get a grip. I searched my contacts. At some

point over the years I had all her friends' numbers. I picked Chrissy and paced in front of the fireplace while it rang.

"Jake? It's like twelve o'clock."

"Chrissy, listen to me, I don't know where Ellie is. Is she with you?"

"Uh, no. But you know I'm like at college."

"Yeah. We had a fight. I thought she might have..."

"No. She's not here. She hasn't called either."

I took a deep breath. "Do you know... was there anyone she was...seeing?"

"Seeing?"

I tried to hang on to my patience. "Dating. Hanging out with. Any guy that you might know of?"

"No. No guy. And she would totally not have held out on me about that."

"Okay. Thanks. Sorry if I woke you."

"No problem."

I disconnected the call and had a serious urge to throw the phone across the room, but I was afraid of breaking the damn thing in case she did call. See, this was bullshit. This was immature eighteen-year-old bullshit. I did not need this kind of drama in my life.

She was pissed off and making me pay, and that was horseshit. I should go to bed and call it a fucking night.

Shit. I was going to have to get Sheriff Barling out of bed.

The phone rang and I let my head fall back on my neck when I saw her name. By the third ring I could answer.

"Where the hell are you?"

"Stop calling my friends. I'm fine. I'm safe. I should have... I didn't have the ringer on. I'm sorry. I didn't mean to freak you out."

"Where are you?"

"You don't need to know that. I need some time away. We need some time apart. I think."

"Ellie...I'm sorry..."

"No. You don't have to apologize. Everything you said was true."

It was. That was the horrible part about it.

"Come home. I'll... I'll move into the bunk house."

"I will. Eventually. I just want some space for a little bit."

Her voice sounded so small. So unlike Ellie. I did that to her.

"I don't know what to say." That was also true.

"You don't have to say anything, Jake. It's okay. I need some time. For a while. But I think I can fix this. Sorry I made you worry. I really didn't mean to."

She hung up and I didn't call her back. She wanted space and I had to respect that.

I closed up the house. I didn't lock the door in case she changed her mind. I went to bed and I wondered what she meant by fixing this.

TEN

Ellie

I DISCONNECTED the call and tossed the phone on the bed. I felt bad he'd been so worried. I felt worse thinking he might believe I would do something like that on purpose to spite him.

It was luck I had picked up the phone when Chrissy called. She wanted to know what we fought about, but I didn't have the energy to tell her. It didn't matter. None of that was important.

Whether Jake did or did not sleep with Carol and let her spend the night wasn't the issue. I guess I believed him when he said that wasn't what happened, but again that wasn't what was important.

That rule was for me. So I wouldn't feel like I felt this morning when I walked in on him and saw him...

"Ugh! Am I ever going to forget that moment?"

The empty room didn't answer.

There were no hotels in town or anything like that. Just the one room for rent over the Hair Stop. But nothing close enough where I could commute back and forth to the ranch. I wasn't going to leave Jake high and dry on the work. The ranch was my responsibility. I just couldn't be in the house with him. Not now.

My father's cabin hadn't been used in years. It took me most of the day to get it stocked. I needed a ton of cut wood for the wood-burning stove, but thankfully it did give off a lot of heat.

I'm grateful Jake didn't nearly bone Carol in the kitchen in February, as this escape plan probably wouldn't have worked.

Escape, however, was temporary and I needed a plan for the future.

What I needed to do was simple. I had to divorce Jake. As soon as possible, if there was any hope of salvaging our relationship.

There was no way we could live together in this limbo until I turned twenty-one. At least there was no way I could do it. Because I was the one messing it up. I was the one with feelings.

Sure, Jake was attracted to me, and he felt things for me, but quite clearly he didn't love me.

I did. Loved him. Like an idiot. I figured it out when he asked me that question so many months ago.

Can you say now you want to spend the rest of your life with me?

I hadn't known until he asked.

The word had come fast and sharp back then.

Yes.

Yes. I did want to live with Jake. I did want to be his partner. I never wanted him to leave me.

Was it because my parents had left me, permanently? I don't know. I just knew when he'd asked me the question I was certain of my answer.

Him asking the question in the first place, I was also certain of his answer. That he wasn't ready to say that about me. I asked him to do this thing, to marry me, as a temporary arrangement and instead of putting his life on hold for sixteen months, I came back and asked for another three years.

He didn't really have to stick it out. He could have bailed. I would have done what I had to do to make sure he got his money.

But he didn't leave, and I didn't think too hard about another solution other than trying to ask the bank for more money.

Financially, we had a decent year, this year. Obviously significantly down from the year before, but given the losses we suffered we did the best we could. Would the bank possibly look at me differently now with nearly a year of ranching under my belt?

It was worth a shot.

I would start looking into things tomorrow.

I made sure the ringer on my phone was on and crawled into bed. I tried very hard not to remember what my dad used this cabin for, instead I focused on ideas on how to fix the problem that was my life.

Because no matter what I had to do, no matter how I needed to make it happen, I needed to give Jake his freedom back.

So that he wouldn't hate me anymore.

"God," I prayed. "Please don't let him really hate me. He's the only person I have left."

I OPENED the door to Howard's office in town and Sue Ann looked up and gave me a big smile.

"Ellie. Good to see you."

"You too. I don't suppose there is any chance Howard has a few minutes for me?"

"You are in luck. His next appointment just canceled. If you give me a second I'll let him know you're here."

"Great," I said as she got up and walked down the short hall to Howard's office.

I didn't feel great. In fact I felt a little sick. This was the first step.

The first step away from Jake. It was like everything in my body was screaming *don't do this*.

Carol was a fling. He'd said it himself. She wasn't planning on sticking around. Maybe someday, in the future Jake would grow to love me and then everything would be fine.

That shit happened all the time in romance novels. Couple had to get married for convenience... and then bang! Next thing you know, they were making babies.

Only that was fiction and this was real life, and I couldn't screw Jake over in case he never did come to love me. Even if Carol wasn't *the one*, I didn't want to stand around and watch him fall in love with someone else.

It was bad enough I had to see him...

Don't think about it. Don't think about it.

"Ellie! What a surprise."

I smiled. It had been a while since I had seen Howard. Just a few times over the summer when Jake and I ran into him at the diner.

I walked up and kissed his cheek. I'm not sure why. I wasn't a cheek kisser in general, but suddenly it felt really

really good to see him. He'd been the orchestrator behind the wedding, and I knew he was the one who could get me out.

Even though I didn't really want out. I wasn't doing this for me, though. This was for Jake. The sacrifice I could make for him this time.

He smiled but he tilted his head, and I could tell he was assessing me.

I couldn't have looked good. A solid few hours of crying yesterday and barely any sleep last night. I imagined I looked pretty gross.

Dad's cabin didn't have mirrors, so I didn't have to confront myself this morning.

"Everything okay?"

"Yes, but I have a problem and I was hoping you could help."

He nodded. "Okay. Follow me."

We walked back down the short hallway and a few seconds later I was sitting in front of his desk. I caught myself wringing my hands.

Cheek kissing and hand wringing. He had to know something was up.

"What do you need, Ellie?"

Don't say it. Don't do it. You're going to ruin everything and there will never be anyone as amazing as Jake Talley in your life again.

I took a deep breath and grabbed onto my courage.

"I need to divorce Jake. Now. I need money to do that and I was hoping you could help with that."

Howard actually looked sad. "I'm sorry to hear that. We all knew after the storm what the situation was. For Jake too, given his house was all but gone. Are you two not getting along? You always seemed so easy with each other."

I hate you for that, Ellie. Can you hear me through your locked door? I hate you for that!

"We're okay. It's just that I can't let him do this for another two and a half years. It isn't fair to him. He deserves to have his life back. His freedom. Now that I'm legal, there is no reason not to do this."

"Other than money."

"Yes."

"Are you asking me for a loan?"

I blinked. "Oh gosh no. Nothing like that. I was thinking about the trust Dad set up for me. I know you said I couldn't have access to it until I was twenty-one, but I'm wondering if there isn't some legal way around that. Some kind of catastrophic clause or something I could use to get the money sooner rather than later."

He seemed to consider that. "I'm not sure I saw any language like that when I was looking over the documents, but how about this? I promise to take another look."

I smiled. "Thank you. I knew you would help."

"I have to say... well, maybe I'm an old romantic at heart, but I kind of always hoped you and Jake would just stay together. You may not realize it, but from the outside looking in, you two look like... I guess you look like a family."

That was the way I wanted it to stay. With Jake thinking of me like family. Not resenting me and hating me.

I nodded. "I hope that doesn't change. Thanks again, Howard."

I left with this odd mix of feelings. As if I couldn't tell if I had done the best thing ever or the worst thing.

I WAS BACK in the cabin and starting to fill up the wood-burning stove. Lighting this thing was always a bitch. Finally a log caught a good burn, and I shut the door on it with the heat glove.

The cabin wasn't much. One large room with a bathroom. It had a couch, a chair, a bed, and the stove.

I lay back on the bed and wondered what my dad used to think about when he came here alone. Sure it had been his little tryst nest with Mrs. Nash for a while, but before that I think he was telling the truth.

Sometimes a man needs a little space and time to think.

Which now that I thought about it was really sexist. Only men need space and thinking time?

My phone beeped and I reached for it.

Jake.

Hey, just checking in.

Of course he was. Because that's what Jake did.

I'm fine. I wasn't. I was the opposite of fine but none of that was his fault.

Figured out where u were. The cabin.

It wasn't the hardest mystery to solve. He must have noticed all my work had been done. I had even taken Petunia out for a long ride. He would have been in and out of the barn so he might have seen her missing. Would have known I was close.

Like father like daughter I guess. Needed some space to think.

Warm enough?

Yes.

...

...

Either he was writing something really long, or he was doing a lot of stopping and starting. My guess was the latter.

Do u believe me? That Carol came over in the morning?

I closed my eyes but it didn't remove the image of him shirtless between her legs.

Still, I knew Jake. Inside out. Upside down. He wouldn't lie to cover his own ass.

Yes

...

...

...

Poor Jake. This really wasn't his strong point. I knew he thought I was mad at him, and he hated the idea of anyone ever being mad at him. Couldn't stand it. I was about to let him off the hook. Tell him I would be back tomorrow and everything was fine. But I suppose I wanted to know what he was trying to say first.

Finally the words popped up.

I'm sorry for what I said. I didn't mean it.

I could feel my chin starting to wobble again and my eyes well up. Crying really was so ugly.

Please tell me u believe that too.

I set the phone down. That was the problem. I didn't. In that moment I knew he meant every word. I couldn't tell him that though, it would only make him feel worse. But I couldn't lie to him either.

I picked up the phone and typed.

It's okay, Jake. I'm going to fix this.

What does that mean?

Trust me.

Ellie, please tell me what u mean.

I couldn't right now. Because there was no plan. I didn't want him to get his hopes up only to find out there was no way to get my hands on the money early. If I told him about the nuclear option, I knew he would go ballistic.

I need time. That's all. Did you make yourself something to eat?

If I wasn't around, he rarely bothered to cook for himself. Which meant he'd work a full physical day and make do with sandwiches.

Sandwiches.

That's not enough.

Not hungry.

Right. Because he felt bad. Over me.

I'll be back tomorrow. I'll shop and cook.

...

...

...

He was struggling again.

Okay

Okay. It was strange, but the simple word made me feel better. Like we were actually going to be okay.

I didn't type anything after that. Just set the phone aside and thought about what I was going to make tomorrow for dinner. Simple. Routine.

It helped.

ELEVEN

Jake
October (Or as I liked to refer to it, the suckiest month ever.)

I STARED down at the phone and waited. No more dots. She was done talking. That was okay. Because she had answered and she had seemed... normal. Yes, I wanted to know what she meant by fixing this. There wasn't anything to fix. What happened, happened and there was no changing the past.

No, that wasn't entirely true. There was one thing I had to fix.

Carol.

I had been thinking about it and thinking about it and truth was I didn't know if I was really that into her. It felt more like I was going through the motions to prove something to myself. Or worse, I was using her as a distraction from Ellie.

That wasn't fair to Carol.

It certainly wasn't fair to Ellie. Because I had seen the look on Ellie's face when she found us. I knew the level of pain I had inflicted on her. That I had been inflicting on her since I started seeing Carol.

I looked at my phone again. It was just after eight. Plenty of time to drive into town and do what I had to do and get home.

I typed in Carol's name.

Hey, can I come see u so we can talk?

A few seconds later she responded.

Yes. We should definitely talk.

She gave me her address, but I didn't pay much attention to it. I knew she lived close to town so I headed out, figuring as I got closer I would worry about getting to her actual home.

It wasn't until I was pulling up to the house that it dawned on me where I was.

This was the MacPherson place.

I got out of my truck, and to be certain checked the address against the number on the house. It was the same.

I rang the doorbell and she opened the door with a wide smile.

"Hey. This is perfect timing," she said as she reached out with her hand to pull me inside. "The family is out so we've got the place to ourselves."

"You're related to the MacPhersons?"

She kept pulling on my arm as if she wanted to lead me to the living room, but I planted myself in the middle of the foyer.

"Yep. Sally is my mom's sister. That's who I'm here for. She's having a rough time with the divorce. Remember? I told you."

"You told me you were helping out your aunt for a while. I didn't know that was Sally MacPherson."

She looked puzzled.

"Does that matter?"

"I guess not."

She smiled again. "You wanted to talk? Is this about the other morning?"

"Yes."

How did I explain any of this?

"You said it was okay for you to be dating," Carol said. "I'm not sure Ellie thinks the same thing."

"No. She understands why I'm doing it. She just didn't... It's her house. She thought you had spent the night."

Carol nodded. "So if we were going to move things forward... then we should do that here? Like if we wanted to pick up where we left off..."

She moved toward me, but I took a step back. I didn't want to think about yesterday morning. That was not a pleasant memory.

I must have communicated my resistance to the idea and her smile faded. "Okay, Jake. What's the deal? What are we really doing here? I thought you said you weren't a tease."

"I told you I wanted to talk," I said.

"Yeah, well I want to fuck," she replied, clearly exasperated.

The word dropped like a brick in the room. Up until then she'd come off as this nice, sweet woman. Her agenda had been hidden behind hand touches, smiles and flirtatious innuendo. Now there was something ugly in her tone.

"You sort of made that clear from the start. Is that why

you came out to the ranch in the first place? Were you looking for some...action?"

Something wasn't sitting right with me. I remembered Ellie saying something about Carol being pretty ballsy to flirt so openly with me right out of the gate. Without even knowing about my situation other than from what she'd heard.

"No. I came because Don told me about your insemination program. Then Bobby told me what the deal was between you and Ellie."

"Bobby." Right. Her cousin.

"Yes. He said you two were married, but it was in name only. He thought you might be my type, and he was right. Because you are my type, Jake."

She was flirting again.

Bobby told her my marriage to Ellie wasn't real. Bobby told his cousin I was her type.

Bobby. Who had a thing for Ellie.

"I told you," she continued. "It's been like forever for me. I liked you, I thought you liked me. It's just sex, Jake. Married, not married. What's the difference?"

What's the difference? The difference was Ellie.

"Is this because Ellie got so freaked out? She's obviously into you. You broke her poor baby heart. That sucks for her, but if you're not into her, then oh well. Her loss."

I broke Ellie's heart. For this.

"I came over to say I don't think it's a good idea we see each other any longer."

Her jaw dropped. "Are you serious? You're telling me after the other morning you don't want to fuck me?"

"Yes. I am very certain I don't want to fuck you. Goodnight, Carol."

"Asshole!"

"Not the first time I've been called that. Good luck with your next conquest."

I shut the door behind me and dropped my head.

I hurt Ellie. I broke Ellie's heart. I told Ellie I hated her.

I did all that because Bobby MacPherson thought I would be his cousin's type.

I wanted to drive out to the cabin. I wanted to explain everything to Ellie, but as I got closer to the ranch I realized it didn't change anything. My reasons for getting involved with Carol in the first place hadn't changed.

Instead I drove up to the house and got out of my truck.

When I opened the door I had this thought that maybe she would have come home. It was in the forties. Even with a fire the cabin had to be cold. She said she was coming home tomorrow anyway, why not come back now? Once inside I jogged up the steps to the second floor, but when I pushed open her door I saw it was still empty.

I had done that. I had driven her out of her own damn home for someone as superficial and one-dimensional as Carol.

And I might have permanently altered my relationship with Ellie. Who was pretty much the only family I had left. My best friend, my family... my wife.

There was no one I could talk to about this. Except of course Ellie. Ellie, who was going to come home tomorrow and cook me dinner. Because she hates it when I only eat sandwiches. She thinks it's not enough given all the physical work I do during a day.

I knew that about her.

So even though I had hurt her, even though she had to witness me about to screw another woman in her kitchen, she was still worried enough about what I ate to overlook that and come home.

I was a rancher. A simple man who got up and worked hard all day. I didn't do complicated. I didn't do dramatic. I didn't ask for much.

Only now I was in this shit storm, and I didn't see any way out of it.

There was only one thing left to do.

It was time to get drunk.

Ellie

I WASN'T certain what woke me. I only know I had been asleep dreaming this crazy dream that Petunia could actually talk to me, and now suddenly I was awake. I was nicely cocooned under a ton of blankets, but I could tell my nose was freezing.

Which meant the fire had long since gone out, which meant it was probably the middle of the night.

"Ellie! Open the door, Ellie!"

Jake was banging on the door. It must have been his knocking that woke me.

There had to be some kind of emergency. Maybe something with one of the horses. I didn't think, I got up and ran to the door, unlocked the dead bolt and swung it open.

The first thing that hit me was the smell. Jake reeked of whiskey. The second thing I noticed was him leaning against the door frame with said bottle of whiskey still in his hand.

Although it didn't seem as if there was that much left.

"It's too cold. You need to come home," he said.

"Jake, you're drunk."

"Shitfaced. Now come home."

He attempted to wave me forward, but it was like he didn't have full use of his arm.

"How did you get here?"

He pointed behind him. I could see his truck parked at an awkward angle on the gravel area in front of the cabin.

"You drove! You are shitfaced and you got in a car!"

"Access road to here."

Which meant the road on the property where there would be no other traffic. Not that it mattered.

"What about cattle? Deer? Did you think of that?"

He opened his mouth and then shut it. Then he shook his head like he was having a hard time forming thoughts. "Get your stuff. You can't sleep here. It's too cold. I want you in your room."

"I was completely fine and you're an idiot."

"Yep. Now, Ellie."

With nothing left to do I turned back into the cabin and found my boots. Then I picked my coat up off the chair and put it on.

"I can't believe for as many times as you've railed at me about the horrors of drinking and driving, you would do this. Where are the keys?"

He patted his pockets. I realized he wasn't even wearing a coat. He had to be the one who was freezing.

"Truck?"

Like that was one possibility. Great. I pushed him a little to get him moving in the general direction of the truck. It was a good thing he could still manage walking, because there was no way I had the strength to get Jake into the truck without his help. He was able to lift himself into the passenger seat and his head fell back against the headrest.

"Do not fall asleep on me or I swear to God I will let you spend the night in your truck."

"I won't. Need to talk to you."

He was not in any shape to talk, so I had no doubt that whatever was going to come out of his mouth would be nonsense. But as long as it kept him awake until I could get us back to the house, then I was all for it.

"Okay Jake, what do you want to talk about?"

"Carol."

Was he kidding me? "I don't want to talk about Carol."

"Did you know she was Bobby's cousin?"

I didn't. But I wasn't sure why it mattered.

"Doesn't matter. I didn't fuck her. I know you think I did. I didn't. I ended it."

He didn't fuck Carol? Was that true? Of course it was true. He wouldn't lie sober, much less shitfaced. It shouldn't have made me feel the way it did. As if I was suddenly ten pounds lighter. But it did.

Still. I had to say the words. "I hope you didn't do that because of me."

"I did."

Swell. Yet another way I was messing up his life, and I didn't need the added pressure. "Damn it, Jake. I know you're drunk, but if you think you can make me feel guilty..."

"Nothing to be guilty about," he interrupted. "I'm the one... I'm the one who hurt you. I don't know why I keep doing that."

"It's okay, Jake."

"It's not okay. But I want to fix it."

He was too late. I already had the plan to fix it.

At least Jake had been right about one thing. The access road that led from the house to the cabin had been completely empty. No cattle roaming. There could have been deer, but he'd gotten lucky. I pulled up to the house and parked in front of the porch instead of under the portico. Less of a walk for him.

"Are you going to be able to get out?"

His head basically rolled in my direction and really I had to laugh. I had never seen Jake like this. He looked almost... vulnerable.

"Yes?"

"Wait for me until I open your door."

I didn't want him falling face-first out of the truck and risking hurting himself. Like the good little boy he was, he waited. I opened the door and steered his legs around and although he was unsteady, he managed to get out and still be on his feet. I took the bottle from his hand, and he let it go as if he didn't realize he was still holding it.

Then he wrapped his arm around my shoulders and I figured that was a good idea to keep him from falling over.

He wasn't putting too much of his weight on me, just enough I could guide him up the front porch steps and toward the door.

Luckily the door wasn't locked, so I turned the knob and pushed it open.

"Okay, you first. Inside."

He stumbled but made his way inside. I followed and locked the door behind him, leaving the whiskey bottle on the small table in the foyer.

"Lockthedoor," he slurred.

"I did lock the door. I'm not going to try and get you up the stairs, so it's couch city for you, my drunk friend."

I walked up to him and he put his arm around me again. I moved us in the direction of the living room. Then he dipped his head and smelled my hair.

"It always smells so good. I love your hair. Did I ever tell you that?"

"You like blondes," I reminded him.

"I liked holding your hair in my hands when I kissed you. Like suddenly it was mine."

Okay, I really didn't want to talk about kissing Jake. It brought up too many memories that seemed pointless. I had to get him to the couch, where I could drop him and he could pass out.

Instead he bumped his knee into the coffee table in the middle of the room.

"Are you hurt?"

"All the time. It's like this ache. You know?"

I didn't. And I didn't really want to speculate on anything. Finally I got him to the couch. I pushed him and he dropped, but then he reached for my hand and pulled me down on top of him.

Drunk Jake was still strong Jake.

His hands were wrapped around me and I was pressing my forearms against his chest, trying to get away.

"Jake, let me go."

"Kiss me."

I froze.

"You're drunk," I reminded him. "You don't really want to do that."

"No, it's okay because I'm drunk. Because tomorrow I can say I wasn't thinking. I'm tired of thinking so much, Ellie."

His hand reached up to cup my face and then his fingers slid into my hair.

"Mine."

I should have pressed harder against him. I should have wiggled away from him. He was drunk, he didn't know what he was doing. And I was pretty sure given the fact that

I was sober, if I did this I would be taking advantage of him. Not cool.

"Kiss me, Ellie."

It had been so long. Months and months. One kiss. One kiss couldn't hurt anything. He wasn't going to remember any of this anyway.

I dropped my head and he did the rest. Cupping my face in both hands, tilting my head just a bit, and then he slid his tongue inside my mouth and my stomach dropped as if I had hit the downside on a roller coaster ride.

It felt like a ride, too. Fast and intense. He tasted like whiskey, but he also tasted like Jake. The same Jake from last time, who was all heat and slickness.

He was holding me and kissing me, and I could feel his erection pressing up against me, so I ground myself against it which made him moan into my mouth, and I thought, *this is it. This is really going to happen.*

Us.

My first time.

My first time with a drunk Jake.

I pulled away from him suddenly, and it startled him enough that he let me go. I scrambled off him until I was standing. That saying about being weak in the knees. So true.

"Ellie..."

I took a few breaths, and then I turned toward his feet and started working on the ties on his boots.

"You're drunk. You don't know what you're doing or who you are doing, and I don't want..." I didn't say I didn't want to lose my virginity to someone who didn't realize who he was banging, so I didn't say anything else.

I got his boots off. I covered him with a blanket.

His eyes were nearly shut, but he wasn't asleep yet.

"Kissing you is the best thing," he muttered. Then he turned a little to get comfortable and passed out. Unable to help myself, I bent down and kissed him on the temple.

I got the trash bucket out of the downstairs bathroom and set it by him, just in case. I left a tall glass of water and two Excedrin on the coffee table for when he woke up.

I made my way upstairs and not going to lie, it was nice to sleep in my bed. It smelled the way it should.

I got under the covers and thought about what had happened.

One thing he was right about. Kissing Jake was the best thing.

It was really sad to think that might have been the last kiss we would ever share.

One he might not even remember.

TWELVE

Jake

I OPENED my eyes and then closed them again. My head felt like it was stuffed with cotton balls. Like I couldn't think because all this white fluffy stuff was in the way. And my mouth—for the love of all that was holy in this world, I needed water.

I blinked again and saw the glass of water on the coffee table. I just needed to get up and reach for it. I sat up, noticed the trash can on the floor, and decided all I needed was the water and whatever two white pills Ellie had left out for me.

Ellie.

I started to put the pieces back together. The drive to the cabin. The drive back. I told her about Carol and...

I kissed her. It wasn't like I was going to forget that. She'd pulled away. I remember that. Because I was drunk, she had said. Then nothing.

All things considered, it could have been worse. Awake now, I realized I smelled food. Sausage, which made my stomach grumble with hunger. Nothing like a greasy breakfast to work off a hangover.

I made my way to the kitchen to in fact find Ellie making me breakfast. It was strange the other day when I came down to find Carol... that had looked so wrong in my head.

I looked at the clock on the microwave and saw it was already eight a.m. Ellie had let me sleep off some of my hangover and now she was making me breakfast. I took this as a good sign.

"On a scale of one to ten, how bad did I screw up last night?"

She whipped her head around. "Ten. You drove drunk! That's the stupidest thing I've ever seen you do in my life. And while there would have been no other cars on the access road, you could have done something else to hurt yourself. Remember Janet last year? You were so pissed at her for doing that. It was not cool."

I wiped my hands over my face and made my way to the fridge for more water. That first glass was only touching the surface of my thirst.

"You're right. It was stupid. I don't even know why I did it."

That wasn't exactly true. I did it because I wanted to not think about shit for five minutes. I forgot that sometimes when you get drunk you think about shit even more.

I had the idea that Ellie was cold and needed to come home, and in my drunken state I had to make that happen.

"Sit. I'll feed you and you'll feel better."

Ellie was fussing over me. Ellie was taking care of me.

Because I broke up with Carol. Made sense. I was no longer hurting her.

I sat down and she filled my plate with half a pound of sausage, three eggs, and four pieces of toast. She set a jar of peanut butter in front of me and I went to town.

"Thank you," I mumbled around a piece of toast. I hadn't realized how hungry I was, and nothing tasted as good as hangover food.

"You're welcome. I have to head out to the grocery store. A little food and a hot shower and I'm sure you'll be as good as new."

She was about to stand up when I reached across the table and caught her hand.

"I meant what I said the other day. If you want me to move to the bunk house, I will."

She shook her head and I watched the sway of her ponytail.

Had I talked about her hair last night?

"You don't have to move. We had a fight. I misunderstood the situation and you were upset. It's over now. Behind us."

"We're good?"

She nodded.

I smiled. "Did I say anything really stupid last night?"

"Not too stupid, no."

I don't know why I said it. Maybe because she hadn't brought it up.

"I know I kissed you."

"You did. You were drunk, you didn't know what you were doing. It's fine. No harm, no foul. You're on cleanup duty."

She slipped her hand out from underneath mine and got up. I watched her pull her stuff together, and she was calling out *bye*, and the whole thing felt pretty surreal. Like what had happened the other day had been a fight and she was over it. As if my apology had actually worked.

Or it was because she knew Carol was no longer a thing, but somehow I didn't think that was it. It was like she was resigned to something. Something only she knew and I didn't.

I didn't know that I liked that. I did know that I didn't correct her when she said I didn't know what I was doing when I kissed her.

I knew exactly what I was doing. I was allowing my drunkenness to give me a free pass. Every day was an exercise in not kissing Ellie. The booze gave me cover to give into my basic instincts.

My stomach filled, my plate clean, my head feeling better now that the pills were doing their thing, I got up and handled the dishes. It wasn't until I was drying the counter where I had splashed some water that I noticed the scales.

The other day I had moved all ten disks on the left side.

Ellie had moved six to the right.

Not five.

Six.

For some reason that made me feel better than I had in weeks.

LATER THAT NIGHT, I was putting away the dishes from dinner.

"You're rocking those casseroles," I told her. "If someone in this town dies, you're going to have start coming up with what will be your I'm-sorry-someone-is-dead food."

She chuckled. Weeks of the silent treatment. Weeks of

her barely acknowledging me, and now I had made her chuckle.

I was a king.

I decided to push my luck.

"Hey, there's another season of that show you really liked last year out on Netflix. Feel like binge watching?"

I waited. I didn't realize I was also holding my breath.

"Sure. I'm not loving the book I'm reading right now."

We got everything put away and we took our normal spots. Me, in the recliner, her on the couch. It felt a little bit like walking on eggshells. As if I made any sudden movements she might bolt.

Then the show started and everything seemed to fall into place.

I had my life back.

I had my wife back.

I glanced over at her, but her attention was on the show. Her hair was loose tonight and a sensory memory of me running my fingers through it was intense.

Mine.

I looked back at the screen and tried not to think about it. Tried not to wonder what she would do if I sat on the couch with her. With her body tucked up against me so I could bend down and smell her hair whenever I wanted to.

Shit, I was staring at her. I forced myself to look at the TV, but if she asked me what I thought about what I was watching I would have no clue.

She didn't ask. Just popped up when the second episode was over and said goodnight.

Yes, something was different. We weren't who we were pre-kiss. We weren't who we were pre-Carol. We weren't who we were during-Carol (Thank you God!).

We were something else now. I wasn't necessarily sure

if that was a good thing or a bad thing, but the next day when I took a break to grab lunch I saw another disk had been added to the right scale.

Seven.

Progress, I thought. But progress towards what?

"HEY, I'm heading to Pete's."

I looked up from the article I was reading in *Montana Weekly* on popular bull sperm donors. Yes, sometimes I spent way too much time focusing on bull sperm.

"Okay."

It was homecoming. I knew Chrissy, Lisa, and Karen were all home this weekend.

"It'll be good, you seeing your girls."

She beamed. "I know. I'm excited."

"You know not to do something as stupid as what I did last week."

"Uh, yeah."

"You drink too much, call me and I'll come pick you up."

"I promise."

I watched her leave and I tried not to stare too hard at her ass. She was wearing tight dark jeans and her cowboy boots. She'd curled her hair so it bounced around her shoulders.

Geezus, sometimes I forgot how freaking gorgeous she was.

She was going to be at a bar, looking like that. I didn't want to think about it.

I went back to reading my article but the words ran together. I got up and decided I needed a shower. Something to do so I wasn't thinking about her out with the girls while every guy at Pete's ogled her.

Okay, not every guy. There would be some who had known Ellie her whole life who wouldn't look at her that way. Like I had up until a year ago.

Fuck.

I turned the hot water on and I thought about maybe heading to Pete's myself. I didn't have to hang out with her. I could just be there. That way she would know if she wanted to let loose a little I would have her back. She wouldn't have to be worried about calling me.

That was a solid plan. Done with the shower, I got out, dried myself off, splashed on some cologne. A birthday present from Ellie this summer. Did I consider the fact that I was picking out what I knew was her favorite shirt to wear?

No.

Okay yes, but I was in denial about it so it didn't matter.

I jogged down the stairs and grabbed my good coat (another present from Ellie), not my working coat, off the hook.

As I got into my truck, I paused for a second.

Was this creepy? Was I going all stalker on her?

No, I thought. It was Friday night. I could head into town for a beer. And if I was there to give her a ride home, no big deal.

We were cool now. She had seven disks on the right side of the scale.

Except as I drove into town and pulled up to park on the street near Pete's, the doubts came back. I didn't want to hone in on her night. She hadn't seen her friends since they went off to college. I didn't want her to think I was shadowing her or something.

I should probably go home. I didn't think she would like it if I was there. Just as I turned the engine on my phone rang. I reached for it thinking it might be her, thinking she might actually be calling me to join her.

Except it wasn't her name on the screen. It was Chrissy's.

My gut clenched. "Chrissy, what is it?"

"Jake, something is wrong I think. Ellie only had one glass of wine, but she started acting really weird. Like *really* weird and I just came back from the bathroom and I can't see her. The place is packed, but still she wouldn't have just left me. I tried to call her, but she's not picking up."

I could see that. The parking lot was full. Cars lined the street.

"Do you know who gave her the wine?"

"Bobby bought all of our drinks."

I didn't need to hear anymore. "You keep looking for her and you text me the second you see her. I'll be right there."

I was turning off the engine and calling Ellie at the same time. Then I was out of my truck, running down the street to Pete's.

Ellie didn't pick up. I stopped long enough to text her.

Get away from Bobby now!

Doug was sitting outside of Pete's, acting as the bouncer.

"Hey, Jake. Place is packed. I don't think I can let any more people in tonight. Homecoming. You know how it is."

"Doug, I've got to get in there. Ellie might be in trouble."

"Oh shit. Yeah, no problem. Just muscle your way through."

Hold on, Ellie. Just hold on.

Ellie

SOMETHING WAS NOT RIGHT. I knew that. I could feel it. I was sipping my wine. Slowly, because I could only have two glasses, because I was not going to do anything as asinine as drive drunk.

But I wasn't halfway through it and already I felt like I was trashed.

Or not exactly. Just like I couldn't think. But at the same time I felt so good. Like the best I had ever felt. I was hanging with my girls, and Bobby was there. He'd offered to buy us our first round.

Lisa didn't even seem to mind despite the fact he'd jerked her around a lot back in high school.

He gave us our drinks. I was the only one who ordered wine. Naturally. And he seemed pretty normal for a while. Simply hanging with us. Then I had this crazy urge to touch him so I reached out to stroke his arm and I thought it was really hard.

"You have hard arms," I told him. Actually I shouted it at him. The place was packed with people. I could barely hear myself.

"Thank you," he shouted back.

"Jake also has hard arms."

"Thanks for sharing."

Then Lisa and Karen went to play pool. Chrissy went to the bathroom and it was me and Bobby. I was weaving a little bit on my stool. Bobby put his arm around my waist to steady me. I put my empty wine glass on the bar and it toppled over. Would have broken if it hadn't been made with such thick glass.

"Want another one?" Bobby asked. Close in my ear so I could hear him.

I was planning on two. That's what I told myself coming in to tonight. I could have that and still be okay to drive home. But the way I felt now, there was no way I was driving. I needed to call Jake.

"No. I don't think so. I feel really..."

Not drunk. Not like I was out of my head. More like I was out of my body. The press of people around me felt like it was all too much.

"Yeah, I can see you don't look so hot. It's too crowded in here. Let me take you out back to get some air."

Air. Cool air on my face and skin. Yes, that was exactly what I wanted.

"But I can't leave Chrissy."

"I'll text her. Let her know I've got you. Karen and Lisa are still here."

That was true. I needed the air so very desperately. Bobby helped me off the stool and I caught myself before almost falling. His arm was around me, and that felt good. I had this longing to touch every part of him, which was crazy because I had never wanted to touch Bobby MacPherson. Ever.

We may have called a truce, but it was not like I was interested in him. Despite what Jake said about him having a thing for me. Although I might be more inclined to be grateful if I could get some air. The crush of people as we moved through the crowd was disturbing, because in some ways I hated it and in other ways I liked the contact.

He was guiding me down the narrow hall where the doors to the bathroom were, and I could see the door at the end with the exit sign over it. Yes, that's what I wanted. To be gone. To be able to breathe. To shake this crazy feeling in my head like I was flying so high. Higher than I ever wanted to fly.

Bobby pushed the door open and there it was. I tilted my head back and breathed in as deeply as I could. As if I hadn't been able to breathe at all and suddenly there was all this oxygen. I teetered a few steps and pressed my back up against the brick wall which was the back of Pete's. There was a light attached to the wall that was shining, then suddenly it went dark.

"Why did it go dark?"

"Don't worry about it."

The next thing I knew, Bobby was trying to kiss me. His lips were on me and I could feel his tongue trying to press into my mouth. I lifted my arms to push him away, but he was too heavy.

"Bobby, no!"

I think I said that. I tried to say that. But I didn't want to open my mouth. I turned my head away from him and he started sucking on my neck.

"Stop. No."

"Come on. You know you want this. You're begging for it."

Begging for it? Hardly. "Seriously, stop. This is not cool."

I tried pushing him again, but he was like this wall that wouldn't move. Then he was spinning me, so that my cheek was pressed against the rough brick.

"I know you want it. I've seen your toys."

I was trying to make sense of what he was saying. But I could not fucking control my brain. He pulled my hips back against his and then I felt his hands on the buttons of my jeans. I bucked against him hard and that moved him away a little.

"See, you're like a bitch in heat," he laughed. "I'll make this so fucking good for you."

"No!"

Not this. This was not happening. I was not about to lose it to Bobby MacPherson behind Pete's bar when I didn't want this to happen. I should have done it with Jake when he was drunk. That would have been better than this.

Jake. God, he was going to be so mad at me.

"Jake!"

"Jake's not here," Bobby growled in my ear. "I am."

Then he was tugging off my jeans, or trying to, when I heard a crash. I turned my head toward the sound. The back door had popped open and there was Jake. Like I had somehow summoned him. He was this amazing superhero who I could see from the light pouring out from the bar behind him.

"Help." I don't know if he heard me. It didn't matter.

Abruptly the weight Bobby had been using to hold me in place was gone. I turned around to see him running, and then Jake was tearing after him. Chrissy, who had followed Jake out of the door, came over to me.

"Ohmygod, ohmygod, ohmygod. Are you okay?"

No. I was shaking. I tugged up my jeans and buttoned them back up. I looked to where Jake had gone after Bobby. Jake had caught him fairly quickly and now he was very clearly beating the shit out of Bobby.

"Help me. We have to stop him."

"Uh...I don't think we're going to stop Jake."

"We have to stop him, Chrissy!" I started to run but my legs felt like noodles so it was more like stumbling. I got close enough to hear the sound of Jake's fist impacting with Bobby's face.

"Stop!"

"What the fuck did you give her?" Jake screamed at him.

"Fuck you," Bobby groaned. "She wanted it."

Jake hit him again and blood spurted out of Bobby's nose.

"Jake, stop..."

"WHAT THE FUCK DID YOU GIVE HER?"

Except this time Bobby couldn't answer, not with his mouth filled with blood.

"Jake." I couldn't stand anymore. I could feel myself falling, my ass hitting the gravel hard, even as my hands tried to brace my fall. Chrissy tried to help me up, but I was too heavy for her.

"You are fucking going to jail for this, you little shit," Jake told Bobby, who was now crumbled in the fetal position in the dirt, moaning.

At least he was still alive. I didn't think Jake would get in trouble for hitting Bobby, but if he had actually killed him I'm pretty sure that would have been bad. Then Jake was bending over to help pull me up. I managed to get to my feet, but he lifted me into his arms.

This was much better.

"Chrissy, you go back inside and stay with Karen and Lisa. I'll make sure Doug knows what to do with Bobby."

We didn't go back through the bar. Instead he walked me around the outside of the two buildings that were connected. I was grateful. I couldn't have handled going back inside. Jake carrying me in his arms, everyone knowing what Bobby almost did to me. What he seriously almost did to me. I started crying, and even doing that my brain still felt wrong.

Jake got me settled in his truck to the point of fastening my seat belt. That's how out of it I was. Then he was gone—

for how long I couldn't tell, but each minute was this tiny agony without him.

Finally, he was back and the relief was palpable.

"Okay, listen to me, Ellie. We're going to have to go to the urgent care."

"Noooo," I cried. "Home."

"I'm sorry, baby. I want them to get a blood sample now, while it's still in your system."

Gosh, needles really? After I was almost... I couldn't even form the word in my mind. If I did, then it would have made it too real. While I was still in this hazy reality, I could pretend it was all a dream.

Jake being Jake, there wasn't a choice. He drove me to the clinic and carried me inside. I told him I thought I could walk, but he wasn't having it. Fortunately, it was empty except for Dr. Jenkins and Mary, who recently graduated from nursing school. Technically she wasn't a nurse yet because she hadn't passed the boards, but in Riverbend she was considered good enough.

They led Jake, who still wouldn't put me down, to one of the two exam rooms and I sat on the edge of the examination table. Mary was nice. She didn't say much. She cleaned up my palms, which I had scraped when I fell.

Dr. Jenkins shone a light in my eyes and asked me to try and describe how I felt.

"Sort of euphoric. Dreamy a little, too. Like I need physical contact, except I'm not a touchy kind of person. It's so strange."

It was the best I could come up with. Jake and the doctor were talking to each other, but I couldn't follow what either was saying.

Then I felt the prick of the needle and winced while Jake held my hand. I thought it was over, but the worst part came when Dr. Jenkins quietly asked Jake if they needed to take a rape kit.

"No! It didn't happen. He just...undid my jeans."

Mary was rubbing my back, and again I started to bawl even though it still felt wrong.

"You'll have that tested," Jake told Dr. Jenkins. "That prick is going to jail for this."

Then Jake was lifting and carrying me again until I was back in the truck.

I didn't say anything for the ride home. Clear thoughts were still hard. But by the time we were home, I felt a little more normal. I was able to get out of the truck and up the stairs of the porch without Jake, even though he was right behind me.

I didn't stop or say anything. I wasn't sure what Jake's mood was like. If he was mad at me because I hadn't followed the rules about making sure I kept my eyes on my glass when I was at a bar.

But it was Bobby. He was... Bobby from high school. He'd been mean to me that one time and then he apologized. Beyond that, and knowing Jake didn't like him, I didn't think much about him at all.

Now I probably wouldn't forget him, which just seemed wrong.

I went through the normal nightly ritual. Changed into my pajama bottoms and tank top. Pulled my hair back and washed my face. Brushed my teeth. Went back to my room and sat on the bed.

Jake knocked on my door and I told him to come in. He had the entire Brita water container in his hand along with a glass.

"Drink this," he said, handing me the full glass. "The doc said it was probably Molly. The more water you drink, the more it will help to flush it out of your system. When you finish that glass, drink another."

I nodded.

"You want me to stay with you? I can sleep on the floor."

I nodded.

He left then and a few minutes later he came back wearing the pajama bottoms I got him for Christmas last year, which looked like he'd just taken them out of the package, and a T-shirt. He had a bunch of pillows and a blanket, which he spread out on the floor next to my bed.

I got under the covers and lay down, but I didn't think I would sleep. I liked that Jake was close. I liked that I could hear him breathing. I wanted him on the bed with me. I still had this crazy urge to touch and be touched, and there was no one else I wanted to be touched by.

"Jake?"

"Yes, baby."

Baby. That was new. That was him trying to be gentle with me.

"Can you hold me for a while?"

It felt like it took a thousand years before he finally said, "Okay."

THIRTEEN

Jake

"CAN YOU HOLD ME FOR A WHILE?"

I sucked in a breath. I was so raw right now I didn't know if it was a good idea. She'd feel the tension in me, and that wouldn't relax her. But the idea of denying her anything right now seemed wrong.

"Okay."

I got up and she was lifting the covers on her bed even as she scooted over to the left. I crawled in behind her and wrapped my arm around her waist. She sighed as she pressed her full body against me.

"That feels so good." Her bottom wiggled against my crotch and I had to bite down on the urge to make a sound.

"It's the drug," I said tightly.

It's what MDMA did. Increased pleasure and feelings of emotional warmth.

She was stroking my arm that was over her stomach, and I thought maybe this wasn't the best idea.

"I don't care. It feels so good." She did this full-on body wave and it felt too damn good to me too. So good I squeezed her a little, telling her, I hoped, she needed to stop.

"Jake..."

"Try to sleep." The sooner she fell asleep, the sooner I could get back to the floor.

"I can't. I'm too awake."

That was the drug too. I was going to have to suck it up. For her.

"Please," she said.

"What?"

"I've... I've never... I mean I've tried, but I've never..."

"What?"

"Had an orgasm."

I closed my eyes and tried to think of anything else except what Ellie would look like coming. It didn't work. I remembered that night I saw her, heard her. I remembered that last groan of frustration.

"I can't stop thinking that if Bobby did that to me, that would be my first experience. Then what if I could never do it again? I would never get to have an orgasm. Ever."

"Shh, shh," I said, trying hush her. It was the drug. It was still in her system. She was feeling the effect of it, but it didn't make hearing what she was saying any easier. In fact it was making *it* a hell of a lot harder.

"I feel like I could now. With you. If you were touching me. I know we can't have sex, but maybe you could do that for me. Just that."

That was it. I needed to get up and get out of the bed now. Go back to my room and let her suffer the effects of the drug on her own. Except I could hear the desperation in her voice.

"Please, Jake."

Fuck.

I tried not to think about how right or wrong this was, but in the end I thought if I could make her feel good, if I could give her her first orgasm, that might be what she remembered most about this night.

I just needed to stay in control. This was just about her and getting her off. It had been a while, but I was pretty sure I remembered how to do that.

I slid my hand that had been around her waist down her stomach. I closed my eyes and tried to be as removed as I could be. I felt the soft hair of her pussy and pressed my fingers against her. Immediately, she pressed back as if she was seeking them out. I dipped further and I could feel that she was already slick. Her neck arched and her body pressed against me. Then she was spreading her thighs, lifting one over mine.

It was the trust that killed me. After what had happened to her, she still trusted me implicitly to do this for her and take nothing else.

I dipped my hand lower and she gasped. I started with gentle strokes just to open her up, and that had her thrashing a bit. I pushed my other arm under her neck and wrapped it over her breasts to hold her more firmly against me, even as I started to slip my middle finger inside of her.

"Jake," she cried. "Please. More. I can feel it. It feels so good."

I pushed my hips away from her. I didn't want her to know how hard I was. Between her arousal, the adrenaline, and the violence that were still pulsing through me, it was impossible to not be fully erect.

Instead I just concentrated on her, and what she liked by the sounds she made. She was so slick and tight, but she was moving her hips in rhythm with my thrusts, pushing my finger deeper inside her.

I pulled away.

"Nooo!" she wailed and brought her hand down over mine. Pressing it against her.

"Trust me, Ellie. Let me do my thing."

She moved her hand away and I brought my thumb down on her clit. It was a hard little nub and her whole body tightened like a bowstring when I found it.

"Oh, Jake. That's it. Please don't stop. Please don't stop. So good!"

I sent two fingers inside her this time and she bucked. She was so damn wet. I tried not to think about how she felt, how she sounded. Only on what I was doing. Her breaths were coming faster, her hips were pumping. I pressed down on her clit again with my thumb.

"Jaaaaaaake."

"Come on baby, come for me. Just let go."

And then she did. I could feel her body jerk. The tug of her pussy squeezing my fingers. Her soft cries as the pleasure overtook her. It was unlike any other sexual experience I had ever had.

I held her as she came down from the pleasure of it. I held her as she started to cry softly. I held her until I knew she was asleep. Then I forced myself to get out of the bed and lay down on the floor next to her instead.

I did that because I liked holding her too damn much.

Soundlessly, I moved the fingers I'd used to make her come under my nose and inhaled.

I think that's when I knew I was completely and totally fucked.

Ellie

I WOKE up feeling as if someone had taken all the joy out of the world. Wow, this sucked. I couldn't believe people actually chose to take drugs like that if the aftereffect was this.

I guess the same could be true of drinking and a hangover. I had never had a hangover, so I couldn't be certain.

Cautiously I looked over the side of my bed. The blanket and pillows were gone. So was Jake.

I tried to wrap my head around what happened between us and how I felt about it. It was going to be super awkward to see him, that was for sure. Also not exactly up on the sexual etiquette of what to do the day after you begged someone to make you come.

Was a thank you enough? Should I be thinking more along the lines of a gift?

What I wasn't thinking about... Bobby.

Or at least not thinking much about him.

Truthfully, there was a certain comfort in doing *that* with Jake. Yes, this thing had happened. He'd touched me. He'd put his fingers inside me. Made me come. It was all super intense. Although in some ways it had seemed... okay. Even right.

At the end of the day, there was no one I trusted more. Who respected me more. Jake wouldn't tease me or taunt me with my confession. He wouldn't use what he'd done to press anything between us. He was the one who understood how powerful sex could be and why we needed to be careful about it.

I understood that better. The physical pleasure of what

he'd done to me had been awesome. Amazing. I really hoped now that I'd crossed that barrier I would be able to figure out how to do it myself.

But it was the intimacy of it all, I thought, that was really profound. Feeling his arms around me, hearing his voice close to my ear. It was like he'd completely wiped away the horrible memory of what Bobby had done by replacing it with a caring and devoted Jake.

If we'd been having sex since June, when I wanted to change our relationship, and he decided at some point he wanted out of the marriage—it would be as devastating as a real divorce for me.

Which meant I needed to move forward with my plan sooner rather than later. Because knowing what it was like to be held by him, to be pleasured by him... I shivered. It was only going to get worse.

I pushed myself out of bed and forced myself through my morning ritual, much like I had through my nightly one. I needed coffee though, if I was going to work up the energy for a shower, and I couldn't help but think the caffeine would help clear this funk I was in.

Downstairs, Jake was sitting at the kitchen table reading one of his scintillating (not—*so* boring) animal husbandry magazines.

"Hey," I said, standing in the doorway of the kitchen, hesitant of what his mood would be.

Come on baby, come for me.

The words were suddenly there in my head. His breath in my ear. The way he made my body feel. I might have been drugged, but obviously I hadn't forgotten anything about last night. I could feel my cheeks flame.

He looked concerned. Not aroused. Sure. Because he hadn't wanted to do that to me. Not really.

"How are you feeling?" he asked.

"Like I've swallowed everyone else's sadness."

He huffed. "It's the..."

"Drug. I figured."

"More water," he grunted.

I did as he suggested, because if water would fix this I would gladly drink a gallon of it. Then I got my cup of coffee and sat down across from him.

He was looking at me again, only this time I could see it in his expression. We'd moved on from the physical impact of the drug to something else.

"So... awkward much?"

"I don't know," he said quietly. "Is it?"

I glanced up at him. He was still just Jake. My Jake. That hadn't changed.

"Maybe not as bad I thought."

"Good. You're... okay then with... what happened?"

I nodded.

"You don't think I took advantage..."

"No," I stopped him. "If anything I'm the one who... you know, who took advantage."

"You didn't," he said tightly. "We both know what it was about. We can leave it at that."

"Right. Let's blame the drug," I offered.

He seemed to like that idea because his eyes got wider. "Yes. It was... the drug."

I nodded, then bit my lip, remembering all the stuff I'd said to him.

"Sorry for all the begging and pleading."

He actually managed a tight chuckle. "Trust me. Guys like the begging and the pleading... at least in bed."

"Uh... thank you for the... you know. It was good."

His mouth got tight, but he said nothing in response to that.

"I understand... better now," I continued. "Why you wanted to keep things platonic. It's super intimate. Us splitting up is going to be hard enough. For both of us, I think."

He didn't say anything to that either.

"Anyway. Thanks again. For the Bobby thing, too. You're always saving me."

Another grunt.

Then it occurred to me. "Wait? Why were you there? It felt like I called your name and you just popped out of the door like my own version of Superman."

"I was bored, so I thought I would stop by Pete's and have a beer. Then if you needed a ride home, you wouldn't have to worry about drinking. I was... just pulling up to the bar when Chrissy called me. Said you were acting funny and you had only had one glass of wine. I had a feeling... I told you to watch yourself around Bobby."

Here it was. Now that the threat was over, it was lecture time.

"I know. I didn't think he was... I mean I knew he was a jerk, but I never thought... Never once..."

"It might have been my fault," Jake muttered.

"Your fault. How?"

"I told him he wasn't good enough for you. He might have seen that as... a challenge. I don't know. Some kind of payback against me. It doesn't matter. He's going to jail for it. You should go up and take your shower. Then we're heading into town to talk to Sheriff Barling."

I knew it was the right thing to do. But I also knew the reality of the situation. Sarah Parker, who was two years ahead of me in school, got super drunk at a bonfire. She said

Jeff Tillerson raped her and no one did anything about it. Jeff said she consented and it was his word against hers.

This was going to be the same thing. Yes, my blood sample would indicate I was drugged, but all Bobby had to say was that I took the drug willingly. Still, at least by going to the sheriff everyone in town would know. Riverbend liked its gossip. If it came down to people believing me or Bobby, I had to think people would be on my side. At the very least this would also make every other girl in town cautious around him.

JAKE SLAMMED the door of the truck closed and I winced.

"That is such total and complete horseshit!"

It wasn't funny. At all. Still, I couldn't help but smile a little at Jake's outrage.

Our meeting with Sheriff Barling went as I suspected. While he believed me, there would need to be a witness who saw Bobby intentionally spiking my drink without my knowledge. Sheriff Barling would talk to Pete, who had been working the bar last night, as well as anybody else who he could find who was there. But unless someone actually saw what Bobby did and came forward, there was not enough evidence to actually charge him for a crime.

"He almost... he almost...."

"Don't say it," I said, patting Jake on arm. "I can't stand the word."

"How come you're taking this so calmly?"

"Because he didn't get away with it. You beat the shit out of him, everyone in town is going to know what a creep he is, and I'm a feminist, remember? I'm well versed in the fact that one of the atrocities in this country is that violence against women is often difficult to prove in court."

"I'm going to kill him."

"You're not going to kill him, Jake. In fact you're lucky he didn't press assault charges against you."

He was practically growling now.

"Thank you for sticking up for me."

"This is wrong."

"Sing it, sister." I raised my fist in the air.

More growling.

"Let's go home. You remember what Dad always used to say. A ranch can't run itself."

"Your father would have killed him."

I considered that. My father would have liked to have killed Bobby. That's for sure. But my father had way more of a hair-trigger temper than Jake did. Jake was always the reasonable and calm one. The guy who could talk two guys down from a fight.

I had never seen him like he was last night. As violent as he was. I remembered thinking if I didn't stop him he would have beaten Bobby indefinitely.

"Jake, if you go to jail for murder think what that would do to Wyatt? He'd be devastated."

More growling.

We were both quiet for a while when he asked me, "Ellie, do you need to talk to someone? You know you can tell me anything and I'll listen, but if you need someone else. Someone who understands..."

"You mean a therapist? Riverbend doesn't have a shrink, Jake. You know that."

"You have a car, Ellie. You can go where you need."

I knew that. I just didn't know if I needed a therapist. I didn't feel traumatized. Obviously there wasn't anything sexually messed up with me or I wouldn't have been begging Jake to get me off last night. If anything I was super pissed. That I was stupid enough to fall for Bobby's *forgive me* bullshit.

"I think I'm okay, Jake."

He reached over and grabbed my hand. "You'll let me know if you're not."

I squeezed his back. Looking down at it, at his fingers and thumb, I thought about what he'd been doing with that hand last night, and I quickly let it go.

He must have guessed where I was going with that too, because he shifted in the car seat and I could see that the muscle at the back of his jaw was flexing.

Yes, it was time to act on the plan.

FOURTEEN

Ellie
November

I GOT BACK from the appointment in town with Howard and tried to predict Jake's reaction. The good news was I didn't have to use the nuclear option. Which was putting the ranch up for sale. The bad news was there was no magic clause in the trust that would let me break it early.

However, what Howard did find were these companies that would buy out the trust my dad had set up for me with my mom's life insurance money. Meaning they take twenty-five percent of the total, but I get my money now. Howard discouraged it as not a financially sound move, but knowing the amount it would leave me with was more than enough to do what I needed to do, the decision was easy.

Twenty- five percent to free Jake was definitely worth it.

I could have told Jake what I was trying to do, but any

time I thought about it I kept coming back to the idea that it was better if I presented it to him as already being done.

This way he couldn't talk me out of it. Because, not going to lie, it probably would have been pretty easy to do. I had to remember I was doing this for him. Saving him for once, and it helped to keep me focused.

I officially signed the paperwork, and the money would be deposited in my account in three to five business days.

I came in the front door and made my way back to the kitchen, where I could hear him.

He was listening to some country music while he was stirring something in pot.

"Smells good."

"Beef stew."

"When did you learn how to make beef stew?"

"When I looked up on Google, *how do you make beef stew*. What's in the bag?"

I pulled out the bottle of champagne I bought. To kind of make this a celebration.

His eyes narrowed. "How did you buy that?"

Right, because it was one thing to drink at Pete's, but another thing to buy alcohol underage.

"I bought it from Pete. Told him I needed something to celebrate."

"Celebrate what?"

I swallowed. I put the champagne down on the kitchen island, took my coat off, and tossed it on one of the kitchen chairs.

Then I couldn't delay it any longer.

"Your freedom," I said and tried to smile. I probably looked really lame.

"What does that mean?"

He was giving me his full attention. He turned the music off and put a lid on the stew.

"Okay, remember when I said that I could fix our problem? Well, I found a way and I did it."

"What problem? Ellie, what are you talking about?"

"The only reason we stayed married was because of the money. I couldn't give you what you needed to buy the land, and we needed to take the loan from the bank to save the ranch. I found a way around all that. We have the money now. We can get divorced. Whenever we want."

I choked a little on the word *divorce*, but other than that I think it all came out as well as it could have.

He crossed his arms over his chest and glared at me. "Ellie, what's this about?"

"It's about what I said. Getting a divorce, giving you your life back. It's what you wanted."

"What I wanted?" he asked quietly.

"When we had that fight and you said you were trapped and you hated me…"

"Damn it, is that what this is about? You said you accepted my apology," he snapped at me.

"I did. I do. That's not what matters, Jake. What you said was the truth. You are trapped and it would be really easy to resent me for that. I couldn't have that. I couldn't have you stay in a situation where you would even be able to think the word *hate*, much less actually feel that about me."

"Ellie, I was pissed. Frustrated. I blew up. You said you were okay, but this whole time you weren't? Talk about holding a grudge."

Okay now I was starting to get pissed off. I was making this huge sacrifice for him and he was angry with me?

Immediately, I realized I needed to calm down. I was dropping what was a pretty big bombshell on him and it was going to take him time to process it. Eventually, he would see that I was right.

"This is not a grudge, Jake. Listen to me. We can't do this for another two and a half years. I can't not be jealous the next time there is another Carol..."

"There won't be another Carol. That was a mistake."

"Then what? You're going to live like a monk for the next two and a half years? You were right. I can't get into bed with you every night, have sex with you every night, and then watch you walk away. But I also can't bear the thought of you being with anyone else. Or me, for that matter. That does make us trapped."

"Why does this constantly have to be about sex, Ellie?"

"It's not sex, Jake it's us! We don't know what we are. We're not lovers. We're not a couple. But we're not just friends anymore. We're in this weird limbo and it's not sustainable. You are the most important person in my life. I'm the most important person in yours. I don't want you to end up hating me."

"I would never hate you," he growled. "I was pissed. I said something I shouldn't have. I thought it was over."

I took a deep breath. I had to hit him with the hard punch. If only to get him to really hear what I was saying.

"Do you want to stay married to me? Forever?"

His mouth opened and then he snapped it closed.

I nodded. "You told me before when you married me, you thought it was temporary. You said sex would complicate everything between us and you were right. We're at this place where if we don't walk away, I think we'll drive each other crazy with everything we're not."

"Walk away? Where the hell am I going to go? I don't have a house, remember?"

This was the second part of the plan. I called it Phase II, a.k.a. Save My Sanity.

"I've been thinking and I decided I want to give college a try. I always knew that ranching would be my life, but I never expected for it to happen so soon. I've never gotten a chance to even think about wanting something else. Now that I have the money, I can do that. I can go to school, branch out a little, and you can live here until you have a chance to get your house fixed. I'll hire someone to replace me in terms of what I was contributing work-wise, so you're not stuck with it all. I can handle the books from school, but you'll still need another pair of hands full time. Howard's already put an ad in most of the ranching magazines for me."

He didn't interrupt my speech, which I thought was a good thing.

"That's what you really want? To leave here and go to school?"

No, it wasn't what I really wanted. But anything else was not fair to him.

"I think if we're going to try and go back to being what we used to be to each other, we're going to need space."

"Space."

He said the word like it was equivalent to *shit*.

"Okay. Then tell me what you think. What do you want?"

His jaw clenched. "It's not about what I want, Ellie. It's about what you want."

"No. It isn't. I asked you to save me, and you did. You lived up to your part of the bargain. Now we can end this. Why are you so angry about that?"

"How?"

"How..."

"The money. How did you get the money?"

"This annuity company bought out my trust fund. They take a pretty steep cut, but I get the money up front."

He ran his hand through this hair. "Son of... That was supposed to be your security blanket."

"Jake, there's enough money to pay off the loan, pay you what you're owed, and send me to school. Beyond that, it gets us out of this situation."

"I didn't think we were *in* a situation. I thought we were living our lives."

"Because it's not the same for you," I cried.

"What the hell does that mean?"

"It means... I have feelings, Jake. And I know what you're going to do. You're going to take those feelings and justify all of them. I've done it too. You're a replacement for my father. What I'm feeling is gratitude. I'm too young to differentiate between what's real and what's not because I've never known anything else. But it doesn't change the fact that they are there. Maybe this really isn't about you. Maybe I'm doing the selfish thing and saving myself two and half years of agony. This split is going to hurt me. I told you that. It will hurt worse the longer we go on like we're doing now."

He stared at me for a second, hands on his hips, like he was processing everything I said.

"If I said I did want to stay married to you, then what?"

For a second it felt like my heart was going to burst. Like he was offering me this dream come true. Except I knew when I'd laid this out in my head, I had to be careful for things like this.

"I would say I have doubts about that. That I would always have doubts because I knew when we married you thought it was temporary and not because you loved me. I think we *have* to do this. For both our sakes."

"When?"

I blinked. "Whenever we want. The money will be in the bank in a few days. I'll settle the loan and sort out the rest. I've already signed up for courses and arranged for a dorm room. I need to be there the first week of January. Actually I was hoping you could take me. I'm not allowed to have a car on campus my first year."

"You've been planning this for weeks," he said as if I cold-cocked him. "And you didn't say a damn thing to me."

"I wanted to wait until I knew I could do it all. The college acceptance came through last week. Also I wasn't really sure how you would react."

"Not sure?" he asked, exasperated.

"You gave up two years of your life, Jake. For me. I couldn't ask you to give up another two and a half. Not when there was something I could do to fix it. I thought you might actually be... relieved. You said when you started seeing Carol, you thought that might be a way to return us to the way were. It wasn't. I only got angry and resentful with you. This is my attempt. Time away. Separation. Then maybe when I come back and you're living on your land, we can find a way to become... friends again."

Jake

SHE WAS RIGHT. I hated that she was so damn right. There was no way we were going to keep this up for two years. No way I was going to keep my hands off her for two more years. Not when I knew what she felt like, what she sounded like when she came.

God, what she sounded like.

Except I had started kind of getting used to the idea that it wasn't such a bad thing. Yes, we came into this marriage in the strangest of ways. Yes, it would be really hard to know if her feelings were legitimately about me and not about the situation. But would it be the worst thing to be married to your best friend?

Still, the idea of her going away... in some ways I hated it. In other ways I thought it was something she needed to do. We married when she was sixteen freaking years old. She'd never spent more than a week away from this ranch her whole life.

She said we needed space for us to become friends again. The truth was she needed time to explore the world if we were going to be something beyond friends. She had to have the opportunity for once in her life to make a choice.

The choice she'd lost the day Sam fell to his knees, clutching his chest.

"Say something," she prompted. "Are you really mad?"

"I'm not mad, Ellie. I'm... stunned. I wasn't expecting this."

"But I'm not wrong. Am I?"

"You were wrong not to discuss this with me. We should have done this together."

"It was my money and my decision."

She lifted her chin then and I had this crazy urge to sit her on the kitchen island and show her exactly who she was messing with. Then I remembered all the reasons I kept myself from touching her.

The same reasons she gave for leaving.

What if I had just fucked her?

I let out a sigh. "Then when?"

"When what?"

"When do you want to do this? Divorce."

Her lip wobbled and I could see she was telling the truth about this hurting. She wasn't alone. It felt like I was asking her when she wanted to cut off my right hand.

"How about after Christmas? Right before I leave. That way no one is asking us a bunch of questions around the holidays."

I nodded. "Okay. Tell Howard to do what he's got to do."

"Should I pop the cork?"

"No." This wasn't something to be happy about. "How about we save it for Christmas? Our last one."

Geez, now I could feel my own damn lip beginning to wobble. Ellie was going to leave me. Ellie was going to go to college and learn new things and meet new people. Everything was going to change.

I hated it but I had to accept it.

"Good idea. Champagne doesn't really go with beef stew anyway. Hey, speaking of Christmas, what do you want this year?"

Her. I wanted her.

"I need socks."

She made a face. "Jake, I'm not getting you socks for Christmas. That's lame."

I turned back to the stove and ran a spoon the through the stew. "You asked. I answered."

"I'll come up with something way better."

She usually did. "Stew is ready. Hang up your coat and for the love of God take your boots that have been sitting by the back door all damn day upstairs."

"Yes, sir. Grouchy much? You would think a man who's just been given his parole would be a lot more chipper."

"I want to live to see my freedom, and if I trip over those boots one more time I may not."

We were going through the motions. Saying the right things. Keeping it as normal as we could.

We were both lying. I knew it.

FIFTEEN

Ellie
Christmas

IT SNOWED. Not the scary snow of the storm. Just enough to make it so we didn't have to go anywhere. Didn't have to see anyone. It was nice. Because it was our official last day as a married couple. We were scheduled to meet Howard tomorrow morning to sign the papers and file them with the court. Next week Jake was going to take me to college.

It was happening. So today was our day.

Jake was burning the bacon just the way I liked it. I was watching him while sipping on my coffee and chatting about school.

"What if I don't make any friends?"

"You'll make friends."

"What if my roommate doesn't like me?"

"Try not to leave your shoes by the door and maybe you'll stand a chance."

"Did you talk to Rich about living in the bunk house?"

Rich was the guy we hired as my stand-in. He was older than Jake, divorced and currently without residence. The good news was Jake would have plenty of time with him to show him the ropes. Then if he worked out he could stay on as the foreman when Jake went back to his ranch.

Because that was the other thing that happened. I gave Jake the money he needed and he put a down payment on the land. Talley land was officially in Talley hands once again.

I thought he'd be happier about it. Talk about his plans for the future more, but he didn't. The truth was, since the divorce was decided we were both really going through the motions. Pretending this thing wasn't happening even though it was.

One thing I was worried about school, I knew it was where Bobby had planned to attend. I was okay after the "incident" but it wasn't like I ever wanted to see him again. Jake, having not been satisfied with the whole no jail thing, took it upon himself to track down Ted MacPherson in Jefferson. Last I heard Bobby was now living and working with his father, so hopefully that settled that.

"He seemed fine with it," Jake said about Rich as he served me my burnt bacon.

I didn't wait for the eggs and I started right in. As always it was delicious.

"What do you want to do after breakfast?" he asked.

"Presents! Presents! Presents!"

"You said, and I quote, *let's wait and do presents after dinner, that way we'll have something to look forward to all day*."

"Yes, and I see now that was stupid."

"We can do presents," he relented.

I thought about it and I started to agree with my former self. Presents could wait until tonight. I had a really big one to give him. One I hoped he would accept. But that would be better done after some champagne.

"Let's go for a ride," I suggested. "It stopped snowing, and who knows when I'll have a chance to ride Petunia again."

"Okay."

So we finished eating and dressed for the cold and headed out to the barn. I mounted up and Jake on Wyatt followed me out. Jake took the lead and I clicked Petunia into a gallop to keep up. Not that I ever needed to encourage her. Wherever Wyatt went, that's where Petunia wanted to go.

Like mother like daughter.

It was so quiet as we rode. A soft layer of snow, no wind, just us and the sound of the horses breathing. I thought we were meandering, but when we got to an overlook I realized where Jake had led us.

From where we were on the ridge, we could see down further into the valley. Across the stream was Talley land.

"Does it feel good? Knowing it's yours again?"

He nodded but he was quiet.

"When are you going to get started on the house?"

"Next week. I talked to a contractor Pete knows. He thinks the best thing is to level it to the ground, clear out the debris, and build on the foundation."

I thought about the irony in that statement. That's what me leaving was also supposed to do. Clear us out, so we could get back to the foundation.

Unless that wasn't what I was doing at all. Unless I was

doing this awful thing that would end us.

What if he met a woman next week? What if he fell in love with her? What if I had to sit at his wedding? What if I had to hold his child by another woman?

It would be heartbreaking. But so would looking up from the kitchen table five years from now, realizing he didn't really love me. That he'd stayed with me only out of loyalty and devotion.

"I'm getting cold," I told him. "I'm heading back."

"Me too."

We finished our ride and didn't talk the rest of the way back. I was trying to believe this was a special day. A good day for us, but the truth was it felt like some heavy weight was sitting on our shoulders.

I made hot chocolate for both of us. That didn't help.

We watched *It's a Wonderful Life* together. That didn't help.

I managed to make a turkey that was pretty darn tasty, if I did say so myself. That helped a little.

Champagne. The trick was the champagne.

"It's like drinking fizzy water," Jake complained.

We were sitting in front of the fire with our stacks of presents opened, the wrapping already cleaned up. I got Jake a new pair of work boots, which he needed; socks, which he wanted; a new pair of pajamas in case he ever had to save another woman's virtue someday and she made him sleep on the floor next to her.

And a picture of me. One he'd taken. Just with his phone one day when I had been goofing around on Petunia. It was one of those rare moments when I was smiling but I didn't think my teeth were too big. I had a print copy of it made and framed. So he wouldn't forget me when I was gone.

I think he liked it. He stared at it for a while.

He got me flannel pajamas with tiny little flowers, which I was currently wearing, and this really cool leather satchel with my initials stitched into it to carry around my school books, he said. I loved it.

"It tickles my nose. I like it." I poured myself another glass and then he took the bottle from me.

"Any more and it will make you sick."

"Killjoy."

"That's me. It's late. I'm going to bed. Big day tomorrow."

"Yeah." He got up and took the nearly empty champagne bottle back to the kitchen. I heard him pour himself some water. Then he made his way back to the living room and poked his head around the corner.

"Night, Ellie. Merry Christmas."

"Night, Jake. Pretty good day today?"

"Very good day today. See you in the morning."

I didn't move for a while. Just sipped my champagne and waited. I had one shot at this and I figured I needed him in the right frame of mind. Lazy, comfortable, near ready to fall asleep but not quite there.

Finally I got up and followed him upstairs. I made a quick stop at my room to pick up what I needed. Then I made my way down the hall to his room. I knocked quietly even as I was opening the door.

Jake had been in bed and was just now swinging his legs to the floor.

"Ellie, what's up? Is something wrong?"

I walked over and stood in front of him. I thought I would be more afraid, but I wasn't scared at all.

"I have something else I want to give you. I want you to hear me out. I want you to be my first, Jake. Because you are everything you said my first time should be. I trust you. I care for you. I know you'll be gentle with me and I just can't imagine doing this for the first time with anyone else. Tomorrow is happening. We both know how this ends. So no chance of either of us getting more hurt. Please, Jake. Just this one last thing. For me."

He reached out and put his hands on my hips and rested his head against my breasts. I stroked his hair because he seemed to need the comfort.

He sighed. "I can't..."

It hurt but I guess understood.

"Not," he finished. "I can't not have you. Okay. Just this once."

My heart started to pound in my chest. I held up the condom I brought and he took it out of my shaky fingers.

I stepped away from him and lifted my flannel top over my head, then quickly pushed my bottoms off and stepped out of them. No underwear, so I was naked. In front of Jake.

"You're right," I whispered. "It's a little scary, but not so bad."

He touched me then and I thought I might faint. Just his finger running along my collarbone, then down the center of my chest. He didn't touch my breasts. He did tickle my belly button.

"You're gorgeous," he whispered.

If he said so.

Then he was lifting me and turning me so I was on the bed. I scrambled under the covers and I saw him bend down to get rid of his boxer briefs. I knew he wore boxer briefs because along with socks and the shoes I bought him a set of those as well.

"We're going to take this slow."

"Okay."

"You sure about this, Ellie?"

"One hundred percent."

He kissed me and that made it easier. I could focus on how wonderful that was, because the few times we did kiss it was electric. I got lost in the taste of him, the feel of him.

Then he moved closer to me. Brought my naked body up against his and oh my god!

It was amazing. His body was so warm, it was like snuggling up against this big bear. I could feel the fuzz of hair on his chest, his legs, his arms and his... dick (remember I promised never to call it by a nickname.)

Then his hand that had been holding my face slipped down and cupped my breast, and that was amazing too. He teased my nipple in a way that kind of hurt and made me bump up against his thigh. He used that thigh to hold my legs down so I couldn't move at all. I had to just feel. His dick was pressed against my belly. It was very hard and very hot and it felt way bigger than I remembered from the towel incident.

As in, I'm not sure it was going to fit big. But I would deal with that when the time came.

For now it was all good. He kissed my neck. He slid down on the bed and kissed the tops of my breasts.

He sucked my nipple into his mouth.

"Jake!" I gasped.

He lifted his head, and while the light wasn't on I could still see the glimmer in his eyes. "Feel it, Ellie. Take it all in."

He slid lower and this time I could feel the stubble of his chin along my stomach. Suddenly his fingers were covering my pussy and I thought about the last time he did this and what it had felt like.

"Yes, that."

"This?" he asked, sliding a finger deep inside.

"Ohhhh yes. Yes please."

"Ellie, I want you to spread your legs for me."

He was sliding again and I did as he asked. Because I trusted him. He was going to make this the best first time ever.

"Holy crap is that your tongue!" I started to back away, but he held my hips in place.

"Relax and enjoy it. I promise you this is going to feel so good."

He was doing chin rub thing over my lower belly and it did feel good, so I did what he asked.

I understood the concept of oral sex. I knew people did it. But he was right there. Like RIGHT THERE. And his tongue—

"Ohmygod, ohmygod." He was soooooo right. His finger was still pushing inside me and his tongue was slithering all around, and it was like all the heat from the center of the universe was focused between my legs.

I twisted, I writhed, but he was relentless and when he pushed a second finger deep I came so hard.

He seemed to have figured it out. It might have been me screaming or clenching my fingers in his hair so hard that if I pulled I might have made him a bald man in an instant.

I felt delicious. I felt replete. I felt like a fucking woman. Except it wasn't over. The main event was still to come. I could hear it happening when he tore open the wrapper on the condom.

Then he was pushing between my legs, spreading them again. "I need you talk to me, Ellie. You have tell me when to stop."

Yeah, that wasn't going to happen. I was not stopping no matter what.

The first push was easy. My body was wet and relaxed. He was slipping in and in and then it started to sting and then oh fuck... "STOP!"

He pulled away and it was better. Then he looked up at me and I swear to god he was smiling. "Nice and slow. We've got all night."

I was less sure of that now, but he seemed to be. He slipped back in and again it was this steady press of pressure. This time it stung a little. Not as bad. And just when it was getting too intense he pulled back.

It was crazy but in that moment, even though I knew it was going to hurt, I wanted him back.

"More," I grunted.

"You ready for that?"

I nodded even as I bit down on my lower lip. My hands were wrapped around his biceps, which where huge as he was using them to hold his weight off me. All of his weight except his big freaking cock, that was.

He pressed in again and I waited for the sting, but it was just pressure this time. Then he was gone and I sighed so he came back again, faster this time.

The next time he did it, I tilted my hips up toward him and he slid even further, deeper.

"That's it, Ellie. Let your body get used to it. It knows how to do this."

It was like he was coaxing me through my first horse riding lesson. Well, I guess technically I was riding something. I whimpered a little but he was inexorable. In and out, in and out.

Until I needed something else. Something more.

I let go of his arm and cupped his ass cheek and tried to push him deeper. He groaned and his head fell back and then his hips started to move a little faster. Yes, that was it, that was what I needed. It kept building and building and it was different than when he had his mouth there—this felt like it was coming from inside me.

"Jake!!!"

And then it happened, this incredible pleasure/pain/pleasure that I couldn't stop. My whole body shattered apart and it was unlike anything I could have ever imagined.

Then I felt his hips snapping against me hard. He was so deep inside me. His breath was harsh against my ear. It was all so animalistic.

"Fuck! Ellie," he shouted even as he continued to thrust into me.

Then he was dropping on top of me and it felt as if Petunia had just landed on me. Still, I wasn't moving. Instead, I stroked his sweaty back and squeezed around his middle with my thighs.

After a minute he lifted his head. "You okay?"

"Fuck yeah."

He laughed and slowly disengaged his body. Then he got up, to deal with the condom I figured. It was weird. Like suddenly I was empty without him. I was sore and achy but I wanted him back. Inside me.

He came back and I wasn't exactly certain what to do. Should I get dressed and go back to my room now that the deed was done? But he settled the matter by climbing into bed and wrapping his arms around me, bringing my back up against his chest. His head on the pillow next to mine.

"Jake...on a scale of one to ten, that was an eleven."

He squeezed me and I couldn't help the tears that came. But he didn't seem to mind.

SIXTEEN

Ellie

I WOKE up to hear the sound of running water. It was disconcerting and even more so because I was in a strange bed.

A strange bed that smelled like Jake.

I felt the smug smile creep over my face. That's right. I got good and fucked last night by Jake Talley. (And no, I was not going to think about how this used to be my father's bed because that was a little gross and I wasn't thinking about my dad at the time so it was okay.)

The running water was the shower and suddenly it occurred to me it was morning and we were going to be getting divorced in a couple of hours. I had a few more things on my sex list I wanted to do before we called it quits.

I bounced out of his bed and ran down the hallway to my bathroom to pee and brush my teeth. Because minty breath was important.

Then I jogged, completely naked—so weird—back to his room, hoping he was still in the shower. He was.

I opened the bathroom door and I saw him behind the glass pop his head up.

"I got to do things last night," I said. "But I really didn't get to see a lot. I think it's only fair."

He was assessing me. Wondering what kind of mental state I was in right now. Was I going to cry and say I changed my mind about everything because we'd had sex?

Or was I going to proceed as planned?

Then he stopped assessing me and started looking at me. Wow. That was a look I could get used to. I shivered and my boobs shook and that seemed to decide him.

He slid the glass door open and stepped back. I stepped inside and closed the door, letting the hot water hit my back.

"Don't take this the wrong way, Jake. You're very handsome and built and I would love to take the time to study your body, but right now I'm mostly interested in your dick."

He huffed out a laugh. "As long as you call it by what it is."

"Right. Not going to call it a peen."

He closed his eyes in what I was sure was embarrassment. "You heard that?"

"Yep. Trust me, stopped listening soon after. Now if you will hold nice and still..."

I slowly dropped to my knees. Then I realized that wasn't comfortable on the tile floor. So I got up, opened the shower door, snagged a towel from the rack to put under my knees, and tried that again. Better.

He was already hard. "Is this a morning thing?" I asked.

"No, it's a you're naked and your tits are jiggling in front of me thing."

Good. I wanted it to be a reaction to me, not some biological function. It was definitely as big as I thought last night. Bigger than the dildo I bought for sure. Heavier. I reached up to stoke him in my hand and his thighs flexed.

"Show me how to do this," I asked, fascinated by how hard it was in contrast to how silky he felt in my hand.

His head leaning back on his shoulders, he told the ceiling, "You're doing fine on your own."

I tugged and pulled, loving the feel of him in my hand. Loving the way his breath grew harsh.

I was working my courage up for the ultimate introduction when Jake said the dirtiest thing I had ever heard.

"Fuck Ellie, you need to suck my cock. Now."

Wow. That was so flipping hot. I didn't hesitate, I popped the head of his cock past my lips, in my mouth along my tongue. Taking him as deep as I could. I could feel his hand in my hair, pulling me closer until it was too much and I had to back off. But then it was just like it was last night—as soon as I eased him out of my mouth, I wanted him back in deep.

I kept bobbing my head like that, shallow then deep, shallow then deep. And his whole body was getting tighter and tighter. I could taste his pre-cum, the salt of it. It wasn't gross at all.

Then Jake said the second dirtiest thing I had ever heard.

"I'm going to come. If you don't want me to come in your mouth, back off. Ellie—shit, I'm serious."

I was too. Deadly serious. If anything I sucked on him harder. I felt the first splash of it hit my tongue. I was still doing my head-bobbing thing even as I swallowed what was in my mouth. When it was over he stepped back. I hadn't even realized I had my fingers dug into his ass cheeks.

I could still taste him. Still feel him in my mouth. My sex was pulsing, but I thought I was still a little too sore to do anything about that. Jake was breathing heavy, like I had put him through some intense workout.

He helped me up and then he hugged me. Just that. The press of our two naked bodies squished together front to font for the first time.

For the last time.

"COME ON, Jake. It's only fair."

"I'm not doing this with you, Ellie."

We were sitting in the kitchen. Our appointment with Howard was in a few hours so we were relaxing until then. He was pouring me coffee and scowling at me. Considering I had only recently had his penis in my mouth, that didn't seem right.

"Why not? Just answer the question. On a scale of one to ten how good was that blow job?"

He glared at me.

"What? I need to know how much room there is for improvement."

"I'm not having this conversation with you right now."

"Uh, we're a little past that aren't we, Jake? Your penis, my vagina, remember?"

Then he did something unpredictable. Something I wasn't expecting. His hand slammed down on the kitchen island and caused me to jump.

"Damn it, Ellie! This is serious. Do you get that? I took your fucking virginity. It's mine. Now and forever. This is not some fucking joke to me."

With that he stormed out of the kitchen and I heard him

go upstairs. I was so startled by it, it took me a few minutes to react. Except I knew what I had to do.

I followed him upstairs and made my way down the hall to his bedroom. The door was open. He was sitting on the bed, his elbows on his knees, his hands linked.

"I'm sorry," I said from the doorway. "I know it's not joke. It was a big deal and I was trying to... I'm scared, Jake. About today, about next week. All of it. I was trying to cover up for that."

He glanced up at me and his eyes were intense.

"Would you believe me if I said I was scared too?"

"No. You're Jake Talley. A badass cowboy, and you're not afraid of anything."

He nodded. "Are we doing the right thing?"

"Yes," I said quickly before I could say anything else. Still, it was the best answer. I don't know why, but I was certain of it in my gut. We needed to take this step, to get to whatever the next step was.

"We better get ready then," he finally said.

"Okay. Let's do this."

Jake

I WAS SUPPOSED to do this. I was supposed to sit in this small conference room, as Howard called it, and do this. Ellie was sitting across from me in her graduation dress. The blue one with the small white flowers. It was too lightweight for the weather today, but it was her favorite and this was supposed to be some kind of event.

So I was supposed to sit here and not think about pulling her across the table, undoing the belt around her waist, ripping her panties off and giving Howard a show he would not soon forget.

No, I was not supposed to be doing that. Instead I was divorcing my wife.

"If you want to read through the documents, it's everything I've already discussed," Howard said.

I didn't want to read the document. I didn't want to be in this conference room.

I didn't want to divorce my wife.

I wanted to fuck my wife.

Howard slid the divorce decree in front of me. He did the same with Ellie. All I had to do was take hers and mine and tear them up. Grab her hand, tell her she was coming home and that this was over.

I couldn't. Because she would never believe it was what I truly wanted. And I would never believe it was what she truly wanted. We would always fall back on the circumstances. How we got here. Not why we were here.

This was our only option.

I wanted her to have this chance. I wanted her to go to college and meet new people and learn new things. I wanted her to have that opportunity to grow.

I didn't want it at my expense. Which was incredibly selfish of me, I guess.

I took a deep breath. I had to be strong enough for the two of us. I hadn't been last night. Last night I'd been weak. But when she gave me her little speech, offering her virginity as my last and best Christmas gift, she'd been right. We'd both known how this was going to end, so there were no surprises.

One time—well, two if you counted this morning (which I wasn't going to rank, but what had been without a doubt the most amazing fucking blow job of my life. Mostly I think because it was Ellie), and that was it.

Now we went our separate ways.

Only I didn't want to go anywhere she wasn't going.

I looked at her across the table. She had the pen in her hand. She seemed to be reading the document. She was probably pretending like I was. Then she looked up at me. I didn't know what she was thinking, but suddenly I felt like I was in a game of chicken. That whoever blinked first would lose.

I picked up the pen next to me and toyed with it. I could say no. I could make this not happen. I could convince her this was wrong. After last night I'm certain she would agree.

I could do that and it would mean taking away all her choices.

She thought she was giving me my freedom back. The reality was, I was giving her hers.

I signed and dated the page in front of me.

I felt sick.

She watched me do it. Waited to see me do it really. She nodded and then did the same.

"Ellie..."

Wait. Wait was the word I had been about to say, but it was too late. She was done. She lifted her chin as if to show how courageous she'd been in doing it.

She was.

Howard collected the papers from us. "I'll file these today."

We both nodded but said nothing.

"You two okay?"

He must have felt it. Whatever it was. I wasn't sure. I just knew that the room felt dark. Devoid of all light.

"Yes," Ellie barked. Like she was forcing the word out of her mouth. "This is a good day. We did it."

I stood and shook Howard's hand. Ellie needed to use the ladies' room, so I waited for her out in Sue Anne's area. Sue Anne was chatting about Christmas, but I wasn't paying much attention.

Eventually, Ellie emerged. I could tell she'd been crying, but she had her shit together now.

We walked outside, no longer married, and for the first time in my life I think I understood what the word *heartbreak* meant.

Ellie reached for my hand and I linked our fingers together.

"It's going to be okay, Jake. We've got this."

I hoped so. For both our sakes.

THE LOVER PART 3

ONE

Ellie
January

"WE SHOULD PROBABLY HAVE THE TALK," I said.

Jake was driving me to college. It was really happening. In another hour we would arrive at the university, and he would drop me off and head back to the ranch. I figured it made sense to get things settled between us.

Because we were divorced now.

Did I tell you that part? Short recap.

Jake married me to save me from a foster home after my dad died.

I fell in love with him.

He didn't fall in love with me.

We were hurting each other, so I came up with a way to divorce him.

Oh... and I gave him my virginity as a consolation prize.

It was really rather generous of me, I thought.

Now it was done. I was going to go to college, and he was going to start building his house so that when I was done school he could go back to living on Talley land.

We were both super excited about our prospects for the future.

Or not. Or we were both super miserable instead.

Still, it was important to me to set the record straight.

"To be clear, so there are no hard feelings. I'm single. You're single. You're free to date who you want, and I'm free to date who I want."

He glanced over at me. "Are you serious? I just took your virginity a few days ago. Can we maybe not talk about you dating someone else right now?"

"Fair point, but I wanted it on the record."

"Noted," he bit out.

I stared out the window, but there was nothing to see. "I think you should get a dog."

"Where is this coming from?"

"I don't want you to be lonely. I'll be at school with all my new friends that I'm hopefully going to make. You'll be on the ranch. Alone until Rich comes. You need company. Remember how much you loved Luke?"

Actually maybe it wasn't the best idea. Jake had adored that dog and it had nearly killed him when it was time to put him down. A sure sign he got too close to his animals. I was convinced he liked them more than people. Well, maybe not me.

"I'll think about it."

More silence. Which was not helping.

"Do you really think I'll make friends?" I asked. I was a person most people liked. It seemed reasonable. Only this was a university, not a small town in the sticks. What if people thought I was corny?

"Yes."

"It's also been a while since I had to do schoolwork."

"You'll be fine."

He was placating me. "I don't want to do fine, I want to do really well."

"You'll do that then."

It had been like this for the entire ride. Me chatting nervously, Jake being Jake.

I had no idea what he was thinking. If he was sad, relieved... heartbroken.

I was sad. I was nervous. I wasn't heartbroken though.

I guess it was because I didn't really see this as an end. Like we weren't quite at the conclusion of our story, but still in the middle of it.

Was it the sex that gave me hope?

I didn't know. The sex had somehow changed us. It was there. This tangible thing that happened. That we had done together. We were altered, and yet the same. It was just that one time. Neither one of us, I think, wanted to keep doing it. It would only make leaving that much harder.

I knew leaving was necessary. I had to go, if only so we could both see clearly what we wanted. Not going to lie, now that I was in the truck, heading away from the ranch, it was starting to dawn on me how truly hard this was going to be.

Finally we got to Missoula and then the university. I had the address for my dorm and Jake carried up all my stuff, mumbling I had brought too much. My scales were carefully packed in a box I kept in the back seat of the truck because I didn't want to risk their safety.

It was the last thing to be carried up, which I could do myself.

I set the box down next to me and waited for Jake to

realize the same thing. It was done. I was here, and there was nothing left to do except say goodbye.

"I don't know how to do this, Ellie. So I won't."

I nodded. I didn't know how to do this either. For the last two years Jake had been the center of my existence. The cause of all my happiness and all my pain. The idea of saying goodbye to him was unacceptable but inevitable too.

"You'll call? Check in?"

I nodded.

He nodded back. I watched him get in his truck. I heard the engine start and realized this was happening.

"Jake!"

He rolled down the window with a look that said *this had better be good*, because Jake was not a guy who liked dramatic farewells.

"We've got this. Right?"

He nodded again and I smiled.

I watched as he pulled away. Stayed there the whole time until his truck was out of sight.

Then I picked up my scales, looked up at my new home, and got ready to start my new life.

Three weeks later

IT WAS SUNDAY. I sat back on my bed in my dorm room and hit Jake's name on my cell.

He answered on the first ring.

"Hey," I said.

"Hey back. How are things going?"

I took a deep breath. "I want to come home. I think I made a mistake."

He sighed. I knew he was going to sigh. I also knew what he was going to say next.

"Ellie, you just got there."

"I know, but Jake, this is so..." I struggled for the word and finally landed on, "pointless."

Another sigh. "I thought you liked your roommate."

"I do." I did. Maryanne was cool and we were starting to get to know each other, but it wasn't home. With Jake.

"You said your business class was interesting."

"It is, but seriously most of it is stuff I've already taught myself over the past two years. I miss the ranch. I miss Petunia."

I missed him, but that didn't need to be said.

"You said you wanted to do this. You said you wanted to try this new experience."

"I know," I grumbled.

"You're homesick, Ellie. It will pass."

I didn't think so, but I knew after only a few weeks he wouldn't let me drop out this soon. He would see it as quitting, and he would remind me I'm not a quitter.

"Fine. I'll stick it out."

"That's my girl."

I smiled. Jake thought I was his girl.

"I got to go, Isabella is acting up. I think she might have an infection in a tooth."

"See? I should totally be there for that."

"That's why I'm here, Ellie. You're where you need to be right now."

Then I couldn't help it. I had to know. "Don't you even miss me a little bit?"

God, I hated how pathetic that sounded.

Another sigh. "This is the right thing for you."

His answer, or should I say his non-answer, didn't surprise me.

"The right thing blows."

"Call me next week?"

It was becoming our thing. Sunday night. One call per week. I wanted to call him every day, talk to him every day. But this seemed more measured. More controlled. As if Jake was a controlled substance I had to limit my use of in order to stay functioning.

"Yep. Tell Petunia I miss her and tell Isabella I hope she feels better."

"I'll get right on that."

"Bye."

"Night, Ellie."

I WAS SITTING in class the next day, listening to the TA drone on about profit and loss and thinking about Jake. About how he hadn't answered my question.

He had to miss me a little bit. I was missable. He'd said it before when I was freezing him out over the whole Carol (which now I sort of automatically hated everyone named Carol) thing.

He didn't say he *didn't* miss me. That would have been awful.

Not that this was much better.

"Who is he?"

I was startled by the guy sitting next to me.

"Who is who?" I asked him.

"Whoever it is you're mooning over?"

"How do you know I'm mooning over anyone?"

"Because you're the only girl in the room not drooling over the TA teaching this class, who by the way is HAWT."

He fanned himself with his hand. It was probably the most feminine gesture I had ever seen a man make except for on TV.

Which prompted me like an idiot to say, "Oh my god, you're gay like on TV."

Which he thought was the most hilarious thing he'd ever heard, to which he replied, "No honey, I'm gay like on reality TV."

"I'm sorry," I said immediately. "I didn't mean to be rude. I've just..."

"Never seen one in real life?"

I shook my head. Everyone in Riverbend had suspected David Tillerson, Jeff Tillerson's older brother, was gay, but nobody ever spoke about it. Certainly not David Tillerson.

"When class is over, you can buy me a coffee to make up for it and tell me all about the guy. I love a good romance."

Denny—he told me his name—walked me to the campus Starbucks. I ordered two coffees, and he looked at me like I had lost my mind. He changed the order to two caramel macchiatos and my life, as I knew it, was changed.

We sat down at a table and I thought I would never be able to have coffee again. Which was a shame, because I really liked coffee, but nothing would ever be as good as a caramel macchiato.

"So... who is he?"

"He's just a guy. From back home." I didn't want to tell him the story. One of the best parts about being here was that I didn't have to be Weird Married Ellie or Weird Divorced Ellie. At least for a while.

"Is he pining for you too?"

"I don't know. I guess if he missed me more, he would come get me and bring me home."

"And leave all this?" Denny said, gesturing around with this hand. It really was so strange to see this handsome man use his hands like that. Denny was definitely handsome, too. Blond, thin, but built. I imagined he did very well for himself with other gay guys, but obviously I wasn't going to go there.

"I don't think I'm cut out for college. I'm a rancher's daughter."

No, that wasn't right. I had been a rancher's daughter. What I'd learned by coming here was that I was rancher. Period. I belonged on my land and not in a classroom.

"Well, if you won't give me the gory details then there is nothing I can do to help. Which means as your new official first gay male friend, let me take this time to tell you that the color orange does NOT work for you."

I looked down at my shirt. I had never really given it much thought, but Denny seemed to know exactly what he was talking about.

Jake
Sunday

THE PHONE RANG and I swiped to connect the call. It was Sunday and I had been waiting for her. She was a little late tonight, but that was all right.

"Hey," she said.

"Hey back. How is it going?"

"Okay."

Okay was better than *can I come home*. She hadn't asked it since I told her no, but I could tell each week she wanted to. This time she sounded a little different. This time her *okay* was a little less depressing.

"Okay?" I prompted.

"I made another friend."

"What's her name?"

"His name is Denny. He's really funny."

Denny. Swell. My hand tightened on the phone.

The pause must have revealed something of my... irritation?

"He's just a friend, Jake. It's not... like that."

"Oh."

"There was a guy who asked me out, though. Which was so weird. Like he didn't know me at all. We had never talked. He just saw me in the bookstore and was like, *want to go out sometime?*"

Sometimes I forgot that about her. She truly didn't get it. How gorgeous she was. Of course any guy in his right mind who saw her would be attracted to her. Why not ask her out if he had a chance?

"What did you say?"

"I said I would think about it... but I don't know. I mean, I don't know him at all and I don't know if I feel comfortable going out with a total stranger."

This was the part where I was supposed to say *how are you ever going to get to know him if you don't go out on a date with him.*

Instead I said, "Go with your gut. If you don't want to go out with the guy, then don't."

"Okay. I won't. How is Isabella?"

"She's finally turning a corner. Sam thinks she's out of the woods for now." Sam was the large-animal vet in town. He'd been making weekly house calls. Probably to put my mind at ease. Everyone, I suppose, knew how I was with the animals in my care. Like an overprotective father.

"Good."

I thought to bring it up. To ask her if she was settling in better, but if she wasn't asking to come home I suppose that said it all.

I was happy about that. Happy she was making more friends. I was.

I was also lonely as hell and missing her like crazy. Not that I could tell her that. If she saw weakness in my armor she might attack, and I couldn't have that because I was fairly certain I might cave.

"Classes are still going good?"

I didn't know what else to ask about. I certainly didn't want to talk about guys in her world anymore. I only knew I wanted her to continue talking. Because it was Sunday night and Sunday night was Ellie night.

She rattled on and I took it all in, and when she finally said goodnight I got that feeling again in my chest.

The feeling that we had gotten this all wrong.

I didn't know it at the time, but Ellie was going to fix that with one really stupid mistake.

TWO

Ellie
February

"DENNY, have you ever been in love?"

We were sitting in the coffee house after class as usual. I had quickly become addicted as expected. See, that was how Starbucks did it. The great con. You drink one damn caramel macchiato, and suddenly the idea of paying four dollars for a cup of coffee doesn't seem like a stupid idea at all.

"Of course. Like a thousand times."

I glared at him. "It couldn't have been love if there were a thousand different guys. Which I'm having a hard time believing there are even a thousand gay guys in the entire state."

He tilted his head. "Okay, maybe not a thousand."

"Is it hard?" I asked, curious about a lifestyle I knew so

little about. "Being gay in Montana? People don't harass you still, do they?"

"Some. But it's not like it was years ago. Besides, being gay in Montana does have its upside."

"What?"

He leaned in and wiggled his eyebrows. "Gay cowboys. Hawt!"

I laughed.

"Why are you asking me about love? Are we back to the guy you are always mooning over but won't tell me about? Sister, have I not explained the advantages of a gay BFF? You can tell me everything you would tell your girl friends, only I can tell you what the guy is thinking from the male perspective. Remember just because I'm gay, doesn't mean I don't still think like a man."

"I told you it's complicated."

"That's the best kind of story!"

I thought about what I had done this week. I knew it was going to be a fight. One I thought I stood a better chance of winning over the phone.

Or not. Either way, this Sunday's call was not going to go well.

But I had made up my mind, and when I did that I could be really stubborn.

Denny was right. I was brooding again. Because Jake and I were going to have this fight first, but the next fight after that was going to be even worse.

I had to be strong.

"Oh my goodness... Speaking of hot cowboys. Yum! Please let him be gay, please let him be gay."

I looked over at the door that had just opened.

Holy shit. Jake! My heart nearly flew out of my chest and up into my mouth. He was here. In person. I was actually looking at him again and it was like this missing piece of my body suddenly reconnected.

"He's not gay," I told Denny almost breathlessly.

"Bitch, how do you know?"

"Because that is my... ex-husband."

Jake was looking around the coffee house as if expecting to find me here.

Denny's jaw dropped. He actually shut it closed with this finger. "You were married."

"I told you it's complicated."

"And you divorced thaattt? Girlfriend, are you insane? Oh look, he saw you. He's coming this way. Oh my goodness, is that scowl real? Holy shit, I think I'm going to crap my pants."

Jake approached the table. Apparently he was a little more pissed at what I had done than I realized. Not that it mattered. He was here, and suddenly for the first time in weeks I felt... happiness.

It was how I knew I had absolutely made the right decision.

"Hi Jake."

"Ellie."

"This is my friend Denny. Denny, this is Jake Talley."

Jake glared at Denny. I recognized it as his typical guy stare-down look. Denny had apparently never been on the receiving end of anything like it, because he popped up out of his chair and raised his hand.

"Don't hurt me. I play for the other team! Bye, Ellie." Then he took off at a near run.

Jake took his seat at the table.

"That's Denny?" he asked.

I lifted my chin. "Yes. You have a problem with him?"

"No."

"What are you doing here, Jake? How did you know where I was anyway?"

"I went to your dorm. Your roommate said you get coffee with your friend after class. As for why I'm here, you know why I'm here."

"You drove three hours to yell at me about the money."

"You're damn right I drove three hours to yell at you about the money. Did you think I wouldn't find it? How the hell did you even have access to my bank account?"

"I do your payroll, remember. Direct deposit."

"You're taking the money back."

I took in a deep breath, because I knew I was going to have to overcome generations of built-in Montana macho to make my argument.

"Jake, after the storm, when we realized we had to stay together, we talked about this. If you were going to put your life on hold, then we would work out a deal where you would be compensated for it. That's all that was. It was money you earned."

He was glaring at me again. "Do you know how that sounds? Like somehow you had to pay me for... for living with you."

I reached across the table and laid my hand on his arm. To make a point sure, but also just to touch him. Jake was here, and even if it was to yell at me it was still worth it.

"That's not it and you know it. Because of you, we got the loan from the bank. Because of you, we got back on our feet faster than I ever imagined. What does that make me if I take all of that and give you nothing in return?"

"A friend," he snapped.

"You said it yourself. It's more than just getting your land back. You have an operation to get up and running. You have a house that has to get built. Last week you told me you have made no progress at all. Take the money you earned and do that."

He said nothing for a while.

"You can afford this?"

I could. He probably wasn't going to like why I could afford it, but that was something I could tell him later. For the next fight. Now was about winning this argument.

"Yep. No problem."

His jaw was flexing, his nose was flaring.

"I'm right, Jake. You know it."

"I haven't even started thinking about what I want to build for a house. I can build anything on the foundation, but how the hell do I know what I want?"

I thought about the timing of that and my plans, but it's not like I had any control over that. Who knew how long it took to build a house? He probably needed to wait until spring anyway, when the weather was a little more forgiving.

"You'll figure it out."

He grunted.

This was a surprisingly easy victory. Given he'd been mad enough to drive out here in the first place. I figured now was a good time to redirect.

"How is Rich working out?"

"He's fine."

There might have been a pause there, but I couldn't tell.

"And Petunia? You're talking to her like I asked?"

"Hours every day. I find she's really easy to talk to."

I made a face at him. "Sarcasm doesn't become you."

He grunted.

I looked down at my coffee cup. I wasn't sure what happened now. Did he just get back in his car and leave now that the fight was over? Although I have to say, all things considered he'd rolled over pretty quickly, which was not like him. Maybe he was getting mellow in his old age. This boded well.

"So..." he said.

"So what?"

"So are you going to show me around this place or not?"

I clapped my hands. "Yes, you're going to stay for a while. Okay, first you have to have a caramel macchiato. It is the most delicious thing in the world."

"I'm not spending four bucks for a cup of coffee."

"Trust me, Jake. This is life-altering and so worth it. Then I'll show you the campus. And then we have to go to Eddy's for burgers later. They have the *best* burgers. Don't tell Frank I said that, but we're talking miles better."

"Miles, huh?"

"Miles and miles."

"All right. After you."

I was thrilled. I was over the moon.

Because Jake was here.

"WELL?" I asked him as he pulled his truck up to my dorm building. It wasn't very late, just after seven, but I knew he had a three-hour drive back.

"Consider my life altered."

I smiled. "I knew it. I told you Starbucks would change your life. Not to mention Eddy's."

"You like it here now," he said. A statement, not a question.

I didn't have the heart to tell him the truth.

"It's okay," I said quietly.

"You're not alone."

"No. I have friends."

"Good."

There didn't seem to be anything say at that point. I suppose I should have opened the door, hopped out, said goodbye and left. Except I didn't want to leave. I didn't want him to leave.

What I really wanted was to kiss him, but I had made that move in the past and had gotten burned by it.

"Fuck this," I heard him growl before he reached for me. His hand coming behind my neck, pulling me toward him. It was just lips and tongues at first. Urgent breaths, nibbling teeth. Except I needed more. More of him touching me, more of me touching him.

Jake must have agreed because he was hauling me over the center console so I was in his lap. The space was tight and awkward. Every time I shifted to rub myself along his body, my ass hit the steering wheel and the car horn let out a little yelp.

"Help me," I said even as I tried to get my hands to the buttons of his jeans.

"No," he grunted. The next thing I knew was being lifted and set back on the passenger seat. I was freaking five foot nine. He really should not have been able to lift me so easily.

I was trying to catch my breath, wondering what happened to make him kiss me and then what happened to make him push me away.

"I'm not fucking you in a truck outside your dorm."

"You seem angry. Are you angry?"

"I'm hard, Ellie. Hard and apparently staying that way. I didn't... I wasn't planning on..."

"Okay. Yeah. I understand. We should probably avoid the kissing and stuff."

"You being three hours away makes that easier. You being a foot away makes that more difficult."

I smiled at him. "Jake Talley, that might be the nicest thing you've ever said to me."

"Go, now. Before I change my mind."

"Okay, but you know I want you to change your mind."

"Ellie," he growled.

"Going. Going." I opened the door and hopped out of the truck. "See ya, Jake."

"Call me Sunday," he snapped.

And that was it. He left and I had to think about what that kiss meant.

That's when I knew I was going to need reinforcements.

THREE

Ellie

I MADE it upstairs to the second floor of the building. I used my key to let myself in the room.

Maryanne was sitting on her bed, reading. She looked up at me. It must have been all over my face. Well, certainly my lips... what I had been doing with Jake.

"Oh yeah," she said. "I'm going to need details."

I took out my phone. "Hold on. Denny is going to want to hear all of this too."

I texted him.

So do you want to hear the story about me and my ex-husband?

...

Yeeeeeessssss. I'm coming over. Doritos or Combos?

Doritos, I texted him back.

Okay, Doritos go best with margaritas. I'll be right over.

True to his word, Denny was right over with what

appeared to be a bucket of pre-made frozen margaritas, tequila included, and an economy-size bag of Cool Ranch.

While he poured drinks I shifted nine disks to the right side of the scale. It was a great day. It was an awesome day. But at the end of the day Jake left.

He was there at the ranch and I was here.

The three of us were on the floor between our two beds, drinking and eating chips, and I told them everything. About my dad dying and Jake marrying me. About the storm and the first kiss. And the second kiss. About Janet and Carol. Finally about us and why I needed to leave.

Denny sniffled. "That. Is. Epic."

"Wait. Back up," Maryanne said. "You had an amazing first time? Did you have an orgasm?"

I thought about it. "Two of them, actually. Before and during."

"During? During sex! Your first time?"

I sipped my on my red solo cup, which was filled with what looked like green slime but actually tasted delicious. "Yes, is that not normal?"

"Uh, no. I squealed like a pig during my first time, then walked around for the next two days with my legs bowed."

"He was really patient," I offered.

"So what happens next?" Denny asked me.

I shrugged. "I don't know. I deposited more money in his account, because I realized I'm not staying and I want to make sure he gets his house done before I go back. That's why he came here today. To yell at me about the money."

Denny made this coughing sound, which came out sounding like *bullshit*.

"Agreed," said Maryanne.

"Agree with what?"

"He did not drive three hours to yell at you," Denny

explained. "The money was an excuse. He drove here to see you. To spend the day with you. To see what your life is like here. Then at the end of the day, he kissed you. That doesn't say pissed-off man, that says... he's missing you."

"It's so messed up," I said, falling back to lie on the floor. The margaritas were starting to kick in and make my head spin.

"Why does it have to be?" Maryanne asked. "Go home, tell you him love him, have all the orgasms in the world and start making babies with the dude."

"What she said," Denny added.

I lifted myself back up to sitting. "That's my point. It's been all me, every time. I tried to change us and he didn't want to. I had to ask him for sex, but if I hadn't then he wouldn't have touched me. At some point he has to go first if I'm going to know where he stands."

"And you don't think driving three hours to see you and make out with you is going first?" Denny asked.

"He was pissed about the money," I insisted. "I knew he was going to be."

"Denny is right. He wanted to see you," Maryanne argued.

"See, you can't do that with Jake," I told them. "You can't assign him motivations. He's completely upfront and honest about everything. If he missed me, if he wanted to see me and that was all, he would have said something."

I could tell neither of them were buying it, but I knew Jake. The kiss. It meant something. There was no getting around that. We were changing again into something else. The weekly calls. He obviously still wanted me. That kiss had been intense. Nothing had changed in that department.

"We need more time," I muttered.

"You've got the rest of the semester," Maryanne reminded me.

"I'm so bummed he's not gay," Denny said.

Then we all kept drinking until we literally kicked the bucket.

Jake

I PARKED the truck under the portico and thought I had made good time getting back. Less than three hours.

I made my way inside and I hated how dark the house was. How quiet. When Ellie left, I considered moving into the bunk house. Figured it might help get me acclimated to what we were now. I wasn't her husband any longer. Not really family anymore.

I was back to being the hired help.

Then, before I could pack, Rich showed up and it seemed stupid for us to share the bunk house when we both could have our own space. Besides, I got the impression Rich liked his privacy. He worked hard during the day, but I knew he was a drinker at night. I wasn't quite sure how heavy a drinker, and unless it interfered with his work, it wasn't any of my business.

Unless he was going to be the solution going forward. Once I left for my ranch. I didn't know if I liked the idea of him out here drunk at night with Ellie in the house.

Ellie. She'd looked so damn beautiful today. I saw her and realized what had been missing these last months.

Her. Her from this house. Her from my life.

I missed her. I missed her every damn day. I hadn't felt like this since... but no, I didn't do that. I didn't think about when my mom left. I never thought about that time. Ever. That whole part of my life had been erased from my memory completely. It had been the only way to compartmentalize it to make it less than what it was.

Besides, there was no point in sharing any of that with Ellie. It was hard enough being away at school for her. She didn't need the added pressure of my feelings to worry about. Presumably she would be there another four years. I didn't know what we would do over the summer. Definitely by then I would have to move out.

Otherwise there would be no shot at maintaining my distance. That line, the one I had kept so diligently between us for a year, had been erased in one night.

Thinking back on it, I did some serious damage to it the night I made her come for the first time too.

Just the memory of that, which would pop up at random times throughout the day, was enough to make me instantly hard.

I never let myself think about the night I took her virginity. If I thought about the sex... if I let myself think about what that night felt like, to be inside her... then it became really damn hard to tell myself it had been a good idea letting Ellie divorce me.

Letting Ellie leave me.

No, when she came back this summer I absolutely had to vacate the house.

I could get started on the plans for my house. It was strange, but what I told Ellie was the truth. When I thought about it, what it might look like, what considerations I might have when rebuilding, it all seemed so amorphous. I had no vision of what the house should be. For someone who spent as many years as I did wanting my land back, saving for it ruthlessly, doing nothing but thinking about the future of the Talley ranch, it was strange that I wasn't more aggressive in making that happen.

Like most things, I tried not to overthink it.

Instead I made my way through the empty house, got some water, headed upstairs and when I climbed into bed, only then did I let myself think about what I had done by kissing Ellie.

I'd wanted to do it the second I saw her. All damn day until finally it was something I couldn't not do.

What I didn't know was what it meant for us going forward?

Was it a question of now that we had crossed the line I thought I had permission to touch her?

Or was she just fucking hot and I liked her a lot, so why not kiss her?

Whatever it was, it wasn't simple. I didn't think it ever would be between me and Ellie.

Ellie
March

I WAS IN THE LIBRARY, trying to focus on what I was reading, but every two seconds the feeling of Jake reaching for me in his truck would overtake me, and I would think about that instead. Maryanne, Denny, and I had analyzed that kiss from every different angle, but at the end of the day the only person who could explain what he'd done, why he'd done it, was Jake.

Did he want me? Did he miss me? Did he want us to be something other than what we were? No one in the universe could explain what we were.

I pulled out my phone and thought, *what if I just called him now?* It was Thursday, just after four in the afternoon. Not our normal call at our normal time. What if he answered and was happy that I called? What if he answered and was grumpy that I called because I had broken what had become a pattern for us?

It wasn't hard to figure out that Jake liked consistency. Probably not all that shocking, given his upbringing. A mother who ditched him, a father who basically did the same by drinking himself to death.

Still, what if I challenged the norm? What if I broke our pattern? What if...

"Hey."

I looked up, expecting to see someone I knew, but instead it was a guy who I had seen before on campus. He was cute, with dark hair and some chin scruff. I figured my age or a year or two older. I knew him because he'd randomly asked me out when he saw me in the campus bookstore. At the time it had freaked me out.

"Hey," I answered back.

He must have taken that as an open invitation, because he took a seat across from me at the table.

"What are you studying?"

"Right now, nothing. I should be reading about statistics."

He snorted. "Statistics are boring."

"Yep." I wasn't sure what else to say. This was something having been Weird Married Ellie I'd missed out on. I had had a boyfriend before Jake. I had attempted to flirt with guys before Jake. I had even tried to have sex with someone before Jake (AKA The Great Prom Debacle).

But for the last few years it had been all about Jake. Whatever flirting muscle I had was obviously out of shape, because not only did I have no idea how to talk to a strange guy, I had no idea if I even wanted to.

"I'm Kevin."

"I'm Ellie."

He smiled. "I know who you are."

Okay. "How?"

"I asked. I wanted to know the name of the girl who shot me down."

That sounded smug. Like no other girl had ever dared. "See, and I thought it was strange you would ask a girl out without knowing her name first."

"Touché."

Also smug, I thought.

"I know your name now," he said pointing out the obvious. "What do you say we grab some food?"

It was happening again. He was asking me out again.

I thought of Jake driving all the way to school to yell at me about the money, and what his real motivations were. I thought about the kiss. I thought about who I wanted to be spending my time with... and it wasn't Kevin.

"Sorry. I'm... involved with someone right now."

"That's cool. Maybe you'll let me know when you're not."

Doubtful. "Maybe," I lied.

Kevin got up and left, seemingly unscathed from being shot down again. I knew this because I saw him walk up to another girl in the library who was also studying alone.

I went back to reading, not really reading, about statistics.

And missing Jake. I guess I had my own patterns too.

That next Sunday night

"YOU KISSED ME."

This was the result of pressure from Denny and Maryanne. I told them about Kevin asking me out, and told them I had said no. And why. They were convinced the time had come, and I needed to confront Jake directly about his intentions. I suppose I knew it, too.

Jake huffed. "Hello to you too. That was a few weeks ago. Why are you bringing it up now?"

"I need to know what it means, Jake. That guy I told you about, the one from the bookstore, his name is Kevin and he asked me out again. I said no."

There was silence on the other end of the line.

"Let me be clear. I said no because of you. Should I be saying no because of you?"

More silence.

"Jake? This is important. This might be the most important thing we ever say to each other."

Jake

"JAKE? This is important. This might be the most important thing we ever say to each other."

She was right. She'd been gone for two and half months, and the pain of not having her here wasn't going away. I waited like a man dying of thirst every week to answer the phone on Sunday night. Frankly, I hated it. Feeling like this.

I drove myself crazy thinking about kissing her, fucking her. Crazier still thinking about her with other guys.

Suddenly it all made sense.

"Yes." It felt good to say it.

"What?"

"Yes. You should be saying no. I don't know what this means, Ellie. I'm... not sure where this is going. But damn it... I don't want you dating anyone while we figure it out."

"Okay."

"This is selfish as hell. Probably the most selfish thing I've ever done."

"Yep."

"You going to school was supposed to be about having choices, and I'm taking that away."

"You're a horrible person, Jake Talley."

I scowled at the phone because she wasn't taking any of this seriously. In fact, she sounded like she was beaming.

"I'm serious, Ellie. I don't know if this is the right answer."

"I don't think there is a right answer, Jake. Have you thought about someone else? About seeing someone else?"

"No."

No. I only thought of Ellie. Or at least I tried real hard *not* to think of her. Which had to mean something. I was willing to admit that to myself at least.

"Then let's call this limbo. We're not dating each other. We're not dating other people. We're taking our time with things. We were married for two years, seems right we should have some time to consider all that."

I nodded. That seemed reasonable. We didn't have to commit to anything right now. Because when I thought about it, that's all Ellie and I had ever done. Commit to the marriage, commit to the divorce. Hard choices at every turn, when all I wanted was a little easy.

"Yes. Right. Limbo. Until we can sort out what this is."
"Okay. Then we're good. I'll call you next week?"
"Yes."
"Night, Jake."
"Night, Ellie."

I disconnected the call and thought limbo might just the best idea we had ever had.

FOUR

Ellie
The next day

"WE'RE IN LIMBO."

Denny scrunched up his face and Maryanne rolled her eyes. We were having lunch together in the cafeteria as I filled them in on my confrontation with Jake.

"Limbo?" Denny said. "What is that?"

"We're not ready to date each other, but we've agreed not to see other people." I thought it was the best idea ever.

"So you're trapped," Maryanne said.

"No. Trapped is what Jake was in our marriage. Trapped is what circumstance and a really bad storm did to us. This is a choice."

I could tell they weren't buying it.

"Guys, this is real progress. Jake is finally admitting he has enough feelings for me that he doesn't want me going out with other guys. This is huge!"

They looked at each other and I could tell they didn't share my excitement.

"What am I missing?"

"Don't you deserve more than that?" Maryanne asked.

Huh. I never really considered that. It had always been so clear for me about what I wanted, which was Jake, that I never thought about what I deserved.

"You're making it out like he hasn't given me enough. When he's given me... everything."

"What he gave you was a divorce," Denny said flatly. "Only to turn around two months later and tell you not to date anyone while he works out his own shit. That's not everything. That's selfish as hell."

Jake knew that. He'd said as much.

I was so excited by the idea he cared enough to stop me from moving on, I didn't really think about everything he didn't say.

That he missed me. That he wanted us to have an actual relationship. That he wanted me to come home.

I threw my hands up in the air. "I was feeling great. Thanks for ruining everything, guys!"

Denny and Maryanne smiled sadly at me and Denny reached over to pat me on the hand. "That's what friends are for."

Jake
Sunday night

ELLIE and I had been chatting for a while when it occurred to me that April was around the corner.

"Hey, what do you want for your birthday?" I asked.

"You," she answered.

I closed my eyes and tried not to imagine what that would be like. Because if I did I would end up hard and frustrated, like I did most times when I thought about Ellie.

"I get it," she quickly added while I was busy trying not to imagine her naked and in my bed. "You've got the ranch and everything. It's spring and things are busy. My birthday falls in the middle of the week, so that would make it even harder. Anyway, you always think of something great. You'll have to surprise me."

I did like to do that. To surprise her on her birthday.

"It's late," she said. "I should probably go." There was something there in her voice. A hint of sadness. Or maybe it was longing.

I could appreciate it, because I felt it too.

"Yeah. Night, Ellie."

I ended the call and thought about how she sounded different. Not her normal cheery self. Since we had agreed to this ridiculous limbo, she hadn't brought up the question of us again. We talked about school, which I felt like there was something she wasn't telling me about. We talked about the ranch. She told me crazy stories about Denny and funny ones about Maryanne.

I asked her if she was okay handling the ranch bookkeeping along with the schoolwork.

Pedantic, dry-as-hell stuff.

Stuff that two people who were in a relationship would share with each other. Except we weren't in a relationship. We weren't out of one, either.

Either way, I wasn't getting laid.

I closed my eyes and tried again not to think about it. Tried not to remember what it had felt like to kiss her, to hold her. To have her.

It was after seven and I needed to get out of my head. Pete's wouldn't be packed on a Sunday night, but there would be someone who could distract me from the running image of Ellie on her knees in my shower, sucking my dick.

Because that one got a lot of air time.

I got to Pete's and found a stool near the bar. Pete gave me a chin nod, and a few minutes later walked over with the draft beer I always ordered.

"What's happening, Jake? Haven't seen you around."

"Busy. The usual."

"How's Ellie? She liking college?"

I didn't know. She liked her friends, but she never seemed overly thrilled with her classes. "She's doing fine. Grades are up."

"Miss having her around here. She was always a ray of sunshine. Not going to lie, I thought it was a shame when I heard you two decided to split."

I set my beer down carefully. "Our marriage was a temporary arrangement. Thought everyone knew that."

"Yeah, but look at what she grew into."

That had me seeing red, and I did the thing I swore I would never do. Asked the question I swore I would never ask. Not a to single soul in Riverbend.

"Pete, do you think I was messing around with her the whole time we were together?"

His reaction was to bark out a laugh. "Jake Talley, you would have cut off your dick before taking advantage of Ellie after Sam died. I know that. All I'm saying is after graduation, when you two were in here that night... she was a woman then. Not a girl any longer. Thought you might see that too, but given how you two grew up together maybe not. I know this. Any man in this town would be lucky to call Ellie Samson his wife, and I know a lot of people think you're a damn fool for having that privilege only to give her up. I'll leave you to your beer and company."

Only I didn't want my company. I wanted Ellie's company.

I thought I had been so damn strong by letting her go. So damn self-sacrificing. Giving her a chance to grow and experience new things. To really have a choice about her future.

But I hadn't let her go at all. Not really.

Only I wasn't sure enough of myself, or her, to do a damn thing to change that.

"Limbo," I told the bar as I took deep gulp of my beer, "blows."

IT WAS morning and sun was streaking through the barn. I stared hard at Petunia, not for one second believing I was going to do this. I started with an apple slice, which she eagerly accepted, nearly taking my fingers with it.

"Ellie says I need to talk to you."

Petunia huffed and lifted her head. Which, sure, could have seemed like a response, but was probably more of an effort to get another apple slice.

I gave her another one.

"It's not as if I've never talked to Wyatt... Usually it's just commands, though. It's not like he needs chit chat, you know what I'm saying?"

Another huff.

I stroked her nose, and as strange as it was it made me

feel closer to Ellie. As if by touching something I knew she loved, it connected us in some way.

"I'm guessing you miss her too. Who wouldn't? All that life. All that energy. All of her spirit. I think that's what's been missing in her voice the last few times we talked on the phone. It's like being away from here, she's lost part of herself. But it was her choice to go away, her decision—all of it. It's not like I can tell her to come home. She's got to make that call on her own. Right?"

"Jake, I hate to interrupt your... conversation, but I need to take Petunia out and clean her stall."

I heard Rich behind me, but my face was too red to actually turn around and face him. "Yep. I was just... Ellie wanted me to..."

"No explanation necessary. No better listener than a horse, in my opinion."

I fed Petunia my last apple slice and then started to make my way out of the barn.

"Not my place," Rich said, almost more to himself than directed at me. "But if I was missing someone, seems to me the easy thing would be to just go see her."

Just go see her. It wasn't the worst idea.

FIVE

Ellie
April 22

IT WAS TUESDAY. Maryanne and Denny had taken me out for my birthday. I was trying to be happy about it, but all I could think about how this was the first birthday in a long time I had spent apart from Jake.

It felt weird.

Officially, Jake and I were still in limbo. The reality was, there wasn't a lot of opportunity to change that. He was three hours away and responsible for running my ranch. It's not like we could casually go out on dates. So we did our thing. We talked each Sunday about school, about the ranch, and we didn't talk about us. Or what us not dating meant.

Denny and Maryanne continued to give me advice as to why limbo was the stupidest thing ever. I continued to ignore that advice in favor of my stubborn belief that I was doing the right thing.

Only one more month to go before the semester was over, and then I was going back to Riverbend. Permanently. I could say that I officially stuck it out for one semester, which wasn't quitting. Jake would fight me on it, but I was done living this half-life. Not when I was clear on what I wanted my future to look like.

Yes, that's when, as Denny would say, shit was going to have to get real. For now I was happy enough to be out with my friends, drinking margaritas and eating more guacamole than was probably healthy.

"Did Jake at least call you?" Denny asked.

"Yep. This morning. He said he had a present for me and that it should be delivered today. I'm hoping it will be waiting for me when I get back to the dorm."

Maryanne smiled. "I know I give you a lot of grief over him... but I do think he's a nice guy."

I smiled. That actually meant a lot to me. Jake *was* a nice guy, and while maybe he was being selfish with the whole limbo thing, I knew he deserved some slack. None of what we had been through had been easy. On either of us. Which meant nothing could be as simple as black and white going forward. We were a work in progress. I knew that even if they didn't.

"And I think he's hot enough to warrant sticking around for," Denny said as he slurped back the last of his margarita.

I made a mental note to let Jake know Denny thought he was hot. He would get all freaked out, and then I could school him on his closeted homophobic fears.

"We do have one surprise for you," Maryanne said with a big smile.

"Is this the part where they come out singing with a cake? Because really guys, that's so embarrassing."

"No, this is the part where I get to give you my present."

I whipped around in my chair. There, standing behind me, holding flowers (ACTUAL FLOWERS) was Jake Talley.

I felt tears spring to my eyes. "You're my present," I said, realizing what he meant on the phone this morning.

"Happy birthday, Ellie."

I jumped up and was in his arms in a second.

"How did you make this happen?"

"Rich, Javier, and Gomez have control of things at the ranch. I could make the time. I called Maryanne this morning and she told me where they were taking you for dinner."

"Surprise!" Maryanne said.

I took the bouquet of wildflowers and pressed my face in them. It was without a doubt the most romantic gesture he'd ever made, and I couldn't stop myself from being thrilled.

Then he held up a small box. "What's this?" I asked.

"Your other present. Open it."

I opened the box and inside was a square plastic card. It looked like a smooth credit card without the numbers.

"What is it?"

"It's my hotel room key. I thought... we could spend a few days together. If you wanted."

I looked up at him. I could see his cheeks were flushed and his jaw was tight. That muscle flexing away. His eyes... He was looking at me like he had that one time when I got in the shower with him. Like he didn't have to hide what he wanted from me any longer.

"Really?" I whispered.

"If you want."

I nodded.

"You can finish dinner with your friends first..."

"No." I turned and looked at Maryanne and Denny, who were watching us like we were a movie being played out for their entertainment. "Guys, you don't care if I go..."

"NO!" Denny shouted. "For the love of God, put us all out of our misery and boink the hell out of him."

I blushed and I could tell Jake wasn't pleased as he glared at Denny, but that was just Denny being Denny.

Jake turned and I followed him out of the restaurant. I didn't say a word in the truck. I didn't really know what to say. This was a massive departure from anything he had ever done before.

Like kissing me first. Like telling me he didn't want me to see anyone else. Like bringing me flowers.

When before it had always been me putting myself out there to him.

I was giddy with the pleasure of this.

We got to the hotel and I jumped out of the truck. I was wearing a jean skirt and wedges and a light sweater. I thought about what I might need for a few days, and then decided since I planned to spend those few days naked it didn't really matter.

It was just a Courtyard Marriott, which I knew wasn't super fancy, but it was my first time staying in a hotel and I was in awe of the cool furniture in the lobby.

A hotel. In Missoula.

"Hey, this isn't the same place you came when you took your trip that summer?"

He glared at me. "No."

"Just checking."

We got to the room, which I thought was really big with

a massive bed. I literally gulped. I heard the door close behind him and I waited, not really sure what was going to happen. Yes, I knew *what* was going to happen, but I wasn't clear on how we got there.

This was us having sex like two people who had no restrictions on doing that. It was almost surreal.

Then I felt him behind me. He put his hand in my hair and ran his fingers through it. He leaned down to inhale it. I found myself trembling. Like I was a virgin all over again. Only I wasn't. That was Jake's too.

"Ellie, you understand this isn't going to be like last time," he whispered into my ear, then bent to kiss my neck.

"It's not? Because I have to say, Jake, last time was pretty awesome."

"It was. But I was very... controlled. Because I had to be. After four months of thinking about this, I don't know if I'm going to have that control at the start. Do you get that?"

I thought I did. He was a guy, he was hard up for sex. The patience I had bragged about might not be there for now. But that was okay. What mattered was that we were doing this, not how many orgasms I came away with.

I pulled away from him and turned to face him. I pulled off my sweater, undid my bra, pulled down my skirt and panties until I was naked. And because the room was fully lit, I crossed my hands over my chest... well because. It probably wasn't the sexiest of strip shows, but I figured he wanted to cut to the chase.

Instead of pouncing, his head fell back on his shoulders and he groaned.

"You're going to kill me."

"Isn't this what you wanted? To go fast?"

He looked at me. Then he *looked* at me. Then he was reaching out to touch me again. A finger down my arm, a hand sweeping up my stomach until he cupped my breast. A kiss pressed against my collarbone.

He reached into the back pocket of his jeans and pulled out a strip of condoms he tossed on the bed. I counted six.

This, I thought, was going to be fun. I stopped thinking about how the lights were on and how strange this was that Jake was doing this. I stopped thinking about everything other than how good his touch felt. How much I'd missed the smell of him.

It was the reverse of that phrase *death by a thousand cuts*. Instead, Jake was giving me pleasure by a thousand touches. He pinched my nipples and pulled on them, watching the whole time what that did to my breasts. He stroked a finger through my pussy lips, barely touching my clit, which made it even hotter. Then he put that finger in his mouth and sucked on it.

Oh my.

Yes, I thought I was starting to understand. The Jake who took my virginity had been patient and sweet and endlessly giving. The Jake who was with me now in this hotel wanted to fuck.

"Get on the bed," he told me.

I did and I watched his eyes as I spread my legs. They got really super dark. Then I watched as he impatiently took off his clothes. His pressed checkered shirt and jeans. He'd ironed everything, which meant this was important to him. That made me happy.

Finally naked, he loomed over me as he crawled onto the bed, his hips between my legs, his cock pressed up hard against my pussy.

"Tell me you can handle this, Ellie. It might be a little... rough."

I wrapped my thighs around his waist and pressed

myself against that cock, making him wet with my desire. Showing without words what I wanted. I'd been turned on since he told me what the hotel key was.

"Jake," I said softly, whispering in his ear. "I would very much like it if you fucked me...hard."

His head dropped down so that his forehead was pressed against mine. He reached for the strip of condoms and this time I watched as he slid it on. Then he was kissing me, his tongue pushing into my mouth even as his dick was pushing inside my pussy. It was tight and it stung again as he worked himself to the hilt, but I didn't tell him stop.

This was no longer about me losing my virginity, or him making it easy for me or any of that.

This was about us and our bodies being together. Because I didn't know how he felt, but for me there was a certainty about us when we were like this. Jake Talley was supposed to be inside me.

His hips started to pump, and it hurt. Then he tilted my hips higher so he could go even deeper, and that hurt. Then he started snapping his hips really hard like he had no control over it, and I reveled in the hurt. Because alongside that pain and pressure of him being inside me came the other feeling. That sense that if he just kept hitting that one spot over and over and over...

"Jake! Yes! Please!"

He growled, pumped himself harder and faster, and now I really understood the difference between what we'd done before and what we're doing now.

This was fucking, and it was glorious.

SIX

Jake

"FUCK YES." I slapped her ass and she gasped. I had her on her knees, her back arched, her face shoved in the pillows catching her cries. This was the first time I was taking her from behind, and it was fucking amazing. Every time with her felt richer and deeper. Like I could get as far into her as I wanted and she would take all of it.

Her hair was spread out over her back in this honey wave.

Mine. All of it mine.

Some instinct had me gathering it in my hand. I tugged on it and it forced her head back, all while fucking her so hard I knew I wouldn't be able to hold back my come. Then I would shoot into her and that would be amazing too.

"Jake. Jake. Stop. Stop!"

It took a second for the words to penetrate. Stop, she

was telling me stop. Immediately I pulled out of her and let go of her hair.

"Shit, Ellie did I hurt you?" Shit, shit, shit. I had let myself lose all control.

She was breathing hard. I was too, for that matter. My dick was about to explode but I wasn't doing a damn thing until she told me what was wrong.

"Ellie? Was I too rough?"

She shook her head.

"Ellie, talk to me."

"I just... It was all so... intense... and I... I don't know. I... It was like there was no controlling it. I'm not making sense."

She made perfect sense. Fuck's sake, this was the only second time she'd had sex, and I had been rutting on her for what felt like hours. It had been the most intense sex I had ever had, and I had experience.

She had none.

I changed our position. I sat on the bed, my back against the headboard. And I brought her on top of me so we were face to face, her knees straddling my hips.

Then I took a hold of my dick and gently slid it inside of her. Because I needed to still be connected to her. I didn't thrust, even though it was killing me, just let her wiggle a bit until she was comfortable.

"I'm sorry," she said, even as she began these gentle hip rolls against me.

"You don't have to be sorry. You're new to this. Sometimes sex is about taking and sometimes it's about giving and sometimes it's about sharing. I've been taking too much."

Because I was finally getting to do what I had been thinking about for months. When I'd asked her a few weeks ago what she wanted for her birthday, she'd said me. Then of course she quickly covered that by saying she knew it would be too hard to get away from the ranch.

It planted a seed that suddenly became clear when Rich said the most obvious thing in the world. If I missed her, I should see her. That's when I knew. Knew I was going to surprise her for her birthday and fuck her without any reservations. Pretty much ending this limbo shit once and for all.

Now we were here, it was the middle of the night, we were on our third condom and I hadn't let her up for air once. And she seemed to embrace all of it. I pushed my thumb between her legs and found her clit, stroking it in time with her hip rolls.

She hummed in the back of her throat. I loved that sound. Almost as much as when I made her gasp.

She had her hands on my shoulders and I watched as she looked down at where we were joined. Watched as I pressed deep inside her. Then she pulled herself up and slowly sank herself down again.

"Now I'm in control," she said.

I smiled. "You like that, you little feminist."

She leaned in to kiss me and I thought it had been too long since I had tasted her. Certainly more than minutes.

"I do like it. Is this me taking and you giving?"

"Yes."

"Do you not like being on the bottom?"

"There is no such thing as not liking sex with you. In any way possible. It's a little harder for me to come this way, but it's all good. I'll get there eventually."

That's when she amazed me in the way only Ellie could. She pulled herself up until I left her heat. I nearly whimpered. Then she climbed off me and turned around on the bed. She rested her cheek on the mattress and kept her ass high in the air. It was the most fucking erotic thing I had ever seen in my life.

"I'm good, Jake. You can go back to taking."

"Ellie..."

"I want to feel it again. In that context. It's okay to be out of control because I'm giving you something. Please. That's how I want you to come."

This was the part where I refused because I was a gentleman, and clearly banging the fuck out of her from behind while I pulled her hair and slapped her ass had been a little scary for her.

Instead I got on my knees, positioned my cock against her wet pussy, and thrust deep. Then I leaned over so that my arms were on either side of her head. And I fucked her as hard as I could. When she came underneath me, screaming my name and reaching around for my ass, I felt like a fucking caveman who had claimed his mate. Then I came so hard all I could see were stars behind my closed eyes.

Ellie

SUCKING DICK WAS DELICIOUS. Almost as fun as what Jake had done to me with his mouth earlier this morning. He said I needed a break from penetration, which I didn't know why, but the word *penetration* seemed ridiculously hot to me. So he sank down between my legs and made me come twice with his tongue.

That was him giving.

Now it was my turn to make him come, although while I was giving it also felt a little like taking too. Because I loved every sound he made. I loved the way he would thrust into my mouth like he couldn't help it. I loved the way he pushed down on my head like that too was out of his control.

Jake liked sex. A lot. I was already coming to understand he liked it better when he could tell me what to do.

"Use your tongue right under the head. That's it. Right there. Fuck yes!"

I was a very good listener and a quick study. I pulled him out of my mouth and lifted myself on my hands so I could get a better angle. That had his cock sitting between my breasts and I saw his eyelids get heavy. When his eyes fell to half-mast that, was when he was super turned on.

I loved that I knew that about him.

Going with it, I shifted myself back and forth so that my nipple touched the tip of his cock.

"Ellie," he growled.

"You like seeing that, Jake? Your dick on my tits," I teased. Then I hunched my shoulders together so that his dick was pressed in between my breasts and I moved up and down like he was fucking them. He lurched as if he couldn't control himself.

"Do you want to come on them?" I asked. I remembered that from my porn-watching debacle. Guys seemed to go crazy when they could do that. Mouth, boobs, it didn't matter to me, just so long as he came. And he made that animal growl noise, which was freaking primitive and hot and a total turn-on.

"Fuck," he barked, and then before I knew what was happening he had me on my back, pushing my breasts together while he fucked them with his cock. Then it was happening, he was coming and I felt splashes of it on my neck and cheek while he made the growling noise.

Total bliss. I smiled and but when I opened my eyes I could see he looked horrified.

"Ellie...I don't... I don't know what to say. I've never done that..."

I leaned up and kissed him on the cheek. "Then I was your first boob fuck. Yeah, me. Now let me up. I want a shower and then you're going to take me somewhere for food. I'm famished."

He rolled off me and I headed for the bathroom.

"Ellie, are you really okay with that?"

I stopped. Suddenly tense. I didn't face him when I asked, "Should I not have been? Was that like... too slutty for you?"

A second later I felt him wrap his arms around me from behind and instantly I relaxed.

"Because slut shaming is not cool, Jake."

"I'm sorry. That's not what I was saying. I was afraid... I feel like I keep pushing you. You have to tell me if it's too much."

"I think I did that before. What just happened was not too much. The point is to have fun and feel good, right?"

"Yes."

"Did I do that for you?"

"Yes. You're the sexiest creature I've ever known."

"Then that's all that matters. Isn't it?"

He kissed the top of my head. "Go take your shower."

Jake

"HI, and if you can, tell them to really burn the bacon for me. As crisp as you can get it," Ellie told our waitress.

"Will do."

We were sitting at a table at a breakfast place not too dissimilar to Frank's. We each had a cup of coffee. Ellie had been pleased to see that I brought some extra clothes from home for her. She was adorable in jeans and a t-shirt and her wedge sandals.

Except I was trying not to look at Ellie too much because when I did all I could see was that phantom splash of my come on her cheek.

In my life I had never been so free with a woman during sex. I knew how to make a woman come, I knew how to get off. This was different. This was like fulfilling any fantasy I'd ever had. My dick between those perfect breasts and Ellie smiling at me wickedly as if she would give me anything I wanted.

I had been helpless. It had been frightening. I wondered if this was what Ellie had felt last night when she told me to stop. Like neither of us could handle the passion of what we were together. It was all too much.

I didn't know what that meant. But I figured I was a cowboy. I could put a rope around anything and eventually make it bend to my will. This was just a mental rope around sex.

One thing for sure was that I needed to be more in control. I couldn't risk doing something that might legitimately put her off, because it was clear she didn't have any boundaries when it came to sex.

So I couldn't do anything as crazy as tell her to get down on her knees under the table and suck me off.

Because I was afraid she might do it.

Instead I reached across the table and took her hand in mine. I brushed my thumb over hers. I looked around at some of the other customers in the tables adjacent to our booth. No one was looking at us funny. No one was staring at us.

"No one knows who we are," I said.

"Huh?" Ellie was looking down at our joined hands. I shocked her, I know. It wasn't like me to do this. I never would have done this if we were at Frank's. But I liked touching her.

I liked knowing I could touch her. No one around here thought we were anything other than two people who were fucking each other.

"Anybody who looks at us thinks we're a normal couple."

She leaned over the table. "We are not a normal couple, Jake."

"I know that, but here we are. Nothing to speculate or wonder about. Just two adults having breakfast together. I like that."

"Is that what we are now?"

I knew what she was asking. She wanted to know what these few days meant for us. What exactly we were now, because Ellie and I weren't anything if we weren't defining ourselves. Friends. Married. Divorced. Limbo.

"We're lovers."

She nodded. "Lovers. I like that. I've gone from teen bride, to virginal wife, to ex-wife lover. It's like a Lifetime movie!"

Still I had to remind her, "The point of you coming here was to give you options. I don't think I did a very good job of that."

"Jake Talley, that might be the most sexist thing you've ever said to me. Have I taught you nothing? You don't control what choices I make. I control them."

She had a point. "You're right. I'm sorry. I only... you know I only want what's best for you. I want the best of everything for you, Ellie. There are times in the past when I've made choices that I don't think were good choices for you."

She scowled at me. "Jake, get over it. I'm nineteen. I own a multi-million-dollar cattle ranch that we've run successfully, both you and me, for two and a half years."

When she said it like that, I had to concede maybe I was a little sexist. Because this whole time all I had been thinking about were how my choices were affecting her. Never once did I consider what her choices meant.

Her choice to kiss me the night she graduated high school. Her choice to offer me her virginity. Her choice not to date anyone. Her choice to stay with me at the hotel.

Her choice to see how the sight of her breasts on my cock aroused me and give me something she knew I wanted. Something I never thought to take before.

The food came and I ate it, but I didn't taste much of it.

"So what should we do for the day?" she asked. As she nibbled on her bacon.

We had the whole day and night. I didn't have to leave until early tomorrow morning. As it was, I knew Ellie was blowing off a day's worth of classes but she didn't seem to be bothered by it.

There was a rodeo in town I saw on signs when I was driving here. A movie theater, too. I could let her pick a girly movie.

Those would have been the sensible things to do. Allow

me to get a rein on this sexual intensity between us rather than dive back in for round two.

Except I wasn't feeling very sensible.

"I think we should go back to the hotel and fuck some more. All damn day if we want to."

She smiled. SHE FUCKING SMILED. Like no woman had ever smiled at me before. Like I was a sex god and she was in perpetual heat.

"That sounds like a plan. Let me just finish my bacon."

I HAD us both on our knees, her back pressed up against my chest, her head leaning back on my shoulder. I was slowly thrusting up inside her, only my hands cupped over her breasts keeping her in place.

We were like a choreographed dance. With each push she tilted her hips back against me. So that with each thrust and parry I got so deep into her. It was unlike anything I had ever done.

It was un-fucking-real.

"Jake. Jake."

She liked to do that. She liked to just say my name.

"I'm going to make you come so hard you're going to scream." I moved my hand down her body, slid a finger through her pussy, circled her clit.

"Yes, yes, please do that!"

My hips were snapping now. I could feel it coming.

"Come for me, baby. Now."

"Ahhhhhhh!"

And there it was. I could feel her squeezing me hard even as I shot my load inside her.

She practically melted back against me. Her head rolling back and forth on my shoulder.

"Is that sharing, Jake?"

"Yes," I puffed out.

"Mmmm. I like sharing." She lifted herself off me and fell face forward on the bed.

"Nap," she said and I watched as she closed her eyes.

Yeah, a nap felt about right after hours of the most amazing sex I had ever had or even expected to have in my life.

But I needed to deal with the condom and take a piss first.

Looking back on it, I don't know what was the truth.

Had I seen it and decided to ignore it and the possible consequences?

Or was it as simple as I wasn't paying attention so I didn't notice the drop of come that was outside the tip of the condom?

Either way I tossed the condom in the trash, pissed, washed my hands, and went back to bed with Ellie.

And I didn't say a thing.

SEVEN

Ellie
The next morning

I ALMOST DID IT. I almost said the words. I woke up and I was facing him. He was already up. He was looking at me and playing with a piece of my hair.

It would have been so easy.

I love you, Jake. Take me home.

But I didn't. Because again, I thought this had to be his move. He had to choose me. He knew how I felt, and in many ways I knew how he felt. But Jake wasn't a man who would fall in love easy. I knew that.

His mother had left him when he was a boy. There had to be scars from that. Trust issues. Not that he ever talked about her leaving, or talked about her at all for that matter. Sometimes it was like she never existed, but of course she had.

He'd dated Janet for nearly two years, and never once

had I ever heard him say he loved her.

Which thank God! Right?

A. Janet would have been horrible for him. B. I wouldn't get to have him.

I had Jake. I mean I HAD Jake. Because in my mind, no two people could share what we did for two days and not want a lifetime of that. It was ridiculous to even think it. But he had to get to that conclusion himself.

"I am really good at sex," I told him.

He laughed.

"Seriously. Who knows how you'll be until you do it? Shy, awkward, hesitant. Not me. I fucking rocked it."

He touched my nose with the tip of his finger. "You destroyed me."

Now I was smiling.

So this was the time to say it. To end this farce of a divorce. To go back home and live with Jake and the whole happily-ever-after thing. Except he didn't say it. Instead, he got us both up and we took a shower together. No funny stuff. I think our bodies were both too worn out for that.

We dressed and I took my bouquet of flowers, which were wilting but not enough for me to consider throwing them out. We got breakfast again at that same place and Jake drove me back to my dorm.

We were quiet for a minute when he turned the engine off, and I thought he might do it then. Ask me to come home. Tell me he loved me.

Instead he sighed, and I knew some really hard stuff was rolling around in his head.

"When should I come back to pick you up? For the summer."

"Uh, actually I might be able to get a ride from someone. There's a girl from Jefferson I know who goes here, and she offered to drop me off."

"We'll need to talk about what happens when you're home. Come up a with a plan."

I nodded. Because there was no one in Riverbend who was going to think it was normal for Jake and me to live together now that we were divorced. Not that I was overly concerned with my reputation, but it was more than that.

Jake and I knew it. If we were going to live in that house together, it was because we would have made a decision. Or at least he would have made one.

I was already there.

So I knew exactly what I had to do.

I leaned over and kissed him on the cheek.

"That's not how lovers say goodbye," he told me. Then he proceeded to kiss me senseless.

Another sigh. This time from me.

I smiled. "Best birthday ever, Jake."

"Yeah. It was. You'll call me Sunday?"

"Yep," I lied.

Then I got out of the car and walked away from him. I didn't even watch to see him leave. Let him see me walk away for a change.

I used my key to get in my dorm, and I was grateful Maryanne wasn't there. She would want details and I wasn't ready to share any of that. These past two days were for me and Jake only.

Then I got started on my plan. The first step was finding a vase for my flowers. The second step was packing.

"YOU'VE GOT to be kidding me," Denny said. "There is literally like one street."

"I told you it was small."

"It's almost like a Hollywood set."

It wasn't. It was home. Jake left me Thursday morning. Now it was Saturday, just past evening, and I was back in Riverbend. Denny had a friend, who he suggested was maybe more than a friend, who had a car. Denny was able to borrow it to offer me a ride home.

I was sad to leave Maryanne, but she obviously understood why I was doing this. I was going to miss Denny too, but he said this separation would allow him to have one other person he could always be texting with, which he liked do in public because he thought it made him look super popular.

"You're sure you can't stay?" I said. He'd pulled over in front of the Hair Stop, which was across the street from the diner. "I'll buy you a burger, but warning they are not as good as Eddy's."

"No, I told Chad I would have the car back tonight."

"Thanks for doing this."

"You are sure you know what you're doing?"

"One hundred percent positive."

"You love him," Denny said.

"Of course I do." I looked over at him and I could see he wanted to say something. "What?"

"You're doing all this for him. Dropping out of school, coming back home. And you're doing it because you think all the signs point to him loving you back, but... what if he doesn't?"

My heart sank. Because wasn't that the one-million-dollar question? What if Jake never did get to that place where he was deeply in love with me? As much in love with me as I was with him? Because if he didn't get there, then *we* would never work. It would be too lopsided and I knew I couldn't live my life that way.

"One hundred percent positive," I repeated stubbornly. "That's how much I believe in what I'm doing."

I had to.

"Okay. Ugh. You suck. No one who is nineteen should be one hundred percent positive about what they want out of life."

I shrugged. "What can I say? Early bloomer."

"Let's get your stuff."

We got out of the car, and the first thing I did was knock on the door next to the Hair Stop. It was a small house where Bella, who owned the Stop, lived. She smiled when she opened the door, and she gave me a hug.

"Welcome home, honey."

"Thanks."

She held out the key. "Why do I think if Jake finds out I helped you with all of this, he'll be madder than a bucking bull?"

"If he is, it will be with me. And trust me, I can handle Jake Talley."

"I bet you can. All right. Here you go. You know there is nothing much to it. A bed, a bathroom, and a kitchenette."

The room over the Hair Stop. The only place to rent in Riverbend. Every husband who had ever been thrown out of his house by his wife would have rented that room at some point. Now it was my turn.

"That's all I need."

"I'll tell you something else. This Monday, Kathy broke her leg. She's all messed up and staying with her sister in Billings. Bernie has been helping Frank out when she can, but you know how clumsy she is."

Bernie—Bernice actually, but everyone called her Bernie—was Frank's wife. She managed the money and the food ordering and stuff. But she did not wait tables. Mostly because when she did, she usually spilled something on someone.

I glanced across the street at the diner, and lo and behold, saw the Help Wanted sign.

Perfect. I was sorry about Kathy's leg, but this couldn't have worked out any better.

Denny carried my suitcase up, and I had my scales and another bag. Maryanne was going to box up all my other stuff and ship it. I left her with enough money to hopefully cover everything.

Denny gave me air kisses on each cheek and then said *ta* in that way he did.

Then I was alone. In my new place. I took my scales out and set them up on the table by the bed. Nine disks on the right side. One on the left.

Because while I was back in Riverbend, I still wasn't where I was supposed to be.

One step closer, though.

I smiled and wondered how Jake was going to react to all this.

I WALKED into Frank's early the next morning. Bernie was running around with coffee, mostly screaming at everyone that she would be there in a minute.

I took a booth and waited. Finally after ten minutes she stopped by.

"What in the hell are you doing here?"

That was about right for Bernie.

"I'm home from school and I'm actually looking for a job."

I could see her hopes rise, only then she scowled at me. "Don't you have Long Valley to run?"

"Jake is doing that for me. He's got to get his house done before he can move out, so I'm staying in town until then. While I'm here, I figure I might as well work."

I could tell she knew there was more to the story. But how did I explain it to Bernie, who had been married to Frank for twenty years?

Jake and I were lovers, but he wasn't ready to commit to me. Which meant I couldn't go back to the house. The cabin too, for that matter, was too close. He hadn't let me spend more than one night there, and I knew that wouldn't change over the summer.

He was probably planning on moving into the bunk house, but I didn't see that working either.

There was no way, after our hump fest, we were going to be able to keep our hands off each other. Which meant more than likely we would end up sleeping together in the house.

All of that was too easy for him.

I kept going back to what Maryanne said that one time about Jake. Didn't I deserve more?

My answer was a resounding yes. I deserved a man who wasn't reluctantly attracted to me. I deserved a man who told me he liked me and he wanted me. I deserved a man who shared himself and his feelings with me. No matter how hard that was for Jake.

I had been a dog at heel for two years, feeding off the scraps Jake was willing to dole out. Loving each and every one of them.

That had to end. If we were going to work we needed a

little more balance, which was why I didn't tell Jake I loved him when I woke up Thursday morning and saw him watching me.

Yes, I was a basic novice when it came to sex, but I wasn't an idiot.

When Jake said I had destroyed him, he was telling the truth. So I had power now. Power in this relationship to ask for what I wanted. What I wanted was simple.

How I got it, was not.

"When can you start?"

I thought about it. "Now?"

"You're hired. Five dollars an hour and tips. Although I have to say the tips aren't all that."

Not when you spilled coffee in their laps, no.

I stood up and she handed me an apron I put it on and got to work.

IT WAS JUST after nine at night when I let myself into my room. I was dead tired, having worked until closing. Ranching wasn't a walk in the park, but Bernie had me work the full eight-hour shift, and eight hours on my feet the entire time was no joke.

I fell on to the bed and thought about just kicking off my shoes and falling asleep, but I smelled a little from the effort I exuded today and I knew I wouldn't be able to sleep. I sat up, making the effort to get undressed and showered, when I felt my cell phone vibrating.

Oh that's right. It was Sunday.

I pulled the phone out of the back pocket of my jeans and smiled.

I answered. "Hey, Jake."

"Hey, is everything okay? You didn't call."

No I didn't. Every Sunday for weeks *I* called *him*. Never once, not that whole time, had he called me first.

That was not balance.

"I'm fine. The time just got away from me."

"Oh. Okay. I was afraid... after my trip..."

"That you fucked my brains out so hard I forgot to call you?"

He laughed.

"I'm not china, Jake. Not something that you have to worry about breaking."

At least not physically. Emotionally, he'd been breaking me for years now.

"I know that. I... I realized I was probably rougher with you than I should have been."

"Guess I'm like her then, because I really like you... rough."

"Her who?"

I smiled again because I could tell his voice had deepened.

"You know. The *Fifty Shades* chick who likes to get her ass slapped around. We might need to look into toys. Whips and cuffs and that sort of thing. But maybe this time you could not open them in public."

"Ellie," he growled.

"Just an idea. Think about it, Jake. Hey, I'm super tired. I was going to grab a shower and go to bed."

"Oh."

Right. Because I had never ever once ended a call when he wanted to keep talking.

"Okay," he said. "I'll let you go."

"Night, Jake."

"Night, Ellie."

"Dream of me."

I didn't wait for his reply. I ended the call and took my shower and thought of Jake spanking my ass. Then I thought about spanking his ass, which resulted in a self-induced orgasm (I had finally mastered the art) followed by a blissful night's sleep.

The next Sunday

I CALLED JAKE. See how that works? He calls me, I call him. Balance. Well, mostly balanced. Sure, I was lying to him about where I was and what I was doing, but eventually he would come into town and we would straighten it all out. In the meantime the regulars at Frank's were loving the fact that Bernie was back in her office and not staining the shirts of Riverbend citizens everywhere.

"Hey," he answered.

"What are you wearing?" I asked him in what I hoped was my sexy voice and not just my raspy voice.

"A pair of jeans and a t-shirt."

"That sounds hot. Are you touching yourself?"

"Ellie," he grumbled. "Knock it off."

"What? We're not allowed to have phone sex?"

"I don't do phone sex."

That made me laugh. It was so... Jake. "Why? It's not that you can't talk dirty. I distinctly remember you saying you were *going to make me come so hard I would scream*. That's some raunchy shit right there."

"That's different. That's during sex."

"So? Phone sex is just sex over the phone."

"It's not private," he said.

"Are you with someone at the house right now?"

"No, I'm alone."

"Okay, I'm a alone too." Again, a little lie there, since I was always alone now in my new room.

"It's different."

"Worried we're going to be intercepted by the NSA? You probably should be, but I have to figure there isn't anything those guys haven't heard when it comes to phone sex."

"I'm not doing it. Sex should be between two people, not between two phones."

"You're such a prude."

"I am not a prude," he snapped.

Rattling Jake was always fun, but rattling Jake about sex was ridiculously fun.

"So you don't want to hear how I'm lying on my bed. Naked. My hand cupping my breast."

Pause.

"No. And should you really be doing that? What if Maryanne walks in on you?"

I winced. I really did hate to lie to him. "I lied, I just wanted to see what you would do."

"Stop messing with me, Ellie."

"Why would I do that when it's so much fun?"

"Tell me how your week is going."

I definitely did not want to do that. "It's fine. Did you get my email I sent on the numbers?"

"I did. I don't think we have any choice but to think about really expanding the insemination program. It's yielding the best results."

"Which is sad in a way," I told him. "The whole science over nature thing. But I can't argue. What about you? Any progress on the house?"

"Some."

That was it. That was all he ever said about the house. I didn't care, because in the end if I had my way he wouldn't need his house, but he had to see he was stalling for a reason. "Let's start with the basics. Are there walls and a roof?"

"No. I'm getting closer on finalizing the plans though."

Finalizing plans? It was so un-Jake to be hesitant about this. I wanted to scream at him for not seeing what was right there in front of his face.

"If you're worried about where I'm going to stay over the summer, I already thought about it. I'll use the cabin," he said.

See, I knew that was what he was thinking. That if he's not physically living in the house, sleeping with me is still okay.

"Okay, but where are we going to have sex? My bedroom? Your old bedroom? Or do you think I should sneak out to the cabin like Mrs. Nash used to?"

Silence.

"Jake?"

"I don't know, Ellie. I hadn't really thought about it."

"You hadn't thought about having sex with me again? You're saying last week was... forgettable?"

I had to bite my bottom lip to stop myself from laughing.

"No. Of course not. You're not understanding... what... I think about having sex with you. All the fucking time. I'm just saying we can't... I mean I don't know how this is supposed to work. Okay?"

Yes, it was okay. Because I knew how it was supposed to work.

"Well we'll work on it," I offered.

"Fine. Yes. I have to go."

Yes, poor Jake. As strong and as tough as he was, I had firmly and solidly knocked him out of his comfort zone.

"Night, Jake."

"Night, Ellie."

I ended the call and wondered when it was going to happen. When Jake was going to learn what I had done. I was guessing sometime next week. He'd have to come into town for something, and when he did he usually ate at Frank's.

Two words. Fire. Works.

Oh, wait, that was actually one word.

One word. Fireworks.

EIGHT

Jake
Tuesday Afternoon

I PARKED my truck and figured I would get lunch first. Then I would drop by the post office to see if my new wire cutters had arrived. I paid way more than I should have, but the reviews in *Rancher's Weekly* had been pretty compelling.

My lips twisted at the memory of Ellie opening her Christmas gift that one year only to find I had given her wire cutters. I might have done better with a lump of coal, she had looked so crestfallen.

I would have to do something special this year. I had a feeling Ellie would want something girly and romantic now that were doing it.

Lovers. It was odd, but the word made me uncomfortable. I wasn't even sure why I told her that. Lovers implied...

I don't know. Something illicit. Despite how all of this had started, we weren't illicit now.

I opened the door to Frank's, wondering if I was in the mood for a burger or some chili, when a girl walked by with honey-brown hair in a ponytail hanging down her back, carrying a coffee pot.

Bernie must have found someone to replace her. Thank God. I took another look because from the back she looked a lot like Ellie. Then she turned around and I saw it was in fact Ellie.

"Hi Jake. Pick any open spot."

"Ellie, what in the hell are you doing here? And why are you holding a coffee pot?"

"I'm a waitress. Waitresses poor coffee."

My eyes narrowed and I didn't have to say anything else. She knew what my expression meant.

"Okay, okay. Hold on. Let me just refresh some coffee and then I'll explain."

She breezed away then as if this wasn't a big deal. This was a fucking big deal!

"Oh no. I told you, once Jake hears about this we're getting Bernie back."

I looked over to see Sam and his wife sitting at a booth, looking at me with concern.

His wife patted his hand and said, "Let's see how it plays out. Ellie obviously has her reasons for being here."

I turned away from them, not able to believe what I was hearing. Ellie was here when she should be at school. Beyond that, she must have been here long enough that Sam and his wife were already making predictions about my reaction.

AND I DIDN'T KNOW ABOUT IT.

Did everyone catch that?

This was a big fucking deal.

I sat in the first open booth and seethed. Then I realized every eye in the place was on me, so I tried to contain my anger.

Ellie came around the booth sans coffee pot and her lower lip between her teeth, which meant she was nervous, which she should be.

"Outside. Now," I said.

"Jake..."

"I mean it, Ellie. I'm not having this conversation in the middle of Frank's." I got out of the booth and grabbed her hand. I made my way down the narrow hall where the bathrooms were and then opened the office door. I knew the back entrance was through there.

Bernie looked up and was about to open her mouth, then she saw me and understood the situation.

"Ellie is on a break."

"Okay, Jake. But don't take her back. I'm not going out there again."

I slammed open the emergency exit, because that felt good, and moved Ellie out the door in front of me. Fortunately the back lot was empty of any smoking dishwashers.

"Talk. Now," I said.

"You know, Jake, I don't think you should be using that tone with me."

"Ellie..."

"But you're surprised, so I'll allow it this time. I quit school."

"Ellie..."

"No. Wait. You can't bark at me to talk and then interrupt me when I do."

I snapped my jaw shut, took a deep breath, and waited.

"Right. So here's the thing. I'm a rancher. I belong on a

ranch. My ranch. The whole school thing felt... stupid and pointless, and I told you that. But you didn't want to listen, and I figured we probably needed more time to work out our stuff. After my birthday, I realized it was even more stupid to stay. I had already made the decision I wasn't going back, so I didn't see the point in sticking around for another month to take tests I could care less about the outcome. I came back here that Saturday. I'm renting the room over the Hair Stop and as you can see, working at Frank's."

I worked through her logic. Then something stuck. "The money! That's how you were able to give me that money."

She nodded. "Yes, it was certainly more important for you to have it to build a house than for me to waste it at school. Except you don't have a house."

"Why does that bother you?"

"Jake, can you say right now you're committed to being with me forever?"

I must have looked like a deer in the headlights. I felt like a deer in the headlights. Like I couldn't blink.

"Exactly. You can't, and that's okay. But if I came back to the house, even if you did *move* to the bunk house or *move* to the cabin, do you really think it would be anything but us boinking twenty-four seven?"

It was harder to know what annoyed me more. The rabbit-ear quotes around *move* or her use of the term *boinking*.

"It would be too easy for you, Jake. We would fall into this pattern, and it wouldn't be about us choosing each other. It would be about us settling. You settling, to be more specific. And damn it, I want more!"

"Okay, that's fine. But why not tell me that? Why not

discuss it with me? This is the second time you've gone off and done what you wanted without once running it by me. We should be making these decisions together!" I shouted back.

"Why!" she shrieked. "Why should we make them together? We weren't an actual married couple. I told you then, it was my money and my decision to go to school. That is still the case. My money, my life, my decision. Not yours. Until we are in a real relationship, I don't have to consult you on any of the decisions I make in my life."

"What is not real to you about our relationship? Because I have to say Ellie, you are pretty much the most real thing in my life."

I didn't know what that meant, I only knew it was true. And it seemed to make Ellie happy because instead of shrieking back, she was smiling at me again.

"I know. We are real. We just have to change things."

"Like what?"

"I want to go on dates. I want to get more flowers. I want you to call me sometimes. I want to be wooed, Jake. That's why I'm staying in town. If I was out at the house it would be too easy for you. You want me, you're going to have to make an effort. Then we can see, like any other normal couple does, if we have what it takes for the long run."

I hated it when she made sense. Because if we were arguing and she made sense, it meant I was wrong.

I worked my way back through the fight to see if I had any justification to hold on to my anger.

"You said you came back here after your birthday. You've been lying to me for weeks."

"I know. I'm sorry about that, but I thought it would be better this way. To let you find out for yourself. You were going to know by the end of the semester anyway. This was always the plan. I just accelerated it."

Always the plan. To come back to Riverbend, but not her own damn house. She was right though. Now that I had her, now that I had reached a place in my head where it was okay to have her, I wouldn't have been able to keep my hands off her if she was at the house regardless of where I kept my clothes.

In fact, I could feel my hands twitching now. Wanting to reach for her because she was standing in front of me.

"I should get back to work. Paying customers and all that."

I nodded. We had to go around the front of the restaurant because we couldn't get in through the back door. It felt like all conversation came to a complete standstill as soon as we walked back inside. Then I took my seat in an open booth. Once everyone could see I wasn't hauling Ellie away, they went back to their own business.

I ordered the chili and a Coke. Ellie cheerfully brought me a refill on the Coke. It was all very civil.

She wanted to be wooed. She wanted flowers. I brought her flowers for her damn birthday.

Then I fucked her brains out. Not exactly romantic.

It was hard to admit I had treated Ellie in any way that was less than respectful. But she was right about that too. I had dated Janet for weeks before I'd ever considered taking her to bed.

And sex with Janet was nothing like being with Ellie.

When I was done I paid the check and left a tip (twenty-five percent, because I was a good tipper normally) and asked if I could have another moment with her outside.

Ellie agreed and walked me to my truck.

"Ellie Samson," I said, because she hadn't changed her

name when she married me. "Will you do me the honor of going out on a date with me sometime?"

She clapped. Then her face got very serious. "Yes, Jake Talley. I would love to go on a date with you."

I leaned down and kissed her on the cheek. "I'll call you."

"Can't wait. Have a good day."

It wasn't until I was halfway back to the ranch that I realized I was still smiling. Because Ellie was back in Riverbed. Because we were going to go on a date.

So yeah. It was a good day.

I STARED at my phone later that night and realized what she said. It was true. I never called her at school. I never reached out to her. Only that one time when she had failed to call me, and I thought now that was probably deliberate on her part.

I wasn't sure why I didn't call her. I guess it all went back to this feeling that Ellie and I weren't normal. That I couldn't push her in any way to be with me. That she needed to have options. For her own protection.

Which in the end I shut down for her by telling her she couldn't date anyone else. Yet she didn't seem to mind.

At some point, just like I had to come to terms with her making decisions for herself, I also had to come to terms with the idea that she had feelings for me and those feelings were real.

Not going to lie. It felt good.

I dialed her number and she answered on the second ring.

"Hey!"

"Hey. I was hoping I could take you out to dinner on Friday."

"Friday works."

And there it was. That simple. Our first date. "Okay, I'll pick you up around six thirty and make the reservations for eight."

"Ooh, reservations. Does that mean what I think it means?"

"Thought I would take you to the Chop House."

"My favorite! I haven't been there since high school graduation."

I didn't say I had been there. With Carol. I was thick sometimes but I wasn't a dumb man.

"Okay. How was the rest of your day?"

"Awesome. I had this really hot guy leave me a twenty-five percent tip."

I smiled. "Probably because the service was super special."

She chuckled. "But seriously, waitressing at that place is no joke. I am on my feet constantly and when I come home all I want to do is sleep."

I looked over at the clock. It was nearly ten.

"Then I'll let you get to it. See you Friday."

"See you Friday. And Jake..."

"Yes?"

"Thanks for calling."

"Good night, Ellie."

"Night, Jake. Dream of me."

The call ended and I decided I was dead tired too. Nothing left to do but go to bed and do as commanded.

Because I did do that at night. I did dream about her.

NINE

Ellie
Friday Night

I HEARD his truck pull up and I nearly squealed like a girl. Or a pig. One of the two. I needed to take a chill pill. This was just Jake. Yes, it was our first official date. And yes, I was out of my skin I was so excited, but I didn't need to let him know that.

Right? Guys liked to chase a little. I told him he needed to woo me and I meant it. I had texted Denny and Maryanne to keep them in the loop. Maryanne had sent back a bunch of smiley faces. Denny had told me what outfit I should wear.

I ignored his advice, despite it being flawless, because I wanted to wear my favorite dress instead. The blue one with the little flowers, that wrapped around my waist. I brushed my hair one more time. Slicked on some pale pink lip gloss and headed for the door, assuming he would beep to let me know he was there.

The knock on my door should have told me this night was going to be a little different. I opened it to see him standing on the landing outside the small apartment with a bunch of daisies in his hands.

He held them out and I buried my face them in again. They weren't exactly the same as my birthday flowers, because those had been the first flowers from Jake ever and this time I sort of had to tell him he needed to get me flowers, but still they were pretty great.

"I have a vase. Let me just put them in water."

"We've got some time."

I stepped back to let him inside and it was a kind of weird. Like I felt almost shy around him, which was ridiculous considering I had had his penis in my mouth more than once.

Still, this was a new dance between us. Not friends. Not fucking. Dating.

Maryanne had shipped all my stuff, but I hadn't taken everything out of the boxes so they were piled up against the wall. I found the one with my vase and made my way into the bathroom to fill it up from the sink.

When I came out Jake had wandered around the small room and focused on the table where I had my scales. Nine on the right. Because let's face it, I was pretty damn happy these days.

I set the flowers next to them. "Ready to go?"

"Yep."

We left the apartment and I locked up. When I got to the truck, Jake was holding the passenger side door open for me. Then he put his hand around my arm to give me a boost.

I had been getting in and out of Jake's truck for years and he'd never, not once, done that.

He shut the door behind me and I struggled what to make of that. Because if this was wooing, this was kind of fun.

"So tell me what it's like working at Frank's," he said as he started the truck and we got on the road.

"It's a little crazy. Not going to lie. I mean I've known all these people most of my life, but who knew they had so many weird habits? Mrs. Petty blew my mind the other day. You know her, she's so nice. She orders the steak, and Frank makes it for her. I put it in front of her and she says it looks funny. That it's not cooked right. Okay, I take it back. Frank doesn't say anything, just makes her another one. Again, not right. I'm like how can you even tell? She just pushes it with her fork. So I go back to Frank with this second steak, thinking he's going to be ticked off, and you know what he does?"

"What?"

"He hands me the first steak and tells me to serve it again and says to trust him. I'm thinking he's crazy, but sure enough I set the first steak in down in front of her and she says, *there, that's perfect.*"

Jake laughed and I laughed with him.

"I asked Frank about it and he says she does it all the time. Which is why he always cooks the second steak to either his or Bernie's preference, because they know it's going to be their dinner that night."

"Mrs. Petty... weird about steak. Who knew?"

I shared a bunch more stories with him. How Howard added extra hot sauce to everything, how Pete had to have his hamburgers cooked until they were burnt, which to both Jake and me was a sacrilege.

Finally he pulled up into the parking lot. When he stopped the car he looked at me and said, "Stay put."

For a second I was thinking he wanted to confirm the reservation or something, but nope. He just came around the truck and opened my door. I unhooked my belt and then he was lifting me (which again, five-nine, I shouldn't be so easily liftable) actually *lifting* me out of the truck until my shoes hit the ground.

"What are you doing?"

"This is a date, Ellie. This is what I do on a date. Just go with it."

"Okay. But I guess this explains why you never went out with Maddie Hornburg, because you would not be lifting her anywhere."

Maddie was in Jake's grade growing up and made me look diminutive.

He shook his head and took my hand (that's right, we were HOLDING HANDS) as we made our way to the restaurant. He held the chair out for me and I sat. And when he pushed the seat back in, he bent down and whispered in my ear.

"You look beautiful tonight."

I blushed. I had to be blushing. This was unlike anything I expected. Maybe a little too over the top.

"Jake," I started as he sat down across from me. "You know you don't have to... I mean I know what I said about the wooing and everything, but I don't... well, I don't want you to force it or anything."

"Force it?"

"Yeah. Like calling me beautiful." I tucked my hair behind my ear and focused on placing my cloth napkin perfectly in my lap.

When I glanced up, he was looking at me strangely. As if I was this new exotic creature to him.

"Ellie, you're one of the most beautiful women I've ever known. Part of that is the way you look and part of that is who you are. I couldn't tell you those things before because... I couldn't. Now I can."

"Oh."

"I get to say that's my favorite dress."

"Mine too."

"I know, because you always wear it on special occasions. Which means you think this is a special occasion, and I like that."

"It's our first date."

"Right. And if I'm going to get you to go out with me again, I'm going to have to both flatter and impress you with my manners."

Who was I to fight it?

"Okay, Jake. Impress away."

JAKE PULLED the truck up to the Hair Stop and turned off the engine.

"Want to come upstairs?" I didn't have to tell you it had been without a doubt the best night of my life. After all it was me and Jake, but with Jake making every effort to be even more perfect.

So naturally I wanted to jump his bones.

"Yes." Only he said it with this deep sigh. "But I'm not going to."

This didn't make sense. "Why?"

He turned to face me. "Because we're not lovers anymore, Ellie."

That totally didn't make sense. "You don't want to have sex with me?"

"Of course I do, but we're dating. Dating means taking things slow."

"But we've already done it. Like a lot."

"Will you cut me some slack here? I'm trying to be a gentleman. Trying to do this the right way."

Okay. I got it. Jake wanted to show me that being with me wasn't all about sex and getting laid.

I was worth more to him than that. Which was sweet. It really was. But also a little disappointing, because apparently I wasn't going to get to jump his bones.

"Okay, Jake."

"May I kiss you?" he asked. Actually asked.

"Yes."

It was beautiful. Soft kisses on my lips. Deep stirring kisses with this tongue. He kissed me slowly and leisurely, like we could sit out here all night and make out. Until finally he pulled away from me. "That's enough. I'm a man, Ellie. There is only so much I can take."

"When can I see you again?"

"Are you working tomorrow?"

I nodded. "A full eight-hour shift, too. But Sunday I'm free after one."

"Why don't you drive out to the ranch and we'll go for a ride? Plus I want to show you some changes I've made."

"Sounds good."

He sighed again like he was reluctant for the night to end, and that made me feel special.

This time I knew to stay put. When he opened my door and lifted me out of the truck I didn't complain. I might have even pressed myself against him, which caused him to moan a little in the back of his throat.

He walked in front of me up the stairs to my room. Took my key and unlocked the door for me.

Then he handed me back my key and waited until I was inside. I started to close the door when he said, "Ellie..."

"Yes?" I held my breath, because I couldn't imagine what he was going to say next when basically everything out of his mouth tonight had been mind blowing.

"On a scale of one to ten, how did I do?"

A ten. He would forever and always be a ten. But I wasn't going to let him know that. I nodded my head as if I was seriously considering my answers. "I'm going with a solid eight. Good start, but let's leave a little room for improvement."

He smiled and I thought he was the most handsome creature on the planet.

"I'll see you Sunday."

"I'll see you Sunday. Night, Jake. Dream of me."

He nodded and then headed down the stairs.

I closed and locked the door behind me, kicked off my shoes right there, and sighed.

Best date ever.

TEN

Jake
Sunday afternoon

IT WAS a little crazy to me how excited I was for her to get here. I had known this girl, now woman, all her life. Dating Ellie should have felt easy. Comfortable. Like putting on a favorite old coat.

It wasn't anything like that. She was new to me in a way I hadn't seen before. She'd blushed when I had called her beautiful, and I thought it was sweet. Of course I didn't know she would do that, because I had never said it to her so directly.

I wanted that blush back. I wanted that blush when she was naked and underneath me.

Although I tried hard not to think about that. I was going to need the same kind of willpower today as I had the other night. I meant what I told Ellie. We should take this slow. I wanted her to know she was worth waiting for. But I had had the sexual experience of my life with her, and she was pretty hard to resist, knowing she wanted me the same way.

Ultimately we would get back there. As long as I knew that, I could keep a grip on my dick. Figuratively, not literally.

Then I heard her truck pull up. I had returned it to her yesterday while she was at work. I had Rich follow me into town so he could take me back to the ranch. I thought about stopping by Frank's, but thought that might make me look too eager. Better to be cool about this.

Although I did get a text from her last night.

New discovery. Mr. Nash has a fear of mayonnaise. Who fears mayonnaise?

I wrote back *Mr. Nash, apparently.*

NOW SHE WAS HERE and we had the rest of the day. And I realized I was happy as shit.

"Jake!"

"In the kitchen," I told her. I wanted to see her expression when saw what I had done.

"Oh my god!" She squealed and clapped. "It's yellow. And that's a new refrigerator and a new oven!"

"The old ones were about to go. I had to replace them, and since you said you always wanted a yellow kitchen I thought I was safe with the paint choice."

"It's perfect."

"I was thinking we could redo the island and counters too. Put a granite top on them. I didn't want to make that call without you."

"That would be awesome. Can we afford it?"

I nodded. Then I reached out to take her hand. "Come on. Let me show you what else I've done."

I took her out to the barn to show her the expansion I put on it. "If we ever have a storm like the one we had, I wanted to make sure we had the extra room."

Then as we walked out to the pen I gave her the numbers breakdown on the herd and the count of calves.

"Jake, how did we do that? We're almost back to full capacity."

"And we've got a new bull," I said, pointing to the pen where Rupert was currently having his way with a cow.

"This is impossible. I've been doing the books. I know every dollar that's been spent. How did you afford all this?'"

I looked at her and that was all it took.

"Jake Talley! You used the money I gave you for your house and spent it on Long Valley instead!"

"Ellie, if you thought there was a chance in hell I was going to keep that money, then you don't know me as well you think do."

She frowned. "I thought you caved too easily."

"There was no use arguing about it."

"But your house! How is that ever going to get built?"

"You spend a lot of time worrying about my house."

"Because Jake, if this thing we're doing doesn't work, if we break up, you need to have somewhere to go."

"If we *break up*," I said (I have no idea why I made rabbit ears around that. I hate rabbit ears. Rabbit ears are stupid unless they are on real rabbits.) "I'll cross that bridge then."

She huffed, but didn't say much after that. I walked her out to the bunk house and knocked on Rich's door. He opened and I could smell the booze on him. It was his day off, but still. At some point I was going to have to address it with him. Especially now that Ellie was back and would be living out here sooner or later.

"Rich, I wanted to introduce you. This is Ellie Samson. Long Valley's owner."

Ellie stretched out her hand and Rich shook it.

"We've talked over the phone, but it's nice to put a face to the person," Ellie said.

"Miss Samson," Rich said in acknowledgement. "Heard a lot of nice things about you."

He didn't slur or stumble. I had to give him that.

"Please. Call me Ellie."

"We're going to ride out," I told Rich.

"I would head north. Ground's still wet to the west."

"Appreciated."

Ellie and I left him to his day and headed back to the barn.

"How old is Rich? I thought he was in his early fifties."

I nodded. I knew where she was going with her question. "That's about right."

"He looks older."

"I get the impression it hasn't been an easy life for Rich."

"Well, I know how he's self-medicating. He reeked of booze."

"I'm aware. But he hasn't missed a day of work. And he doesn't drink while he's working. I'm not saying I'm thrilled about the situation, but I can't tell a man what to do on his down time."

"You're the boss."

That stopped me. "No, Ellie. You are. I'm an employee. So is Rich. If you want him gone, all you have to do is say the word and it will be done. He probably won't be the last person you have to hire or fire."

She nodded. "I understand. It's a man's life we're talking about and not a decision that should be made lightly."

"You said you wanted to be a rancher. It's all yours now, Ellie."

Ellie

ALL MINE. Only I didn't want it to be all mine. I wanted it to be all ours. I didn't say that, though. That was a lot of pressure on date two. Instead we made our way to the barn and I got to shower all my love on Petunia.

"Petunia! Did you miss me? I missed you. Did Jake talk to you?" She huffed and I thought I could hear a distinct *not really* in that answer.

"If you're done with the reunion, can you put a saddle on her?"

I did that after I fed her a few apple slices I had in my pocket.

We headed north along the access road and it felt great. "See, this where I belong. On Petunia and on my land."

"You can move back whenever you want to, Ellie. I can stay at the cabin and still manage to buy you flowers."

"You forget about the boinking," I reminded him.

"Can we stop calling it boinking? It sounds ridiculous."

"You prefer banging?"

"I prefer not discussing it out loud."

"Because you're a prude."

"I am NOT a prude," he said, clearly offended.

"I think you're going to have to prove that. You know I once read this historical western romance where the couple did it while riding horseback."

"What! I would no sooner... On Wyatt?! That's just disrespectful. Apologize to my horse."

I threw my head back and laughed. "Sorry. Didn't mean to offend you, Wyatt. But you know Jake, we are heading in the direction of the cabin..."

"I know what direction we're heading."

"We could maybe stop there for a... break," I suggested.

"Ellie, what did I tell you?" He was growling, so I knew he was at least thinking about it.

"Yeah, yeah, yeah. You respect the hell out of me. But Jake, it's been WEEKS! Can't you go back to respecting me on our next date?"

"Ellie..."

"If you're worried about condoms, there are some at the cabin. Remember I stocked up for my prom date."

"Okay, first of all I'm not using a two-year-old condom. Second of all, I'm not using a condom you intended for someone else to use. That's also flat out wrong."

"Do we even need condoms? We can do the other stuff. You know, try that... oh the number thing. Sixty-nine!"

"Ellie," Jake barked. "Stop talking right now!"

"Because you're imagining the number thing now, aren't you?"

"Hell yes, I'm imagining the number thing, and riding a horse with an erection, despite what your romance novel education taught you, is not comfortable!"

"Sorry to hear that, but I for one am heading to the

cabin. I'm feeling awfully tired. So I think I'm just going to go there, take off all my clothes, slide into bed and see if I can sleep."

I put pressure on Petunia with my thighs and clicked my tongue and she started to run. Which meant Jake was going to have to chase me, and the idea of it sounded hot. I let Petunia go at a full gallop and it was like flying. There was no other feeling like it in the world. Freedom. Exhilaration. Talk about an aphrodisiac. As we came up on the overhang that would lead down to the cabin, I slowed her up. She was breathing heavy so she walked us down the ridge to the cabin. I climbed off her and tied her reins to the post out front.

I stepped into the cabin and it was exactly like I had left it. I had both boots and socks off when the front door slammed open.

Jake didn't hesitate. He just rushed toward me, picked me up around the waist, and the next thing I knew I was on my back on the bed with Jake's tongue in my mouth and his body pressing down against mine.

It was crazy, and wild, and more fun than running Petunia at a full gallop. I was only wearing a t-shirt and jeans, but he almost seemed annoyed that he even had to bother with that. Together we pushed my shirt over my head and even as I was trying to undo my bra from behind he was pulling the cups down so that he could get to my nipples.

God, that felt so good. I had no idea how sensitive I was there until he pulled and pinched and sucked them into his mouth. Finally I was free of the bra and I arched my back and let him play with my body. Back and forth between teasing them and biting them gently.

"Jake, I think I could come from this." I didn't know if

that was a good thing or a bad thing. That it was happening so fast, because I didn't want it to end.

He lifted his head and his eyes had that heavy half-mast look that told me how turned on he was.

"You were supposed to be naked."

"Wyatt's faster than I thought."

"Get naked now."

He rolled off me and got off the bed to watch. I unbuttoned my jeans and took them off first, leaving my panties on. (I wore my sexiest just in case—they were white and a little see-through). I loved watching him look at them as if just seeing them was making him hotter.

"Off," he commanded.

I quickly obeyed. I slid my fingers into them and tugged them slowly down my legs. Until I was as promised. Naked and on the bed. Then I got to watch him. He stripped off his shirt first. Then he reached into his jean pocket and pulled out a condom and tossed it on the bed.

"Respect my ass," I said even as I was smiling.

"I had a thought I should be prepared. That's all." He sat on the bed to take off his boots and I came up to him from behind, pressing my breasts against his back. Letting him feel how hard my nipples still were.

"Ellie, I swear to God... you have to... let me."

I don't know why I thought of it. But I opened my mouth and bit down on the spot where his neck met his shoulder. Just enough pressure for him to feel it. He made this low bark, then shot off the bed.

Then in seconds his jeans were off and he was rolling the condom down over his very hard dick. He was on me and in me and it was just like the last time. A little snug, a little sting, but oh so good.

"You drive me insane," he said into my ear as he started

rolling his hips against me. "I can't control myself around you."

That might have been the second best thing he'd ever told me. Then he pulled out and I whimpered, but it was only so he could get on his knees between my legs.

"I haven't... I should do more for you," he said with an expression on his face that made me think he was in pain.

"I don't want more. I want you," I said, reaching for him.

He wrapped his hands around my hips and pulled me toward him and then he lifted my legs so they were around his waist. I squeezed him like I would Petunia when I wanted to go faster.

He reached down between his legs and then he was inside me again, only so deep this time I thought I could feel him against my heart. I tilted my hips and arched my back and the same feelings I had when I was flying on the back of Petunia came back. Freedom. Exhilaration. Then there was more. The slow build of pleasure. That sense that he was working me toward something with each thrust. I could hear my harsh breathing, his low grunts.

"Jake!"

Then it happened. That all-over body-consuming pleasure, like every muscle was being stretched and stroked at the same time. I felt his hips snapping against me. Felt that last thrust as he groaned the word *fuck*. And then he fell on top of me, crushing me in a way that was so delicious. Because while he was heavy, when he was on top of me like this I had this feeling of being consumed by him.

After a moment he lifted his weight from me and rolled onto his back. I rolled with him and tucked myself up against him. He stroked my hair and we didn't talk. We didn't need to. Because this was bliss.

Oh and the number thing—because while Jake came prepared, he only came prepared with one condom—was also super freaking hot.

ELEVEN

Jake
June

"JAKE. A MINUTE."

I was heading out to the barn when I heard Rich call out to me. I stopped and waited for him to catch up.

"What's up, Rich?"

"I'm not exactly sure how to say this. And as you know, I'm not one for poking into another man's business. Unless it affects me, which I think this does."

"I'm not following."

"Saw Ellie's car here this morning. Saw it here last night too."

Immediately, I felt defensive about it. "Rich, if you've got a point you best get to it."

"I'm wondering why the owner of this ranch doesn't live in her house but you do."

It was a good question, because from the outside looking

in, it didn't make any sense. I didn't think I needed to explain any of that to an employee. "It's complicated. Let's leave it at that."

"I'm guessing, what with her car here some nights and gone in the morning, that she's your girlfriend now."

Technically she was my ex-wife, former lover, and the girl I was presently dating. Although in the last few weeks it felt more solid than simply dating. "Yes, she's my girlfriend. You got a problem with that?"

"No, I'm only asking because... I'm guessing at some point she's going to come back to the ranch. That's what the young people do now, isn't it? Live together? Imagine you won't need an extra set of hands unless she's more of a hands-off operator."

"She's not. She can do everything that needs to be done. She struggles cutting fence line, but that's about it."

"Right. Again, I'm only asking because if I can get heads up on when that's about to happen, so I know when I need to start looking for work. At my age I'm looking for something permanent."

"Understood. If things do change I'll make sure you know about it. And you'll have all the time you need to find something."

"'Preciate it."

He walked off and I thought about it. Between me driving in to town to see Ellie and her driving out here to see me, we were putting a lot of miles on trucks so that she could feel... what did she call it the other day? Balance. Said something about how balance was important and wasn't our relationship perfect.

We never talked about the next step, which as Rich said would be her moving home. Us living together. With Janet that had never been option, because she lived with her parents and I lived in the bunk house. But if she had had a place, would we have lived together?

It might have ended things sooner if we had. Living together certainly speeds up the learning curve on a relationship. Like how Ellie leaves her shoes by the door for you to trip over them every day.

I hadn't tripped once since she left.

I would have to think about it. Right now things were good between us. No point in moving too quickly.

Ellie

"SO YOU'RE TELLING me you're dating your ex-husband?"

When Chrissy said it like that, it sounded strange but I didn't care.

"Yes. Jake Talley is one hundred percent officially, my former ex-husband and current boyfriend."

"You guys are so weird."

I couldn't help but laugh. Chrissy was home from school, and we decided to hang out on Friday night. We were at Pete's, she was having a beer but I had decided I didn't want to drink. I told myself it was because I had to be up early for my shift tomorrow, but the reality was my last time drinking at Pete's didn't end so well. Like nearly getting raped by Bobby MacPherson. So I wanted to keep a completely clear head.

"We are Weird Jake and Ellie."

"But you are so freaking lucky! Jake Talley is the hottest guy in town. I'm bummed I didn't even have a chance with him."

"Sorry. All mine."

"But what if you guys get married? I mean married again. Then you will have had Jake and only Jake forever. Doesn't that worry you?"

"Uh, that's a big no. Besides, you say it like it's so unusual. Maybe it's not the norm now, but plenty of couples around here married their high school sweethearts. Look at the Pettys. I think Mrs. Petty said she started dating Mr. Petty when she was like fourteen. They are probably each other's only."

"Ewww, can we please not discuss the Pettys and their sex life?"

"Fine. Then let's talk about yours. Anyone interesting at school?"

Chrissy huffed. "First there was Greg, and he turned out to be a jerk. Then there was David, and he just wanted in my pants, which can I just say was not all that great when I finally caved. Then he just dumped me. Now there is Eric, but I'm not sure if we're going to make it over the summer."

I didn't say anything. Just sipped my soda and thought how not-awful it was that Jake might be my one and only. The sex was mind blowing, he was definitely not an ass, instead he was the opposite.

Everything was perfect. My scale was set to ten daily. I wasn't even bothered by the fact that he hadn't said he loved me or anything. It was too soon for that anyway. Just because I was there didn't mean we both had to be at the same place, at the same time. Eventually he would get there.

I was certain of it.

"Oh, and did I tell you about Bobby MacPherson?"

"There is nothing I want to know about him," I told her.

"No, seriously. He's in jail."

"Oh my god, tell me he didn't drug another girl."

"No. It was drugs. Cocaine. Not just possession either, but intent to sell. How is that for justice?"

I didn't want to feel good about someone being in jail, but yeah, I kind of liked that he had to pay for something he'd done. Jake, I knew, would be thrilled. I almost texted him, but I didn't want to be one of *those* girls. The ones where as soon as they had a boyfriend, he became the world and everyone else got shoved to the side. Chrissy was home and this was our night and I was going to stay focused on her.

"Hey Chrissy, I didn't know you were home. Buy you a beer?"

I looked up and saw that it was Alex, who Chrissy had dated junior year, standing by our table.

"Hey Alex, I didn't know you were home either."

"A couple weeks. You?"

"Just last week."

"Hey Ellie."

"Hi Alex."

"Let me go get you a beer and we can catch up. You too, Ellie... Jake's not around anywhere, is he?"

Yet another example of the Jake intimidation factor at work. It was a good thing we actually ended up being a thing, or I really might have gone to my grave as a permavirg.

"No. But I don't need anything, thanks."

"I'll take an Ultra bottle," Chrissy said.

As soon as he was out of earshot, Chrissy leaned over the table. "You don't mind if he joins us, do you? I haven't seen him in a while and he's even hotter than I remember."

So much for just a me and Chrissy night. No, I didn't mind. Because unlike me, she was still searching for her guy and I would never want to get in the way of a good love story. "Nope. Flirt away."

"You're the best."

I didn't know about that, but I since I was feeling pretty smug in the relationship department I was willing to be magnanimous.

IN THE END I went home alone. Alex claimed it made way more sense for him to drop off Chrissy than me, since she was on his way home. All I knew was, I was pretty sure Chrissy was right about her and the other guy from school not lasting over the summer. That girl was smitten.

I was happy for her too. I had this delicious feeling inside, as if love was contagious. I wanted everyone to be as happy and as lucky as I was. Which is why when I pulled up in front of the Hair Spot I was grinning like a loony bird.

Because that was Jake's truck parked in front.

He came to see me!

I got out of my truck and practically ran up the steps. I had given him a key for this very reason. In case he wanted to stop by and wait for me until my work shift was done. The TV was on and he was already in bed.

I slipped my shoes off, dropped my purse, and then walked over and hopped on the bed next to him.

"This is a surprise," I said.

He turned the TV off with the remote and looked at me. God, he was hot. Big shoulders, awesome chest. Sometimes I forgot and it took my breath away.

"I'm not going to be able to see you for a few days, so I thought I would come into town tonight."

"When are you leaving?" This was a planned trip down to Colorado to see his friend Don Simmons. So they could talk about bull semen in person. Yuck! The plan was to go camping and fishing too.

"I fly out tomorrow afternoon. But you know, out where we go fishing there's spotty to virtually no cell coverage, so don't worry if I don't call."

"I won't." I would probably, but I wasn't about to be a clingy girlfriend. "And you're sure you don't want me to stay at the ranch to watch over things?"

"It's up to you, but Rich is fine for a few days on his own."

"Thanks for driving into town to see me."

"I didn't want to deprive you of my company for that long," he said with a small smile around his lips.

"Oh I see. Very generous of you not to leave me pining for you. Of course it had nothing to do with maybe you missing me a little?"

"Nooooo. Absolutely not. Men don't miss people. It's a thing about us."

"You're full of shit, Jake Talley."

Then he rolled over me and settled his body between my legs.

"I'm full of something, Ellie Samson," he said even as he pushed his erection against me and dipped his head to kiss my neck. Was this ever going to get old? I couldn't see how.

"I think you better let me have it then."

"That was the plan. Now let's get you naked so I can fuck you goodbye."

"Oh Jake," I sighed. "You're such a romantic."

Jake

I WOKE up to the sound of the shower running. I reached for my phone on the table next to the bed and saw it was almost six. Ellie must be working the morning shift today, so she had to be at the diner by six thirty.

I got up and stretched. Then found my boxer briefs and put them on. I needed to drive back to the ranch, finish packing, then head to the airport. My flight wasn't until later, which made the trip into town doable last night.

Still, all this back and forth between town and the ranch was starting to get old. When I got back we were going to have to sit down and talk about living together. It only made sense. I had been worried about changing things, and it was true it would be a big change, but this was about practicality. Ellie had a ranch to run. Frank needed to find a replacement for her, which was going to take time.

We would have to see if Ellie thought I had done enough wooing of her, and if we had balance, whatever the hell that meant.

Which also meant a conversation with Rich and his future at Long Valley. I supposed I could keep him on full time, but then Javier and Gomez would be out of work. Although with those two it was never certain if they would come back year in and year out.

I pulled on my jeans and threw on my t-shirt. Then I sat on the bed to pull on my boots. The shower stopped and I gave her another few minutes to dry herself. Then I knocked on the door.

"Ellie, hurry. I want to get in there and take a piss before I have to get on the road."

The door opened and she came out with a towel around her head and a towel around her body. Except she had this weird look on her face. Like something had shocked her.

"You okay?"

"Huh?"

"Ellie, you look like you saw a ghost."

"Oh no. Nothing. No, I'm just... You need to hurry. I still need to finish my hair and I don't want to be late."

I did my business and when I came out she was already dressed (not going to lie, a little disappointed I wasn't going to get to watch the show).

I walked over to her and cupped her chin in my hand. "Seriously, did something upset you?"

She smiled. "No, I'm fine. Really. Have fun on your trip."

I bent down to kiss her, a quick taste because neither one of us had time for anything else.

"I'll be back on Wednesday."

"Yep."

"This is the part where you tell me how much you'll miss me."

"But you've already said you won't miss me, so I can't tell you that I'll miss you. Because that would be unbalanced."

"Right. I keep forgetting," I said even as I rolled my eyes. I pecked her lips again, because I could, and then left her to her hair.

"Balance," I muttered to myself even as I made my way down the steps that ran along the side of the building. I seriously didn't even know what that meant.

Still, I was pretty sure she was going to miss me.

TWELVE

Ellie
That same morning

DON'T PANIC. It was the first thing I told myself.

Dontpanicdontpanicdontpanic.

Except when you do it like that, really fast in your head... it was basically doing the opposite.

I was panicking. It was so stupid. I got out of the shower and dried off, and then I opened the cabinet doors under the sink because I wanted to get a nail clipper and trim my toenails.

I don't even know why I paid attention to them. I mean they were always there. In any bathroom I've ever used.

Always pads and Tampax tampons.

But suddenly it occurred to me it was June. And I hadn't needed them since coming home.

Then Jake knocked on the door, which pushed me past

the panicking part, although I obviously didn't do a good job of hiding it because he could clearly see I was freaked.

Fortunately I assured him I was fine, and he left quickly. Then I started doing the math. I was not a fan of math in general without a calculator, but this was girl math and the numbers added up pretty quickly in my head.

My last period was in April. Which meant I'd completely skipped May. How did I not realize that I SKIPPED MAY?

Because I wasn't thinking about anything other than Jake. Jake and sex and dating and balance and more sex. Now it was June. Which meant I should have had my period a second time already and I didn't.

Maybe it was a hormonal thing? All the sex and orgasms were throwing me off my normal cycle.

Okay, totally reaching.

First things first. I called Frank and told him I was sick and couldn't come in today. I didn't feel at all guilty, because I basically worked almost around the clock for him since taking the job.

He told me to feel better and that was that.

I knew I couldn't go to Nash's to get a pregnancy test. Good Lord, the whole town would know in minutes that I was knocked up.

No. Not knocked up. I wasn't anything until a test proved otherwise.

Jefferson. It was my only option.

I got ready, ran down to my truck, and drove the hour to Jefferson. Then of course not realizing what time it was had to wait almost forty minutes outside the pharmacy until it opened. I was the first customer of the day and fortunately alone.

I made my way down the aisle almost clandestinely.

Dumdeedum. Nothing to see here. I picked up three different brands of pregnancy tests, then some mouthwash and a can of hairspray to hide them.

See, just a pile of normal stuff. Nothing strange going on here. Not a thing. I stood at the counter while a seemingly nice old man rang me up.

Hairspray, check, mouthwash, check. Three pregnancy tests... check.

To his credit he didn't say a thing. He handed me the bag, my receipt, and I was out.

The drive back to Riverbend was killer. I was practically coming out of my skin as a dozen different what-ifs ran through my mind.

Every time, I had to cut myself off. Nothing was real yet, until it was real.

I got back to my room and started chugging water from the kitchenette sink. Ten minutes later I felt confident I had enough to pee.

I did the deed, set the stick on top of the toilet tank, and left the bathroom to wait. The test said three minutes. I took my cell phone out and set the timer.

When it buzzed, I literally jumped off the bed.

Then, like a dead man walking, I made my way back to the bathroom. From the door I could see that stick was pink as shit.

Of course, it wasn't the final result. No. I had two more tests to take. Nothing was official until all three brands were in agreement.

Eighteen hours later, because I think I read somewhere that first-thing morning pee was the best to use, I took the third test.

It was real.

I was pregnant.

Wednesday

I SAT at the kitchen table and waited. I knew Jake's flight landed in the morning, but he still had a three-hour drive from the airport. I had no idea what I was going to say to him. Because I knew exactly how this was going to go down.

For four days I had cried and despaired. Then in the really dark moments, I thought about making it go away before he came home and never telling him about it. After all, wasn't it my decision?

But I couldn't. Because it wasn't. This was something we had done together. If he ever knew I had done that without letting him know, it would end us. Any semblance of what we were. And even if he never found out, I would still know I had done that to him. I couldn't live with myself knowing that.

It would hurt him to know I had even had the thought.

But he wasn't going to see this like I saw it. He wasn't going to see how I had trapped him again. How a relationship where both people didn't chose each other was ultimately doomed to failure.

There was this one dream I had. Hope really. That maybe he would walk through the front door to find me waiting for him, and without any prompting he would tell me how much he missed me. How much he loved me.

I heard his truck pull up and felt my stomach drop. This was it. Every practiced speech, every thought in my head of how I could make this not horrible was about to go down.

"Ellie, you here?" Jake called out as he opened the front door.

"In the kitchen," I called back. I took a sip of water and I could see my hand was shaking.

I swallowed.

"Hey, I didn't know this was the plan, but I like it," he said as he bent down to kiss me on the lips. "Not working today?"

I shook my head. I wasn't ready to talk over the lump in my throat.

When I could, I started with the easy stuff. "How was the trip?"

"Hey, can you hold that thought? I just want to run out and check in with Rich first. Make sure there are no fires. Then I'll tell you all about it."

I nodded and listened as he made his way out the back door.

A reprieve. Still, the fantasy was gone. No immediate declarations of love.

I got up to fill up my glass. There was soda in the fridge, but truthfully I had no idea what I could or could not drink yet. Alcohol was out obviously, but what about coffee or did I have to drink tea? And I thought there were new rules about lunch meat.

I didn't know. My head was too wrapped around what this meant for me, for Jake, that I hadn't been ready to go into research mode quite yet.

What was going to be a surprise was his reaction. What he did after that, was not in doubt. But I wondered if he would be angry or sad. Or if he might be happy. He'd always wanted a family. He might in some ways be thrilled, which meant I had to make sure he didn't know how devastated I was.

After all, it was Jake's baby. I was probably going to love the thing.

After another ten minutes passed I heard the back door open and close, and then he was in the kitchen. Smoking hot in jeans and a black t-shirt. The father of my baby.

Yeah, maybe once all the sadness passed about how this would dramatically change the path we were on...I would start to think how lucky I was.

He made his way to fridge and got out a beer. He sat down and stretched out his legs and sighed.

"Long trip. Man, I hate flying. The seats I swear are made for five-foot, hundred-pound women and that's it. Anybody else and you're out of luck. And of course the guy in front of me had to have his seat back all the way. I'm serious, Ellie. Not going to lie, I get a little claustrophobic on those damn things."

I nodded.

This was it. This was the moment. I just had to say it.

"Sorry about that. I'm pregnant."

"So you want to know about the trip... Wait, what did you just say?"

I took in a big girl breath and said it again. "I'm pregnant. I realized the day you left that I missed my period for May and again for June. So I bought three tests and took them and... I'm pregnant."

Jake

"AND... I'M PREGNANT."

It was weird, but it felt the exact way it did when Sam died. We'd been herding the cows to the south pasture. I had been maybe a half a mile away when I saw him grab his arm. Then he'd just teetered off his horse. I'd rode to him as fast as I could and by the time I got there he was dead. CPR hadn't worked. After thirty minutes of breathing and chest compressions, I knew he was dead. And everything was changed and nothing was ever going to be like it was before.

I had that same feeling now. Like I couldn't process it.

Ellie was pregnant. With my baby.

Ellie was pregnant with my baby.

It was shocking. It was life-altering, but it had happened.

"Yeah. Pretty heady stuff," she said.

I looked up at her and thought how amazing she was. Because once again this *thing* happened to her. We'd used a condom every time. She didn't want to get pregnant. Just like she didn't want to lose her dad, or get married at sixteen, or lose half her herd. Yet every time life punched her in the face, she didn't cry or wail or say how unfair it was.

No, she just took it in stride and kept moving forward.

I should have said that to her. I should have said just that. That Ellie Samson was the most amazing, strong, beautiful woman I had ever met. That I was the luckiest sonofabitch in the world because she wanted to be with me.

That this woman was going to be mother of my child.

I didn't say that. Why didn't I say that?

"We have to get married." That's what I said.

She bit her bottom lip and nodded. "That's what I figured you would say."

I reached across the table and put my hand on top of hers. I had to make her understand.

"Ellie, you know we do. This is Riverbend. People aren't going to..."

She slid her hand out from mine.

Why was I talking about what people would think? Why did I care?

I should have asked her. I should have asked her to marry me. That would have been better. But it's not like we had a choice.

"Yep. I know, Jake."

"We can go back to the courtroom. Get the judge to marry us. Howard made that all happen in a couple of weeks."

"Sure. But we've got time. I won't show for a couple of months. I figure it happened on my birthday. Some present, huh?" She smiled tentatively and I thought that was a good sign.

I smiled tentatively back. I didn't want to jump up and down with joy if she was wrecked by this. Then again, I didn't want her to be wrecked by this at all.

"Ellie..." I swallowed. "It's not such a bad thing, is it?"

She stood up and came over and patted me on the shoulder. "No, Jake. It's not such a bad thing. Listen, I'm feeling tired. I was stressing this conversation hard. And I do have to work tomorrow. I'm going to head back to my room, and then tomorrow or whenever we can start making plans."

I grasped her hand in mine. "I'm sorry you had to be alone with this for four days."

"It was probably a good thing. Gave me a chance to process it before I had to tell you." Another small smile.

"Yeah."

"I'll call."

"Okay." I squeezed her hand in mine. "We've got this? Right?"

She squeezed it back. "Yeah, Jake. We'll be fine."

I let her go and she made her way out of the kitchen and I heard the front door close.

That didn't go well. In my gut, I knew that didn't go well, but I... what the fuck? You don't get news that your girlfriend is pregnant and just know what to do. What to say. I said the most important thing. The thing that mattered.

We would be married. Period. The end.

Then the kid would come, and like everything else in our lives Ellie and I would handle it together.

Yes, I told myself. We had this.

Then why was I suddenly so afraid?

THIRTEEN

Ellie

BEE DU BEEP.

I heard the sound of the text and cringed. Cringed. I was cringing when Jake was texting me. That was so not right.

Don't ask me how I knew it was Jake, I just did. As if I could discern a Chrissy vs. Maryanne vs. Denny text. I didn't have different sounds loaded for them, I just knew.

It was late. I was lying in bed. Everything felt unsettled, and when I heard the *bee du beep*, I just knew. And I cringed.

I rolled over and picked up the phone from the nightstand. It wasn't too late. Just after ten, but when I saw his name I knew it meant he was having a hard time sleeping.

Hey. Checking in.

Because that's what Jake did. I sighed and texted back.

All good.

...

...

...

Oh no, I thought. The dots with Jake meant he was struggling.

I feel like I didn't say the right thing today.

He didn't. He was supposed to get down on his knees and profess his undying love for me. In a perfect world, he was supposed to do that before I told him about the baby, but I would have accepted it after as well. But there was nothing I could share with him.

I struggled with what to text back. I was in this weird place with no outs. Before, when I knew how he felt, being trapped in the marriage, it had motivated me to find a way out. For both of us. There was no way out of this. This was a baby. So I was going to have to find a way to get over this horrible melancholy. (Please note, anytime I thought or said this word I did it the same way Will Ferrell did it in the movie *Megamind*.)

I landed on the following:

There is no right thing to say. It was big news. U did ok.

...

...

...

I want us to be happy.

Happy. Could I get there? Could I do that knowing the man I was married to, the man who was the father of my child, didn't love me? Or I should say, wasn't in love with me. Jake loved me. I couldn't not feel that. But there was something holding him back from a full-blown commitment.

It could have been something as simple as my age. Or something as hopeless as he just never thought of me in a romantic light. That even though he wanted me physically, he still wasn't at a place in his head where he could see me as anything other than little Ellie Samson.

Me too, I texted him back quickly. I didn't want him to know how much I was thinking about all of this. Jake liked to keep things simple. We had sex. We made a baby. We got married. We would be happy.

We're going to have a baby! he wrote.

That made the tears come. I wiped them away and tried to sniff them back. I knew he would be thrilled by the idea. Once he got his head around the concept. Once he started thinking about what this meant. I knew it. He'd want a boy. Then he would change his mind and want a girl.

I would get there. I would get on the *JakeandElliewerehavingababy* train eventually. I just wasn't there tonight.

We are tired again.. must be a baby thing Night, Jake

...

...

...

Night

It wasn't the greatest answer to his exclamation mark, but it was the best I could do for now.

I put the phone back on the table next to the bed and then put my hand over my belly. It was just a dot right now. This bean that was going to change our lives forever. I knew eventually I was going to love it. It was Jake's, after all. That love, my love, it would have to be enough for both of us. Yes, soon I would love the heck out of the thing. But right now I couldn't help but think this kid had really poor timing.

"YOU ARE the weirdest person on the planet."

I was sitting across from Chrissy the next day at Frank's.

I was on a shift, but taking a break and stealing her fries when I told her the situation.

"I know, right?"

"No, seriously," she said. "This is like, bizarre the way bad stuff that happens to you."

That was my first moment of parental guilt. I didn't want anyone to think I thought my baby was a "bad" thing that happened to me.

"I wouldn't say bizarre," I mumbled.

Slightly unusual at best.

Then Chrissy started counting stuff off. "Your mom died. Your dad died. You had to get married at sixteen. You had to get divorced at eighteen. And now you are part of the two percent population in the WORLD where the condom didn't do the job. And you have to marry your ex-husband."

When she said it like that, I suppose bizarre was back on the table.

"And that's just you. Jake's mom ran out on him when he was a boy, completely wrote off her only son. His dad drank himself to death, his mentor and stand-in father died. He has to marry a sixteen-year-old so the whole town wonders if he might be a perv. Then he divorces you, which makes everyone think he's a jerk. Now he's knocked you up and everyone is going to think...I guess I don't know what I think."

"Jake is not a perv," I said, angry at the use of the word. Then I thought about everything she listed and thought about how hard life had been for him too. I always thought about things from my perspective, but had I really considered Jake's? I was sad that he couldn't find a way to love me, but now I could see again why being that vulnerable would be so hard for him.

He'd lost so much, too.

"*I* know that. I'm just saying it looked... funny. From the outside. You have to admit that."

I shrugged. I really didn't care what people thought about us.

"So do you want the gig or not?" I asked.

She smiled then. "Yes, I would love to be your maid of honor."

"It's not going to be a big thing. The wedding, I mean. We're going to do it at the court house. But I don't want it to be like last time. I want friends there. I want it to be an occasion."

Karen, Lisa, Maryanne, Denny. Howard and Mirry. Frank and Bernie. Don Simpson and his wife. Rich. A small gathering. A nice dinner back at the house. It wasn't a lot to ask. I hadn't told Jake about my idea yet, but I was planning to next time I saw him.

This time I was going to get a dress. Not a real wedding dress or anything, but something nice and new. I was going to hold flowers. Because this time it was for real.

"You can pick out the ugliest dress in the world and I will wear it. I promise."

I swiped another fry. "Thank you."

"You know, if you were going to get knocked up by anyone, at least it was Jake Talley."

"That's why you're my maid of honor, Chrissy. You always see the silver lining. I better get back to work."

I slid out of the booth, but she caught my hand as I walked by. She had this strange expression on her face, like she was trying to be serious. Only Chrissy was never serious.

"Ellie... I hope... I really super hope... you're happy. After everything. You deserve it. You both do."

Deserve. It was such a crazy word. What someone

deserved in life was pointless. Because what someone got in life... well, that was out of anyone's control really.

I squeezed her fingers. "Thanks. But I'm still going to make you wear yellow or maybe orange."

She laughed, which was my intent, and I went back to work.

Jake

"YOU NEED to tell Frank he has to find a replacement."

It had been two days since I had seen Ellie. There was a problem with a bad birth and we lost a both cow and calf. I had been dealing with that, so I hadn't been able to make it into town. It dawned on me this morning that I needed to fix that.

Ellie was taking her lunch break with me, and I watched her picking at her food. Ellie wasn't a picker. She worked hard at anything she did, so she always had an appetite.

I wondered if she was feeling sick.

"Why?"

"What do you mean why? You need to move back to the ranch. Hell, I would have had you back there today, if I didn't know how much everyone in town would be pissed at me for inflicting Bernie on them again. But that's Frank's problem to solve. I'll give you two weeks and that's it."

"You'll *give* me two weeks?"

I sighed. I hated when she did that. Like what I was saying wasn't totally reasonable.

"Ellie, we're getting married." I leaned in closer because I didn't want anyone to overhear. "You're pregnant. We need to pack up your stuff and you need to come home. All of that has to happen in the next few weeks. Telling Frank now you're leaving only makes sense."

"We have some time, Jake. It's going to be at least another month, maybe two before I start to show anything."

I shook my head. "Ellie this has nothing to do with you showing anything. You need to be at the ranch so I can take care of you. Fuck that, you need to be at the ranch because it's your damn home."

"You're getting mad."

I was. I was getting mad at why she was even remotely making this difficult. This was a no-brainer and I didn't understand her reticence.

That's when it occurred to me. What she might be thinking.

"Are you mad at me?"

"What? No. Why?"

"For putting you in this situation. For...for getting you pregnant in the first place."

"Jake Talley, your sexist phone is ringing."

"Ellie, I'm serious."

"We did this together. We used protection. It didn't work, but there is no blame in this. I don't blame you any more than you could blame me for getting knocked up. It happened. I'm just thinking all of this is happening really fast. We don't have to move at lightning speed."

Lightning speed was exactly the pace I wanted to go. I wanted it done. I wanted us married, I wanted her back home, I wanted her in my bed as my wife. Then our life could start. Our future. With our kid.

Our kid. Every time I thought about it, I got a little crazy. Could I really do this? What if I was like *them*? What if I was the kind of person to skip out on a kid and a wife? The type of person who could forget he even had a child...

I checked myself. I wasn't that person. I knew I wasn't that person. Which is why I knew marrying Ellie now wasn't some kind of knee-jerk reaction to her being pregnant.

"I want to marry you, Ellie. I should have told you that. I should have handled everything better but I was stunned."

"You do?" she asked me quietly.

"Yes." Wasn't that obvious?

She bit her lower lip and seemed to think about that. "But you didn't want to before. When we fought about me staying in town and I asked you..."

"You didn't really give me time to think, Ellie. I get why you took the room over the Hair Stop. And I was fine with dating and taking things slow and wooing you, but..."

"But I'm pregnant," she said. Said it like it was a bad thing.

"Ellie, I'm not marrying you because of that. I want us. Yes, and the baby. I want us to be a family. I want that now. As soon as we can make that happen."

She smiled. A full-blown Ellie smile. Finally, FINALLY, I knew I had said the right thing.

"Okay. I'll tell Frank. Two weeks."

I nodded, satisfied. I looked down at my plate and realized I hadn't taken a bite and it was because I had this feeling of dread in my stomach. Like Ellie was going to tell me she didn't want me or the baby. But of course that didn't happen. So I was hungry again.

"Speaking of the wedding..."

See, that was awesome. She was talking about the wedding. The wedding that was going to happen between us. Soon. Making us husband and wife. Officially for real this time.

"Yep," I said even as I took a large bite of the burger I'd ordered.

"I want it to be more than just us. I want friends there. I already asked Chrissy to be my maid of honor. I think you should invite Don and his wife. They're your friends."

I rolled the idea around in my head. Part of me was hesitant. I didn't want people to know why we were doing this so fast. I also didn't want people to think... that I was just marrying her because of this.

Maybe I didn't want to people to think she was marrying me just because of this.

But Ellie gave me a legitimate smile today, and it was the first one I had had since before leaving on my fishing trip. I would give her anything she wanted.

"Sure. We can do that. Plan a nice reception back at the house."

Another full-blown smile. And she was clapping, in that way that she did like I had just given her the universe. Had I ever told her how that made me feel? Probably not. It wasn't like I was someone who shared emotions easily, but when she did that, when she clapped like a little girl on Christmas morning getting her first toy, it always made me feel as if I had achieved something. I had made Ellie happy, ergo I had accomplished a victory.

"Okay. But that means we have to wait at least a month. You have to give people notice. They need a chance to put it in their calendars. Plus I want to shop for a dress, not some big deal dress or anything, just something nice and pretty.

We'll need to plan a guest list and a menu for the reception. All of that takes time."

I frowned.

"One month, Jake, and don't go all eighteen hundreds on me. I know you think you're going to be able to hide it from everyone about why we needed to get married. That we'll just say the baby was a little early or something, but it's the twenty-first century. People know better."

She was right. People were going to know, but that didn't mean I had to like it. Still, one month didn't seem too long to wait.

"Okay. Whatever that Saturday is a month from now."

"You won't regret it," she said with a bit of smug satisfaction.

"But you move home next week."

"Yes, Jake," she agreed. I knew she was placating me, but I didn't care. The good news was after our talk, she was eating again.

Which was good. Because she was eating for two.

FOURTEEN

Ellie
July

"ARE YOU KIDDING ME RIGHT NOW?"

It was my first night back home. We had packed up all my stuff, and when I say *we* I meant Jake because he wouldn't let me lift anything that was heavier than a pound. I had given Frank notice that day after Jake and I had lunch. He hadn't been thrilled about it, but he'd seemed resigned. After all, he knew eventually I had to go home. I did tell him Chrissy was looking for summer work, and then he'd looked at me like I had two heads.

Chrissy didn't exactly have a reputation for being super reliable, but at least she wouldn't spill stuff on people. At least I didn't think she would, but that was Frank's call to make.

Meanwhile I'd let Bella know I was heading home. She'd just smiled at me and said it was about time.

Two weeks later, Jake had driven out to town and took all my stuff to his truck, and then I'd followed him home in my truck. He'd grilled steak for dinner while I unpacked the essentials. Mostly my toothbrush, moisturizer, brush, hair dryer, some clothes, and my scales.

It had been hard call on what number to give the scale. On the one hand I was thrilled to have them back where they belonged. On my kitchen counter. On the other hand they were only back on the kitchen counter because I was knocked up.

Ultimately, I had settled on seven. It was a good number for how I felt.

Now we were in bed, which was kind of weird because this was how it was going to be for the rest of our lives. Not that we hadn't slept together. I had stayed over some nights and Jake had stayed over with me some nights, obviously. But this was it. This was official.

This was the start of our life together.

Which I thought should begin with awesome and amazing sex.

He thought otherwise.

Which is why I asked him, "Are you kidding me right now?"

He was reading one of his ranching magazines, so he wasn't looking at me when he said, "You've had a long day on your feet, up and down the steps, packing and unpacking. You need to rest."

I flopped back on the bed. "Ugh! Jake Talley! Please tell me you're not going to do this through the entire pregnancy."

"Make sure you're well fed, well rested, and looked after. Yes, Ellie I am."

"How many times do I have to tell you, I'm not china.

I'm perfectly healthy and sex isn't going to hurt me. It's going to make me feel good."

He glanced at me and I knew he was caving, but then he seemed to make up his mind.

"Not tonight."

"You're being ridiculous," I said as I settled under the covers.

"I don't think I am."

The worst part was as soon as I put my head down on the pillow I let out this massive yawn.

"Told you," he muttered.

"Know-it-all."

I turned on my side to watch him read for a bit. "This is a first for us."

"How so?"

"It's the first time we're sleeping together without having sex first."

He looked down at me. "You know we're going to be married. For life. It's not like we're going to have sex every single night."

"Why not?"

He laughed. "You're going kill me."

I settled into my pillow and then I reached out to touch his arm. Just because I could.

He didn't pull back or shrug me off. Instead he let me stroke him with my fingers.

"Are you scared at all?" I wondered. "You know, about the whole parenting thing."

He looked up from his magazine and then he got this strange faraway expression on his face, like he was looking into the past or the future, it was hard to tell.

"Desperately, Ellie. But I can promise you I'm going try my best."

"Of course you are, Jake."

Then I got drowsy and I could feel myself drifting off to sleep.

I guess I was tired after all.

Jake

SHE WAS ASLEEP IN MINUTES. She couldn't see it, but I could. The dark circles under her eyes, the slump of her shoulders. She'd been bone tired by the time she got into bed, and the last thing she needed was me between her legs.

I couldn't help but watch her for a while. Ellie was a beautiful girl, but not while she was sleeping. She wasn't like Snow White or Sleeping Beauty. All serenity and loveliness.

Nope, she usually slept with her face half smushed into the pillow, with her mouth open a little. In a couple more minutes she would make this small snoring noise. It wasn't loud or obnoxious. Just a sound I would come to know as part of the soundtrack that was Ellie.

Hopefully, a sound I would sleep with every night of my life from here on out.

It was one of those things I liked knowing about her. Because I was the only one who did. I was the only one, would be the only one, to ever know how Ellie looked and sounded as she slept.

Her scales were set to seven. I knew because I checked right after she set them up. It was a decent number, and I thought maybe she did it because of how she was feeling about the baby. Obviously she was just as scared as I was. Her question suggested as much. We would get through that, too.

Still, in that moment, I had committed to making those scales go higher.

To be the man who, day in and day out, made Ellie happy. A ten, on a scale of one to ten. I turned the light off on my side of the bed and tossed the magazine on the nightstand. Then I settled down next to Ellie and thought about how right this all felt.

I listened to the sound of her soft snores until I drifted off to sleep.

I WOKE UP HARD. Not a shock when Ellie had her hands inside my boxer briefs and was stroking me. I glanced over at her to see she was awake with this playful smile on her lips and a glimmer of mischief in her eyes.

"I'm nice and rested now, Jake."

"So it would seem."

The sun was coming up. I had a thousand chores to take care of, but I wasn't going anywhere. Instead I just lay there as she worked my cock, knowing now how I liked pressure on the head of it, knowing just what grip to use.

"Fuck, that feels good."

She sat up then and lifted off her tank top. I reached for her breasts and I tried to feel if there was any difference. If they were bigger or more sensitive. Nothing yet so far, but that would change. I tweaked and tugged on her nipple until she squirmed. Then she pulled the covers down and straddled me.

She pushed my boxer briefs down just far enough to have my cock out. Then, helpless against her, I watched as she positioned herself over me and took me inside. She was wet and I slid in so easily. This was my first time doing it without a condom and it felt fucking mind-blowing. So hot, so wet. Her skin on mine. I had no idea.

I started to put my hands on her hips to guide her, but she moved them to her breasts. Then she slowly rolled herself up and down, and it was outstanding. Because I knew it was going to take me forever to come like this, so it would last. And last. Just the feel of her sliding up and down on my cock, her nipples hard bullets against the center of my palms.

Then she was grinding against me hard, using me to get off. I watched her face as it came over her. Her beautiful fucking face.

"Ahhhhhhh... haaaaa... so good. Every time it's so good," she muttered.

She was right.

And then because she knew, because I had once told her about not coming when I was on the bottom, she slid off me and just waited there on her hands and knees. Then she wiggled her bottom and winked at me.

I barked out a laugh, but I didn't hesitate. Sure, I would have come eventually, but I wanted this now. I got behind her on my knees, took my wet dick in my hand and eased my way back inside her.

She gasped and sighed as I started to pump my hips and I thought I could do this. I could so easily fuck Ellie and no one else for the rest of my life. I reached around with my hand and slid my fingers between her slit.

I could feel her working her clit against them even as I worked my dick inside her pussy.

"Ellie, I need you to get there," I told her. Because I wanted her to come again and I knew I wasn't going to last. I could feel it already in my balls.

"Jake, Jake, Jake."

I loved that. I loved when she called my name. I thrust deep and hard. Then I could feel her fingers on top of mine, pressing me harder against her, and then she was moaning again.

"Yessssss!" she cried out.

It overtook me. The release. So intense and powerful it felt like I was pouring my come into her. She slumped underneath me and I slid out of her and spooned her from behind.

"Happy first day of the rest of our life together," she said.

I kissed her on the shoulder in response. I gave myself five minutes. Five minutes to feel that post-orgasm bliss. But I was a rancher and there were chores to do.

I started to get up.

"Noooo," she crooned.

I liked that. I liked that she was upset I was leaving her. I pulled up my underwear and walked around the other side of the bed. I bent down to give her a kiss on her temple.

"A ranch doesn't run itself, Ellie."

"So you say... but have we ever tried?"

I pulled the covers up over her. "Go back to sleep. It's early."

She mumbled something but she didn't get up. I did my normal morning routine but stopped before I left to give her another kiss. She was already asleep again. That was something else I knew about Ellie. She always got a little sleepy after sex.

Or maybe it was the baby. Fatigue, I knew, was part of

the whole pregnancy thing. I left for work with what I knew was a shit-eating grin on my face.

Ellie

IT WASN'T A BIG DEAL. According to the internet it could mean nothing. Still, I had to be careful. I didn't tell Jake because I knew it would freak him out.

It was just a little spotting.

I had been back at the house for a few days. Things were pretty great between us. I had resumed mostly my normal role. I fed chickens, I rode Petunia, I shoveled shit out of the barn. I was barred from any heavy lifting by Jake, which I had already concluded myself. I wasn't a total idiot. But I considered myself a young, healthy person.

There was no reason to change my workload just because I was pregnant.

But this morning when I woke up and went to the bathroom, I noticed a few drops of dried blood in my panties. So I told Jake I needed to grocery shop, which was true, and took the truck into town.

I stopped first at the clinic. As I walked through the door there was always that *uhg, I'm here again* moment. My memories of this place were nothing but bad ones. Broken bones, horrible flus, and then of course the *thing* that happened last year with Bobby.

The good news however was that Mary had officially passed her boards, so she was an actual nurse now. She was behind the front desk and it looked like she was filling out some paperwork.

"Hey, Mary."

"Ellie." She smiled. "I heard you were back in town. And that you and Jake were a thing."

That was Riverbend. Everyone knew everyone else's business and had absolutely no problem getting confirmation from the source.

"Yep. Jake and I are definitely a thing." Big, massive thing.

"That's not why you're here, though. What's up?"

"Uh, where is Dr. Jenkins?"

"Sorry, he just left to grab lunch. I'm all you've got."

Mary would probably be the one to examine me anyway. "Can we use the examination room? Just in case someone comes in."

"Sure."

She led me down a short hall to one of two examination rooms. We stopped at the first one and I stepped inside and sat on the paper-covered examining table.

"Okay, now tell me what's wrong."

"Not wrong really. I'm pregnant."

Her eyes got wide, but she said nothing.

"At least that's what three different little sticks told me."

She smiled. "Okay, well first we're going to get that confirmed. You're going to need to pee in a cup for me. When was your last period?"

"April ninth or tenth, somewhere around there. Not exactly sure. It's not like I put it on the calendar or anything."

"Got it."

"But here's the thing. We can do this like a normal visit, but I actually came down here today because... well, this morning I had a little blood in my underwear. I checked online and read that it could be normal..."

"It can be. Especially in the first trimester. Any cramping?"

I shook my head. "Nothing that made me go ow."

Although there had been a feeling of... tightness. I guess that was the best way to describe it.

"What about nausea?"

I shook my head again. "No, nothing like that."

"Okay. Well, let's get that sample and we'll confirm you are pregnant. Then what you're going to want to do is just watch the bleeding. See if it intensifies. In the meantime, rest, avoid heavy work, no sex for a few weeks, sorry, and pads only. No tampons."

I nodded and then went to pee in a cup.

I left with a sample of prenatal vitamins and sense of dread. If sex was off the table then I was going to have to tell Jake, and that meant he was going to freak out on me. I had no doubt if he could wrap me in bubble wrap for nine months he would.

I headed over to Nash's and bought the groceries, and thought about how to tell Jake there might be a problem.

Or could I get away with *I just wasn't in the mood* for a few weeks?

Given the other day I woke him up with my hand down his underwear, practically begging for his dick, probably not.

Besides, this was probably something he would get really pissed about if I didn't tell him. He got mad when I sold the trust fund without telling him, but my excuse was that it had been my money, so it was my choice. Then again when I chose to drop out of college.

But this baby was half him, so he had to be included in

the process. I wasn't going to track him down on the ranch, but tonight when he got home I would tell him about the spotting, the visit to the clinic, and that we would have to abstain from intercourse.

Then I would give him a blowjob. That might help contain the freak out.

It was a solid plan.

Until the cramping started.

FIFTEEN

JAKE

I HAD JUST PUT Wyatt in his stall and was making my way out of the barn when I heard Ellie scream my name. It wasn't a good scream either. Not the kind she gave me in bed.

That sound. That was the sound of Ellie in pain. I started running as fast as I could and I could see her at the back door of the house. Holding on to the door frame, bent over and obviously in a lot of pain.

I rushed to her and found her crying.

"Something's wrong, something's wrong. There was some spotting and I went to the clinic and I was going tell you tonight I swear, but now it really hurts."

I wasn't listening to any of that. Instead I was focused on the on hand towel she was holding between her legs that was red with her blood.

I didn't think, I didn't ask any questions. I just scooped her up in my arms and ran as fast as I could to the truck parked under the portico. My keys were in it, out of habit, and as gently as I could I slid Ellie in the back seat. Immediately she curled up in pain.

"Shit," I cursed. Then I hopped in behind the wheel and drove as fast as I knew how to drive.

"I'm sorry, I'm sorry," she said.

"Stop saying that."

She was writhing in pain in the back seat and trying to tell me she was sorry.

"No, it's my fault," she sobbed. "It's because I was upset at first. I didn't want to be pregnant. So this happened."

"Nothing is your fault, Ellie. You did nothing wrong!"

"I'm so sorry, Jake. I'm sorry."

"Stop saying that."

It was horrible. I would glance behind me, but when I did I would see the blood and I could not handle the sight of Ellie bleeding. I wasn't so stupid that I didn't know what it meant, but I couldn't think about that right now. My focus had to be on Ellie.

Ellie was in pain. Ellie was bleeding.

I needed to make those things stop.

It felt like forever, but in reality it was the shortest drive into town ever. I pulled up in front of the clinic and jumped out. It wasn't easy because she was having another cramp, but I managed to pull Ellie out of the back seat so that she was in my arms.

"Breathe through it, Ellie," I told her. "Short pants, then deep breaths."

I was a rancher. I had watched any number of things give birth. Breathing was the only thing you could do to not tighten up against the pain.

"Dr. Jenkins!" I shouted as soon as I got through the door.

Mary bounced up and took one look at me and seemed to know immediately what was happening.

Right. Ellie had said something about the clinic. She must have been here earlier today, maybe worried about the bleeding. I had been pushing her these last two weeks that she needed to make an official appointment.

"Follow me," Mary said and led me to the examination room straight ahead. She opened the door and I put Ellie on the table.

"The doctor is in with someone, but I'll get him now."

Ellie rolled to her side with a groan. She was sobbing now, but I didn't know if it was from the pain or...

I couldn't think about that now.

Dr. Jenkins came in and then immediately turned to me. "I need you to step out."

"I'm not leaving her."

"Jake, I'm telling you now. Step out of the room."

"Go, Jake," Ellie cried from the table even as her hands were pressed against her belly. "Please go. I don't want you to see."

I had never felt more useless in my life. I walked out of the room and the door closed behind me and it was like nothing I had ever felt before. I walked down the short hallway and sat in one of chairs in the waiting area, my head in my hands as I thought about what just happened.

I had been so freaking happy today. Had been every day since she'd been home. As happy as I had been, was as sad as I was now.

Why couldn't Ellie and I ever get a break? One fucking time, a break. From pain and loss and sadness.

A half hour later I looked up and Dr. Jenkins was standing in front of me.

"It's done, Jake. As far as I can tell, she was about ten weeks along."

I knew exactly how far along she was. It happened on her birthday. I closed my eyes against the pain.

"I'm going to send her in the ambulance to Jefferson."

"Why?" I asked with a new sense of fear. "Is something else wrong? Is there some kind of complication?"

He shook his head and put his hand on my shoulder, I suppose to calm me. "No. But given how far along she was, there is a procedure to make sure everything has been expelled from the uterus. I don't have the facility for it here. She'll go to Jefferson, they'll probably do it first thing tomorrow morning, and then you can take her home after that. You know where you're going?"

I nodded. "Jefferson Hospital." It wasn't like there was more than one hospital.

"You okay to drive?"

I looked up at him. "Yeah. Can I see her?"

He had that sad somber look I assumed all doctors must practice when they had to deliver bad news. "She's a little upset right now, Jake. I would give her some time. You'll see her once they put her in a room at the hospital."

She didn't want to see me. Okay. I got it. That made sense. Maybe it was a good thing. We were both a little raw.

"Jake, she's a young, healthy girl. Miscarriages happen. She'll pull through this."

"Yeah."

Dazed, I made my way outside and back to my truck. I had left the keys inside and the back door open. I suppose that was some luck thrown my way. That some passing car thief hadn't stumbled across it.

I sat for a moment and tried to deal with what had just happened. Then I saw the ambulance, which was always parked behind the clinic, pull out and instinctively I knew I had to follow it.

The whole time I kept my eyes on it, wondering what Ellie must be going through.

She thought it was her fault. Because at first she hadn't wanted to be pregnant. Of course she hadn't. It's not like we had planned this. I knew she wasn't happy with the idea of having to get married, but in the end she'd come around. These past few days...

We had been so damn happy.

I lost the ambulance when it pulled into the Emergency Room entrance way. I had to go around back to visitor parking. I entered through the front doors and the first thing that hit me was that smell. Hospital smell. A combination of sickness and antiseptic. I hated that smell. That was the smell of Ernie when he died. Sam too, although Sam had been dead long before he reached the hospital.

Now it was the smell of Ellie and our lost baby.

I asked the receptionist for Ellie's room, but they said it would take some time to process her. She asked me about health insurance and I shook my head. Neither Ellie nor I had it. We talked about signing up for one of those self-employed insurance plans, but we were probably both too young and too stupid to think we needed it.

The last thing I cared about though was the money. I just wanted to see Ellie. Finally, after what felt like forever, the receptionist gave me a room number. I made my way up two floors and down the hallway and turned a corner. I stood outside the door, wondered what the hell I was going to say to her, and then took a deep breath.

I knocked on the door to give her warning, but she didn't look at the door. She was in the bed closest to the window and was staring out of it. The other bed in the room was empty.

I walked over and slowly sat down in the chair next to her. She still wouldn't look at me. I reached across the bed and tried to take her hand, but she made it a fist.

"Ellie..."

"I can't, Jake," she said and I could hear her voice cracking. "I can't talk to you right now. Please don't make me."

Make her? Hell, I wasn't going to make her do anything.

"Can I get you anything? Something to drink?"

She shook her head tightly.

"You don't have to talk to me, Ellie. But I need to be here. You need to let me stay here. Is that okay?"

She nodded.

"Okay."

Ellie
The next day

MAYBE THE HARDEST part was the car ride home from the hospital. The two of us in this tight space. I still couldn't talk to him. I didn't have any words. *I'm sorry* wasn't enough. I didn't know if he was sad or relieved or what he felt.

I was numb. Full-on numb.

As upset as I had been about finding out I was pregnant, the miscarriage should have meant nothing to me. If anything it should have been a relief. Now we didn't *need* to get married. I should be happy. That only made sense.

Except as soon as the cramping started I had this bolt of fear and I prayed with everything I had in me that it wouldn't happen. This dot that I hardly let myself think about became the most important thing in the universe in that moment, and I didn't want to let it go.

Only I couldn't stop it.

Now it was gone and everything was over. And it was like I would never feel anything ever again.

It reminded me of when my dad died.

Shock.

That's what Jake had called it back then. We got back to Long Valley and instead of parking Jake pulled up to the front of the house.

"Stay here."

It was the first words he said to me since we left the hospital. After he asked me how I was.

Then the car door opened and he was lifting me out and holding me in his arms.

"Jake, I can walk."

"You're not walking."

I didn't have the energy to fight him. He brought me inside, carried me up the stairs like I weighed nothing, and then started walking me toward his room.

"I should stay in my room," I said. I wasn't sure where that came from, but I just knew I didn't want to go back to his room. I didn't want to lie in that bed where we had been so happy. Not when I felt like this.

"Why?"

"It's better if I sleep alone, so you don't jostle me in the middle of the night."

It was awful. To imply even obliquely that he might do

something to cause me more pain. But I knew it was something he wouldn't argue with me about.

He didn't. Instead he took me to my room and set me gently down on the bed.

"You must be hungry," he said. "It's almost five in the afternoon and you haven't eaten since yesterday. I'll go put together some sandwiches quick."

"Actually I'm not hungry. Just really tired. Is it okay if I take a nap instead?"

"Yes," he blurted. "Of course. Whatever you want to do. Are you comfortable?"

The doctor told me what to expect. Some minor cramping and bleeding over the next two days or so. They had given me an ibuprofen for the pain, so actually I felt fine. They had given me a pair of scrub pants because my jeans had been ruined...

Don't think about it.

But yes, between the scrubs and the t-shirt I was wearing I was fine. I didn't have shoes on, because I hadn't been wearing any when it all went down, so I pulled the covers down around me and then slid into bed.

"Yes. I'm fine."

"Ellie..."

I turned away from him then, which was rude, but I didn't want him to see me crying and I still didn't have any words for him.

"Please... talk to me. Let me help you."

"Later, okay Jake?" I sniffed. "I really am super tired."

Jake

I WANTED to yell at her. I wanted to shake her. Force to her say something. Anything. Yell at me, hit me, blame me for every sadness in her life. Something other than this.

Because this was worse. This felt like she was shutting me out. I carried her up the stairs and I remembered the last time I had done it. The day of the snowstorm when she'd unhooked herself from the damn safety line to try and save a calf.

I remembered freaking out then because I thought I might lose her to hypothermia.

Only now I was the one who was frozen.

Because she was shutting me out and it was crushing me.

Quietly, I left the room because there was nothing I could actually do. I made my way downstairs toward the study, because a drink was the only thing that made sense right now.

I poured the whiskey and sat down in the chair behind the desk. The one that used to belong to Sam. I thought about the horsewhipping he might give me if he was here right now.

"Yeah, Sam," I said to the empty room. "Sorry about taking her virginity and knocking her up. For putting her through this crushing ordeal. But I'm sure you would understand... I really wanted her."

I took a hard gulp. I tried to think about what this might mean going forward, but it was like my brain didn't want to go there. All I knew for certain was that for next few days she was supposed to stay off her feet and rest as much as possible.

That, right now, was all I could handle.

SIXTEEN

Ellie
August

IT WAS TIME. I was fully recovered. Really I had been after a few days, but the only thing Jake could do for me was pamper me, so he insisted I stay in bed for five days and then wouldn't let me leave the house for another three after that.

Then it was another few days of walking on eggshells around me until I couldn't stand it anymore.

So it was time. I had my most important stuff packed and already in the truck, just a suitcase and my scales. I would come back for the rest later. I wasn't even really sure why I was taking my scales. It's not like I wouldn't eventually be coming back here, but the thought of being without them was too upsetting.

I was sitting at the kitchen table, thinking about twelve weeks ago when I had told Jake I was pregnant. I had said those words like they were the words of doom. I knew Jake wanted kids. I had always known that about him. And the first experience of having children that I gave him was a really crappy announcement followed up by a miscarriage.

What a particularly horrible way for our story to end.

I heard the back door open, and I tensed.

I was not going to cry through this. I was not. I was going to say what I had to say and then I was going to leave with some modicum of dignity. At the very least our story deserved that.

"Hey, how are you feeling?" he asked as soon as he came into the kitchen.

So damn beautiful, I thought. Just a stupid t-shirt and jeans and he was smoking hot. And he was mine. Or had been for a little while. I could at least have that.

"Fine," I answered. The same thing I answered any time he asked.

"Ellie, what is it? I can tell something is wrong."

"I'm leaving."

There, I said it. I let out this woosh of breath.

"I don't... what do you mean?"

"I'm going back to the room above the Hair Stop. I'll see if I can get my job back at Frank's. Chrissy will be heading back to school soon."

He was shaking his head.

"I'm not following."

"I'm done, Jake. I can't do *this* anymore. We're not married. We have no reason to be married now, and I'm done."

"Done with me," he said tightly. "You don't want me anymore. Why don't you say it one more time? I've been feeling it for the past two weeks!"

I looked up at him then. His face was blank but that muscle was twitching at the back of his jaw.

"Oh no. You don't get to make this about me." I could feel my anger bubbling. Anger would be good right now. Anger would get me through this.

"How can I not make this about you? You're sitting there telling me you want to go. You're done with me. I don't want *you* to go. I want you to stay. So yes, Ellie, this is about you and your choices. Not mine. Never mine."

I was nearly incredulous. Was he kidding me right now?

"Hey Jake." I stood then, my hands braced on the table. "Breaking news just in. I LOVE YOU. I HAVE LOVED YOU FOR YEARS. And you know it! You goddamn well know it. But you don't love me. Oh yes, you care for me. I'm family. But you're not in love with me. You know how I know? Because when we woke up after my birthday you should have said *I love you, Ellie. Come home with me.* Because when I told you I was pregnant you should have said *I love you Ellie, please marry me and make me the happiest man alive.* But you didn't. Not one *I love you*. Not once. So yes, I'm done, Jake. I deserve to be loved as much I love you. I deserve the kind of happiness my parents had. I do."

He said nothing and I straightened my back until I was as tall as I had ever been.

"I'm going to go back to the room over the Hair Stop. You are going to build your house as quickly as you can and move onto your land. Some day in the future we'll find a way to get along somehow. And that is the end of the Jake and Ellie story. Goodbye, Jake."

I made it to the front door when I heard him.

"Don't go."

I turned around to tell him not to make this any harder,

but when I did I saw he hadn't been looking at me when he said it. His gaze was off as if staring at a ghost over my shoulder.

"That's what I said to my mother the night she left. She came into my room. I was eleven at the time. You don't remember her, I know, you were just a baby. Anyway, she came in to tell me that she was leaving. That she couldn't stay in Montana anymore and that it was better if I stayed with Dad. Then she said it would be cleaner this way. I didn't realize at the time she meant she was just going to forget she ever had a son. Then she left the room, and I ran after her down the hall and I said, *Mom, I love you. Please don't go.* And she left."

The tears came and I couldn't stop them. "You never told me."

He shrugged his shoulders. "Who wants to tell that story? I told myself I would never say those words again. That wasn't going to happen. No way. That... being rejected like that...that just hurt too much."

"Oh Jake, I'm so sorry."

"I tried to show you. I thought I... did. I tried to give you presents I knew you would love so you would see. I tried to be there for you when you needed me. I tried to be the man someone like you deserved. I... in bed... I mean I tried to show you what I was feeling the whole time. I thought you knew. You had to see it. Feel it. Yeah, I thought if I could show you. It would be enough."

He walked toward me then and I was shaking so hard I couldn't move.

He fell to his knees in front of me and rested his head on the womb that used to carry his child.

"I love you, Ellie. Please don't go."

Then he did something in my life I had never seen Jake Talley do. Not when his dad died. Not when my dad died.

He sobbed. He wrapped his arms around me and sobbed and it was the most heartbreaking sound I had ever heard in my life.

Jake

I CAME in through the back door with a sense of dread of another night like the last few nights had been. Ellie still couldn't talk to me about what happened. She was just this zombie going through the motions. I was trying to be as careful as I could around her, but I felt this distancing from her. Like our lives were tied together with a hundred pieces of string that she was cutting one by one.

"Hey, how are you feeling?" I asked when I saw her sitting at the kitchen table.

So damn beautiful, I thought. Just a stupid t-shirt and jeans. No makeup. There were times I couldn't believe she was really mine.

"Fine," she answered. In that short clipped way she had been since it happened. Like I was some distant stranger she barely knew.

Maybe it was the fact there was no food on the table, or cooking on the stove. But for some reason this felt like it had twelve weeks ago. When she had a bombshell to drop on my head.

"Ellie, what is it? I can tell something is wrong."

"I'm leaving."

I heard the words. But they didn't make sense.

"I don't... what do you mean?"

"I'm going back to the room above the Hair Stop. I'll see if I can get my job back at Frank's. Chrissy will be heading back to school soon."

I shook my head. Why the hell would she do that? This was her home.

"I'm not following."

"I'm done, Jake. I can't do *this* anymore. We're not married. We have no reason to be married now, and I'm done."

This. She waved her finger back and forth between her and me when she said it. Our relationship. That's what she meant by *this*. Only she said it like it was some foul thing.

And she was done. With. Me.

"Done with me," I repeated. I suppose it made sense, given how she had been acting. But I wanted her to say it again. I wanted her to say it completely so that I would hear it and understand what was happening right now.

"You don't want me anymore," I said again. "Why don't you say it one more time? I've been feeling it for the past two weeks!"

Yes, I was mad. That she could even think about leaving me. We were happy. So fucking happy. Yes, a horrible thing happened. We'd had horrible things happen to us before. We had survived so damn much together, and now she was just *done?*

"Oh no. You don't get to make this about me."

Was she getting pissed? She was sitting there dumping me, and she was getting pissed at me? Was she serious right now?

"How can I not make this about you?" I charged at her. "You're sitting there telling me you want to go. You're done with me. I don't want *you* to go. I want you to stay. So yes, Ellie, this is about you and your choices. Not mine. Never mine."

"Hey Jake." She stood up then and braced her hands on the table. "Breaking news just in. I LOVE YOU. I HAVE LOVED YOU FOR YEARS. And you know it! You goddamn well know it. But you don't love me. Oh yes, you care for me. I'm family. But you're not in love with me. You know how I know? Because when we woke after my birthday you should have said *I love you Ellie. Come home with me.* Because when I told you I was pregnant you should have said *I love you Ellie, please marry me and make me the happiest man alive.* But you didn't. Not one *I love you.* Not once. So yes, I'm done, Jake. I deserve to be loved as much as I love you. I deserve the kind of happiness my parents had. I do."

Wait. What? She thought I didn't love her? She thought I wasn't in love with her. How was that fucking possible? Yes, I screwed it up when she told me about the baby, I knew I should have said probably exactly that, but I couldn't say those things. I wasn't the kind of man who could just say those things out loud. It was about actions, not about words.

Because of her.

It felt like a ghost running across the back of my neck.

"I'm going to go back to the room over the Hair Stop. You are going to build your house as quickly as you can and move onto your land. Some day in the future we'll find a way to get along somehow. And that is the end of the Jake and Ellie story. Goodbye, Jake."

I watched her turn her back on me, watched her walk out of the kitchen, and I thought *oh hell no.* That was not how our story was going to end.

I wasn't letting this happen because of my goddamn mother. I chased after her and caught up to her at the door.

"Don't go." I remembered. That's what I had said to her that day so long ago.

She turned around but I didn't see Ellie. I saw her. My mother.

"That's what I said to her the night she left. She came into my room. I was eleven at the time. You don't remember her, I know, you were just a baby. Anyway, she came in to tell me that she was leaving. That she couldn't stay in Montana anymore and that it was better if I stayed with Dad. Then she said it would be cleaner this way. I didn't realize at the time she meant she was just going to forget she ever had a son. Then she left the room, and I ran after her down the hall and I said, *Mom, I love you. Please don't go.* And she left."

"You never told me."

I shrugged my shoulders. "Who wants to tell that story? I told myself I would never say those words again. That wasn't going to happen. No way. That... being rejected like that...that just hurt too much."

I would certainly never ever beg. Never again. That's what I told myself.

"Oh Jake, I'm so sorry."

"I tried to show you. I thought I... did. I tried to give you presents I knew you would love so you would see. I tried to be there for you when you needed me. I tried to be the man someone like you deserved. I... in bed... I mean I tried to show you what I was feeling the whole time. I thought you knew. You had to see it. Feel it. Yeah, I thought if I could show you. It would be enough."

But it wasn't. This whole time I thought I was giving

her everything I had. More than I'd given to anyone in my life. And she thought I didn't love her.

Right. Because you had to say the scary words. Out loud. So I had to tell her. If I was going to keep her, I had to tell her.

I fell to my knees in front of her and rested my head on the womb that used to carry our child. I had never felt a sense of loss so strongly as I had when I realized she'd lost the baby.

Until ten minutes ago, when she said she was leaving me. So I did the thing I thought I would never be able to do again.

"I love you, Ellie. Please don't go."

Then I couldn't control it. I did something I had never done in my life. I cried. I cried for the boy who lost his mother. I cried for my father and her father. I cried for the baby. But most of all I cried because the idea of losing Ellie, the best part of my life, was so damn scary there was nothing else I could do.

She soothed and rubbed my head. Told me to hush, and that everything was going to be okay.

Did she mean that? I pulled away and looked up at her but she was getting on her knees too. She took my face between her hands, looked me dead in the eye, and said the thing that I had so badly wanted my mom to say all those years ago.

"Okay, Jake. I'll stay."

"I love you." It was easier the second time.

"I know that now."

"I love you," I sighed. It felt like some huge weight had been lifted off my chest. "I have. For years. I didn't realize until now... why I couldn't tell you. All this time I thought I was protecting you, making you sure you had choices...I was really just protecting that eleven-year-old boy. Ellie Samson, I love you."

She smiled, and swear to God it was the most beautiful thing I had ever seen in my life.

"See, was that so hard to say?"

She laughed and I laughed too. Then we kissed. Not a romantic kiss, but a hard one. One that felt like we had sealed some kind of deal.

SEVENTEEN

Ellie
April 22

I STARED down at the ring on my finger and wondered if I was going to pass out. I was sitting in a small vestibule, trying to keep my arms away from my body so I wasn't all pitted out in my white dress, while Chrissy constantly checked her hair in the small mirror on the wall.

You're probably wondering how it all went down at this point?

After Jake told me he loved me, we'd both decided we didn't want a rushed wedding. He'd said he wanted it done right, so that everyone would know we were doing this because we were in love and for no other reason.

That meant a church, a white dress, not just a few friends, but all of our friends (which was basically the town of Riverbend) and a big party afterward.

Together we'd mourned the loss of our baby. I had told

him everything I felt, why I'd felt it. Some of it had hurt him, but it was the only way I knew how to really heal. To forgive myself for the feelings I had when I first learned I was pregnant. Then I had gone on the pill, because we both knew we weren't ready for children yet and it turned out Jake loved sex without condoms. (Like really loved it.)

For Christmas, he'd given me an engagement ring. Something totally useless, as a rancher and jewelry didn't often go together, but still I loved it.

The ranch was once again at full capacity. Thriving really. Enough so that we could offer Rich a full time position and still have work for Gomez and Javier whenever they showed up.

I told them both about the wedding when they came in February. I think they had a hard time understanding that we weren't already married. But they had left at the beginning of April, so that was two less guests.

Still, the church was packed. I knew this because between checking her hair in the mirror Chrissy would walk over to the door of the vestibule and crack it open and tell me it was packed.

We picked my birthday, even though it was a Wednesday in April. We picked my birthday because I wanted the best present Jake could ever give me. Himself. Obviously the town didn't seem to mind.

There was a knock on the door.

"Come in," I said.

It was Howard. "Ellie, you ready?"

Howard was going to give me away. I thought back to that first wedding, when Howard had come to get me then. How different everything had been. It felt like a hundred years ago.

I stood up, and he smiled. "You look beautiful."

"Thank you."

I heard the organ music start to play. Chrissy did one last hair check, and then air-kissed me as she made her way out of the vestibule. I could see her measured steps as she started up the aisle. Then Howard held his arm out and I took it.

"A lot different then last time," he said, chuckling, echoing my earlier thoughts.

"I don't know. I think I might be more nervous."

"That's because this time it's for real."

Yes. This time it was for real. Including changing my name to Talley. Of course I had a long conversation explaining the feminist position of keeping my maiden name to Jake. To which he'd said *Please. I like the way Ellie Talley sounds.*

I totally caved. Because I liked the way it sounded too.

Howard and I turned the corner and everyone stood. It was without a doubt the craziest moment in my life. Everyone was there. Frank and Bernie, Pete, the Pettys, crazy enough both Mr. and Mrs. Nash came together, Karen and Lisa, Denny and Maryanne, the Simpsons. Bella, who had done my hair earlier that morning. Rich, who cleaned up pretty well for an old ranch hand.

My life. My people. My family. All standing up and looking at me.

And then I saw Jake, and they all went away. He wore a suit and tie. His hair was freshly cut. He was smiling. Beaming actually, and it was because he was happy.

I made Jake Talley happy, and to me there was no greater honor on this earth.

Howard gave me a little tug and I made my way to him. Then Jake was taking my hand and we were standing together in front of the minister.

"I'm nervous," I whispered to him. "I don't want to forget my vows."

Then he squeezed my hand and reminded me of something I think I always knew.

"Don't worry. We've got this."

Jake
April 22nd Ten Years Later
On a road between Long Valley and Riverbend

"OH JAKE!!!! I think you need pull over."

"Do not do this to me, Ellie. We've got about ten more minutes until we get to the clinic."

I hit the gas even harder, but then she reached over and grabbed my arm. I could tell by the force of her grip the level of pain she was in.

"You may have ten more minutes. This kid does not. It wants out. Like now!"

Fuck!

"Jake, you've brought a thousand calves into this world, you can do this. Ohhhhhhh. Jake, hurry. I need to push. Seriously."

She was panting with short pants to control the pain, but I could see it wash over her body, the way it tightened her belly.

There was no hope for it. I pulled the truck over to the side of the road.

"Ellie, you're going to need to get into the back seat.

Can you do that? Wait for the next ease of the contraction and then move."

"Move," she muttered. "Like I'm not the size of a beached whale." Still, she was undoing her seat belt.

I got out and opened the back door of the truck. I probably should have taken the minivan, but when her water broke I hadn't been thinking of a side of the road delivery. Just getting her into town as fast as possible.

"Okay, see this?" I pointed to the handle bar above the window. "Grab on to that with both hands. You can use that for leverage."

She'd worn one of her light, maxi-length maternity dresses. I pushed the material up over her belly and then ripped her underwear off. Which, don't ask me why because she was screaming in pain with an enormous belly and gigantic maternity panties, was still a little hot. Because it was Ellie, and anything to do with Ellie was hot. I made a mental note when she was recovered to try this trick again.

Then I focused on the task at hand. I spread her knees wide, and holy shit she was right. The head was already crowning.

I looked up at her. "Good call."

She puffed through a contraction. "Third time. I got this nailed."

"All right, let's do this. Let's give Jack and Sam their newest sibling."

Jack was for Jackson Talley Jr. Ellie loved my name, and while she felt Jake was a suitable nickname wanted to keep the Jack in Jackson. Sam, well that was obvious. For this baby we'd decided not to know the sex in advance. For a boy we were torn between Tom and Alex. I had no idea what she was thinking if it was girl. I just told her she couldn't name it Petunia.

It was messy, but it was almost too easy. Ellie bore down on one long push, and my daughter slid out head first, then a shoulder like she simply could not wait to meet us. Finally she was free and I laid her on Ellie's chest. While Ellie checked that her mouth and throat were clear of any mucus, I ripped off the bottom of Ellie's dress to dry the baby and wrap her up as best I could.

Then I hopped back in the car and drove us the last of the way, where Dr. Jenkins was waiting for us to deliver the afterbirth and cut the cord.

Ellie

A BABY GIRL. I glanced down at the pink bundle in my arms and promptly fell even more in love than I already had when Jake first laid her on my chest. Just like I had done with Jack and Sam. It was this bottomless well of love that never seemed to end.

We were driving home now. Dr. Jenkins had given me and the baby a thumbs up, so there was no point in staying at the clinic. I was sore as heck sitting in the truck, and we hadn't had time to bring the baby seat, so Jake was driving twenty-five miles an hour which meant the trip would take even longer, but none of that mattered.

Not when I was so blessed.

"I told you we should have stayed and done it at the house," I told Jake.

What we knew after two previous pregnancies was I

gave birth at record pace. Jack had been the longest at three hours, but we'd barely made it last time with Sam.

"What I should have done was have Mary come. Well, too late worrying about it now. We're just lucky there weren't any complications."

I reached over to rub his arm, because I knew he'd been scared.

"You did good, Dad."

He grunted.

"Did you call Howard and Mirry?"

"Yes. I told them what happened. Howard thought it was funny. It was not funny. They are going to take the boys to their place tonight. Let them have a sleepover and give you a break."

Howard and Mirry had basically become our kids' de facto grandparents. They had been over for dinner, which was just lucky timing, when my water broke. Which was a surprise, since the baby wasn't due until the first week of May.

Clearly this girl was in a rush to get started with life.

"What are you going to name her?" Jake asked.

"You're going to think this is hokey..."

"Ellie. Do not go crazy on me."

I didn't think it was crazy. I thought it was just another in a long line of amazing birthday gifts Jake had given me over the years.

"I want to name her April," I said, looking down at her, wondering if she agreed. Then I looked over at Jake and I could see him nodding. He understood. Every April he gave me a gift that in some way showed me how much he loved me. This April was no different. To me it was a word synonymous with love.

"April," he said. "I like it."

"April," I repeated.

AND THAT'S how it went, really. Our story. We loved each other, we loved our kids. We had hard times and good times. Sometimes really hard times, but then really great times.

Overall on a scale of one to ten, I would say my life with Jake was...

One million. Or a billion. Or a trillion. Did it get bigger than a trillion?

See what happens when you break the scale?

JAKE AND ELLIE'S STORY CONTINUES IN... THE BABY

Read an excerpt

The Baby

Chapter One

Ellie

June

You're probably wondering what I'm doing here sitting on the toilet. No, no, nothing gross or anything. I'm just taking a test. You know... to see if I'm preggers or not.

I'm not going to lie... I'm freaking out about it.

Quick recap.

My dad died when I was almost seventeen, leaving me an orphan. I fake-married Jake, a longtime family friend and our ranch foreman, so I could continue to live and work on my cattle ranch in Montana. Then I fell in love with him. Then he kissed me. Then... Carol happened. Still can't stand the name Carol to this day. Then I divorced his ass. Not because of Carol really, but because I was still in love with him. But then he fell in love with me. Sort of.

Then I got pregnant.

And there were those five minutes when I thought about not being pregnant. About making myself not pregnant.

I didn't do it. Looking back on it, I know I could never have done it. Not to Jake's baby.

I lost the baby. I'd thought it was all my fault. I thought I had lost Jake too, but it turned out he just had serious mommy issues. With good reason. The bitch left him when he was eleven years old and never looked back.

Fortunately he was able to work through those, and we found a way to be together.

Then we got married for real. It really was a beautiful wedding.

That was three years ago.

Being married to Jake ever since has been the best. I mean it was like a nonstop sex fest there in the beginning, which was fun. We were nearly gross with how we couldn't keep our hands off each other.

People called us the Starbucks Unicorn couple because we were so freaking sweet. (Not that many people here in Riverbend, Montana have ever been to a Starbucks, but they see stuff on the internet.)

Things were great. We had a successful cattle ranch,

which we could expand because of the addition of Talley land. We added goats because I always wanted goats. (Don't get Jake started on the goats!)

Most of all we had each other, and it was more than enough.

Then Christmas happened, and we started talking about what we wanted our future Christmases to look like. You know, with kids running around screaming with anticipation and writing letters to Santa Claus. Christmas cookies and stockings. Getting us up at three a.m. because of how excited they were, and then tearing into gifts in minutes.

We decided we were ready to talk about the future.

Did we want kids?

Definitely.

How many, if we were fortunate enough to have them?

Still up in the air.

After a couple of weeks of haggling, we took the plunge. I tossed the birth control pills. Jake kept on doing what he did best, which was to fill me up in the best sort of ways.

Now six months later I'm sitting on the toilet, seat down, waiting to see if it worked.

I'm afraid it did. I'm afraid it didn't. I'm afraid if I am pregnant I might lose the baby again. Because let me tell you, that day ranks as one of the shittiest days of my life. And I've had a lot of bad ones.

Jake says I shouldn't be afraid. That it was just one of those things.

Jake has never had a miscarriage.

I think I'm ready to handle this. No matter what happens. Except there really is no way to tell what a person can handle until something does actually happen.

I looked over at the counter, where my phone was ticking down on the timer. The white plastic pee stick sitting there waiting to define my life. Of course I had to drive to Jefferson again. No chance that I could casually pick up one of those bad boys in town without everyone knowing what Jake and I were doing.

Were trying.

It was the same person behind the counter as last time. I'm pretty sure he didn't recognize me from three years ago. Still, I couldn't help but wonder if that was a bad omen.

My phone dinged and I practically fell off the seat. My heart was pounding as I stood and picked up the stick.

Positive.

Pregnant.

PREGNANT.

HOLY SHIT PREGNANT!

There it was. I sat back down on the lid and tried to take deep, calming breaths. Then I thought about what to tell Jake.

All I knew was that this time had to be different. Last time, it was like I was giving him the worst news ever. He understood. He knew it was because I was afraid he was going to want to get married... again, which he did, without me knowing if he really loved me. Because back then he hadn't been able to say it.

Now I knew he really loved me. That fear was completely gone.

It was just the other fear. The fear that maybe there was something wrong with me. Maybe I could get pregnant, but I couldn't carry a baby full term. That because... in those few moments of wondering if I should undo the last pregnancy... I had cursed myself forever.

Which was ridiculous of course. It's not like I actually believed in curses.

Much.

I didn't have to tell him right now. I had time to come up with a plan. Maybe a nice dinner. Something different and special. With that in mind I put the test back in the cardboard box, then I put it in the trash and took the bag out of the small pail and tied it off.

I ran downstairs, even though I knew I was in the house alone, and stuffed the small bag of trash in the main kitchen trash and covered it with a bunch of towels. Now it was my secret.

I looked over at my scales. Jake and I had had yet another fight about the goats last night, so I had willfully moved the disks to seven on the right.

Jake's mission in life was to keep me at a nine and above on the scale of one to ten of happiness. But when he threatened to murder Gary the Goat, that was obviously not going to make me happy.

I couldn't move them to ten now. He would know something was up. I would wait. Until we both knew that we were going to have a baby.

I tried not to be afraid. I really really tried.

ALSO BY S DOYLE

The Baby

The Homecoming

Made in United States
Orlando, FL
17 January 2022